Linda Fairstein is a former prosecutor and America's foremost expert on sex crimes. Her first novel, *Final Jeopardy*, which introduced Alexandra Cooper, was published in 1996. Since then, Linda Fairstein, who lives in New York and Martha's Vineyard, has written several Alex Cooper thrillers. Her sixth, *The Kills*, was an international bestseller. *Entombed* is the seventh.

Praise for the Alexandra Cooper series

'Engaging characters, an intelligent story full of twists' *The Times*

'Chilling stuff' *Hello!*

'Fascinating reading in a mystery which stretches far beyond New York' *Sunday Telegraph*

'Romantic tension, the fast-paced plotting, and the New York setting will keep fans of Fairstein's series engrossed' *Booklist*

'There are so many legal functionaries showing up in fiction . . . that it's a mark of Linda Fairstein's class that she stands out' *The Weekend Australian*

'Impeccably plotted and thoroughly engrossing novels' *Daily Mail*

'Her novels pulsate with catchy police jargon and a bustling, warm, down-to-earth reality' *TV Week*

Entombed

LINDA FAIRSTEIN

TIME WARNER
BOOKS

TIME WARNER BOOKS

First published in the United States in 2004 by Scribner
First published in Great Britain in 2004 by Little, Brown
This paperback edition published in 2005 by Time Warner Books
Reprinted 2005 (twice)

A CIP catalogue record for this book
is available from the British Library.

ISBN 0 7515 3572 9

Typeset in AGaramond by Palimpsest Book Production Limited,
Polmont, Stirlingshire

Printed and bound in Great Britain by
Clays Ltd, St Ives plc

Time Warner Books
An imprint of
Time Warner Book Group UK
Brettenham House
Lancaster Place
London WC2E 7EN

www.twbg.co.uk

For the Fairsteins—

GUY AND MARISA,
LISA AND MARC

With love, laughter, and admiration

Acknowledgments

My first encounter with Edgar Allan Poe's *Tales of the Grotesque and Arabesque* made an indelible impression on my adolescent imagination. A dead man's heart beating beneath the floorboards, the huge pendulum descending on a prisoner in the pit, the Red Death invading the festive masquerade, and the repeated torment of premature burial and entombment behind cellar walls – each of these narratives was responsible for youthful nightmares, and all of them have lured me back over the years to delight in their dramatic power and poetic elegance.

That Poe was capable of such a body of work – stories, poems, journalistic pieces, and literary criticism – is even more remarkable when one considers his short life and the tragic circumstances of it. Several cities claim the great master of crime fiction as their own – Richmond, Baltimore, Philadelphia, Boston. To my surprise, though, were the many places in New York where Poe lived and in which some of his greatest works were written, and the inspiration he drew from the landscape he so loved to walk.

My greatest pleasure in plotting this book was the opportunity it provided to reread all of Poe's writings. My source was the ten volume collection published by Stone and Kimball in 1894, including the memoir by George E. Woodberry. Poe's life is well-described by Kenneth Silverman in *Edgar A. Poe: Mournful and Never-ending Remembrance*; and by Arthur H. Quinn in *Edgar Allan Poe – A Critical Biography*.

The Bronx County Historical Society maintains Poe Cottage in remarkable condition, for tourists and scholars alike. Kathleen McAuley is not only its knowledgeable curator, but an enchanting guide. The splendid setting that is the New York Botanical Garden is one of the city's true jewels, as I saw in the hands of Dr Kim Tripp, and a far less threatening site than it appears in my novel. I am grateful to both institutions for opening their doors to me.

Thanks once again to everyone at Scribner and Pocket Books – Susan Moldow, Roz Lippel, Louise Burke, Mitchell Ivers, Pat Eisemann, Erin Cox, Sarah Knight, Angella Baker – and to John Fulbrook, for my own elegant raven.

To Susanne Kirk, who has guided my hand and spirit from the first pages of *Final Jeopardy* through the last edit of *Entombed*, may you always be sitting on my shoulder as I write, through your long and happy retirement.

To Hilary Hale and David Young at Time Warner UK, my gratitude for taking Alex Cooper around the world in such grand style. And to Esther Newberg, the best in the business, I'm glad to have had you at my side since the outset.

My family and friends are my inspiration and source of sustenance. Librarians and booksellers are the generous souls who put my books in readers' hands. And my beloved Justin Feldman – whose childhood playground, in the Bronx, was actually Poe Park – remains my steadfast partner in law and literature, which gives me happiness beyond imagining.

To be buried while alive is, beyond question, the most terrific of . . . extremes which has ever fallen to the lot of mere mortality. . . . We know of nothing so agonizing upon Earth – we can dream of nothing half so hideous in the realms of the nethermost Hell.

—Edgar Allan Poe
The Premature Burial

Chapter 1

I looked at the pool of dried blood that covered the third-floor landing of a brownstone on one of the safest residential blocks in Manhattan and wondered how the young woman who'd been left here to die yesterday, her chest pierced by a steak knife, could still be alive this afternoon.

Mercer Wallace crouched beside the stained flooring, pointing out for me the smaller areas of discoloration. 'These smudges, I figure, are partial imprints of the perp's shoe. He must have lost his footing over there.'

The blood streaked away from the door of the victim's apartment, as though her attacker had slid in the slippery fluid and stumbled to the top of the staircase.

'So there's likely to be some of this on his clothing?'

'Pants leg and shoes for certain, until he cleans them. Look here,' he said, and my eyes followed the tip of the pen he was using as a pointer. Outlined on the light gray paint of the door to 3B was another bloody design. 'That's hers, Alex. She must have braced herself with one foot against that panel to push the guy off. She put up a fierce struggle.'

I could make out the V-shaped tip of a woman's shoe

sole, and inches lower the circular mark that confirmed it was a pump rather than a flat.

'High heels and all, she did pretty well for herself. Just lucky.' The uniformed cop who had been assigned to safeguard the crime scene for the past twenty-four hours spoke to Mercer as he straightened up.

'That's what we're calling it now when someone resists a rapist and ends up in the intensive care unit with a few holes in her chest and a collapsed lung?'

'Sorry, Ms Cooper. I mean the girl is fortunate to be alive. You know she went DOA when they pulled up to the docking bay at the emergency room?'

Mercer had told me that. Annika Jelt had stopped breathing on the short ride to New York Hospital. The cops who were dispatched to a neighbor's 911 call reporting screams in the stairwell knew there was no time to wait for an ambulance. The young officer who carried the victim down to the patrol car had served in the army reserves as a medic during the war in Iraq. Annika owed her life to the fact that he revived her in the backseat of the RMP, on the way to the ER, before she was rushed into surgery to inflate her lung and staunch the bleeding.

Mercer led the way down the staircase. The traces of black fingerprint dust on the banister and walls reminded me that the Crime Scene Unit had done a thorough workup of the building when they were summoned by Mercer, shortly after the 3 A.M. attack on a frigid morning in late January.

'He never got her inside the apartment?'

'Nope. She fought like hell to keep him out.'

'Did he take anything?' I asked.

'Keys. He took the ring with the keys to both the

2

vestibule door and the apartment. The super's changed both locks already.'

'But money? Jewelry?'

'Her pocketbook was lying on the ground next to her. Cash and credit cards were inside and she still had on her earrings and bracelet. He wasn't there for the money.'

Mercer had double-parked outside the five-story walk-up on East Sixty-sixth Street. He had awakened me yesterday at six o'clock to tell me about the case. We had worked together for the better part of the decade that I had run the sex crimes prosecution unit of the Manhattan District Attorney's Office, while he had been assigned to the police department's Special Victims Squad. He knew I'd want the first heads-up about the crime, before it was reported on the local network news and before the DA, Paul Battaglia, hunted me down to get enough details so that he could answer the flood of calls from local politicians, concerned citizens, and the ever-curious media. Violent crime, especially sexual assault, was always fodder for headlines when it happened in the high-rent district of the Upper East Side.

I left my desk in the criminal courthouse this afternoon to join Mercer at the victim's apartment. It always helped me begin to frame an investigation and prosecution if I could see exactly where the attack had occurred and what evidence there was of a struggle, or any clues to the perpetrator's method of operation. What the lighting conditions were, the size of the area involved and distances between the beginning of the attack and its conclusion, as well as potential evidence that might be cleaned up or altered in the days to follow – I liked to see those things with my own eyes. The cops had still been too busy processing the scene themselves to allow me access when Mercer called me yesterday morning, but now they had given the green light to let him walk me through it.

In addition, my years of work on these cases often added another experienced perspective to that of the police team – and sometimes it resulted in recalling a distinctive detail or trait that would lead the investigators to a repeat offender in this category of crimes in which the recidivist rate was so extraordinarily high.

Mercer started the engine and turned up the heat in the old department Crown Vic that had responded to more sexual assaults than most officers ever would in a lifetime. 'So, did anything there speak to you?' Mercer said, smiling at me.

I rubbed my gloved hands together against the harsh winter chill that had seeped through the cracks around the car windows. Lots of veteran cops got vibes at crime scenes, claiming to be able to figure out something about the assailant by being in the same space. I shook my head. 'Nothing you don't already know. Yet one more sick puppy who was somehow aroused by forcing a woman he'd never seen before to engage in a sexual act.'

'There are buildings with doormen on both corners of the block. This is a fully occupied brownstone on a well-lighted street. He's a cool case, this guy. He got her at the front door on top of the stoop, as she was unlocking it—'

'She told you that?'

Mercer had been waiting at the hospital when the young woman emerged from the anesthetic late last evening. 'Too many tubes coming out of the kid to speak, and the docs only gave me fifteen minutes with her. I asked some

4

basics until she ran out of steam. She squeezed my hand like I told her for some yes-and-no kind of questions.'

We were driving to the hospital, just a few blocks away on York Avenue at Sixty-eighth Street. Mercer stopped in to check on his victim on the way to his office this morning, and insisted on seeing her again, as he would every day until she recovered. He wanted to tell the young exchange student that he had telephoned her parents, in Sweden, and that they were flying here tomorrow. Until they arrived, he would be the closest thing to family she would have at her side.

'Did Annika know he had the knife when he accosted her?'

'She never even heard him coming. I figure the first thing she felt was his arm yoking her neck and the blade of the knife scratching the side of her throat.'

'Not a particularly distinctive MO,' I said.

'You looking for creative, too, Alex?'

I shook my head.

'It's all in the details, as you know. Exactly what words he said, how he touched her, what he smelled like. It may be a couple of days until we can get all that from her.'

'And hope in the meantime that he doesn't feel it necessary to finish the job with another victim tonight or tomorrow.'

Mercer flashed his badge at the security guard in front of the hospital driveway, who motioned him to leave the car right at the curb.

Sophisticated monitors beeped their familiar noises as we pushed open the doors into the surgical ICU. Nurses were engaged in every one of the eight cubicles, tending to patients in the most critical phase of care.

Mercer walked to the glass-enclosed area where Annika Jelt lay in bed.

'She's awake, Detective. You can come in,' the nurse said.

I remained in the doorway as Mercer took a step to the bedside. He reached out his large hand and placed it on Annika's arm, above the intravenous needle that carried fluids back into her slim body. As she felt his touch, the young woman turned her head toward us and tried to smile, recognizing her new friend and protector.

'Hello,' she whispered, barely able to move her mouth because of the tubes coming out of her nostrils.

Mercer leaned his six-foot-six-inch frame over the bed railing and gently stroked Annika's forehead. 'Don't try to talk. I just came back to check on you. Make sure they're treating you right.'

The nurse walked to the far side of the bed and adjusted the pillows behind her head. 'Detective Wallace told me he'd haul me off to the clink if we don't get you up and out of here as soon as possible.'

She twisted her head back toward the nurse and forced another smile.

'I spoke with your mother, Annika. It's okay. She and your dad will be here tomorrow.'

At the mention of her parents, the girl's eyes filled with tears and a guttural cry escaped from her mouth. She wanted to speak but couldn't find the strength, or the right words.

'They know you're going to be fine. They want to come over here and be with you.'

I couldn't understand what she was mumbling. Her head was moving back and forth, causing all the monitors to go into high gear. It was something about what she wanted.

'I know you want to go home,' Mercer said. Her hand was clasped in his and he continued to try to calm her by stroking her hair.

I bit my lip and thought of how isolated and frightened she must be. Alone in a foreign country, victim of a crime that almost took her life, and not even able to speak on the telephone to assure her family that she would survive.

'Remember the lady I told you about, my friend Alex? I've brought her here to meet you,' Mercer said, stepping back from the bed that was surrounded with medical equipment so that Annika could see me.

I came in closer and she dropped his hand, gesturing toward mine. I took his place by her side, covering her cold fingers with my own, and let Mercer finish speaking. 'Alex and I are going to find this man, Annika. All you have to do is get strong again. That's your only assignment.'

'Mercer's right. You need to get all the rest you can. We'll be back to see you every day. We'll get you everything you need.'

'Home?' This time I could hear her clearly.

'Of course you can go home as soon as you're well enough to travel,' I said.

'She's almost due for her pain medication,' the nurse said. 'She gets agitated whenever anyone mentions her family. She doesn't want them to see her this way and she worries about how upset they must be. They never wanted her to come to New York for school.'

We waited until she had composed herself, and the

MorphiDex that the nurse added to the drip began to take effect.

Annika's watery brown eyes blinked repeatedly, like she was fighting sleep, determined to make sure that Mercer stayed by her side. She closed them at last, her small head barely making a dent in the firm pillows behind her, looking pale and sallow against the crisp white hospital linens. The lifesaving machinery that surrounded her outweighed her twofold. Its blinking lights and beeping noises wouldn't disturb her medicated slumber, and I hoped as well that nightmare visions of her attacker couldn't penetrate the veil drawn around her by the strong painkillers.

It was not even five o'clock when we got back into the car for the ride downtown to my office, but it was already pitch-black and the windchill factor had dropped several notches.

Mercer's cell phone vibrated and he unhitched it from his belt to flip it open as he pulled out of the driveway onto York Avenue.

'Sure, Bob. I'll take a preliminary,' he said, looking over at me.

It was Bob Thaler, the chief serologist at the medical examiner's office, who had worked up a quick analysis, less than twenty-four hours after getting the evidence found at the scene of Annika's assault. These tentative findings would later be validated with further testing. This first run wouldn't hold up in court, but it would give us an immediate idea if there was evidence of value.

'Yeah, we picked up those four cigarette butts from the stoop in front of the building. You find something?'

Thaler gave him an answer, which caused Mercer to turn and wink at me. Good news, I assumed.

8

But their conversation went on, and as he listened, Mercer's smile faded to a serious expression, almost an angry one. He hung up the phone, dropped it on the seat between us, and accelerated onto the FDR Drive.

'There's that word "lucky" again. I was afraid we were hopeless on the serology because there was no semen. Thaler's got Annika's blood on one of the cigarette stubs. That's why he wanted to know where we found them. Looks like the guy stepped on it on his way out of the building, with wet fluid still in the creases of his shoes from where he dropped her on the landing.'

'You heard something else you didn't like.'

'They were able to work up a profile from the saliva on the same butt, too. I'd say it's our man, without a doubt.'

It would be a stretch for Mercer to get excited about a random item that wasn't even found inside the apartment hallway, where the crime occurred. He knew better.

'Didn't you just say there were four—'

'I'm not talking about a foreign profile, Alex. It's a very familiar one. Three of the cigarettes are useless. The butt with both blood *and* saliva on it was dropped there – maybe on his way up the steps when he spotted his prey – by someone you and I haven't seen in a very long time.'

'We know him?' Someone we sent away who got out of jail, I expected Mercer to tell me. Someone we'd put away who was back to haunt us. A paroled convict who would be easy to track down through new sex offender monitoring laws. The surprise chance of something breaking in our favor so early shot through me like a burst of adrenaline.

'If I knew who he was, if I could tell you his name,

then I wouldn't be cruising you downtown right now. I'd be knocking on his door and throwing the cuffs on him tonight,' he said. 'The bastard beat us cold four years ago then disappeared long enough for me to begin to believe he'd come to his own violent end. Now here he is again, obviously more dangerous than before.'

'You think you know—?'

'I do know, Alex. Thaler just confirmed it for me. The Silk Stocking Rapist is back in business.'

Chapter 2

I looked at the grid of the Manhattan street map mounted on poster board behind my desk and pressed a red plastic pushpin into the location of Annika Jelt's apartment. The distance between the building in which she had been attacked and the one in which I lived was less than the width of my fingernail, barely five blocks away.

I turned around to face the district attorney of New York County. 'I'm ready to go to the grand jury tomorrow and start taking testimony.'

'You've got to catch the creep first, Alex. You have to know who committed the crimes before you indict anyone for them.'

'I *do* know who he is, boss.'

'You got a name? You come up with something I'm not aware of?'

'I've got a DNA profile. I have five women—'

'What, from four years ago?'

You can interrupt me but you can't shut me down. 'I said we've got five women whose cases were matched up to each other's by the serology lab and four more victims of attempts that scream his MO loud and clear, even

11

without a trace of physical evidence. Now we have a fresh hit.'

Paul Battaglia turned away from me and took a step toward the door. 'So I'm supposed to tell the press that this maniac is back on the loose, and I've decided to indict some indecipherable genetic markers to make the public feel safe? Come back to me when Mercer has someone in handcuffs. Give me a name, a date of birth, and a mug shot I can plaster all over the newspapers. Am I right, Detective?'

The expression on Mercer's face was obscured by Battaglia's cigar smoke.

'I'd like your permission to indict him.'

'Indict who, Alex?'

'John Doe. I want to charge this rapist as John Doe. Would you just stay here long enough to listen to what we've put together?' What I really wanted to tell him was not to be so dismissive of me without letting me make my case, but even after running his sex crimes prosecution unit for almost ten years, there were some lines I couldn't cross with Paul Battaglia.

'You've done this before, haven't you? Why do you need me—'

'I'm not wasting your time, Paul. We've only done it twice here, on cases that didn't have any ink. No press coverage. Sort of slipped it under the radar screen.'

It had been a risky move the first time I decided to indict a rapist when all we knew about his identification was the unique combination of alleles that made up his DNA profile. No flesh-and-blood image to go with it, no clue what his name was or where to find him. I wasn't even sure Battaglia had been aware that I'd tried the novel approach.

12

'Once the commissioner goes public tonight with the fact that the Silk Stocking Rapist is back, you'll have the entire Upper East Side squeezing you for a solution.'

I had his attention now. Maybe Battaglia's election campaign slogan assured Manhattan's citizens that you can't play politics with people's lives, but he would again be on the ballot in November and vulnerable to concerns about every spike in violent crime statistics.

He leaned against the doorframe and talked out of the side of his mouth, his cigar wedged firmly in the center. 'What advantage does it give me, this John Doe indictment?'

'Two things. This new case isn't the issue. But the older attacks took place more than four years ago. If we don't get the guy soon, the statute of limitations runs out on those and he can't be charged for any of the cases.'

Unlike murder, which could be prosecuted whenever the killer was caught, sexual assault cases in New York had to be brought within five years of the occurrence of the crime, barring special circumstances that the courts had recently allowed.

'So by charging him now, this, uh, this—'

'This John Doe, whose genetic profile we literally spell out in place of the defendant's name on the front of the indictment, has a combination of DNA alleles that the chief serologist is going to tell you is expected to be found in only one in a trillion African-American men. Once the squad puts a face and name to this evidence, I promise you we'll get a conviction on all counts.'

Mercer's back was against a row of file cabinets in my crowded office. His soft, deep voice added the latest news from the NYPD's press office. 'The commissioner's called

13

a conference for seven o'clock. He's releasing the composite sketch from the last reign of terror. This new victim won't be able to work with the artist for days, but we don't have to worry about that with the match Thaler gave us. All of the women from four years ago signed off on the accuracy of the sketch back then. Same face as last time, same skills.'

'When we get him, we make sure he never sees daylight again,' I said. 'He goes away for this case and anything else that he does from this point on. And trust me, Paul, he isn't stopping with Annika Jelt.'

Mercer agreed with me. 'He's way too frenzied now. Coop's plan gets him for every attack the first time he was in town. We beat the statute and ask for a sentence of life imprisonment – plus how's another two hundred fifty years for good measure?'

'Annika's mother and father are flying in from Sweden tomorrow. All she wants to do is go home, and all her parents want is to get her out of big, bad Gotham City. I've got to take her testimony as soon as she's able to move from the hospital bed.'

'What else? You said there were two advantages to indicting Mr Doe.'

'We enter the profile in the data bank. Upload it to CODIS.' The Combined DNA Index System collected results from both convicted offender databases and unsolved casework from every contributing lab in the country. Our evidence was routinely transmitted to Albany as well as to the federal system.

Battaglia shifted his position and chewed the cigar over to the corner of his mouth. 'Why isn't it already in CODIS from the time the old cases were tested?'

Mercer spoke. 'We weren't linked to the feds when the first cases occurred.'

'And the profile had to be reworked, Paul. Four years ago, DNA matches were declared with as few as eight loci in common. Now we can't upload a sample unless we've got a sixteen-loci hit.'

The reason that DNA had become such a critical tool in identifying individuals is because no two people, with the exception of identical twins, have the same genetic fingerprint. Lab analysis doesn't look at all of a person's DNA, because more than 95 percent of it is exactly the same among every human on earth – two arms, two legs, one head, and so on. What makes us unique is the area of DNA within our chromosomes that is different, and that's called a locus, or location. The more loci that are compared in the laboratory, the more valid the DNA match.

'I assume you hope to find something if you put this information in CODIS. What good is it if it doesn't tell you who he is?'

'Maybe we learn where he's been. I'd settle for that, for starters. Cold hits on serial rape patterns in other cities, a connection to a relative, or a jurisdiction he relocated to for a few years. Rapists this successful don't go dormant, Paul. If he wasn't in jail somewhere – which CODIS also finds out for us – then you can bet he was committing these crimes on somebody else's watch. Maybe the national data bank will tell us where.'

I could see the frown lines setting in on Battaglia's face. 'So if I follow the commissioner's press conference with one of my own next week – the day you get your first grand jury filing – telling them about my idea to indict the DNA of this monster, you'll give me a briefing on all this, right? Loci and alleles and the rest of the scientific lingo. I'll be able to handle questions on this, in English?'

He was a very quick study. Half an hour in his office before the press corps arrived and the district attorney would be explaining the process of polymerase chain reaction testing and short tandem repeats to them as well as the best serologists would do it on the witness stand at trial.

'This John Doe business stands up on appeal?' he asked.

It was still a controversial technique, used first on a serial pedophile case in Milwaukee and not yet litigated before our appellate jurists. 'Our cases were both pleas. It hasn't been tested yet in New York. But the higher courts in Wisconsin, California, and Texas have all upheld it.'

'Yeah, well, those judges won't be close enough to this courthouse to see the egg on my face if there's a screwup at 100 Centre Street, will they? You got law for me to read?'

It didn't pay to try to put anything past Battaglia. 'I'll give you cases, but yes – there's a slight distinction.'

He started to shake his head at me.

'We're solid, Paul. Really. Those other states don't have grand jury systems, so they don't have to go forward by way of indictment. The prosecutors simply issued warrants with sworn affidavits from witnesses and lab techs. It's not that the law is different, it's just an easier way for their lawyers to proceed. Think of it like this, boss. You can announce that you're the first district attorney in the country to do John Doe DNA indictments.'

He liked being first at everything. Creating specialized

investigative units, taking down international banking firms that no other government agency dared touch, putting deadly drug cartels out of business – originality was a hallmark of his prosecutorial style.

'So it was a good idea, then, for me to think of doing this, wasn't it?' Battaglia said, smiling at Mercer.

He was in a better mood for the second part of my request. 'I'm going to need money, Paul. The ME's office will have to retest all of the old samples to conform to the current standard number of loci. We may need to outsource some of them to private labs, which gets pretty expensive. And Mercer's got some interesting approaches that are going to cost us a bit of—'

'Whatever happened to old-fashioned legwork, Detective? Pounding the pavement, spreading some five-dollar bills around town till somebody drops a dime on the perp?'

'Mr Lincoln's portrait? I haven't broken a case using small change like that since I was in the Academy. This guy beat me first time around, Mr Battaglia, and I'm damned if it will happen again. He's escalated the violence already.'

'I thought this case wasn't completed. He didn't rape her, did he?'

'Only because she fought with every ounce of strength she had to stop him. That's why she was almost killed,' I said. 'Resisting him – probably because he tried to tie her up.'

This predator was fuel for a tabloid feeding frenzy. Not only did he target women in one of Manhattan's toniest residential neighborhoods, long known as the Silk Stocking District because of the wealthy New Yorkers who

17

built mansions there a century ago. He also used panty hose to bind his victims' hands together after he had subdued the women at knifepoint. It didn't matter to the *New York Post* that most hosiery hadn't been made of silk since the Second World War. Nylon, Lycra, and spandex didn't quite have the same ring on the front page of the morning papers.

The police commissioner's press release tonight would be cause for flooding the area with additional street cops in a precinct already stretched thin by manning security posts on the consulates, diplomatic residences, and high-profile public buildings like art museums that sat within its borders.

'So, no stocking to tie her up this time, but you're willing to go with some drool on the cigarette butt to confirm it's the same man?'

'We don't even know what he did to her, Mr Battaglia. She hasn't been able to talk yet. The docs have only let me in long enough to ask a handful of questions. I'm not sure how he tried to restrain her. She may have started to kick and fight because of the weapon alone, or because he actually brought out the stocking to tie her. Now that I have the hit from Thaler, I'll go back up to the hospital and see if she's ready to give me more.'

'Maybe I can put together an array of composite sketches,' I said, 'to see whether she picks out our man from the old drawing.'

'When I interviewed her briefly, it was before I knew about the DNA match. This time, I can ask her if she saw any panty hose. With or without the hosiery, science will prove it to an absolute certainty.'

'Mercer wants me to hire a geographic profiler, Paul. There's a guy in Vancouver who's willing to fly in and—'

'I thought you didn't believe in that profiling mumbo jumbo, Alex.'

'I don't. Not the psychological crap. "You're looking for a guy who had a bad experience with a woman when he was nine, Ms Cooper. Your rapist probably has trouble expressing himself to women in a normal sexual setting." "No kidding, Doc. I'll keep that in mind." We're not talking about that nonsense, Paul.'

'This fellow I've introduced Alex to has solved pattern crimes all over the country. You bring him in and he studies each of the scenes, same time of night, same lighting conditions as when the crimes happened,' Mercer said. 'Helps us figure out how our perp conceals himself from victims who never see him coming until they've got the key in the brownstone lock. And more important, gives us a clue how he gets away afterwards when we've had the area saturated with police.'

'Don't you remember, Paul? Four years back the task force beefed up street patrol, anti-crime units, under-covers on foot and in unmarked cars. They had heli-copters on standby, canine on the sidewalk within minutes of each attack. Cops were at subway entrances and cruising in medallion cabs. Even the tollbooths at the bridges and tunnels were doing car checks.'

I reached for the poster board, which had been wedged behind one of my file cabinets for the last four years until I pulled it out on our return from the hospital to add the new site to the old pattern. I lifted it onto my desk so Battaglia could see it better and circled the line of pushpins that ran from Annika's building through the locations of the older cases. Every attack had occurred between Sixty-sixth and Eighty-fourth Streets, Second

Avenue to the river, two long blocks east of the nearest subway line.

'The rapist likes it here, boss. He moves around easily, he's confident that he can strike and get away without being caught. Every time he can score and make an escape, he'll get more arrogant about his ability.'

'Which means?'

'He works right in here, maybe,' Mercer said. 'Or he lives here. He's back off the street too fast to be hoofing it over to Lexington Avenue to grab a subway. He's got an anchor point somewhere right in this 'hood, even though it's a lily-white part of town and his complexion is as dark as mine. It's where he leaves from and it's where he returns right after the attack. It's his bat cave.'

'You think flying your expert in will make a difference?' Battaglia asked, looking at his watch. He ignored the racial observation, which raised the potential of an ugly campaign problem.

'We've got very little to lose,' Mercer said. 'This is the first time the perp has drawn blood. If he liked it, if it didn't bother him to leave his prey for dead, then we're going to see him do that again.'

I fished in the old case folder and pulled out a yellowed piece of newspaper. Battaglia was turning to the door as he told us to go ahead with our plans, but I thought I saw him flinch as I opened the clipping to show him a headline he probably recalled from several years back, shortly before election day in his last race: SNAG IN SILK STOCKING – Prosecutor's Promises to End Serial Attacks Gets Hosed.

Chapter 3

Mercer reached into my closet for his leather jacket and handed me my winter coat and scarf. 'Are you serious about tomorrow? You want me to have one of my complainants down here to testify?'

'I already reserved an hour in an afternoon grand jury, just in case Battaglia saw the light,' I said. 'They were impaneled on Monday so they'll be sitting through the end of February. Do you think you can reach any of the old witnesses tonight?'

Mercer was religious about staying in contact with his victims. In the decade since we started using DNA to solve stranger-rape cases, even the civilians were aware that investigations that seemed to have gone cold could be revived instantly as the input from data banks all over America grew and became standardized.

He listed the names of the women he had to call this evening. Neither of us wanted them to hear from the media that the man who had attacked them was suddenly active again. Each of their lives had been traumatized by these events, and all had recovered to different degrees. I was a firm believer that a successful prosecution would further aid their recovery.

'I'd like to start with Darra Goldswit. She's solid, she's always been ready to do whatever you think is best, and she still lives in the tristate area.'

I flipped through her case file, which Mercer and I regularly updated with contact information as she and the other witnesses moved to new homes, graduated from schools, changed jobs, married, and generally got on with their lives. 'Need the number? I'll read over the police reports and be ready for her by the time you get here.'

He copied her home telephone number and cell from my folder.

'If you can have her here at one, we'll be the first in the afternoon jury at two o'clock. I can put the medical evidence and lab report in after she finishes.' There were at least six grand juries that sat in Manhattan every weekday, three that convened in the morning and the others in the afternoon.

'I'm off to headquarters. The commissioner wants me right by his side when he makes the announcement.'

It was usually tough for the PC to decide when to publicly declare a crime series a pattern. Too early and it might create unnecessary panic within the community, while too late would lead to criticism about failure to keep those at risk from knowing the danger. This was an easy call because the cases had been such big news stories four years earlier, and now the reliability of DNA technology left no doubt that the new attack was the work of the same man.

The news reporters would want details of Annika Jelt's assault and though they were few at this point, Mercer Wallace knew them better than anyone else. He and I were the only people who had interviewed every one of the women who had been brutalized in the older cases. He would stand on the podium behind the commissioner, alongside the very somber chief of detectives, and provide whatever information they deemed appropriate to release at this point.

'I'll watch for you on the eleven o'clock news. Call me if anything interesting develops tonight, okay?'

'You going to be home, Alex?'

'Girls' night out. But a very tame one. There's a seminar at NYU Law School and Nan Toth is dragging four of us with her. We get our continuing legal education credit if we show up for the two-hour lecture, made painless by stopping at the alumni reception first with Nan. She promises enough wine and cheese to tolerate a panel of legal experts explaining the most significant Supreme Court decisions of the last year.'

We rode down in the elevator together and walked out onto Hogan Place, the narrow side street that housed both buildings of the DA's office. The wind and biting cold embraced me.

'You meeting them here?' Mercer asked.

I looped the scarf around my neck and shook my head. 'They gave up on me when they heard Battaglia was stopping by my office at six. I'll grab a cab up to Washington Square.'

Mercer waved one down in front of the courthouse and tugged on the fringe of my scarf as he said good night. He was three short blocks from One Police Plaza.

The law school was on Fourth Street, the southern border of the square, and a very short ride from my office. I got out of the cab in front of the main building, careful to step around the icy patches of sidewalk left over from the weekend storm.

A security guard stopped me at the front door and asked where I was going. 'The reception has already started, miss. It's in the new building, not here.'

'But I thought—'

'Eighty-five West Third Street.'

My dismay was obvious. I had rushed Nan off the phone and never asked the exact address. Now I didn't feature going back out into the cold.

'Just around the corner, miss,' the guard said. 'Not very far. The block between Sullivan and Thompson Streets.'

It felt like it was twenty degrees or below outside. I put my head down and fought the wind as I made my way down the narrow street, so typical of Greenwich Village. I followed several men with litigation bags up the steps of the small brick building in the middle of the block, moving against the flow of other partygoers on their way out.

'Your coat, madam?' A young man standing beside a metal rack checked my things and I continued inside until I saw my friends from the office.

'I recommend the red,' Catherine Dashfer said, holding up her glass. 'Enough of the wine and you won't feel quite the urge to punch out Scalia when they discuss his opinions.'

'Sorry it took me so long. I went to the law school first. What's this?' I looked around at the bare walls of this shell of a building, which looked more like a tenement than a major academic facility.

'They're tearing this dump down and putting up an enormous new structure in its place,' Nan said. 'Check it out downstairs.'

'Check what out?'

'The dean's got a construction crew in the basement, using crowbars to break down pieces of the wall.'

'Seven o'clock at night? With that kind of overtime, no wonder the tuition here is so high.'

'It's all part of the show for this evening's alumni dedication ceremony for the new school building.'

The bartender handed me a glass of red wine. 'Am I supposed to say that sounds like a riveting evening? Worth skipping the lecture to see?'

'Not exactly. But this brownstone is more than two hundred years old. The excavation has turned up all sorts of artifacts from colonial days. Teacups, silverware, pewter bowls. You'd love it.'

'Why now? Why tonight?'

'Give the big donors a show. How often do you get to see a bit of New York City history uncovered before your very eyes? C'mon.'

'I've seen enough. It's claustrophobic down there,' Marisa Bourgis said to Sarah Brenner, the deputy of my unit, who was nodding in agreement.

'I'm game,' I said, and followed Nan and Catherine to the staircase that led down to the basement.

Two dozen men in a variety of pin-striped and chalk-striped suits mingled with a handful of lady lawyers, while three other guys in hard hats chipped away at discolored old bricks. A table in the corner held the assorted debris recovered from behind the eastern portion of the wall that had been revealed in the hours before I arrived. I sipped at my wine and examined a wooden implement – some kind of primitive kitchen tool, I assumed – while Nan stopped to speak with one of her former professors.

'What would you guess this is?' Catherine asked me,

holding up a twisted piece of black metal. 'A pair of spectacles or—'

The crowded space reverberated with the shrill screech of a woman who looked as though she had been one of the earliest female graduates of the distinguished law school. She was on the far side of the room and several of the men rushed to help her to a chair.

'Poor old dame probably got nailed by the backswing of a crowbar,' Catherine said. 'Every ambulance chaser in the house will be looking for a piece of the action.'

We walked toward the site of the commotion. A couple of well-dressed visitors had moved to the staircase to hold off onlookers from above, while others clustered in front of the fractured bricks, staring into a dark hole and murmuring their surprise. One man moved aside and I stepped into his place.

Perfectly smooth ivory-colored bones framed the empty orbital sockets that met my horrified stare. I was face-to-face with a human skull, buried behind the ancient wall.

Chapter 4

Mike Chapman stood in front of the skeletal head that had been exposed in the basement of the Third Street building. 'The Thin Man, eh, Coop? What homicide dick wouldn't give his left leg to come face-to-face with the Thin Man?'

The professor assigned by the law school dean to wait out the arrival of the police didn't seem to appreciate Mike's humor and had no reason to know that every unidentified corpse he encountered was given a nickname, some way for him to personalize the task at hand.

'Whaddaya expect me to do here?' Mike said, turning to Nan and me. 'It's not even my jurisdiction.'

'You think I'd call those guys at Manhattan South after the way they treated me on that last case?' I said.

'I'm not talking geography.' Mike was the very best detective assigned to Manhattan North Homicide, the elite squad responsible for all unnatural deaths from the farthest tip of the island down to Fifty-ninth Street, and we had worked scores of investigations together. 'I'm talking centuries. I got people tripping over me and my partner to get to the morgue – they're shooting and stabbing each other, sticking up bodegas for nickels and dimes, throwing babies out windows like there were trampolines on the sidewalk, filling hypodermics with poison and poppin' 'em in their veins. Current events are overwhelming me and you broads call me down here 'cause some old colonial codger got buried in the basement two hundred years ago?'

The construction workers had started to pull the bricks away to about chest level. The figure seemed frozen in place, raised arms bent and fingers outstretched, as though they had been pressing against the wall that had entombed them.

But the workmen stopped at that point – at our urging – as the bones began to shift and several ribs dropped away to the floor of the dark hole in which the fully articulated skeleton stood.

'I called Hal Sherman at the Crime Scene Unit while Alex was looking for you,' Nan said to Mike. Every prosecutor had a favorite detective and we each hoped to get one of them to respond as quickly as possible this time. 'I think I can still hear him laughing.'

'You picked the right night, bright eyes. CSU's got a pile of body parts sticking out of a snow mound that was plowed off a street in TriBeCa last weekend and a domestic with five down, the perp still out looking for his wife's goombah. You bet Sherman's laughing at you. This antique bag of bones is not going to be a priority for him or anybody else in the department until the spring thaw. It'll probably take the docs that long to figure out what they've got and how long it's been here.'

Professor Walter Davis stepped away from the skeleton. 'What do you propose to do about this, Mr Chapman?'

'I've got a call into the medical examiner's office. They'll

28

send a death investigator over to figure out how to dismantle this character properly and give him a place to lay down for a while. Long time to be on your feet.'

'Who's coming?' I asked.

Mike shrugged. 'I asked for Dorfman. Andy Dorfman.'

The office had only one forensic anthropologist. The overwhelming number of old bones that people came across in an urban setting belonged to animals that had once roamed the place more freely, and sometimes to humans who had died of natural causes. Every now and then, the remains could be linked to a homicidal death.

'That's why you stopped the digging?'

'You got it. Andy doesn't like anybody touching his bones until he's eyeballed the setup for himself. I'm just waiting to see if he's available so I can help him get started.'

Dorfman was a perfectionist, a brilliant detail man who at thirty-eight had been a leader in this specialty long before recent television shows and popular media made his work seem chic. We had recently consulted him to determine the identity of a body that had been reduced to charred pieces of bone and left in the furnace of an abandoned building in Harlem. The ex-lover who killed his pregnant girlfriend was convicted on the basis of the forensic work, and as a result of Dorfman's success, the chief medical examiner hired him away from his academic position at a Texas university.

'Look, Mr Chapman. Can we just lock up the basement and get about our business? Surely this . . . this' – Professor Davis waved his hand at the silent skeleton – 'this can wait until tomorrow.'

'You got somebody's briefs you got to get into? We can handle this without you.'

Davis fidgeted and kept looking to the staircase. It was not unusual for people to be uncomfortable in the presence of death, but these remains looked more like an exhibit in a museum or medical school display case than those of someone who had recently shuffled off his mortal coil.

'The dean asked me to wait with you. Of course I'll stay.'

'How old's this tenement?' Mike asked.

Nan had gone upstairs to refresh our glasses of wine and bring one for Mike. The dean had swept everyone else out of the building, including the bartenders, who had abandoned their station but left their cargo behind.

'It was built more than two hundred years ago,' Davis said. 'That's what all the community fuss was about when the law school trustees bought the place. Neighborhood people wanting to declare it a historic landmark, even though it wasn't architecturally significant. I handled the lawsuit for the university.'

Mike lifted his glass to the Thin Man. 'Cheers, buddy. We'll have you out of that wall in no time.'

'Can these scientists actually tell, Detective, how long this body has been here?'

'It's a little bit of modern forensics and a lot of circumstantial evidence. Me, I like when you find one of these guys clutching an old newspaper with the date on it. The 1805 town crier, with the latest reports on Napoleon's victory over the Austrians at Austerlitz. Short of that, I turn it all over to the medical examiner,' Mike said.

'Strange way for someone to go to his eternal rest, isn't it?' I asked. 'Standing up inside a brick coffin.'

'And naked. Unless his drawers fell down to his kneecaps and I just can't see them in there, he's stark

30

naked. Somebody could have had the decency to spring for a black suit, don't you think?' Mike said, turning back to the professor. 'Were there people living here when the university bought the building?'

Davis nodded. 'Yes, it was completely occupied until a couple of years ago. This basement was the original kitchen of the house, which explains some of the pottery and cooking tools that have been dug up. Then in the 1940s it was a restaurant called Bertololloti's, refitted for apartments in the sixties. In fact, it's generally been students and faculty who've lived in here going back decades. The way the campus has grown, it's conveniently in the middle of things.'

'I know a few guys who are gonna hate you for this, Coop. Some poor slob over at the cold case squad will be digging through occupancy records and census data till his pension vests, trying to figure out whether any tenants disappeared or people were reported missing over the past few centuries.'

Professor Davis had seated himself on the edge of the table in the far corner, where the recently dug artifacts were displayed. 'You don't hear a heartbeat, do you?'

Mike smiled at him. 'I didn't see you drinking, Mr Davis. These bones have been picked clean.'

'The floorboards, Detective. I'm not talking about the chest cavity.'

Mike looked at me quizzically but I was just as puzzled as he.

'No telltale heart, Mr Chapman? I'll give your colleagues a head start. This building was once the home of Edgar Allan Poe. This grim little structure was known to the neighbors as Poe House.'

31

Chapter 5

Mike Chapman ushered Andy Dorfman down the narrow staircase shortly after 9 P.M. 'The last place that Poe lived in Manhattan, that's what the professor was telling us. Eighteen forty-five, right?'

'Eighteen forty-five, forty-six. It was called Amity Street then. Number Eighty-five Amity Street. Greenwich Village,' Davis said.

Dorfman was as excited by the find as I was. The literature major in me thought it extraordinary to be in these haunting surroundings that Poe had actually inhabited. The literary provenance seemed to matter not at all to the forensic anthropologist. He made straight for the skeleton and spent several minutes just staring at it, his two technicians over his shoulder, before he set his large metal case on the floor and opened it to remove some of his tools and a camera.

Mike leaned in to talk to Andy. 'What can I do to be useful? Imagine you've got the greatest American writer of his time, the man who created the first fictional detective – damn, I bet Coop can recite his poetry, can't you? – and all the while he's living next door to a corpse.'

Andy waved him off. 'Back off, Mike. Let me get some

shots before we open this up. Any bets that Poe himself was the perp?'

I thought of all the stories I had read from adolescence on by the master who created the genre that had become modern crime writing, including everything from mystery and detection to horror.

'That's like suggesting someone in my own family's a murderer,' Nan said. 'Don't break my heart.'

'You have to admit,' I said, as Andy's flash went off repeatedly and his assistant loaded film into a second camera, 'he was fascinated with premature burial and entombing people in odd ways.'

'These bones are gonna talk to Andy. They're gonna tell him everything,' Mike said. 'Seven hundred homicides a year citywide. How many are like this – skeletal remains?'

'Only one for the last twelve months,' Andy answered.

'No wonder you're so frisky. You might earn your keep, starting out the new year with something to dig your teeth into.'

Pathologists worked with soft tissue – flesh, brains, organs. Anthropologists worked with bone, and rarely in New York City did Andy get the chance to do only that.

'Here's what we're going to do. The three of us will try to take another section of brickwork down. You got gloves, Mike? I may need you to hold on to your friend here as we remove the support in front of him. Then we'll see whether there's anything inside with him, on the ground, to give us a sense of date.'

Mike pulled a pair of rubber gloves out of his rear pants pocket and started to put them on, while Andy's assistant tossed some to Nan and to me.

'So, where's his fingers?' Mike asked, stepping toward the wall.

'The phalanges probably dropped off. Small bones do that,' Andy said, shining his flashlight over the side of the brick column and looking down. 'The spinal ligament's still in place. That's what connects the bones to each other, so it keeps the body and head together – for the moment. But your friend's never going to come out of here in one piece. This will be a long night.'

Andy and his team were suited for work in white lab coats and boots, and they laid out a sheet on the floor in front of the skeleton's vertical coffin. Professor Davis watched us from his remote corner of the room.

With construction tools that they had brought with them, Andy's assistants began to chip carefully away at the layer of bricks. The first four came out easily, and still the upper torso remained in place.

'Mind if I try something?' Mike said, lifting one of the stones and carrying it over to the table. He compared it with several others that had been mounted there and labeled as objects from the original foundation. 'Looks like it could be as old as the ones removed from another part of the wall earlier today.'

'This building has been restored and rehabilitated so many times over the years that it's entirely possible there were piles of the old materials just stored down here in the basement, maybe used and reused,' Professor Davis said.

Andy was bagging a couple of the bricks, and into another envelope he was scraping the substance that had bonded each of them to the others. 'Whatever this cement-like compound is might give us a clue about age.'

He laid the bags carefully on the floor, to be tagged and numbered, just as each piece of stone had come down from the wall.

I picked one up and ran my gloved finger over the surface, smoothing out the plastic so I could examine the stone. It was the color of a burnt sienna Crayola, faded from its once red glaze. It was pocked and pitted on the exterior surface, smooth on the sides where it had been resting against one of its mates. The taupe-colored sealant was clumped on the top and bottom, some substance that had fixed it in place for all the years it had been here.

'You and Alex mind holding hands with him for a minute?' Andy asked. 'Gently, Mike. Not like he's a suspect in a homicide.'

We stood on either side of the Thin Man, an arm under each elbow, as Andy directed us while he worked below us to free the last foot of space to ease the rest of the removal. I had handled bones before at the morgue, and I had seen my share of human skeletons on late-night visits to the medical school at the University of Virginia when I was engaged to a student there. This was eerily different and discomforting, as I wondered what brought our unfortunate soul to such a macabre resting place, naturally or unnaturally.

'You see anything down there?' Mike asked.

'Nothing from this angle, but it's too dark to tell.' He picked up his camera and took more photographs, including close-ups from head to legs. 'Okay, guys, let's go.'

The technicians who were assisting Andy moved in next to him. They replaced Mike and me, one of them taking hold of the arms and the other of the skull, while

Andy secured the lower torso. Together they moved the skeleton slowly and painstakingly out of the brick niche and swiveled it onto the sheet, laying it out flat. Leg bones fell away and clattered to the bottom of the brick shaft, and Andy returned to reach in to retrieve them. One by one, he kneeled and laid them out to complete his human jigsaw puzzle, gently and deliberately.

'First thing we're going to do, Mike, is give your pal a new name,' Andy said, leaning back on his heels.

'Because?'

'Because I think he's a she.'

'Ah-hah! Once some more of the bricks came down I was beginning to wonder. But then I've been told you need a magnifying glass to see *my* private parts, too.'

'The hips on this one give her away.'

'Why's that?'

'See where this flares out over here?' Andy said, pointing his finger to the large bones coming out of the lower vertebrae. 'Nature's way of accommodating childbirth. The sciatic notch spreads as a young woman matures, and the pelvis gets wider to be able to hold a fetus. Look at the forehead, too.'

'What?'

'Vertical. Straight up and down. Men's foreheads tend to slope more, form a brow ridge above the eye sockets, while women's generally are like this.' He turned to one of the techs. 'Want to pass the big torch?'

'What are you looking for?' Mike asked.

'You want to know who this is, right? We've got a start on gender. We need to figure out her age, race, height – anything that will direct the scope of your investigation.'

'How about when she went missing behind the wall?'

36

'That's what I'm about to dig for.' Andy turned on the light and moved it slowly over the surface of the crude wooden floor behind the remaining few inches of bricks.

He lifted out some tiny sepia-colored chips, pieces of bone that seemed to have absorbed color from the brown earth on which they had rested. He turned them over and examined them, placing them next to the digitless hands. 'Fingers, probably. Toes are down there, too. Camera, please.'

The tech passed the equipment back to Andy, who took the shots himself. When he finished that task, he bent down close to the wall and reached in again, sifting through some of the remains and scooping a small sampling into a glassine envelope, which he studied before passing it on to Mike.

'See those little fragments?' Andy asked. 'Like small caramelized bits?'

'Yeah.'

'Good chance they're her fingernails, broken off when the bones dropped to the ground years ago. Submit them to the lab along with one of the older bricks. Betcha fifty bucks you'll find some of that sealant stuck to them.'

Mike looked up at Andy. 'You're telling me this lady was clawing at a brick wall to try to get out from behind it?'

Andy nodded.

'So this isn't just a coffin, right? You're saying she was probably still breathing when she went in here, just from what you think is underneath her nail bed?'

Buried alive. I shuddered at the terrifying thought of such a ghoulish demise, at the hopelessness of her delicate fingernails scraping against the stones that had been cemented in place. Nan and I exchanged glances.

Mike was pumping Andy for his techniques, unfamiliar as we both were with skeletal remains.

'Last year's case in midtown, some hard hats found the bones in a concrete slab when they were digging a storage room for an Eighth Avenue pizza shop,' Andy said. 'The girl still had the hair on her head and some ligature around her wrists. Hey, can you get a shot of this?'

One of the techs moved closer and focused his camera on an object on the ground.

'What do you see in there?' Mike asked.

'Looks like a sock. Like a man's sock. I was hoping it would be something of hers.'

Clothing would be a big help in the identification process, Andy explained. If it had great age or distinctive markings, it might lead the detectives to a specific period in time. Modern pieces with logos, labels, and trademarks could pinpoint a year and guide them directly to the place of purchase.

'Big enough to be a restraint?'

'I'll let you see it in a few minutes. Maybe a gag, stuffed in the mouth, but nothing long enough to tie her up, I don't think,' Andy said, as he painstakingly covered every crevice of the small space with his light.

Mike was readying a brown paper bag. 'That'd be good. Get some saliva off it for DNA evaluation.'

'Don't be too excited about that until we know how long she was in here. There are some holes in the back wall of the building. Professor, you still here?' Andy called over his shoulder.

'Yes.'

'What abuts this basement on the outside?'

'A small yard, actually.'

'That's why she's picked clean, Mike. May not mean she's been here two hundred years.'

'Maggots?'

'More likely mice have gotten in and out. Field mice, squirrels, some kind of vermin could have squeezed through these crevices. Picked the flesh clean, but the ligaments would have been left just like they are. Kind of dried out, almost mummified.'

'How'd you date the bones you found uptown?'

'One shiny dime,' Andy said. 'A 1966 ten-cent piece in the cement coffin. We knew that wasn't necessarily the year she was killed, but it couldn't have been any earlier than that.'

He lifted the dark sock with a pair of tweezers and passed it out to be bagged.

'Any pocket change?' Mike asked.

'Nope. But there's something cylindrical standing on its edge.' He reached in again and removed what appeared to be a small ring. An assistant sealed and labeled the package before passing it to me.

The gold-toned band was now tarnished and caked on its surface with some sort of debris. At its widest place, I could make out an engraving in cursive black lines. 'Could be initials. Maybe an *A* and a *T.*'

There was no date, no hallmark. It looked like an inexpensive ring that a young woman would wear.

'Come in close on this, will you?' Andy said, lying prone and making room on the basement floor for Mike as he passed the flashlight to him. 'There's some writing.'

'Where?'

'It looks like a piece of canvas that got caught in the cement on one of the bricks over to the left. See it?'

Mike focused the beam into the recessed brickwork and read aloud: "'Cappozelli's Rat Poison. Manufactured in" – first three letters are all I can get – probably going to be Detroit. I'm making out the *d-e-t*.'

'Does it show a date?'

'Patience is a virtue, blondie.' Mike had his nose pressed against the bottom edge of the wall. 'It's got one of those drawings of a skull and crossbones. "Keep out of reach of children." Looks like Poe is exonerated. The poison was packaged in 1978.'

Chapter 6

Dorfman's team continued to work at dismantling the bricks above the scrap of canvas so that it could be inventoried with the other items. 'So I'm thinking this lady went behind the wall no earlier than 1978.'

'Gagged and naked?'

'Probably. Although that kind of poison is so caustic it could have eaten away clothing or paper, anything that might have been in there with her.'

'You're convinced she was alive when she was bricked in?' I asked. I couldn't shake the image of this woman's final torture, a premature burial evoking a very primal fear.

Mike and Andy looked at each other before answering me. 'Doesn't seem any point in gagging someone already dead, does there, Mike?'

'Depends what kind of games they were playing. What's next?'

'We close up shop for the night,' Andy said. 'You get the PD to secure the building. I come back tomorrow and start a head-to-toe workup on the skeleton. I don't even want to turn her over now.'

'Looking for what?'

'Signs of blunt force trauma. Broken bones from old injuries. Anything that might help determine cause of death, in the unlikely event it wasn't a shortage of oxygen. The kinds of fractures or dental work that can be compared against existing medical records for identification purposes.'

'So sometime about twenty-five, twenty-six years ago, Miss A.T. disappeared, and all we have to do is figure out who she is and why somebody put her here,' Mike said.

Now I was looking for the identities of both Jane Doe and the rapist we were calling John Doe, even though they bore no relation to each other. I'd like to be able to put names and faces to both of them.

'The working conditions are far from ideal here,' Andy said. 'We'll get a team in and then transfer her back to the morgue in the morning.'

Mike called his lieutenant to get the local precinct commander to send patrol cops to safeguard the site. Waiting for them, we walked outside to put Nan Toth in a taxi for the ride home to her husband and kids.

'You got your car?' Mike asked.

I shook my head.

'Put your mittens on. I'm parked around the corner. Aren't you hungry?'

It was after eleven and the audible rumbling from my stomach reminded me that the dinner hour had long since passed.

'Borborygmi.'

'What's that, the *Jeopardy!* final question?' I asked. 'I'll give you twenty bucks without even guessing. Just feed me as fast as you can.'

For as long as I could remember, Mike and Mercer

had bet against me on *Jeopardy!*'s final question every evening that we were together. Whether in a bar or at a crime scene, Mike found a way to interrupt the proceedings to step to the television. He had studied military history in college and could detail more battles, biographies of generals, and the colors of the horses they rode in on than anyone I had ever met.

'Double or nothing. Borborygmi.'

He had seated himself in the driver's seat and wasn't about to let me in from the cold unless I gave in to him.

I banged on the car window. 'I'll buy dinner. I don't have a clue. Open up, okay?'

He unlocked the door and tossed several case folders onto the backseat. The half-eaten bologna sandwich at my feet had some other cop's bootmarks all over it.

'The muscular contractions and expansions of peristalsis that move the contents of your intestines up and down.'

'That was tonight's question?'

'Nope. That's what my doctor told me that rumbling noise is I can hear your flat little belly making. When your stomach's full of food, it mutes the noise. But that disgusting sound you're making now? It's deafening. Can you hold out until we get to Primola?'

'Sure. And there I was, ready to concede that the Battle of Borborygmi was the turning point in the Crimean War.'

Mike drove east and headed uptown to my favorite Italian restaurant, on Second Avenue at Sixty-fourth Street. The sidewalks were empty as predictions for frigid temperatures the next few nights seemed to have driven people inside earlier than usual.

'*Ciao, Signorina Cooper.*' The owner, Giuliano, called to Adolfo, the headwaiter, 'Set up that table in the corner for Mr Chapman. *Subito.* I'll have Fenton send your drinks right over.'

The restaurant had long been my favorite, not just for the good food, but because we were treated like family. It was always pleasant, at the end of a long day, to be greeted warmly by Giuliano, whose hard work and great kitchen made his restaurant a well-known watering hole for New Yorkers with fussy palates.

'Kitchen still open?'

'For you, Mr Mike? Even if I had to boil the water myself.'

'Skip the usual cocktail, Giuliano. I don't want anything with ice cubes in it. Give us a nice bottle of red wine,' Mike said.

No matter how cold the weather, Mike never wore an overcoat. His navy blazer was a trademark, along with his thick head of dark hair and an infectious grin that only the most depraved crime scenes could suppress.

'You know what you'd like to eat or you want to see a menu?' Adolfo asked.

'Anything but ribs,' Mike said. 'I've had enough of them tonight.'

'I'll take the hottest bowl of soup you can cook up. Stracciatelle? And then some risotto with sausage and mushrooms.'

'A veal chop for me. Biggest one you've got back there. String beans, potatoes, throw everything in the kitchen on the side, okay? And tell Giuliano to come back and join us.'

The owner was as tall as Mercer – six feet six – with

an expansive personality, at once charming and tough. He had come to the States from a small town in northern Italy and worked his way up from a position as a waiter in a well-known restaurant to running his own chic eatery.

Adolfo poured the wine for us and went off to place the order. I told Mike about the new case with my old silk stocking nemesis and explained how Mercer and I had convinced Battaglia to let us go ahead with our idea to indict his genetic profile to allow us to connect the newest cases to the older ones.

The soup arrived and I began to eat while Mike chewed on bread sticks. 'Tell me how Val is,' I said. 'I thought she looked fantastic last week.'

Mike had fallen in love with an architect he met almost two years ago, while she was recovering from surgery for breast cancer. It was the first serious relationship he had been involved in since we started working together ten years earlier.

'Yeah, she's in great shape. That was my best Christmas present, after the scare we had last fall. She got a clean bill of health in December.'

Mike Chapman had just celebrated his thirty-seventh birthday a few months back, half a year before I would. We came from vastly different backgrounds and had grown to be great friends. There were no two people I would rather have covering my back than Mike and Mercer, and I delighted in the happiness that had so radically changed both their lives recently.

Michael Patrick Chapman was the adored son of a legendary cop who, as a second-generation immigrant, had returned to Ireland and married a girl from the family home in Cork. Their three daughters and Mike were raised in Yorkville, and Brian was fiercely proud that Mike chose to be the first in the Chapman line to attend college. While in his third year at Fordham, where he immersed himself in military history when he wasn't waiting tables to supplement his student loans, Mike's father suffered a fatal coronary the day after he retired and surrendered his gun and shield. Mike graduated the next year, but enrolled in the Police Academy immediately, determined to follow in the giant footsteps of the man he most admired.

'Val looked like a natural with Logan in her arms,' I said. We had all been together for dinner at Mercer's house in Queens. He and his wife, Vickee, were the parents of a little boy, born last year and named Logan.

At forty-three, Mercer had a new stability in his life, with his remarriage to Vickee and with fatherhood, a role he took so seriously. There were not many first-grade detectives in the NYPD, and Mercer was one of the few African-Americans to hold that distinction. He had once been assigned to homicide with Mike, but preferred – as I did – the opportunity to work with victims, whose recovery from their trauma could be aided by the relationship with a compassionate investigator.

'Six months ago I probably would have snapped at you for going in that direction. Now I'm starting to think it wouldn't be so bad. A kid is all Val wants,' Mike said.

I smiled at him. 'Think of all the broken hearts there'll be when she takes you off the market. Officially, I mean.'

'Yeah, well, I'm trying to buy up every deck of Old Maid in the toy stores around town. You're wearing that logo like it's embedded in your forehead. You don't even look upset about it.'

'I actually feel kind of relieved,' I said, as Adolfo

replaced the empty soup bowl with our entrées. My relationship with television newsman Jake Tyler had ended abruptly last October, after a long period during which I could feel our emotions unraveling and tangling both of us in their debris.

'First-class jerk if you ask me. Shit, I would have married you just for the house on the Vineyard.'

'You still can,' I said, reaching to refill my wineglass.

'Too much angst, Coop. You and me? You'd probably cut off my balls the first time I rolled over in bed and closed my eyes. It's bad enough you're always telling me what to do on the job. Think what would happen the first time you tried that between the sheets. Talk about murder.'

I had grown up in a loving family, too, but came to public service from a completely different direction. My two older brothers and I were young kids when my father, Benjamin Cooper, revolutionized the field of cardiology with an invention that he and his partner created for use in surgical procedures. The small piece of plastic tubing known as the Cooper-Hoffman valve remained an essential component in every operation done in this country for the fifteen years thereafter.

The trust fund that my father established for each of us was a cushion while he encouraged us to find ways to give back to society by working in the public sector. My schooling in Westchester was followed by a degree from Wellesley College, and then law school at the University of Virginia. It was in Charlottesville that I fell in love with Adam Nyman, the young physician who was killed in an automobile accident as he drove to the Vineyard to be married at the beautiful old farmhouse we had bought together.

'It's odd sometimes. So many of my pals saw that it wasn't going to work with Jake before I did.'

Nina Baum, my college roommate and closest friend, had been the first to tell me to step back. There had been a point early on when I was certain enough of my love for Jake that I had moved into his apartment so we could try living together.

'Hard to miss the clues, kid. He just wasn't there when you needed him.'

'Or when you thought I needed him.'

Mike was devouring the chop while I pushed the risotto around my plate. 'Eat up before I start on your meal,' he said, pointing his fork at my food. 'Mercer and I have it all figured out. What you need is a nice brainiac kind of guy who has a solid nine-to-five job, with no emergencies, no summit meetings in Asia to cover.'

Jake had been a reporter for network news. He spent more time on airplanes than I did at crime scenes. 'It's not just the travel—'

'Whoa, I'm not done. He's got to have a lot of self-confidence and—'

'I can wait till you stop eating.'

'See what I mean? What you really wanted to say right now was to tell me not to talk until I'm finished chewing, right? You just can't help yourself, can you? Most important, this guy should be mute.'

''Cause you think I don't let him get to say what he wants?'

'No, 'cause I think the urge to tell you to shut up would be powerful.'

'What to know something interesting?' I asked.

'Don't change the subject. You don't think that's going

48

to stop me from starting a search committee to find a mate for you? Otherwise you'll take out all your frustration on Mercer and me.'

'I'm not the least bit frustrated at the moment. I've just been thinking about this. Tonight was the second time I've actually been in a room that Edgar Allan Poe lived in.'

'Body or no body?'

'Guess we have to go back and check under the floorboards. He spent a year at the University of Virginia, 1826. I think it was only the second year Jefferson's school had been open. Poe lived on the west range of the Lawn. The room's been restored to look like it did when he was there: fireplace, small bed, chair, and desk. Number thirteen.'

'Superstitious? Wouldn't have worked for me to live there.'

Giuliano came over to the table and pulled out a chair to sit with us. 'I was just in my office, watching the late news. So this guy, this Silk Stocking guy. This is your case, Alexandra?'

'Yes, he is. Again.'

'I know you're going to think this is crazy, but I swear to you: that sketch they just showed on television? That man was in here a couple nights ago. He was right over there at the bar, drinking with a group of guys for an hour or two. I swear it was your rapist.'

Chapter 7

'That's just a sketch they showed on the news, Giuliano. It's not a photograph.'

'I know that. But he's got an unusual face, no?'

The Silk Stocking Rapist was distinctive-looking to me, if in fact he closely resembled the inked rendering. Most often the portraits created by police artists looked like a generic composite that would not enable anyone to pick the assailant out of a crowd.

This perp had features that each of his victims had described to the man who worked, four years ago, on the drawing they all agreed resembled their attacker. He had almost a cherubic affect, with soft, puffy cheeks that rounded the shape of his face and seemed to push his eyes into a permanent squint. His dark black skin made it hard to notice the fine mustache that traced the outline of his upper lip, but several women described the way it felt when it brushed against their skin.

'What night was he in here?' Mike asked.

Giuliano had a great mind for his business. Customers came in once and it was rare that he would forget them when they reappeared weeks later. A nod of his head and Adolfo would know whether to seat the arrivals in the front, with his most prominent clientele, or bury them in Siberia, near the kitchen, or by the steps to the rest rooms.

'A couple, maybe three nights ago. Late, like close to midnight.'

'Was it two nights or three?' I pushed him, knowing that two nights would place him here drinking just hours before Annika Jelt was accosted.

'Fenton,' he said, stepping away from the table and whispering to the bartender, who thought for a few seconds and shrugged before responding to his boss.

'He's pretty sure it was the night before last. He remembers the guy, too,' Giuliano said, 'and Fenton was off three nights ago.'

'You know the people he was here with?'

'Three guys. Investment bankers, maybe. You know the type. Two of them on their cell phones the whole time, talking about the market and deals. Money, money, money. No talk about broads even – nothing but money. And flashing lots of cash,' Giuliano said, describing their manners and clothing, down to the brand of gold watch each was wearing. 'Not regulars. Maybe Fenton knows them.'

He waved to the bartender, who came over to the table. Fenton, too, agreed that no one in the group was familiar to him.

'None of them? No one you ever saw before? Nobody paid by credit card?'

'Two of them put hundred-dollar bills on the bar. I checked them myself.'

'This isn't exactly a halfway house, Giuliano,' Mike said. Local politicians, celebrities, sports stars, and well-to-do

New Yorkers sat elbow to elbow at the tables that were turned over three times a night. 'The cheapest scotch you serve is eight bucks a pop, so who were these guys? You hear their conversation, Fenton?'

'Some of it. The guy who put the first bill down, I think he was French. He did most of the talking. Sounded like they had all come from a party together and just dropped in here before they split.'

'Was there only one black guy in the group?'

'Yup.'

'He talk a lot?'

'Drank mostly. Don't remember him saying much.'

Mike looked at me. 'You and Mercer got room for me on the task force? If you can arrange for me to have this post – just park me here at Primola's bar – I can help keep the city safe.'

'That's a deal. This one's a real long shot, Giuliano. Just promise me you'll call nine-one-one if you think you see this guy again.'

'You're not convinced?' Mike asked. 'You're the one who spent the better part of a year going to every community meeting and school association, if I recall correctly, telling people in this very neighborhood that the Silk Stocking Rapist lived or worked right among them.'

What a thankless assignment that had been for Mercer and me. Some rapists were opportunists who attacked whenever the moment presented itself, whether the prey was fifteen or seventy-five years old. If she was in the wrong place at the right time for the perp, and she was vulnerable, he struck. This one was different. He targeted a physical type – most were tall, slim young women, in their twenties – and so far he had never deviated from his profile. Week after week we'd respond to requests to talk to citizens groups about the Silk Stocking Rapist's pattern and the risks posed in his targeted residential community. Rarely did any women under the age of sixty show up to listen to us, and the seniors who came could have passed our suspect on the street without his thinking twice about committing a crime.

'Look at the man in your corner deli,' I used to tell everybody, 'the dishwasher in the restaurant on your block whose shift ends at one A.M., right before the attacks started. Your doorman, the super down the street, the guy next to you on the subway platform.'

'So why couldn't he show up in your favorite restaurant, Coop?'

'It's certainly in the zone. So next time, Giuliano, make sure you get the glass he was drinking from before it goes in the dishwasher. A little saliva for his DNA is all we need. C'mon, Mike. I'm whipped.'

He drove me the short distance to my apartment and waited until one of the doormen let me inside and walked me to the elevator.

I flipped on the lights and stopped to hang up my coat and scarf in the hall closet. I picked up the pile of mail that my housekeeper had left on the credenza and carried it into my bedroom. There was no flashing light on my answering machine, one more sign of my newly unattached lifestyle. Somehow, wherever in the world Jake Tyler had been on assignment, he left loving messages for me that cheered me when I returned at whatever ungodly hour from a day too full of violence and heartbreak.

I clicked on the television and listened to the local all-news channel as I undressed, washed up, and crawled into bed. After reports of a suspicious breach of security at a nuclear power plant upstate and a car accident in Times Square that killed three tourists, the commentator replayed the police commissioner's seven o'clock statement.

Mercer was behind the commissioner's shoulder as he announced that the Manhattan Special Victims Squad had identified a sexual assault pattern within the confines of the Nineteenth Precinct on the Upper East Side. Reporters at the foot of the podium furiously scribbled details of the cases, holding Xeroxed copies of the sketch that was posted on an easel next to Mercer.

'This is Manhattan SVS pattern number three of the new year,' he said.

'How'd you slip the first two by us?' the *Post* veteran, Mickey Diamond, called out.

Here it was, only the last week in January, and three serial rapists had each claimed a corner of the island to terrorize.

'The first is in Chinatown, Mickey. Three cases involving abductions of women who are here illegally. Their status has not in any way affected our investigation of the cases, but it has made some of the victims' families reluctant to report details to us, and we're happy for any information the public has to offer.' The subliminal message was that the rest of us weren't in danger from a criminal targeting poor immigrant women, who were unlikely to seek police assistance because of their immigration status.

'Pattern number two is in Washington Heights,' the commissioner continued. 'Five cases, starting at the end of last year. These have all occurred at known drug locations.'

'Junkies?' Mickey interrupted again. 'Junkies and hookers?'

'The victims have alternative lifestyles, Mickey. So far, they've been very cooperative. We have a couple of suspects and are making great progress on the investigation.'

No wonder there had not been a press conference to announce patterns one and two, which my unit had been working on with the crew at SVS, around the clock and on all cylinders. Those cases weren't seen as impacting the lives of most Manhattan residents. Location, location, location, as they say in real estate. The Upper East Side made for different concerns and flashier headlines.

The commissioner tried to pick up his narrative about the new case. 'On January twenty-sixth, at 0300 hours, a twenty-two-year-old female was attacked as she entered a brownstone at Three Thirty-seven East Sixty-sixth Street, between Second and First Avenues.'

He described the physical assault in graphic detail. The stabbing would raise more alarm and attract more attention than a sex crime. Often, when people heard the word 'rape,' they foolishly assumed something had occurred as much because of the woman's behavior as the man's. Rape remained the only crime that too many people considered 'victim precipitated,' and scores of listeners would thereby distance themselves from their potential vulnerability by assuming it was an act that couldn't happen to people like them.

Now the commissioner gave the press hounds the news hook they were waiting for. 'You may recall that several years back, the department declared a pattern of cases, also in the Nineteenth Precinct, that remained unsolved when the perpetrator seemed to have vanished four years ago. You gentlemen and ladies dubbed him the Silk Stocking Rapist, which is far too elegant a name for the vile things he does.'

The gallery came alive. 'Same guy?' one reporter called out.

'The ME's office has confirmed through serological testing that—'

'I thought this week's case wasn't a rape. How'd you get DNA?' another said.

'We're not going to tell you what physical evidence we do have, but a match to genetic material from the crime scene has been declared by the lab, so that we have confirmed our belief that the cases are related. We have reassembled a task force and we'll give you the details of that,' the commissioner said, stepping back so the chief of detectives could describe the operation he had hurriedly put in place.

'Last time around, how many cases were there?' a young kid on the City Hall beat asked.

'Five completed rapes, four other attempts,' the chief answered.

I thought of another eight crimes that rested in my case folder, which had not been connected by forensics but which had the same nuances of language and order of sexual acts the rapist performed to make me certain it was the work of the same man. The mayor had ordered the PC not to heighten the public's fear by including those other cases.

'This new attack, what'd the girl look like?'

A question like that could only have come out of the mouth of Mickey Diamond. In no other kind of case would a news reporter ask for a description of the woman.

But the tabloid's titillating version of sexual assault stories required the flaxen-haired filly or the buxom blue-eyed beauty to fill in the blanks occasioned by the media rule of not naming rape victims in their stories.

'Still using silk stockings, or has he aged into support hose since the last time we saw him?' Diamond asked, to amuse the reporters around him.

I clicked off as they were appealing for the public's help and offering reward money for tips leading to the arrest of the attacker.

When I opened my door at seven the next morning, the rapist's face stared up at me from the front page of both tabloids, and above the fold on the Metro section of the *Times*. I showered and dressed for work, and drove downtown in my SUV to grab a parking space as close to my building as possible, sparing myself a cold, slippery walk.

I spent the morning reviewing notes of phone messages that my secretary, Laura Wilkie, had downloaded from the unit's hotline. For a bit of reward money, people were willing to turn in ex-husbands, unfaithful lovers, and ne'er-do-well nephews. All the leads would be turned over to Special Victims for follow-up calls.

Then I studied the file of Darra Goldswit's case, readying a checklist of questions for her grand jury presentation.

I heard Chapman's voice outside my office, in Laura's cubicle, just after 11 A.M. 'Morning, Moneypenny. Give us a kiss, will you?'

I knew she'd be in a good mood for the rest of the week. Laura was a perfect foil for Mike's flirtatious humor.

He ambled through the door, ran his fingers through

the thick slice of black hair that rested on his forehead. 'Carmine Cappozelli, purveyor of the purest and most potent rat poison this side of the Mississippi, sends his warmest personal regards. Told me he manufactured his first batch of rodent botulism in 1978.'

'We knew that from the label you read.'

'Yeah, but none of it was shipped until 1979. So that's the revised earliest date our skeleton went into the closet. That's why you need a good detective, instead of going on the stupid assumptions you lawyers make. Saves you a year of unnecessary digging.'

'What other useful calls have you made?'

'Cold Case Squad. Scotty Taren caught the squeal. He's meeting me here later so we can run up to the morgue. See how far Dorfman gets today.'

'Where does he even start on something like this that happened a quarter of a century ago?'

'My old man was walking a beat back then. Wouldn't it be a kick to think it was a case he could have solved? You just got to put yourself there in that time and place, think of the world the victim was living in.'

'Easy to say.'

'Think culture, Coop. *Kramer vs. Kramer* won the Oscar, Mother Teresa got the Nobel Peace Prize, Margaret Thatcher became prime minister of England, the Shah was booted out of Iran, *Sophie's Choice* was the bestselling book in America, *Saturday Night Fever* was the album of the year, Pittsburgh won the World Series, Martina beat Chrissie at Wimbledon, Spectacular Bid won the Kentucky Derby, and both John Wayne and Nelson Rockefeller died – but only one of them went in the saddle and it wasn't the guy who was supposed to. Are you there yet?'

'Close.'

'There were eight hundred fifty-four homicides in the city, and two hundred sixty-three missing persons. Our babe fits somewhere in the middle of those numbers. I'm handing this to Scotty on a silver platter. I expect an ID by Monday. Where's Mercer?'

'He'll be here at one.'

'I've got trial prep on a shooting from last summer with your psycho-colleague, Pedro de Jesus. If we start now, he may get himself up to speed by the spring thaw. I'll swing by later on.'

He turned and bumped into Mickey Diamond, who was on the prowl to see what I knew about the rape pattern.

'I owe you a few rounds, Chapman. Lunch on me at Forlini's?'

'Not today, buddy,' Mike said, trying to brush past the reporter.

'Did Chapman tell you he bet me fifty large that you'd be playing solitaire on Valentine's Day? I was dumb enough to think this was the real deal for you and Jake—'

No wonder Mike was trying to make a quick exit. 'Wagering on my love life? Counting the days until Jake threw me back in the water? The sign of a true friend, Detective Chapman. Old maid, solitaire . . . nice to know you feel my pain.'

I cracked open the window behind me and reached for a handful of snow off the top of the air-conditioning unit while Mike tried to apologize to me and shut Diamond up at the same time.

'Can you give me any scoops on the East Side case, Alex? Something I can quote to keep it on the front page tomorrow?'

'Nada. Scram, will you? I'll have news for you at the beginning of the week. Get lost. Follow Chapman and steer clear of me, okay?'

I finished rounding the icy slush into a ball and lobbed it at the back of Mike's head. 'Don't write me off yet for Valentine's Day, sucker. The *Post* can always run another personal ad for me.'

'Can't do worse than the first one,' Mike said, wiping off the snow.

Several years back, on a very slow news day after I had taken over the unit, Diamond had written a piece that he titled 'Legal Miss Who Misses Kisses.' His theory was that I was crazy to take this job because no man in his right mind would want to date a woman who might confuse the first pass with an inappropriate touch – a criminal one.

'Harpo Marx, is he still alive? He's mute, right? Perfect for you. I'll see if I can find a number for him, blondie. Let me tell you what we ran into last night,' Mike said, sauntering out of the office with Diamond at his side.

'Mike!' I tried to stop him but he didn't turn back. I didn't want him to leak word of the skeleton before I had a chance to tell the district attorney about it. It might come to nothing, but Battaglia would have my head if I made the wrong call on a story like that.

Chapter 8

'Raise your right hand, place your left hand on the Bible, please. Do you solemnly swear to tell the truth, the whole truth, and nothing but the truth?'

Darra Goldswit answered me. 'I do.'

I was standing at the back of the room, behind the two tiers of seats in which twenty of the twenty-three grand jurors were arrayed in amphitheatrical fashion, facing the witness. To my left sat the foreman and his assistant, along with the secretary. The stenographer was seated beside the young woman to record every word spoken.

I had tried to calm Darra by assuring her there would be no surprises at this proceeding. The defendant had no right to be present. There was no defense attorney to cross-examine her. The questions I had reviewed with her would likely be the only ones she had to answer, unless I left out something relevant that a juror caught at the end of my presentation. I had done this enough times to be confident that would not happen.

Two of the young lawyers from the unit had asked to sit in as observers, and the warden leaned against the door, interested in the charges that I had submitted on the slip of paper I had filed with him earlier in the day.

'Would you tell the jurors, please, what your name is and where you live?'

'Darra Goldswit. I live in New Jersey now. I moved there from Manhattan.'

'I'm going to direct your attention to March eighth,' I said, giving her the date of her attack, emphasizing that it had occurred almost five years ago. There was audible murmuring among the jurors now, as they did exactly what I had reminded them was improper just moments ago. They nodded and winked at each other, puffing up with pride as the one grand jury among six that was getting to decide the front-page news.

'How old are you now?'

'Twenty-seven. I turned twenty-seven earlier this month.'

'Are you employed?'

'Yes. I'm the assistant to the manager of public relations at Madison Square Garden. I've worked in that office since I graduated from college six years ago.' Smart, stable, responsible – qualities all summarized in a job description and title. A trial jury would get more detail, but in these bare bones presentations, this would do the trick.

'Can you tell us what you did on the evening of March eighth?'

'Certainly.' I could see that her hands were trembling slightly as she kept them clasped on the table in front of her. 'I was at the Garden that evening. There was a special event, a basketball game with professional athletes who were raising money for charity. I had to stay at my office until the event ended, shortly after midnight.'

'Did you leave the Garden alone?'

'No, no, I didn't. My boss had a car service waiting to take him home. It picked us up on Thirty-fourth Street and Eighth Avenue.' She pressed her fingers tightly together. 'He was tired and wanted to get home to his apartment on Park Avenue, so he asked me if it was okay to drop me at the corner of Park and Seventy-sixth Street. It was about one A.M.'

I could have started my questions at the front door of her building, but wanted this jury to hear that this victim, unlike several of the others targeted by the rapist, had not been walking from a neighborhood bar or coming from a party.

'I lived between First and Second back then, so I just walked east on Seventy-sixth Street.'

'Did you talk to anyone on the way?'

'No. I didn't see a soul.'

'What happened next?'

'My building's a brownstone. I climbed the six steps with my key in my hand. I stopped to unlock the door, and just as I opened it I felt this body on my back – suddenly, out of nowhere.'

She paused to compose herself. 'His left arm was around my neck and he was holding a really sharp object – I couldn't see it but I could feel it sticking into my neck. That was in his right hand. I – I froze. He was talking the whole time, really softly. "Don't scream and you won't get hurt. I don't want to cut you. I just want your money." He kept pushing me inside until he could close the door behind us.'

Jurors were slinking down in their seats, all of them staring in Darra's direction. They were fidgeting as they watched her try to calm herself. This would be the hard

63

part, I had warned her. Looking twenty-three strangers in the eye and telling them the story of the most intimate assault one human could commit upon another.

'What did he do next, Darra?'

'I handed him my pocketbook and he told me to keep walking. He pushed again, this time toward the staircase, and told me to go upstairs.' She stopped. 'I wouldn't move.'

'Did he say anything else?'

'Yes,' she answered, nodding her head. '"Go upstairs or I'll kill you."'

She stopped to take a breath and most of the jurors seemed to hold theirs.

'He dug the knife into my neck then. I, um, we went up slowly, 'cause he wouldn't take his arm away from my throat, and when we got to the landing at the top he handed me back my bag and told me to take out my wallet so he could count my money.'

'What did you do?'

Darra looked away from me and the jurors, toward the clock on the wall. 'I was stupid enough to believe that's what he wanted.'

'Did you open your wallet?'

'Sorry. Yes, I did.' Darra's head was down. 'He slammed me into the wall and crushed my face against it while he went through my wallet. He wasn't looking for money – he never took a thing from me. He wanted my ID to see which apartment I lived in, 2D – it was right on my license. He said it out loud.'

I waited for her to go on.

'Then he dragged me by my hair, still with the knife to my throat, up another flight and right to my apartment door. He made me open the door.'

She was trying to talk even as the words got wrapped up in her tears. She was reliving the events and getting to the worst moment.

'Take a deep breath, Darra. Would you like to step outside?'

'I want to get this over with, Ms Cooper,' she said, shaking her head. 'He made me open the door. I tried to beg him not to but he smacked my ear with the handle of the knife. He closed the door behind us and told me to get on the bed, and that's when he saw my fiancé.'

'Where was your fiancé?'

'We had a studio apartment. Henry – Henry Tepper is his name. Henry was asleep in the bed, right next to the door.'

'What did the man do?'

'He made me stand beside the bed, next to Henry,' she said, now sitting on her hands and looking up at me. 'He put the knife next to my eye. Like this.'

'For the record, Ms Goldswit is holding her finger against her left eye.'

'Yeah, he was sticking the knifepoint in my eyelid. He handed me something. I couldn't tell what it was, 'cause my eyes were half closed. I looked down and it was panty hose.'

'What happened next?' There weren't a lot of different ways to ask the questions that moved the story along and elicited all the elements of the crime.

'"Wake him up," he said. I leaned over to touch Henry's arm and he woke up, sort of groggy. The guy told him that if he moved a muscle, the knife was going to go right into my eye.' Darra leaned an elbow on the table and rested her forehead in her hand.

'What did Henry—?'

'He didn't do anything. He couldn't do anything. The guy made me tie his hands behind his back. I tried to do it loose but it wouldn't have mattered. He never took the knife away from my eye, so Henry never moved. Didn't say a word.'

She described how the man made her undress and lie down next to Henry before he lowered his pants and straddled her. There were never more than five seconds that the blade of the knife was not next to her eyelid. When the attack was completed, the rapist used more hosiery to tie Darra's hands and feet, as well as tighten Henry's bonds. He ripped the telephone cord out of the wall and walked out the door of the apartment.

It took more than ten minutes before they could untie each other and pound on a neighbor's door to ask her to call the police.

I needed to establish that Darra had not recently had intercourse with Henry, to prove that he was not the source of the seminal deposits recovered. Her testimony ended with the hospital examination that yielded the sample for DNA analysis, through which her assailant would ultimately be identified.

'Did you sustain any injuries during the assault?'

'There were some scrapes and superficial marks on my face and neck, where the knife was poking me the whole time. Nothing that needed stitches or medical treatment.'

'The man who attacked you, have you ever seen him again?'

'No, I have not.'

'Thank you, Ms Goldswit. I have no further questions. If there are—'

I had tried to make this clean and get out without irrelevant inquiries from jurors.

Two hands shot up to make it clear I had not succeeded.

I walked down the steps to juror number nine and he leaned over to ask me, 'Where's Henry? What happened to Henry?'

Henry Tepper was not essential to my presentation, but since he had been an eyewitness to the assault on Darra – and himself a victim – it was natural that jurors would be curious about him. They didn't need to know that he had been unable to handle the guilt of not being able to prevent his fiancée from being raped – secondary victimization, as the shrinks called it. They didn't need to know that he had broken their engagement a month after the attack and moved back to Phoenix.

'When is the last time you spoke with Mr Tepper?'

'Last night. I called him last night. I hadn't heard from him in a couple of years. He lives in Arizona now.'

The gentleman who asked the question sat back, satisfied somehow to know that Henry was out of town, and out of Darra's life.

Juror number eleven was still waving frantically to me. I circled the front of the room to take her question before putting it on the record. 'Is it still rape,' the elderly woman asked, 'even if she didn't fight the man? I mean, he didn't actually cut her with the knife, did he?'

It had been more than twenty years since the last of the archaic legal requirements had been stricken from the books. How is it that people still clung to these medieval attitudes? Well into the 1980s the law in New York State had demanded that sexual assault victims resist their attackers to the utmost, even when confronted with deadly physical force. Too many women were injured and killed resisting assailants who were armed and stronger than their prey.

'After the testimony is completed, I'm going to charge you on the specific elements of each of the crimes. I'll give you the definitions of every term used in the indictment.' I would be telling this nitwit that the crime was accomplished if the sexual act was compelled by physical force, present here, or by the threat that placed either of the witnesses in fear of immediate death or serious physical injury. How much worse could it get than having a blade held against your eyelid, accompanied by threats to kill? 'I expect it will be clearer to you then.'

'Thank you, Ms Goldswit. You may step out now.'

The warden held open the door and she walked out. Mercer was waiting for Darra in the witness room. Like he had done dozens of other times over the years, he would take her back to my office and close the door, calming and reassuring her that those twelve minutes of discomfort would be worth the price of nailing the miserable bastard once we had him in our sights.

My next witness was Marie Travis, the serologist who had done the laboratory examination on the seminal fluid recovered from the body and bed linens of Darra Goldswit.

I took her through her training and credentials, and the duties she had performed for eight years at the forensic biology lab of the medical examiner's office.

'Four years ago were you assigned to the matter designated as the Manhattan Special Victims Squad pattern number five?'

'Yes, I was.'

'And included in that group of investigations, is there

the matter of Darra Goldswit, known by a particular forensic biology number?'

'Yes. That case was FB number 1334.'

'Did you personally conduct the testing in this case?'

'Yes.'

'Did you receive a rape evidence collection kit to examine in this matter?'

'Yes, that kit contained vaginal swabs and slides prepared with samples taken from sheets at the crime scene. Both items tested positive for the presence of semen, from which I was able to extract a sperm cell fraction.'

'Were you able to determine a genetic profile from either of those samples?'

'Yes, from both of them, actually.'

'What determinations did you make?'

'The DNA profile from the victim's vaginal vault was identical to that from the sample on her sheets.'

'Did you compare that profile to others then entered in your data bank?'

'Our data bank was very small at that time, Ms Cooper. We had just gone online several months earlier. I entered the profile but got no matches at that moment.'

Darra's case was the earliest strike, to our knowledge, of the Silk Stocking Rapist, just weeks away from being lost to the statute of limitations.

'Did you undertake a statistical analysis to determine the probability of that profile appearing in the African-American population?'

'Yes, we knew from the victim's physical description of the assailant that he was a black man. We used the probability guidelines established by the National Research Council.'

'In the African-American population, what are the odds of finding the exact profile that you identified and matched on the two samples in Ms Goldswit's case?'

'We would find this, Ms Cooper, only once – one time – in ninety-five billion African-Americans. We could put ninety-five billion men in one place, if we had a big enough room, and only one of them will fit this genetic profile.'

Finding John Doe and pulling him out of that enormous haystack was the only major obstacle left in this operation.

I finished the questions I needed to prove the scientific aspect of the case, linking this crime scene evidence to the human phantom we were about to indict, and followed Marie from the jury room. She knew her way out of the courthouse, and I returned to read the definitions of the various crime categories charged and ask the grand jurors to vote.

When I left the room so they could deliberate, I found Mercer Wallace waiting at the warden's desk. 'Got your vote?'

'Give them five minutes. The novelty of it will take them longer than usual.'

'We've got a problem at Kennedy Airport. You can wait the jury out or come with me,' he said, striding to the hallway.

'What—?'

'Annika Jelt's parents just landed. They've never been more than twenty miles away from their farm before. They don't have proper documentation and immigration won't let them into the country.'

Chapter 9

We both had our gold shields and identification badges in our hands, having been left by an angry immigration officer to cool our heels – and our tempers – while she fetched her supervisor.

'Put the hardware away,' the supervisor said when he joined us in the glass cubicle. 'Rules is rules and I don't break them for anybody.'

I pointed across the corridor to the middle-aged couple, sitting stone-faced on folding wooden chairs like a pair of nineteenth-century Ellis Island immigrants. 'Their daughter is in the intensive care unit of New York Hospital, fighting for her life. We'll vouch for them, sign for them, deliver them back here in a week. What more—?'

'Welcome to America, post nine-eleven. I don't know who let them board without the papers they need, but this is as far as they get on my turf.'

'The Swedish consulate arranged the whole thing. They were escorted onto the plane by an envoy from the American embassy, who gave them a letter that was hand-signed by the ambassador. He was promised by an NYPD captain that they'd be met on this end by a Port Authority official who would arrange everything from this point on.'

'Maybe they can cut corners in Stockholm, lady, but I call the shots at this airport. The paperwork they got at the consulate is outdated.'

Mercer was trying to restrain me, taking the reins with his unflappable demeanor. 'We can do this your way, or we can do it the way the police commissioner just recommended to me. The mayor drives out here with the key to the city and a phalanx of reporters – and you continue to get in his way, or you just bend the regulations a bit and let us get these nice folks on the road.'

We wrangled until after six o'clock, when the shifts changed and a new supervisor appeared. I had called the grand jury warden before the office closed to confirm the indictment had been voted. Within the hour we were on the Belt Parkway back to the city with our charges, who were more frightened than exhausted. The English they had not spoken since high school was basic enough for us to communicate, and I told them as much as I could about their daughter's experience and the news of her great recovery.

Mercer entered Manhattan through the Midtown Tunnel. 'Let me out on First Avenue. I'll catch up with Mike and Andy Dorfman at the morgue.'

I knew the nurses would not allow all of us into Annika's tiny room, and that it was more important for Mercer to be present at the parents' reunion with their child, in case there was any further conversation about the facts of the attack. For me, it would be less stressful, less emotional, to watch the processing of the skeletal remains. Without flesh and blood, the bones seemed too far removed from anyone with whom I could identify.

I had never been in Andy's cubicle in the basement of the medical examiner's office.

The familiar odor of formalin wafted through the dim hallways, and empty steel gurneys lined the walls, waiting for their lifeless loads.

No need to look for room numbers. I could hear Alex Trebek's voice as I passed an open door. Andy was hunched over the left femur of the skeleton, while Mike sat in a chair with his feet on the desk, noshing on a bag of pretzels and looking at the small portable television set on a bookshelf across the room.

'European Literature. You're just in time.'

Our usual bet was twenty dollars. 'Double or nothing,' I said. This was one of my few areas of strength against Mike's concentration on military history and general trivia.

'Not a prayer. Twenty is max. Don't get too cocky, kid. You in, Andy?'

'Nope,' he said, dipping a toothbrush in a bowl of cloudy water and gently scrubbing against the bones.

'He hasn't stopped working since we left him last night,' Mike said. 'A little toothpaste, a little soap – our girl will be cleaned up in no time.'

'Writer who lost an arm at the Battle of Lepanto,' Trebek read aloud from the answer board to the three finalists, each of whom looked as pained as I did by the question.

'That category's a mischaracterization,' I said. 'You just got lucky. It's war in the guise of literature.'

Mike lifted a Polaroid of the skull from the top of a pile in front of him and scribbled something on the back. 'You first, Coop.'

'Who was . . . ? Give me a hint, will you?' I knew Lepanto was in Greece, but couldn't begin to figure whether the battle was an ancient or modern one.

'No, I'm sorry,' Trebek said to the three-time champion, a waiter from Oregon who was trailing the other two players. 'It was not Alexandre Dumas.'

'Time's up,' Mike said, tapping the photo on which he'd written the question on the tabletop while he twirled Andy's calipers in the other hand.

'Who was Sophocles?'

'Very lame. Bad answer.'

'He was a playwright and a general, wasn't he?'

'Yeah, but he never lost a body part,' Mike said. None of the contestants answered the question correctly. 'Who is Miguel Cervantes? You didn't know he was called El Manco, the one-armed man? Lepanto was the first defeat of the Ottomans by the Christians – Spanish and Venetian mostly. Fifteen seventy-one. Jane Austen and those brooding Englishmen you like to read never left the sheep farm, Coop. I would have won the bundle tonight.'

He held out his hand for the twenty.

'I'll buy dinner. Put it towards that.'

'No can do, Miss Lonelyhearts. Valerie leaves for California tomorrow. Family ski trip for her parents' fortieth anniversary. Going to her place for a home-cooked meal. You know what that is, home cooking?'

'I have a vague childhood recollection.' I had grown up in a close-knit family. My grandmother, who emigrated from Finland as an adolescent, lived with us for many years. Both she and my mother were superb cooks who prepared complicated meals every day of the week and made it seem effortless. We'd spend less than an hour at the dinner table when my father returned home from his surgical rounds, and then the women had to deal with the mounds of plates and pots that had been used in the process. Somehow I never inherited the love for standing over a hot stove that had run through my maternal line.

'Andy's making great progress,' Mike said. 'Scotty and I got up here at five. He's already running with it.'

'With what?' I asked, glancing around the shelves that were lined with fragments of bone and assorted animal skeletons – snakes, an armadillo, and an elegantly horned antelope head among them.

'Basic 'scrip. Enough for Scotty to start looking at old police records and calling other agencies. Explain it to her.'

Andy kept rubbing the surface of the leg bones with his toothbrush. 'We've got a woman – and I'd say a young one, in her early twenties.'

'How can you tell that?'

'Get used to it, Andy. Coop's gonna keep interrupting. All she knows how to do is cross-examine.'

'First thing is getting the bones clean, laying her out in a proper anatomical position. That was easy here. Usually when we find them so many years later, the skeletal pieces are scattered around the scene, or they've been moved by animals. This one had nowhere to go in that brick coffin.'

'But age, how can you tell that?'

'Bones stop growing basically by the time we're twenty-five years old. Up until then they keep changing and fusing together. After that, you begin to see deterioration, which helps us make estimates. They sort of break down, with everything from signs of arthritis to osteoporosis.'

'And here?'

'She's in her early twenties, most probably. It's the pelvis again, and the ribs. She's got good height. How tall are you, Alex?'

75

'Five-ten.'

'I'd say she was somewhere between five-six and five-eight.'

'I was this big by the time I was sixteen. Could she have been a teenager?'

Andy's attention shifted to the skull, and he pointed the toothbrush at the woman's mouth. 'The teeth are interesting. Can you see?'

I stepped closer to the table.

'Some pretty expensive dental work went into this girl. Quality dentistry, including a pricey porcelain crown in one of the back molars.'

I could see the neat and well-crafted denture in the lower part of the jaw.

'Now look up here,' Andy said. 'These teeth evidence some pretty severe rotting.'

'That's an odd combination, isn't it?'

'What it suggests is a kid from a family of means, parents who would pay for first-class dental work throughout her youth and at some stage of young adulthood. The multiple sites of decay are consistent with some other kind of dysfunction going on in her life. Most often it's a slip into addiction or alcoholism. Her mouth exhibits classic signs of someone who has stopped taking care of herself, someone who didn't get medical or dental attention because the substance abuse would be discovered once she was in the hands of a health care professional.'

It was astounding to me how this empty shell of a being was revealing herself to Andy Dorfman. 'Can you tell anything else about her?'

'Give me the calipers, Mike,' he said, reaching across

the table. 'We try to figure out race from the facial character-istics, using tools like this. The distinctions are pretty subtle for the most part – the set of the cheekbones, how far apart the eyes are, the shape and width of the nose. You need the skull to do it, so we're fortunate she was intact – without that, I couldn't even make an educated guess.'

'And here?'

'Caucasian. I'm sure of it. I've put my calculations into FORDISC—'

'What's that?' I asked.

'University of Tennessee keeps a database of cranial measurements, a few thousand of them going back a century. Forensic Discriminant Functions, it's called. Sometimes the facial mask is more obtuse than this one. No question in my mind about this one.'

'So we got a white female in her early twenties,' Mike said. 'Possibly a drug addict or alcoholic. If the ring is hers, her initials are A.T.'

'Anything that tells you how she died?'

Andy ran his eyes up and down the length of the silent specimen on the table. 'Nope. I thought for sure once we turned her over today I'd find a fracture on the back of her skull. I really wanted to.'

'Why?'

He looked up at me. 'Because the alternative is pretty frightening.'

'Nothing worse that I can think of,' I said, recalling the undersides of the broken fingernails, caked with a layer of cement.

'It's one thing to find that she died – say of an over-dose – or was killed, even, and then bricked up inside this wall. But if she was alive, and gagged, and then watched herself being entombed – well, can you think of a more miserable death?'

'Twenty-five years ago, huh?' Mike said. 'I just hope the guy who did this to her is still breathing so I can be there when Scotty slaps the cuffs on.'

'Are you still looking for something else?' I asked.

'The pathologists reviewed it with me – both the X-rays and the bones. They agree there's no other gross cause of trauma. There won't be any kind of death certificate for months down the road, Alex. Whatever fancy medical term they come up with, we're talking buried alive here.'

'Why months?' Mike asked.

'I'm going over the works once more to clean her up. I've got to check more thoroughly for any individualizing characteristics to compare to old records.'

'Like what?'

'Pathologies, like fractures that had healed. I think we've got a hairline fracture of the tibia here. We've x-rayed it and I'll document it with detail and measurements.'

'Will you attempt any kind of facial reconstruction?'

'Sure, Alex, and that slows down the process, too.' First the computer would attempt several forms, based on the shape of the skull and Andy's measurements. Then a forensic sculptor would come in to add texture, to try to humanize the portrait. 'You'll be lucky to have that by April or May. It's a skill very few artists have. The ball's in Mike's court.'

'The NYPD's computer system only has missing persons' reports online back through 1995. Everything earlier has to be a hand-search,' Mike said. 'From there, Scotty's got to notify every jurisdiction in the Northeast. No saying where this chick got here from.'

'And the feds, of course.' New York was a mecca to hundreds of thousands of young men and women, coming to the big city from every corner of the country – to find jobs or go to school, if their heads were on right – or to get caught up in the alternative street life of drugs, alcohol, prostitution, and crime if they were unstable or unwise.

'So you go home and get some beauty rest, Coop. Andy's given us a jump-start on the basics. By the time we go public with the story, we'll have a pretty fair idea of who we're looking for.'

I walked along the green-tiled hallway to the elevator that carried me upstairs to the lobby and out the front door onto First Avenue, where I hailed a cab to go home.

Despite the low temperature, the sidewalks in the Fifties and Sixties were full of pedestrians, making their way to and from the bistros and bars. Friday-night burgers and shooters were staples of the end of the long workweek for many young people looking to socialize before heading to the bridges and tunnels.

How many of the women hoping to hook up with guys tonight knew that a dangerous rapist had this very neighborhood in his scope, I thought, as the cab cruised under the Fifty-ninth Street Bridge overpass? How many of them would walk out alone after four or five drinks – intoxicated and oblivious to their vulnerability – and make their way down the side streets in the early hours of the morning?

I unlocked my door at eight-thirty and dropped my files and pocketbook in the entryway. Next to my bed, the answering machine flashed that there were three messages, and I played them back as I undressed.

'Alex? You there? It's Lesley. How about a movie and

late supper? Give a shout.' Girlfriends were stepping in to try to fill the void left by my breakup with Jake.

That one was followed by a call from Nina Baum, my college roommate and best friend, who lives in Los Angeles. 'No feeling sorry for yourself this weekend. If you get lonely, I'm around all weekend. You did the right thing.' Nina had been the most outspoken about how wrong Jake was for me and tried to keep my spirits up after the split.

'It's Mercer, Alexandra. We're on for tomorrow night. Greg Karras is coming in from the coast. Let me know if you're riding with us.' The geographic profiler was ready to start the hunt for John Doe, and I was game to go.

I returned all three calls – gave Mercer a yes, chatted with Nina about my week, and left Lesley a message telling her I had gotten home too late to accept her offer. I soaked in the bathtub with a stack of magazines beside me, wrapped myself in a warm robe, and settled into the den with a Dewar's, an English muffin, and a Faulkner novel that Jake had left behind.

When I awakened at 7 A.M. I was relieved that I had slept through the night without a call from anyone at Special Victims. My Silk Stocking nemesis had taken another night off.

I opened the door to pick up the newspapers. The *Times* had the latest on Middle East peace talks and presidential gaffes. The tabloids were beneath it and I bent to retrieve them. There on the front page of the *Post* was a photograph of the doomed building on Third Street with a cartoonlike skeleton dangling below a three-inch banner headline: POE'S CRYPT?

Chapter 10

'Did you see the damn article on the cover of that rag this morning?' Paul Battaglia shouted into the phone about five minutes later.

'Yes, boss. I haven't had a chance to read it yet—'

He was quoting from its opening. '"Police sources are puzzling out whether the skeleton found in the basement of an NYU building is just a sad postscript to another age, or actually Edgar Allan Poe's crypt." What the hell is this, Alex?'

'You want to give me a chance to look at it before—'

'Pat McKinney just called me. Says you know all about it. Says you gave this story to Diamond.'

McKinney was deputy chief of the trial division, a wretchedly petty supervisor who seemed to take great pleasure in undermining my work. The week before Christmas his wife had thrown him out, embarrassed by his long-term affair with a coworker, and McKinney was flailing out in all directions as though making other people miserable would ease his own suffering.

'I do know all about it and I should have come in to tell you. I know how Diamond got the tip but it wasn't from me. I'm sorry – I was just so busy in the grand jury yesterday and I never imagined this would be of any press interest. Certainly not before the police figured out who she was and how she died.'

Falling on one's sword often helped with Battaglia, but sometimes you had to do it repeatedly before he'd back off.

'What's the deal on these bones? Tell me everything.'

I gave him the scant information I knew and he asked another dozen questions for which I had no answers.

The rest of my day was planned to be relaxing. I dressed for my Saturday morning ballet class, and covered my tights with warm-up pants and fleece-lined boots to trek through Central Park to the dance studio. I stayed for two hours of lessons, stretching and bending before taking my place at the barre for the exercise routine that helped relieve the week's tension.

Then I hiked back across town to the salon where Elsa and Nana would pamper me, highlighting my blonde hair and cutting it for a midwinter lift.

On the way home I stopped at Grace's Marketplace for some takeout, a lemon chicken breast and steamed broccoli that I could nuke at dinnertime. Mercer would pick me up at midnight and we would remain on our patrol until 4 A.M., so I decided to nap in the early evening and eat dinner before going out on our profiling expedition.

When the doorman called up to tell me Mercer was waiting, I pulled on a black ski jacket over my jeans and went down to the car.

Mercer opened the rear door to let me in a beat-up old Chevy Malibu with chipped paint that had once been a deep navy blue. 'Whose wheels?'

'My next door neighbor's kid. Won't stand out quite as much as a department car or medallion cab. Alex, this is Greg Karras.'

I reached over the seat back and we shook hands. 'Good to meet you. Thanks for flying in. How do we do this?'

'You've got your hands full with this guy. I've studied the old reports and Mercer confirms this is about the time of night he starts to strike, right?'

'Nothing earlier.'

'I'd like to visit each of the locations to get a sense of what his approach has been, what the egress opportunities are.'

Mercer and I had graphed out the crimes for Karras. We decided to start at the northern end of the map and drove to the quiet street where one of the earliest attacks had occurred. Mercer stopped the car in the middle of the block and pointed to a stoop thirty feet farther on. 'Left-hand side, the steps with the wrought-iron handrail.'

Karras got out of the car and walked from our position midblock to the corner of the avenue. A couple sauntered down the street with their arms around each other's waist, stopping to kiss under a streetlight, the guy looking back over his shoulder at Karras. There were no trees anywhere near the victim's building and no place for an assailant to hide in waiting.

'Look at this, Mercer,' I said, pointing at someone approaching the rear of our parked car. 'She's likely to be in my office on Monday if she isn't careful.'

The heavyset young woman was unsteady on her feet. She looked as though she was intoxicated, talking to herself and fishing in her purse for her keys. She stood between two buildings with her back to me, trying to decide which one was her destination.

'I almost want to get out and help her,' Mercer said, 'but she'd probably start screaming bloody murder.'

She pulled herself up the six steps by leaning on the handrail and then fumbled for the right key on the ring to open the door. She would have been an easy target for any thug.

Karras got back into the car and asked us to go to the next location. He was quiet as he made notes on a PalmPilot. Mercer circled down to York Avenue and back to Seventy-eighth Street. Scene after scene, we watched the profiler walk each block and check the intersecting cross streets. He measured distances between street-lamps by walking between them, counting the steps as he put one booted foot in front of the next, and made notations of fire hydrants and the occasional tree.

After the round of visits, we went to an all-night coffee shop on Second Avenue. I was ready to put toothpicks in my eyelids to hold them open.

'What ideas did the task force work on last time?' Karras asked.

'Our first thoughts were businesses in the area. The fact that nothing started until after midnight made us think the guy worked here, got off a duty shift at midnight or one A.M. Victims told us he was clean and that he smelled good. We were thinking restaurants or bodegas. Someone who washed up when he left work,' Mercer said.

'How about hospitals?'

'We've got two big ones in this zone – New York Hospital and Lenox Hill. Same thing – it's a natural fit with shift turnovers. We subpoenaed the files of every male who worked there, from brain surgeons to male nurses to orderlies. Took months to get them all. By the time we'd gone through most of them, he had vanished.'

'And we swabbed plenty of the employees, too,' I said. 'They've been entered in the data bank against the profile.'

'I studied all the police reports Mercer sent me while I was on the plane. Can you give me more details – personal details – about your victims?'

'Everything you want to know,' I said.

'Alex and the lawyers do the most thorough interviews you can imagine. There's nothing we can't tell you about these women.'

I operated on the theory that I needed to know as much about the victim as the defendant knew, and more than the best defense investigator could find out if he applied every resource he had. We also tried to reconstruct every second of the victim's interaction with the offender, things that might help us connect to a suspect and give us probable cause to swab his saliva for DNA comparison.

'Can you bring the task force members together for a brainstorming?' Karras asked.

'Of course. Alex and Sarah Brenner, her deputy, have handled all the victims themselves. I'll round up the team of detectives. For when?'

'I'll let you know when I'm ready.'

'Sure. What do you do now?'

'All this data on street locations that I've been mapping, this tracks the spatial characteristics of the pattern. There's a prototype computer system called Rigel. Once I dump in every crime scene – every hospital, store, school, possible physical boundaries—'

'There are no physical boundaries.'

'You can't have linkage blindness, Alex. There may be more clues that I can pick up on than you're even aware of. This case is going to create a very colorful map.'

'We've already got a map.' I was tired and impatient, growing fearful that this was as useless as the psychological crap.

'I'll give you a jeopardy surface, the rapist's center of operation. You haven't had that yet. The perp's most likely base or anchor point.'

I rolled my eyes at Mercer. 'A jeopardy surface, that's what it's called? Don't tell Mike Chapman, okay?'

'Yeah, I try to pinpoint that – his home or his job. It gets superimposed on the scene locations, which are the virtual fingerprints of the perp. The more crime sites there are, the better the predictive power of this system.'

So Karras's goal was the exact opposite of ours – he'd be happy with even more crimes to fill his colorful grid. I was looking at one of his old samples. A bright red dot for the jeopardy center, orange shading for the offender's preferred area of operation, changing to yellow and then green, blue, and purple for the outer limits of his quarry.

'You basically provide us with where he selects his victims,' Karras said. 'He's got a clear comfort zone, and we know that some of the women are low risk – from his perspective – because he thinks they're alone and in some cases intoxicated. His signatures are obvious – the weapon, the kind of binds, not much profanity, minimal verbalization, the way he subdues his prey. The computer uses his movement patterns and his previous hunting habits.'

'To do what?'

'Statistics tell us that right-handed criminals in a hurry to flee generally make their escape to the left. But they discard their weapons to the right. You haven't charted that fact yourselves, have you? See what happens if you take him left out of every one of these buildings. Where does it lead him? That's what I'm supposed to figure out.'

'Oh,' I said grudgingly, toying with my scrambled eggs and lukewarm decaf.

'Did you know that when lost or confused, men go downhill but women go up?'

He was losing me now. 'It's a perfectly flat neighborhood, Greg. This isn't San Francisco.'

'The guy who first developed this program ten years ago? He did it with a serial rapist in Vancouver. Came up with exactly the same kind of map I'm going to create. Charted seventy-nine crime scenes and the computer spit out a red dot on the exact spot in which his perp lived. Nailed him the next day.'

I wasn't focused on the good news. 'Seventy-nine cases before he got a solution? Couldn't have been many places left in Vancouver to look for the guy by that time. I'll be too old to celebrate if I live through that many more attacks.'

'Wait that long and neither one of us will have a job,' Mercer said.

Mercer's cell phone vibrated and he picked it up off the Formica tabletop. 'Wallace here. Hey, loo, what's up?'

It was 4:17 A.M. and I was fading. The lieutenant was undoubtedly worried about how much overtime he would have to authorize for Mercer on this untested caper.

He stood up and walked to the front of the shop to finish the conversation, scribbling something on a napkin the waitress handed him at the counter. He flipped the phone closed, motioned to us to come as he paid the tab.

'Can you take a cab back to your hotel, Greg? Alex and I have business.'

Mercer moved away from the register and pushed open the front door. The blast of cold air revived me as I stepped onto the sidewalk.

'East Eighty-third Street, between First and York. Brownstone with a locked front door. Female white, panty hose, knifepoint assault.'

Karras had his PalmPilot in his hand, entering the address. 'Boy, once they get good at something, these perverts don't change their style.'

'This one's different, Alex,' Mercer said, ignoring the profiler. 'This time the girl is dead.'

Chapter 11

Mike Chapman was whistling a Sam Cooke tune, meant to get under my skin, as he opened the door to let us into the vestibule of the small building. "'Another Saturday night and I ain't got nobody . . .'"

'Don't you have better things to do with your time, Coop?' he asked, handing us the rubber gloves and mesh booties we needed to enter the crime scene, which was still being worked by Hal Sherman and his crew.

'Where to?' Mercer asked.

'C'mon up to three. It's a floor-through,' Mike said, telling us that the deceased had lived in an apartment that occupied the entire third floor of the building.

I trailed behind them, up the staircase where the clean yellow paint on the walls and banister had now been coated with black fingerprint dust.

'Is she here?' Mercer asked.

'We just got her out fifteen minutes ago. I didn't want to deal with the neighbors and a body bag first thing on Sunday morning.'

The third-floor landing was full of Sherman's baggage – metal trunks that held every piece of equipment necessary to process a crime scene. I stepped over them and into the entryway of the victim's apartment.

Hal was on his knees, taking a series of photographs of smudges – probably blood – on the area rug that covered the hallway. I squeezed his shoulder and stayed behind him until he finished shooting and greeted us.

'You got a time of death?' Mercer asked. A death investigator from the medical examiner's office responded to every homicide in the city. The body wasn't removed from the scene until that had happened.

'He thinks she'd been dead only a couple of hours,' Mike said. 'A friend of the deceased let himself in downstairs at two. They were supposed to meet earlier but she didn't show up. Claims he had a duplicate key, for emergencies. That's when we got the call. The ME was here within an hour.'

'The friend – you holding on to him?'

'Yep. He's cooling his heels at the precinct, writing out a statement. Trust me, he's not the man.'

'Is there a story?'

Mike led us from the entry through the living room, kitchen, bathroom, and into the bedroom, a series of long narrow cubicles that gave the feel of walking through the cars of a railroad train.

I clasped my hand to my mouth to stifle the involuntary noise that gurgled up when I saw the blood that covered the beige linen bedspread. It made the stains outside Annika Jelt's apartment look as if they could have been stemmed by a couple of Band-Aids.

The lamp on the table next to the bed had been knocked to the floor and the telephone line had been pulled out of the wall.

'Emily Upshaw. Forty-three years old,' Mike said,

referring to his notepad. 'Single, lived alone. Been in this apartment almost fifteen years.'

I scanned the room for photographs.

'Brunette, about five foot seven, slightly overweight.'

Mercer frowned. 'She's too old for my boy. And a little too fleshy.'

Mike wasn't bothered by the physical discrepancies. 'She had a ski jacket on – it's in the living room. Hood up, from behind, hard to tell her age – or the size of her waist. Your rapist is older now, too. Maybe he's less picky.'

Mercer shook his head and looked around the room.

There were several pictures on the dresser, all of two or three individuals. Perhaps she was in one of those. Groups of people in a beach scene, on a hiking trail, riding bicycles, and in a wedding party.

'What does – did she do?' I asked. The walls were hung with museum reproduction posters in cheap metal frames, about one step up from college dorm room decor.

'Writer. Freelance magazine pieces, book and movie reviews. Whatever paid the rent, her buddy tells me.'

Mike motioned to us as he walked into the last room, which was set up like an office.

'And she drank, too. Have I mentioned that?'

The overturned wastebasket was crammed with crumpled paper and empty bottles, spilling out of it as it lay on its side. Vodka, mostly, and cheap red wine.

'Screw tops,' he said, lifting a half-filled Burgundy off the desk. 'Girl after my own heart. Slainte, Emily.'

Next to the desk was a stack of newspapers. I flipped through them, all from the preceding week. Yesterday's headlines were on top of the pile.

'The computer?' I asked. 'You checked it?'

'Haven't touched it. It was turned off like this when we got here. I'm going to take the hard drive to be downloaded.'

The computer tech cops were experts at the forensic examination of the machines. Emily's files and e-mails might give some hint of her activities and correspondence, and the 'cookies' on her Web browser would tell us exactly what sites she had been searching in the days before her death. The only likelihood of relevance would be if the killer had not picked her at random and there had been some connection between them before this evening.

I shuffled the files on the desk while Mike talked to us. 'Teddy – that's her friend, Theodore Kroon – Teddy's known Emily for almost fifteen years.'

'Romance?'

'Not the way Teddy swings. I didn't ask him how they met. They were supposed to hook up tonight, around midnight, at a bar on York Avenue.'

'Midnight? Why so late?' I asked.

'Emily had to do a piece on a performance artist who was appearing at the Beacon Theater. Some musical geek who plays Burt Bacharach songs in the style of Beethoven, reciting the lyrics in German. Wasn't due to break until almost eleven. She planned to come home to drop off her notes and change clothes since she had to pass right by the apartment on her way to York Avenue. Then she was joining Teddy for cocktails.'

Mercer picked up the thread. 'So you figure she got popped on the stoop?'

'Probably. Can't find any witnesses yet, but that's how the others got it, isn't it? Her handbag's in that front room with the keys inside it.'

'How'd you find her?'

They started back to the bedroom. The articles she'd been working on could not have produced much income. A search for the best homemade ice creams in Brooklyn, the controversy over whether owls should be sold as domesticated pets, and the effect of winter weather on the projected population of deer ticks in the Hamptons for the coming summer. I replaced the folders and joined up with the guys.

'Facedown on the bed. Naked.'

'Completely?' Mercer asked.

'Yeah. Her clothes were in a pile next to the bed.'

'Did she undress or were they cut off?'

'See for yourself,' Mike said. He pointed to a row of brown paper bags, each tagged and labeled. 'I looked everything over – didn't notice any holes. The lab can work 'em up for blood and semen.'

Mercer crouched next to the bags and started to open each one, removing the single piece of clothing inside and holding it up for a look.

'Her arms were tied together behind her back. Ankles were bound, too. Stabbed five times in the back. Carving knife, about fourteen inches long, with the blade. Still in her when Teddy stumbled in.'

'Her own knife?' Mercer asked. We didn't think our perp carried anything that big when he prowled the streets.

'Matches a set in the kitchen. Maybe he took a look at her and figured a pocketknife wouldn't get the job done,' Mike said, glancing back at Mercer. 'Those last bags? That's the panty hose. They're bloody, man. Maybe he cut himself in the process and we've got his fluid on them as well as hers.'

I watched as Mercer opened the last two paper bags

and removed the items one by one. Dried blood had formed clumps on the pale taupe surface of the hosiery, caught in the fine mesh webbing. The empty outline of a foot dangled from his hand, part of the knot that had restrained Emily for the kill.

'Something else bothering you, Mercer?' Mike asked. He knew his old partner well enough to recognize the puzzled expression on his face.

Mercer passed me one of the bags. 'Little things.'

'Like what?'

'Our man never hit before midnight. Never stabbed anybody in the back before—'

'Shit, he never stabbed anybody at all till that Swedish kid fought him last week. Maybe he liked doing it. Maybe thinking he'd killed a girl satisfied him even more.'

'Always had his own knife – the small folding kind,' Mercer said, ticking off a punch list of distinctions from the four-year-old case details he knew so well. 'Her keys shouldn't be inside her pocketbook, like she had time to replace them and close it up. They'd be on the floor or a tabletop. The jacket would be in here, with the pile of clothes.'

'Three, four years is a long time in a pervert's life. Maybe his style changed, maybe his whole approach.'

'It's not just the little things,' I said, twisting the piece of bloodstained evidence and holding it up by the toe. 'This isn't panty hose.'

'Then what the hell have I been fumbling with all these years, trying to get inside the damn stuff? Could have fooled me,' Mike said.

'Maybe you should try it with the lights on and your eyes open once in a while,' I said. 'You might enjoy it.'

'What have you got?'

'Something bigger to add to Mercer's instincts. Stockings. Old-fashioned, expensive, hard to come by, and totally useless without garter belts. Not the cheap Lycra waist-high pull-ups from a local drugstore that all our other girls were tied with.'

'So, what's your point?'

'That this killer's a copycat who's read the news accounts of the case pattern, took the headlines literally, and is trying to imitate our rapist to cover up a murder,' I said, passing the bloody hosiery to Mike. 'These really are silk stockings.'

Chapter 12

'I'll take your twenty dollars and bet it on this. They're not going to find semen when they autopsy her,' I said to Mike as we climbed the staircase to the squad room in the Nineteenth Precinct station house at 5 A.M. 'This wasn't a rape.'

We walked in, greeted by the frightened or sullen faces of more than a dozen men – black men – seated on every available chair. The metal gate of the holding pen was thrown open so that others could sit on the benches usually reserved for prisoners.

'What the hell's happening here? Somebody holding auditions for *The Jeffersons*?' Mike asked Mercer, who was coming up behind us. 'One look around and I know it ain't hockey tryouts.'

'Same damn thing as last time. This is where the RoboCop business gets ugly.'

After the serial rapist task force had been formed several years back, the moment there was a report of an attack that fit the pattern, police swept the neighborhood for every dark-skinned man who was on the street. A single glance around and it was obvious that no one in this crowd even remotely resembled the round-cheeked suspect depicted in the victims' composite sketch.

A lone detective sat in a corner in front of a computer monitor, entering pedigree information into the system. 'What are you doing, DeGraw?' Mercer asked.

'I'm trying to get these guys out of here as fast as I can. Two doctors – they're the quiet ones behind bars over there. One partner at some fancy-dancy law firm – he's the one screaming about the racial-profiling suit he's gonna file on behalf of everyone who's keeping me company this dark and lonely night. A banker, two cooks, a fireman, a hot dog vendor, a paroled burglar with six misdemeanor convictions, a couple of lounge lizards hanging out at the local bars looking for a lonely piece of ass.'

'Why are they here at all?' I asked. 'This is appalling.' The usual procedure was to do a stop-and-frisk on the street, fill out the necessary paperwork that accompanied the search, and let the men go.

'The guys stopped so many people they ran out of forms. We had to bring the rest of them in to process.'

Mercer was making the rounds, shaking everyone's hand and apologizing for this outrageous fallout from the murder investigation.

'You swabbing 'em?' Mike asked.

'I've been asking for volunteers. So far, the legal eagle told them they don't gotta do it. One of the docs went along with the program,' DeGraw said, showing me a single Q-tips in a glassine envelope. 'Nobody else is in the mood.'

'You want to take a shot at it, Mercer?' I asked. 'Just for elimination purposes?'

'That is one mean assignment, Ms Cooper. Me, leaning

97

on the brothers to help elevate the African-American statistics in the population genetics pool of the data bank,' Mercer said, doubling back to ask again whether any of the men were willing to give us a saliva sample.

'Where's m' man Teddy?'

DeGraw pointed Mike in the direction of the lieutenant's office at the far end of the room. 'He's in there, unless he flung himself out the window already. Go easy on him – he's a wreck.'

Theodore Kroon lifted his head from his folded arms on the desktop when he heard the door open. His lean, pale face was streaked with tears and his reddish-brown hair was tousled and unkempt. There were bloodstains on the front of his shirt and pants.

He began to wail as soon as he saw Mike Chapman. 'I touched everything, Detective. I couldn't help it. I didn't know what I was supposed to do.'

'It's okay, buddy. I wouldn't expect anything else.'

'But I mean my fingerprints must be everywhere in Emily's apartment. I tried to see if she was alive, I untied her hands, I . . . I even held the handle of the knife. I wrote it all out for you, just like you asked.' Teddy thrust several pieces of paper at Mike.

'First thing you're gonna do is go into the men's room and wash up. You're no good to me if you don't calm down. This is Alexandra Cooper. She's from the DA's office. I'd like to go over everything with you again, so Ms Cooper can hear it.'

Kroon closed his eyes and breathed deeply before he stood up and left the small room.

'See what I mean? Too light in the loafers for a job like this murder.'

The political correctness of the nineties had not even been a blip on Mike's radar screen. 'Please stop with that kind of talk. You know it drives me crazy. And what if I'm right that Emily wasn't raped?'

'I realize you're tired but you're never gonna change my spots, kid. It's just my bad mouth – inside you know I'm like butter.'

'Yes, but it's your mouth that makes such an indelible impression.'

'My cousin Sean – did I tell you he's getting married in June? I'm the best man. The bride's a guy he met playing soccer in Ireland. I got twenty-two first cousins, and if you don't think the odds are that at least five of them are gay, then you can sit there praying with my aunt Bridget and her rosary beads, trying to pretend it only happens in other people's families. Now I have to take Teddy seriously as a suspect – that's what you're telling me?'

'Is it all right for me to come in?' Teddy said, pushing open the door.

Mike put a hand on Teddy's shoulder and steadied him as he walked back to the lieutenant's chair. We seated ourselves across the desk from him.

I opened the coffee I needed to keep myself going and the bag of bagels that I had stopped to pick up for the detectives and witnesses. Mike asked Teddy Kroon to tell us about himself.

'I was born forty-eight years ago in Bangor, Maine. My parents—'

'How about we fast-forward and start from this end. What do you do?'

'Retail, Mr Chapman. I own a shop in TriBeCa that

sells high-end cooking utensils – pots and pans, table toppings—'

'Carving knives?'

'Yes, sir. The one – um – the one that's in Emily's back? I gave her that set for her birthday last year.' He shook his head and tried to open a packet of sugar with his shaking hands.

'You work in the shop, too?'

'Six days a week. I get down there at eight before we open and stay late most nights to do all the paperwork. We're closed on Sundays.'

'And Emily Upshaw, what's your relationship been with her?'

'She's my best friend, Detective.' Teddy's eyes welled up with tears again. 'She's been my very dearest friend for almost a decade.'

'How'd you meet?'

He paused. 'Fifteen years ago. At an AA meeting.'

'Alcoholics Anonymous? Since when did they start holding sessions in a bar on York Avenue?'

Teddy flashed a glare at Mike. 'I didn't make it, Mr Chapman. Neither did Emily. That's why we got along so well.'

'Take me through it.'

'I was new to the whole twelve-step-program idea. We were a small group, meeting in a church basement on Lexington Avenue late in the evening so those of us who worked long hours could keep up. Emily was doing really well then. She had a steady job at a woman's magazine doing some editing, in addition to her writing.'

'Did you see her outside the meetings?'

'Not at first. We'd sometimes walk home together. She was very smart and I liked to listen to her talk about her work. She was always interviewing someone interesting.'

'You bonded right away?'

'It was just a few months and then her schedule changed completely. She had a good offer from a travel magazine. The only problem was that it required her to be on the road a great deal of time. She started to miss meetings. Lots of them.'

'There's hardly a place you can go that doesn't have a branch of AA,' I said.

'True. But the reality was that Emily couldn't manage it. She assured herself that she could skip a session every now and then, but traveling offered too many temptations. There were time changes that left her jet-lagged and more resistant to squeezing in a meeting. There were minibars in the hotel room and expense accounts to charge them to. There was that beverage cart on the airplanes that pulled right up next to her seat. So we fell out of touch for a while.'

'No contact at all?'

'Not for almost four years. By that time she had been fired from the magazine and was ready to try AA again. I had just lost my partner to AIDS and was pretty desperate. Emily and I kind of reinforced each other through some of our darkest hours. From that point on we've been really close.'

'So when did you fall off the wagon?' Mike asked.

'September twelfth, 2001. One of my sisters worked for the Port Authority. My shop was just six blocks away from the World Trade Center and I tried to get there—'

'You don't have to explain that one, Teddy.' Mike was

still fighting his own demons from that tragic day. 'And Emily?'

'She hung in till about a year ago. She'd lost another job and run through most of the small inheritance her parents had left her. I loaned her some money, of course, but she really struggled to make a living. Three strikes, she kept telling me. She was out.'

'What did she mean by three strikes?' I asked.

'This was the third time she'd busted out of the program. The usual alcoholic's denial. Emily just convinced herself it wasn't meant to be.'

'So we know about the second and third times she tried. Do you know anything about the first?'

Teddy thought for a minute. 'It was right after college. She'd been drinking and doing drugs since she was a teenager. Cocaine mostly. One of her professors introduced her to a self-help group like AA. I know she was clean and sober for a couple of years. She did some really good writing then and published a few serious pieces.'

'But lapsed?'

'Yes. She got into a relationship with one of the young men in the program. Something that happened when they were together just scared her to death. I don't know why – that's just the expression she always used. Emily used to say she liked it better being drunk and alone than living with a coke-snorting madman.'

'That's what she called him – a madman?'

'Exactly.'

'You know his name?' Mike asked.

'It was Monty, I think. I don't know whether that was his first or last name. But I'm pretty sure it was Monty.'

'Ever meet him?'

'No, no, Detective. Emily never saw him again. He was someone she ran into in the program, the first time she was in rehab. She was a kid, right out of school. She moved in with him and they lived together for a while, but once they broke up she wanted no part of him.'

'Because?'

'I never got into that kind of bedroom talk with her. I don't know whether it was the sex or the drugs, or some other problem he had.'

'Were there any men in her life since then?'

'No one significant that I'm aware of. Friends, but nothing more serious.'

'How often did you see Emily?'

'Well, we talked almost every day. We tried to have dinner together once or twice a week. Like last night, just something casual in the neighborhood.'

'Did you speak with her yesterday? Was she alarmed about anything, or did she have any plans to meet someone before joining you?' I asked.

He shook his head. 'No. I was too busy to talk when she called the store. She just left a message early in the day telling me what time she'd meet me for burgers at Hudson Bay. Around midnight, she said.'

'But she didn't show. So what'd you do?'

'Naturally I was concerned. I called several times,' Teddy said, looking at Mike for confirmation. 'You must have heard the messages I left on her machine, didn't you?'

'Concerned about her safety?'

'No, not that,' he said quietly. 'I was afraid she might have started drinking at home. Maybe blacked out. Sometimes when she binges I worry – sorry, I mean I worried that she was going to wind up in the hospital, without any coverage to pay for the treatment.' It usually took weeks for people to talk about the dead in the past tense.

'You had a spare key?'

'Yes. We had each other's keys, in case of emergency. Not this kind, of course.'

'Has she got family?'

'Not in New York. Two sisters back home in Michigan.' He leaned back and covered his eyes with his hand. 'Lord, I guess I have to be calling them today, too. I'm not sure I can deal with it all.'

Teddy continued to tell me about his friendship with Emily as Mike walked out of the room. He returned with a cotton-tipped swab and broke into the conversation long enough to ask the nervous witness if he minded rubbing the inside of his cheek for a sample of his DNA.

'Why do you need this?'

'Just routine. Have to run it against all the samples we find at the crime scene.'

Teddy looked back and forth between us but seemed too cowed to question our authority. He poked around and handed Mike the slim wooden stick.

'Ever been arrested, Teddy?'

'Twice. Driving under the influence.' His mood was now alternating between grief-stricken and surly. 'I suppose you'll want to fingerprint me, too.'

'I will, actually,' Mike said. 'There's bloody fingerprints all over the bedroom. We've got to eliminate yours. See if any of them don't match yours or Emily's.'

Mike left the room again to voucher the swab and package it for the lab.

Teddy put his elbows on the lieutenant's desk and

leaned forward as though to whisper to me. The whites of his eyes were shot through with red lines, and the tremor in his hands – probably DT's rather than anxiety – was more pronounced.

'You'll do me a favor, won't you, Miss Cooper?'

'If I can.'

'You'll see Emily, won't you? I mean, at the morgue?'

'Well, I don't necessarily have to go there on this case, but Mike will certainly—'

'No, you must. You must promise me you'll go.' He stopped talking and took my hands in his own. 'Mr Chapman will think this is crazy, but you have to make sure that Emily is dead. Really dead.'

Spare me one more flaky witness, I thought to myself. The friend he had found eviscerated on her bed, a carving knife impaled in her back, had no more chance of breathing again than Ted Williams.

I squeezed Teddy Kroon's hands. 'I'm not sure I understand. You want Emily to be dead?'

'No, no, no. What I mean is that Emily made me promise that if something ever happened to her, I'd make absolutely certain that she was dead. It terrified her more than anything.'

He was agitated now, and I tried to calm him. There was no rational way to do that when I thought of how dreadful her last minutes must have been, but he didn't sound rational anymore either. 'Most people are frightened of death, Mr Kroon. This attack tonight was so quick, so cataclysmic—'

'Not death. It's burial before death that haunted her.'

'Premature burial? That's what Emily was worried about?'

'Exactly, Miss Cooper.'

I pulled myself away from him and stood up. I may not have seen the body bag on its way to the morgue, but I had seen the blood-drenched crime scene. 'That's a promise I can make to you, Mr Kroon. You have my word you won't have to worry about that. The medical examiner's office is the best in the country – Emily's in very capable hands, and there's no question that she's dead. This isn't fiction we're dealing with, so you need to get hold of yourself.'

Teddy Kroon leaned back and rubbed his eyes with his hands. He laughed for the first time since I had come into the room. 'You're right, Miss Cooper. Too much Poe. I guess Emily had an unhealthy obsession with Edgar Allan Poe.'

Chapter 13

'I'm telling you this murder and the skeleton behind the brick wall are connected,' I said, after Teddy Kroon left the station house. 'A skeleton is found in the house where Poe once lived. Buried alive, in all probability. You blab it to the press and it winds up in the headlines on a slow news day. Twenty-four hours later, Emily's dead. And her scene is manipulated to look like the elusive Silk Stocking Rapist just escalated out of control. Emily Upshaw's death has nothing to do with our East Side serial rapist.'

'What's the link, Coop?' Mike's feet were on the lieutenant's desk and I was slumped back in a chair opposite him when Mercer returned to the room. It was after 6 A.M. 'She liked Poe? There's not a literate adult in America who grew up without reading him.'

'An obsession with premature burial? C'mon,' I said.

'You weren't creeped out the first time you read that story? It's impossible to forget those images. The lever in the family vault that throws the iron portals back, the padded coffin with a lid and springs, the rope attached to the big bell, fastened to the hands of the corpse. Living inhumation, isn't that what he called it? Nothing so agonizing on earth. I must have been twelve or thirteen but I didn't sleep for weeks.'

'Mike, we're talking about an intelligent adult. Not likely she was spooked for the rest of her life by a short story she read in grade school. Something happened to her, you heard what Teddy said. It's related to some bad experience with a guy she met in rehab who was a madman. About twenty years ago. It's only a madman who would have entombed a young woman alive, too. Straight out of Poe, in the basement of the very house he lived in.'

'You're going "woo-woo" on us, Coop.'

'The guy reads in the newspaper that we found the skeleton. The same day's paper has the story of the return of the Silk Stocking Rapist. Emily was some kind of danger to him,' I said, my mind racing to think of reasons why, 'so he killed her. I think it makes sense.'

'So, now what do you want us to do? I know, let's dig up every building foundation in New York City. You think we got buried bones all over town? Or this lunatic only comes out of the blue once every quarter of a century to murder somebody? A bit unusual for a serial killer, isn't it?'

'Find that guy, you solve both cases.'

'This bagel is hard as a rock. That's the best you could do for me?' Mike asked, slathering the remaining half with cream cheese.

'I'm with Alex on this one,' Mercer said.

'What a stretch. You think DCPI is gonna go with that kind of long shot? Don't ever tell them it's a brainstorm from the mind of Alexandra Cooper,' Mike said. 'They're likely to flop you back to street patrol in Harlem for taking your cues from blondie.'

108

The NYPD's deputy commissioner of public information would have to advise his boss on this decision. News of a murder on the Upper East Side was a story with legs. Give out an essential clue that might only be known to the killer – the use of actual silk stockings instead of cheap panty hose – and it might blow the chance to score solid points when it came time to interrogate suspects. But if Mike was right and the original serial rapist had escalated to murder, not warning people about this more frenzied attack could prove to be a fatal error.

'The commish is screwed either way. Letting everyone think this new kill is part of the task force operation gives us more wiggle room to work the case quietly,' Mercer said. 'The murderer will think he's got us duped.'

'Mind if I finish this?' Mike asked, reaching over and taking the food Teddy Kroon had left behind. Murder rarely affected Mike's desire for something to chew on. 'You know I hate it when Mercer sides with you. But this time, just on some nitwit literary hunch? It almost takes my appetite away.'

'It's not her hunch.'

'What then?' We both looked at Mercer. His chair was tipped back against the wall, but his long legs were planted firmly on the floor.

'The teeth. It's the skeleton's teeth,' he said.

'How so?'

'Well, Andy Dorfman gives us an age on those bones that wouldn't be so different from Emily Upshaw's age today – forty-three years old – if the other woman had lived. And her teeth suggest that in the last few years of her life she spun out of control – like a drug addict or alcoholic who didn't get any medical or dental attention.'

109

'You two are beginning to scare me,' Mike said.

Mercer ignored him. 'The skeleton lady and Emily Upshaw – we know she sucked the bottle a bit too much way back then – might have moved in the same small world.'

'Yeah, well, that's like telling me it's a quarter of the population of this or any other big city. Dope, alcohol, people who are scared of the dentist's drill. Both of you are leaping to conclusions that seem pretty absurd.'

I looked at my watch and yawned. 'What do you say we carry this discussion forward on Monday, when you get an autopsy report on Emily? Mercer and I have to finish up in the grand jury and file our John Doe indictment on the rapist. And Mike, can I ask a special favor? No leaks this time.'

'Nevermore, blondie. Nevermore.'

The Nineteenth Precinct was only a few blocks from my apartment. Daylight was just beginning to break on this next-to-last morning of January as I walked home at about 7 A.M. Sanitation trucks blocked the cross streets as they loaded huge piles of green plastic trash bags into their bellies, gypsy cabdrivers honked to get my attention as I jaywalked across Third Avenue, and what was left of the snow and ice that skirted my path was now coated in soot. The doormen were huddled in their long uniform coats, with hats and gloves, grudgingly opening the door to let me in. I picked up the Sunday paper from the mat in my hallway, went inside to undress and climb into bed.

I slept until noon. After I had called Battaglia to alert him about the murder of Emily Upshaw and the question about whether it was part of the recurring rapist's pattern, the rest of the day was a lazy mix of reading the

110

Times, catching up with friends and family by e-mail and phone, and rearranging my closets. There were empty spaces and shelves where Jake had kept clothes and toiletries and books, and I tried to fill the gaps – constant reminders of the breakup – with things of my own that I had moved back then to make room for him.

On Monday morning, a light dusting of snow fell as I hailed a cab to go down to the office. I spent the first hour drafting the indictment of the Silk Stocking Rapist for Laura to type, so that it could be signed by the foreman of the afternoon grand jury and filed with the court. Brenda Whitney, in charge of media relations, came in to discuss all the relevant facts so that she could prepare a statement for Battaglia to release to the press. Since there was not yet an arrest, I needed an unsealing order to make the news public. Completing the essential paperwork was as time-consuming as prepping the case.

'Got time for a headache?' Alan Vandomir asked as he knocked on my open door shortly after ten.

'Another one?'

'A little lighter than what you were dealing with all weekend.' Vandomir was one of the best detectives in Manhattan's Special Victims Squad and I liked working with him. 'I want you to hear this story – we'll make it as quick as we can.'

'Bring it on.'

He walked to the waiting area across the hall and returned with a teenaged girl dressed in a lavender velour warm-up suit and chewing on some sticks of red licorice. Vandomir motioned her to one of the chairs in front of my desk and sat next to her while he introduced us and got her to start talking.

Seventeen-year-old Darcy Hallin told me she was a high school student on Staten Island and had been dating a classmate for the first half of senior year. She was tall and big-breasted, with frizzy blonde hair. She went into the details of their sexual relationship, which included the assurance that they had protected sex. Most of the time.

'Last month I missed my period, and then I started getting sick and stuff, so when I told my boyfriend about it he said he had an uncle who could solve the problem.'

'How?'

'That he was a doctor. That he would – you know – take care of things for me. So Friday I went to his office.'

'Where?' I asked, to make sure that whatever event brought her to me was something over which I had jurisdiction. 'In Manhattan?'

'Yeah. But I don't know the street. Somewhere in midtown,' she said, smiling at Vandomir and waiting for him to agree with her. 'Right?'

'What happened at his office?'

'First thing he did was make me undress.'

'Was there a nurse in the room, or any kind of assistant?'

'Just Dr Foster and me.'

'Did he give you a gown to put on?'

'No. He told me to take all my clothes off and put them on a chair.'

'Have you ever had a gynecological exam before?'

'Nope.'

'Did the doctor know that?'

'Uh-huh. He asked me who did the last one and I told him I never had one.'

The fact that it was the first time the girl was going

through the procedure made it impossible for her to know what the standard practice should be in such exams. It was the perfect moment for someone to take advantage of her.

'What did Dr Foster do next?'

'First he told me he had to do a breast exam.'

'How did he do that?'

'Like he was feeling up on me, is what I thought.'

'Can you tell us exactly how and where he touched you?'

First Darcy told us how the doctor rubbed his hands around her chest, then she demonstrated on herself. The long caresses and manipulation of the girl's ample breasts bore no resemblance to the steps physicians took in legitimate examinations. Neither did his repeated questioning, asking her whether it felt good while he touched her.

'What was next?'

'He made me lie down on the table and put his fingers inside me. He was touching me funny and poking me inside with some kind of instrument that I couldn't see, and that's when the man knocked on the door.'

'What man? Touching you how? Slow down, Darcy.'

'Somebody just banged and Dr Foster, he like got real nervous. He told me to get up and get dressed, and he started to hide all his medical tools back in his bag.'

'Did the other man come into the room?'

'Nope. He kept calling the name Pierre – telling him to open up. But he didn't. Not then. Not till he threatened me.'

'What did he say?'

'"If you tell anybody about this, I'll get you. I know how to find you and I'll make sure you never talk again."

Then he took me by the arm and made me walk through the waiting area, out the back door to the alleyway. He tossed his case with all the stuff in it into the Dumpster, which I thought was really weird.'

'How did you get away from him?'

'He made me walk to the subway station and he waited until I got on the downtown train to go home. Said if I told anyone about this except my boyfriend I'd never see my mother again.'

'I'm glad you decided to tell someone, Darcy.'

'I didn't have a choice, really. I was bleeding so badly that night that I had to get my mother to take me to the hospital.' She smiled at Alan Vandomir. 'They're the ones who called the police.'

'So you paid a visit to Dr Foster?' I asked Vandomir.

'By way of the back door on Saturday morning. That's where we found all the equipment inside the Dumpster. And Lucky Pierre was right at his desk.'

'What kind of medicine is he licensed to practice?'

'None, actually. That's why we're here.'

I looked at the vulnerable teen and wondered what would have happened to her had there not been such an opportune knock on the door. 'Don't tell me he's a gardener or a hairdresser?'

'Nah. He's a phlebotomist. All he's trained to do is to draw blood for lab tests. Doesn't know the first thing about gynecology or anything else medical. And you're certainly not going to like where he works, Alex.'

'I'm afraid to ask.'

'Try the court system. He's employed by the Midtown Community Court. His assignment is to draw blood from hookers to test for sexually transmitted diseases.'

'Public service is a wonderful thing, isn't it? Now I'll have the chief administrative judge on my back for embarrassing him with this arrest.'

The MCC had been a controversial innovation from the outset, almost a decade ago. The mayor and the judicial head of the criminal court system had been allies in moving some misdemeanor cases out of the Centre Street courthouse and handling them in the neighborhood in which they'd occurred. It hardly made a difference to any of us in the DA's office to have the cases – mostly prostitution and low-level drug dealing – out from under our feet. But Battaglia had been hell-bent on maintaining jurisdiction over every offense, no matter how petty, and he would revel in this bit of mismanagement by his adversaries.

'I'll have it written up as sexual abuse and throw in an unauthorized medical practice. We can have Darcy sign the affidavit and send her on her way, for today.'

By two o'clock, I had finished charging Vandomir's case and when Mercer arrived, I had the John Doe serial rapist indictment signed and filed. By the time I made the rounds from my eighth-floor office to the ninth-floor grand jury rooms to the tenth-floor Supreme Court clerk's office and then up to fifteen so the judge overseeing grand jury matters could unseal the indictment, it was after three and Mike Chapman was sitting at my desk.

'The plot thickens, Coop.'

'Were you there for the autopsy this morning?'

'Yeah. Tell your pal Mr Kroon you kept your promise. If Emily Upshaw wasn't already dead before she met Dr Kirschner today, it's a sure thing now.'

'Was it as obvious as what it looked like?'

'Five stab wounds to the back with a carving knife. Got the heart, one lung, the kidney, and anything else that matters.'

'Was she—?'

'Sexually assaulted? The jury's out on that one. No semen in the vaginal vault, but don't gloat about it yet. There's some bruising on her inner thighs, like it was an attempt. Your perp had attempts that weren't consummated, didn't he?'

Mercer and I looked at each other and nodded our heads.

'Plus Crime Scene found something unusual in the bathroom.'

'What?'

Mike took a Polaroid photo out of his pocket and showed it to us. 'See the sink counter on the right? There's a plastic bottle of bleach on top.'

'Okay, so?'

'Emily wasn't exactly a meticulous housekeeper. Look at the dingy towels and the ring in the bathtub.'

The photo made it obvious that the only clean surfaces in the room were the toilet seat and bowl.

'Hal thinks the killer finished in the bathroom what he started in the bedroom. Masturbated here and then wiped the toilet bowl to clean off anything that would leave a trace of DNA. Ever seen that before?'

'No.'

'Well, Hal has. There was a case in Queens last October. Perp had only been out of jail a week, paroled on an old sex offense. Did a push-in burglary in Astoria and when he couldn't get it up to complete the rape, he went into the bathroom and played with himself.'

'And the Mr Clean routine?'

'Just before his release from prison he'd been swabbed, by law, to put his profile in the convicted offender data bank. He knew that was a surefire way to identify him in the new venture, so he scoured away the DNA.'

'All that tells me is that Emily's killer was smart enough to eliminate any traces of himself. It doesn't help to figure out whether or not he's our East Side rapist.'

'Damn, you're stubborn. Mr Silk Stockings didn't complete the assault on Annika Jelt, did he? I'm sure he wasn't even aware you'd be able to connect the cigarette outside on the stoop to that crime. Maybe Emily's killer is keen to the fact that if you don't match him to the old cases, you can't identify him or even link the two series. Maybe this is a leopard who actually has changed his spots.'

'No other DNA in Emily's apartment?' Mercer asked.

'Oh, did I neglect to mention that? Coop's pal, Teddy Kroon. His prints are—'

'That's the first thing he told us last night,' I said. 'Of course they're everywhere. He found the body of his best friend and tried to see if there was anything he could do to save her.'

'You know how you hate to be interrupted? Same goes for me. The prints don't surprise me too much – that's exactly what I was going to say. And neither does his DNA on a wineglass. Maybe it's a little tacky that he sat there swilling her lukewarm Chianti while he waited for the men in blue, but it's not a crime. On the other hand, it makes me wonder whether he was in the apartment earlier than he admitted to us – maybe even drinking there while he waited for Emily to come home.'

117

'But the messages he left on the answering machine, from the bar they were supposed to meet in?'

'It's the oddest thing, Coop. Somebody erased them. I didn't want to say it in front of Teddy, but there were no recordings on it by the time I responded the other morning. And Teddy's got one more thing to explain.'

'What's that?' Mercer asked.

'Why his DNA was all over the computer mouse on Emily's desk.'

Chapter 14

'How'd they get a genetic profile from a computer mouse?' Battaglia asked. 'This guy drool on it?'

'Skin cells, Paul. They slough off with ordinary use. It probably means that Teddy Kroon was holding on to the mouse for several minutes, long enough to be opening files or surfing the Web without realizing he was leaving his own DNA fingerprint on it.'

The scientific methodology of DNA had changed so radically since its forensic introduction in the last twenty years that it was not only possible to develop identifying evidence from minute samples of genetic material, but also to work from trace evidence, not just blood, semen, and saliva. Sweatbands inside baseball caps, tearstained clothing, and steering columns on stolen cars that had been handled by thieves to get them started could yield enough data to amplify and match to suspects or convicted offenders.

'What was he looking for?'

I was trying to brief Battaglia on the latest developments in the Upshaw case before he called in the media to give them news of our innovative John Doe strategy. As usual, he was asking questions to which I did not yet have answers. The computer forensics cops would have been livid if any of us at the scene tried to open the files.

'I don't know. We have to get him back in, boss. He never mentioned anything about the computer. I didn't think to ask him about it at the time.'

Battaglia scowled and kept reading the remarks that Brenda had outlined for him. 'How come it's only the house press?'

He liked it better when all the major networks covered his releases. This one would just be attended by the stringers assigned to the courthouse from each of the daily newspapers and the crime reporters from the local TV stations. 'Short notice. Brenda didn't contact them until this morning.'

The district attorney walked to the conference table at the far end of the room. He didn't need to tell me the rules again, but he always liked to do it. 'I'll give them the story and take questions. If I need you to fill in any blanks, I'll just look over at you and you'll know you can answer. Tell Rose to let them in.' He seated himself in a high-backed green leather chair, behind which a blowup of the rapist's sketch was propped against a bookshelf.

I stepped out to his executive assistant's desk and gave her the nod. Mercer followed me back in to flank Battaglia at the head of the table. The twelve journalists filed in and greeted the district attorney while cameramen set up tripods behind the old wooden chairs.

He read stiffly from the papers in front of him. 'Good afternoon to all of you. What we've decided to undertake here is a bold new initiative – one more major step in our battle against sexual assault.

'This will be a joint effort on the part of prosecutors,

police, and scientists to use both the latest technology and an innovative legal strategy to indict the Silk Stocking Rapist – as you people think you've so cleverly named him – on the basis of his DNA profile. We are going to stop the clock on the statute of limitations that would sooner or later allow him to escape the consequences of his crimes. Whenever we find him, he will have his day in court.

'This effort is smart, it's creative, it's proactive,' Battaglia said. He pointed over his head at the artist's sketch. 'But we need your help in capturing this predator. Then we'll make sure he never walks among us again. Thank you.'

'Have you done this before, Mr B?' the CBS newswoman called out.

'Twice. Very quietly. Now it's going to be business as usual when these monsters think they can beat us just because the legislature's too lazy to take a few minutes to eliminate the statute of limitations.'

'Is this about sticking it to Albany then, Mr District Attorney?'

'Those statutes were designed to protect against the dangers of faulty memories and lost witnesses. They're anachronisms,' Battaglia said, a smile drawing slowly across his face. 'Like the legislators themselves. Talk about faulty memories. Those last remarks were off the record, right?'

'When are you gonna catch this guy?' Mickey Diamond asked.

'The commissioner has stepped up his efforts and we've brought in some outside eyes to help review the situation. I'd expect that—'

'Outside? From where?'

'I'm not going to comment on that. Whose side are you on anyway?'

'If you think he's done so many of the cases, how come you only indicted him on this one charge?' the all-news-radio reporter asked.

'We wanted to get started with the oldest case, so we don't risk losing it. We'll be presenting the others later in the month to do a superseding indictment. But this gets us out there in the public awareness and into the national data banks without wasting any more time. This rapist can run but he won't be able to hide for very long.'

'This weekend's murder, Mr B, you have any idea why the police commissioner is hedging on calling it part of the Silk Stocking pattern?'

'It's premature to do that kind of thing and alarm the public until all the evidence is analyzed,' Battaglia said, scowling again.

'Alarm the public?' Diamond said. 'You got women running around the Upper East Side like it was the January white sale at Bloomingdale's. It's sheer bedlam today. I think panic is a better word for it.'

'That's exactly what we're trying to avoid. Let me give you ladies and gents some of the latest statistics. The numbers for last year – violent crimes in Manhattan – are way down over the previous twelve-month period.' I had heard this drill more times in ten years than I would ever be able to count. Battaglia's next sentence was predictable. 'Figures don't lie, but liars figure.'

He chuckled but most of the reporters rolled their eyes. 'Homicides are lower, robberies are down—'

'Rape is the only category of felonies that went up. Why so, Mr B?'

The side of his mouth twisted in my direction and he gave me an almost imperceptible nod, in gratitude for the briefing I'd done earlier. 'There are two issues involved here,' I said. 'First, I think all of us involved in this work accept that there is more reporting of these crimes, not actually more victimization. We have so many more services available for survivors now – legally, medically, and psychological counseling, too.

'The second thing is that you have to make a distinction between stranger and acquaintance rapes. Stranger attacks represent fewer than twenty percent of reported sex crimes. That number has been very stable and has shown no significant increase anywhere in the city for more than five years.'

'So why is that any different for acquaintance rape?' the local NBC reporter asked.

'Because effective NYPD strategies – like anticrime units, community policing, an aggressive sex offender monitoring unit, and a smart SVS – they can keep the stranger rapists off the street with greater success. Acquaintance rapes are cases in which the victim is with the offender because she thinks she knows him, she trusts him. He's a family member or coworker or friend. She walks right past the cop on the beat to go to his home or her apartment or a hotel room. Law enforcement can't prevent this kind of case from happening, and that's why you see the numbers going up from time to time.'

Mickey Diamond brought us back to the moment. 'How come nobody prevented that foreign student from getting stabbed last week? How about yesterday's murder?'

Battaglia took control again. 'That's precisely why we're taking this very aggressive approach, this John Doe indictment. No serial rapist is entitled to put his hands around the throat of this city and strangle it with fear.'

He stood up to signal the end of the questioning period and started toward his desk.

'So you're saying these attacks are the work of one man, Paul?' Diamond asked.

Battaglia pretended not to hear him. He wanted nothing on the record that could be quoted back to him if he guessed wrong. 'Rose, you want to get me the mayor on the phone? And help clear these crews out of here as fast as you can.'

Diamond was relentless. 'Heard you came face-to-face with that skull in the basement over at NYU the other night, Alex. Want to comment on what you thought about the experience? Tell us where that investigation is going?'

Battaglia's head whipped around and he glared at me to ensure that if I had thought for a second that I might respond to the question, I'd think better of it.

'That's entirely a matter for the police and the medical examiner. They've got to figure out who the woman is and how she died before there's any reason for my office to be involved. Alexandra has nothing to say about it. We're closing up shop here so you'd better scram before you miss your deadlines.'

'So I guess that means the commissioner hasn't told you about the call that came into the tip hotline this afternoon?'

Battaglia hated to be out of the loop on anything. He looked to me for help. I shrugged my shoulders and shook my head, knowing he would blame me for not having the latest information. 'I've been tied up most of the day,' he mumbled to Diamond. 'I'm sure the PC called but I haven't gotten back to him yet. Which tip are you talking about?'

'Some shrink from the Village saw my piece over the weekend,' Diamond said proudly. 'Says he thinks he knows who the girl in the brick coffin is. Claims that one of his patients whose initials were A. T. went missing almost twenty-five years ago.'

Chapter 15

'Would you please tell us, Dr Ichiko, why you changed your mind this evening and decided against revealing the identity of your former patient?' The New York One reporter had sandbagged the psychiatrist outside his Sixth Avenue office as he closed up, and the interview was running at the top of the seven o'clock news.

The doctor raised his coat collar and walked briskly away from the cameras, trying to shield his face more than to protect himself from the biting-cold air.

'Is it true you've been offered a substantial amount of money to tell her story tomorrow night on a network reality show?'

The doctor waved his hand in front of the camera and tried to dodge the reporter by stepping off the curb between two parked cars.

'The police believe they have a homicide on their hands and yet you refuse to talk to them, Doctor. Am I right?' The reporter gave up and turned back to the camera. 'That was Dr Wo-Jin Ichiko, who may hold the clues to the mysterious discovery of a woman's skeleton that we told you about last week. It seems that the good doctor is willing to spill the beans . . . but only for a price.'

Brenda Whitney had left her office – Battaglia's public relations bureau – unlocked so that Mike, Mercer, and I could watch the breaking story on the evening news. I had beeped Mike at five-thirty, when Battaglia ejected the press corps, and he gave us the strange development about the doctor.

'Ichiko's just trying to cash in on his fifteen minutes of fame. He's got a bullshit practice treating derelicts, drunks, and druggies and he finally smells a score,' Mike said, talking over the reporter.

'Who'd he call first?' Mercer asked.

'The good doctor started at the *Post* after he read their story. They leaped at the chance to get an exclusive with him. The police department only found out because the editors checked with headquarters to make sure the guy wasn't a quack. Meanwhile, Ichiko liked the press reaction so much he began to call the networks to drum up a little bidding competition for his story.'

'I thought the media can't pay sources for news. I thought they had some kind of ethical guidelines,' I said.

'You use "ethics" in the same sentence as "the media"? I figured you had more brains than that, Coop. The news producer got Dr Ichiko a twofer. Flipped him over to that reality show – *Crime Factor* – the one where ex-cons tell about their worst offenses and how they beat the system. They're willing to pay him twenty-five thousand dollars for what he knows about the girl's disappearance, and then the evening news show uses outtakes from that. We get leftovers.'

'Déjà vu?' I asked Mike.

'All over again.'

We had handled a high-profile homicide several years

back in which a young woman had been strangled. Friends of the defendant had made a videotape of him while he was partying during the trial. He was high on cocaine at the time and playing with a doll, laughing into the camera as he broke its neck. Rather than talk to police about what the perp had been saying off-camera about the murder, or even telling us about the existence of the tape, the enterprising teen filmmaker sold it to a tabloid television show for use after the trial was over.

'Does Scotty know?' I asked, referring to the Cold Case Squad detective who was assigned to the matter.

'He heard about it on the radio and dashed over to the doc's office. Couldn't get past the receptionist.'

'Tell Scotty to be here first thing in the morning,' I said. 'We'll open a grand jury investigation and give him a subpoena. The doctor doesn't want to talk to the police, then let him tell the jurors his story. He clams up, we hit him with contempt.'

Mike made some calls from Brenda's desk while Mercer and I watched the rest of the news. One of Emily Upshaw's sisters had flown in to accompany her body back home to Michigan for burial. She was due at the morgue shortly and had agreed to talk to us at eight o'clock tonight, after her meeting with the medical examiner.

At twenty-five after seven, Mike clicked the buttons to change the channel on the small TV set Brenda kept on top of an old green filing cabinet.

Trebek was announcing the topic of the final answer: 'Benjamin Franklin's Firsts.'

'Twenty bucks,' I said.

'I'm only good on Founding Fathers who were warriors, not statesmen.'

'Cough it up, Mike. Mercer?'

He removed a bill from his wallet and put it on the desktop. 'You're taking food right out of my baby's mouth, Alex. Lightning rods, bifocals, lending libraries. I just know the easy things he invented that you learn in grade school.'

The big board slid back. Trebek read it to us. 'Franklin's printing press published this novel, first ever in America, in 1744.'

Mike crumpled a wad of paper and threw it at the screen. 'A setup if I've ever seen one. Literature in the guise of history, to borrow one of your regular gripes. Nobody was writing novels then. They all should have been plotting the revolution or fighting against the French and Indians.'

'Show me the money.'

'Payday's next Friday. You guessing, Mercer?'

He pointed at the screen. Two of the contestants had left blank spaces where the question should have been. 'I'm no further along than they are.'

'I'm sorry to say you're wrong, Josh,' Trebek told the dog obedience school owner from Wichita.

'You must be one lousy poker player, Coop. You got that shit-eating-I-majored-in-literature-at-Wellesley grin on your face,' Mike said, walking to the door. 'Subtlety will never be your strong suit. So, what was—?'

'*Pamela.* By Samuel Richardson. Published in England in 1740 and reprinted by Franklin. It was subtitled *Virtue Rewarded,* 'cause it's about a young woman who eludes the lecherous advances of the man she works for,' I said, folding and pocketing Mercer's money.

'C'mon. Add the twenty to my tab and let's go find

out more about Emily Upshaw. If you spent a little less time with your nose in your books and a little more effort practicing your social skills, you might be able to hold on to a guy once he makes it into your bedroom and under the sheets.'

'Is that where you think I lose my men?'

'Gotta be, blondie. You're doing something wrong there.'

Mercer put his arm around me as Mike walked ahead of us down the dark hallway.

'I guess what I really need is an expert like you to teach me, Mike. Hands-on. How come it never occurred to me before now? You up for a lesson tonight?'

Mike stopped in his tracks. He turned around to face us and began to comb his fingers through the lock of dark hair that framed his forehead. The overhead lights were dim but I could swear he was blushing.

'Mercer, did you hear what I think I just heard?'

'Yeah, and it sounds as though my lawyer is calling your bluff.'

'Just like you, Coop. You wait until I get a girl of my own. Then she leaves town and in a heartbeat you try to throw temptation in my path. It won't work this time.'

'Why are you doing that stroking thing with your hair? Am I making you nervous?'

He put his hands in his pants pocket and started walking to the elevator. 'The way I figure it is I've got the best of both worlds. There isn't anyone in either of our jobs who doesn't think we've slept together already – which may be great for my reputation or really bad, depending on what they think of you. But it means I don't actually have to risk finding out whether you really do have a set of razor-sharp teeth in the lining of your—'

'You're a dog, Chapman,' Mercer said.

'Unhand that woman, Mercer. Here she is, propositioning me – and you're trying to hold her back.'

'As far as I'm concerned, you either come home with me tonight or you stop yapping about my sex life.'

'I told you I'm just worried about Valentine's Day. You're gonna be cold and lonely.'

'I'm booked. You can relax.'

'Who? What unwitting sucker stepped into the batter's box this time?'

The elevator doors opened and we got on. 'Tell him nothing, Alex,' Mercer said.

Mike teased me all the way down to the lobby and out to his car. By the time we reached the morgue, I had gotten him off the subject and back to the sobering topic of Emily Upshaw's death.

Dr Chet Kirschner, the chief medical examiner, left instructions for us to use his office for our meeting with Emily's sister. The attendant admitted us, and we found the woman sitting alone, her head bowed with eyes closed and her fingers twisting an already crumpled handkerchief.

We introduced ourselves and explained our roles in the investigation. Sally Brandon appeared to be close to fifty, taller and slimmer than her younger sister. She had just viewed the body and was trying to compose herself as she spoke to us.

Mike and Mercer answered most of the questions Brandon asked about her sister's murder. Mercer took the lead; his firm but compassionate manner, practiced with great frequency in the Special Victims Unit, was usually comforting to victims and survivors. Mike's preference for working homicides was in no small measure based on his aversion to the emotional hand-holding that always slowed down an investigation that he was eager to solve.

When the two of them ran out of answers for Sally Brandon, they started to ask her about Emily.

'She was the youngest, Mr Wallace. I'm seven years older, and our other sister was right in between. We were a close family growing up, but when I went off to college at eighteen, Emily was only eleven.'

'What was your relationship like, as adults?'

Sally fumbled with the handkerchief. 'We didn't have one, I'm afraid. I married right after college and had children of my own. She moved to New York, and that's when Emily really began to make my parents' lives miserable.'

'In what way?'

She sighed before answering. 'I'm still so resentful of all the trouble she caused back then. It sounds pretty rough, I guess, now that she's dead.'

'Tell us about it.'

'Betsy and I – she's the middle sister – were a tough pair for Emily to follow. Our parents were very serious, churchgoing Presbyterians, and we were the two daughters who never caused them to lose a minute's sleep. Emily was a rebel from the moment she hit adolescence. She hung out with a fast crowd of older kids and started drinking by the time she was in middle school.'

'Drugs, too?' Mercer asked.

'Nobody knew at the time. Just because no one in the family imagined anything like that. I was away at college and don't even know what symptoms Emily was presenting to them. Mother was in complete denial, and my father thought that the power of prayer would solve all his concerns. Nobody talked about it.'

'Did she stay in school?'

'That was the only thing that grounded her. Emily loved school, enjoyed everything that had to do with books. She'd always been able to escape through her writing.' Sally Brandon stopping wrapping her handkerchief around her finger and looked up at me. 'Don't ask me how she did it, but she managed to get high grades and test well, even when she was in the middle of a binge.'

'Was she ever in treatment back home?'

She shook her head. 'That wasn't a concept my parents understood. It would have meant admitting that Emily had a problem.'

'They ignored everything?'

'Not everything, Mr Wallace. It was hard to look the other way when she was six months pregnant.'

'When was that, Mrs Brandon?'

'During Emily's senior year of high school. Not that it should have come as a great surprise to any of us, but it certainly shocked my parents. They couldn't—' She stopped to compose herself before going on. 'In their little town of eighteen hundred people, it was unacceptable at the time. So they sent her to live with me.'

'And she had her baby?'

Sally Brandon nodded and the tears started again. 'A little girl. Yes.'

'What became of the baby? Did she give her up for adoption?'

'No, Miss Cooper. I agreed to raise the child as my own. I had two boys at the time. I took her into my family on one condition: that Emily never have anything to do with her daughter or with me again. Ever.'

That seemed like an awfully harsh resolution to the situation. 'She agreed to that?'

'It seemed to suit her just fine,' Brandon said, sitting bolt upright and looking me in the eye. 'A month before she delivered, we left Emily at home babysitting our two boys while we went to a neighbor's house for dinner. She was into her second bottle of wine, asleep on the sofa, when her cigarette dropped out of her hand and set fire to the slipcovers. She and my sons escaped unhurt, by the grace of God, but if I ever saw her again it would be too soon for me.'

'I understand,' Mercer said, refilling her water glass from the sink behind her.

'So she graduated from high school and got a scholarship to go to New York University, pleased to leave me with her baby. Emily resented all of us with our happy little families and thought the big city would be the place to live her life unencumbered by the conventions of small-town mores.'

'And her deal with you? Did she keep it?'

'Quite faithfully. Her baby was conceived in a haze of bourbon and marijuana during a one-night stand. My husband figures it happened the weekend she went to New York for the first time, to interview for admission to the college. I mean, that date fits with the birth nine months later. For Emily, a baby was just a great inconvenience and another element to include in her great American novel. She simply didn't care about motherhood. No one in the family meant anything to her. Everything was material for a book.'

'So you don't know very much about her life after she left you?'

'Only indirectly. My mother and I talked about Emily a lot. For Mother, the estrangement of her little girl was the greatest tragedy of her life, of course. My middle sister and I were the only two people she could cry to about it. By the time she was able to acknowledge that Emily needed serious intervention to deal with alcohol and drugs, Emily was already away at NYU and rejecting everything about our parents' lifestyle. For my part, the conversations were just a way for me to make sure that she wasn't coming back.'

'And she didn't?'

'She tried only once. But that was more than twenty years ago, and my husband made it clear she wasn't welcome. We never heard from her again.'

'Her daughter? She never contacted—'

'My daughter, Miss Cooper. Amelia is *my* daughter, can you understand that?'

'What exactly can you tell us about Emily?' Mike asked. 'Do you know what she's been working on lately?'

'Writing, I assume.' It was obviously just a guess.

'Anything specific that you know of? Anything that could have created a dangerous situation for her?'

I figured Mike was thinking of the fact that Teddy Kroon had been searching her computer for some document or file.

'Both my parents are dead, Mr Chapman. There is nothing I can tell you about the last two years of Emily's life. That door between us was closed.'

'Let's start at the beginning then,' Mike said, his notepad already open and only the letters *NYU* and a question mark written on the page. 'Do you know whether she finished college?'

'Yes, she graduated. A year late, I believe, because she was in and out of trouble from the time she got to New York.'

'You mean, problems with abuse?'

'Well, alcohol, of course,' Sally said, leaning back and resting her hands on the top of the table. 'But then she was also caught shoplifting in a department store. I – uh, I feel awful talking about all these things, but I'm sure you can find them in the police records anyway. The case was dismissed, from what I understand, because it was her first arrest. But then there was bigger trouble, personally, when she graduated to more sophisticated drugs like cocaine, according to what Mother used to tell me at the time.'

'Where'd she get the money for these things?' I asked.

Sally Brandon pursed her lips. 'I know you must think I'm terribly hostile, but you're touching all the right buttons. Mother sent her money. Anything she thought my father wouldn't miss. Every time Dad gave her money to treat herself to some little thing that might have made her own life a bit more pleasant, my mother mailed it to Emily. I didn't know about it for years or I would have put a stop to it earlier.'

'Was your sister ever in any relationships that she talked about?' Mike asked.

Sally laughed. 'I guess I'd have to paint you a better picture of my father. There was no one who could have crossed Emily's path who would have been appropriate to bring into a social conversation at home. It's nothing she would have raised with my parents.'

'So Monty – the name Monty – that doesn't mean anything to you?'

Sally Brandon thought for a few seconds and shook her head. 'Nothing at all. She lived with someone for a few months – it was when she was breaking up with him that she wanted to move back to Michigan, back in with us.'

She paused again. 'And then there was that policeman who took an interest in Emily, at least for a while. I think Mother actually thought he'd be good for her, but I doubt that it was a serious relationship. I don't believe either of the men was named Monty but I'm not really sure. I'm not even certain they were two different people.'

Confusion seemed to be overwhelming Sally Brandon as she struggled to think about things she had tried to repress for so many years.

'What policeman?'

'He had something to do with her arrest. I don't know his name, but he actually phoned to speak with Mother several times. I understood he was attempting to help Emily straighten herself out. He and that literature teacher of hers who convinced her to go into rehab the first time. I think they're the only two men who ever tried to do something good for Emily without taking advantage of her from the time she was a twelve-year-old child.'

Kroon had mentioned a professor who had encouraged Emily to get into rehab.

'Perhaps my husband will remember the names. You can call and ask him about it. He was the one who spoke to Emily the one time she called us for help. You know, when I said she wanted to come to stay with us for a while?'

Mike took down the Brandons' home telephone.

'And I'll look in the apartment for her old manuscripts when I go through her things tomorrow,' Sally Brandon said dismissively. 'If it wasn't just another of Emily's alcohol deliriums, I'm sure she would have written the mad boyfriend into one of her novels.'

'What do you mean, "mad boyfriend"?' I asked, reminded again of Kroon's words.

'Oh, that was just the excuse she used when she tried to worm her way back into our lives, Miss Cooper. But by then I'd talked to a psychiatrist, an expert in substance abuse. I found out how manipulative addicts are, and neither my husband nor I was going to let Emily under our roof, no matter what story she made up to weaken our resolve. The doctor assured us she was just spinning a tale.'

'What did she tell your husband?'

'That she had to leave New York because her life was in danger,' Brandon said, waving the idea off with the back of her hand. 'That was Emily. Always exaggerating things, always over-the-top with her storytelling.'

'But was there someone in particular she was afraid of?' I wanted to make clear to Sally Brandon that Emily's murder suggested she might have had some legitimate reason to be terrified at the time she had sent out her SOS.

'It was this boyfriend of hers, she claimed. He'd moved in with her – we could only imagine what kind of problems that young man must have had. I guess she couldn't get him out of her apartment when she was ready to, so she wanted to come back to the country for a spell.'

'But was he abusive to her?' I asked. 'Is that what she was worried about?'

'She never mentioned anything hurtful he did to her,' Sally Brandon said softly. 'I might have believed that. No, this was – well, frankly, this sounded like Emily in one of her drunken stupors.'

'How so?'

'Emily told my husband her boyfriend had killed a woman. She said that's why she was so frightened of him. She was convinced he had buried someone alive.'

Chapter 16

'Early to bed, early to rise. I didn't think you'd beat me in this morning,' Mike said. 'Hope you bought breakfast. I'm dead broke and starving.'

I pointed at the bag on Laura's desk. 'The two bagels are yours. What's with you and the money lately? I'm happy to float you a loan.'

'Long story. I'll tell you next week. And I'd love to borrow a couple of hundred to get through till payday, if it's not a problem. I know my *Jeopardy!* tab is sky-high.'

'Take whatever you need from my wallet,' I said, turning my attention back to the computer screen. I had come in at seven-thirty to try to find the old case records of Emily Upshaw's drug arrest in the office archives. It was nine by the time Mike arrived.

'Any luck?'

'I don't think the system goes back far enough. Besides that, if it was her first arrest, it was most likely ACD'd.' With an adjournment in contemplation of dismissal, Emily's first brush with the law would have been put over for a six-month probationary period. If she had not been rearrested, the charges against her would automatically have been dismissed.

Mike walked behind my chair and picked up the phone. 'Who's this? Yo, Ralph. That Upshaw woman who was autopsied yesterday, would you check if they did a fingerprint card? Yeah, I'll hold.'

It was standard practice for the medical examiner to take prints of the deceased. In many cases there was an issue of identification, and in others they could be helpful in resolving criminal investigations.

'Excellent. Want to rush those down to Police Plaza? Send them to Ident, will you, please?' Mike said, hanging up the receiver. 'Chances are whatever sleazeball lawyer stood up on her case never went the extra yard to have the prints expunged.'

'So this will give us the name of the arresting officer.'

'And maybe the guy she was hanging out with, if he was a codefendant in the case.'

I swiveled back to my desktop. 'Let's break down what we need to do. Is Scotty going to get property and tax records for the building on Third Street, so we can check the list of names of people who lived there twenty to thirty years ago?'

'I figured we'd ask him when he comes in—'

'You two talkin' about me?'

'Speak of the devil,' Mike said, getting up to shake hands with Detective Scotty Taren. A thirty-year veteran of the job, he was a heavyset man, about Mike's height, with silver hair and a nose that looked like it had been flattened by one too many fists.

'That's what you'll be calling me, all right. I've gone over to the dark side,' he said, not moving from the doorframe of my office.

'Good timing.' I stood up and extended my hand to

Taren, trying to pass him Dr Ichiko's subpoena to appear before the grand jury, which I had just finished typing. 'C'mon, I've got coffee and your favorite croissant. Take your coat off and let's sort out where we're going.'

'No can do, Alex.' Taren held up his fingers, crossed in the sign that wards off vampires and evil spirits. 'I've been ordered not to take direction from you. I will grab the coffee, though. I'm freezing my ass off.'

'What are you talking about?'

'The wicked prick of the east – your pal McKinney. Called me at home last night about the bones-in-the-basement case when he saw Dr Ichiko on the late news. Had the same idea you did about hitting him with a subpoena. Lit into me when I told him you were running with it.'

'Yeah? Well, that's exactly what I'm doing. Would you take this—?'

'He's pulling rank, Alex. Says he's deputy chief of the division and he hasn't yet assigned anyone to the case. I'm to scoop Ichiko up and bring him directly to McKinney. And your pet cop here, Mr Chapman – well, it wouldn't be polite for me to tell you what I was told to do with him.'

I picked up the phone to leave a message demanding to meet with Battaglia. Mike saw me put my finger on the button that hotlined me directly to his assistant. He pushed my hand away and took the receiver from me, replacing it in the cradle.

'Pick your battles, Coop. I realize this gets your goat, but you're jumping to all kinds of conclusions about that skeleton before you even know who she is or what happened to her. McKinney wants to throw this whackjob doctor into the grand jury, let him. We got business to do. Scotty won't hold back on us.'

'Just keep feeding me, Alex. I'll tell you whatever you want to know.'

'Property records?'

'I started on it yesterday. We should have something by later in the week. We're getting calls from missing persons units all over the country. Once we send dental information, we should be able to eliminate some of those.'

'Coop thinks your old case is connected to Sunday's homicide on the Upper East Side. You got time to sit down with me later on?' Mike asked.

'Sounds like a long shot, but I'll beep you when I get back here with Ichiko. Let me not be late for Mr McKinney. I've never known him to be in before ten-thirty, but he promised a special arrival time just for me.' Scotty Taren saluted me with his right hand as he turned back into the hallway.

'What's your day like?' Mike asked.

'Without Dr Ichiko? I'm putting Annika Jelt, the Swedish girl, into the jury this afternoon, and helping one of the kids with a difficult witness this morning.'

'Then I'll ski on down to headquarters and try to find Emily Upshaw's old paperwork. Check with you later.'

Stewart Webster was a young prosecutor who had only been in the unit for five months. He was being supervised by one of my favorite colleagues, Ryan Blackmer, but the week before they had met a brick wall in the form of an uncooperative eighteen-year-old witness. I had asked them to have her in my office at ten.

Ryan got there first to tell me the facts. 'You've got to

have the last word about this because it's going to get press if it goes forward.'

'Why?'

'Yolanda – that's the witness – she says he raped her on a moving subway train, just as it pulled into Times Square.'

The location was a sure way to grab a headline, making every straphanger in town fear for her safety.

'But you think otherwise?'

'BFL.'

Our informal unit code name for a big fat liar. 'You couldn't break her?'

'Her older sister kept interrupting the questioning. Thought we were being too tough on her. I tried to keep her out of the room but she kept bursting back in.'

'You figure any motive to lie?' There always was one in a false report, and discerning what it was could usually break the story.

'It might be she got caught by a transit cop. Somebody got off the train and reported some kind of sexual encounter near the rear of the car. When the cop approached, Yolanda stuck her head up and cried rape.'

'Was he going to lock them up for public lewdness?'

'He tells me he never got that far – she started wailing first,' said Ryan. 'And then there's the fact that the sister came home from work early – around midnight – and Yolanda still wasn't in the house like she was supposed to be.'

'What kind of job does the sister have?'

'Exotic dancer. The Pink Pussycat Lounge on Varick Street. That's how she supports her college education.'

'Exotic? That's a lot classier than what I'd call it.'

Webster knocked on the door. I waved him in and he stepped aside to introduce me to Yolanda and her sister, Wanda.

'Why don't you sit right here, Yolanda? And Wanda, I'm going to ask you to wait in the conference room until I'm ready for you.'

'How long's this gonna be? I got school this afternoon,' Wanda said.

'The more candid Yolanda is with us, the faster this will go.' Wanda seemed to be pouring out of a costume from a late-night dance performance, and I couldn't begin to guess in what kind of class she was enrolled.

Wanda tilted her baby sister's chin up so their eyes met. 'You tell the lady the troof now. Don't be wasting anybody's time when I got things to do.'

The young high school dropout claimed that she met Laquon at six o'clock in the evening the previous Wednesday in front of a Starbucks on Broadway.

'What did you and Laquon talk about?'

'Nothin'.'

'Well, how did it begin? What's the very first thing he said?'

'You know, like, he just approached me and told me he thought I was cute, and like that.'

'What were you doing when he came up to you, Yolanda?'

'Nothin'.'

'It was about ten degrees outside, and dark, at six o'clock last Wednesday. Why were you just standing there on the street?'

'I don't remember.' Yolanda was looking at her inch-long fingernails, picking at the glitter that coated each of them in a different color.

'I'd like you to look at me when you answer me, okay? We're talking about things that happened less than a week ago,' I said firmly. 'I expect that you can remember them, so give it a try.'

She glanced up at me and went back to rearranging the pattern on her nails. 'I think I was waiting for my boyfriend to get off his shift.'

'Does he work at Starbucks?'

'Yeah. He do.'

'What time did he finish work?'

'I don't 'xactly know. It was supposed to be six, but when he didn't be out by a quarter after, I couldn't wait no more.'

'Why was that?'

'Because of Laquon. He wanted to take me to a movie.'

'How long had you two been talking before you agreed to go to the movies with Laquon?'

''Bout ten minutes. Till I knew him good.' Yolanda was scratching at the surface of her nails, sweeping the glitter that fell in her lap onto my carpet.

'What movie did you go to?'

'I don't remember.'

'Where was the theater?'

'Near where we was. Broadway and Lincoln Center.'

'What was the movie about?'

'Some kind of Jackie Chan action thing.'

'Well, Yolanda, if you testify in court, you're going to have to tell the jury every detail about what happened from the time Laquon first started talking to you. They're not going to be too happy with "I don't know" or "I don't remember." Juries and judges don't send guys to jail when you can't tell them everything that went on.'

146

She flicked her nail at me, in disgust, and neon green glitter wafted all over my desk. 'It's not my fault I fell asleep in the movie.'

'That's not what Laquon says.' If she could bullshit me, I could certainly bluff her, too. 'He told the cop there was a different reason you two weren't watching the movie.'

'Yeah, well, why you be all believin' him? What'd he say?'

'What would you guess he said?'

Yolanda started chewing on a nail. 'I don't know.'

'Do me a favor and sit on your hands. Stop playing with your polish and sit on your hands while we talk.' I waited while she tucked her pitted nails under her substantial thighs. 'What if I tell you the manager of the theater told the cops exactly the same thing Laquon said?'

She cocked an eye and stared at me. 'He be lying, too.' She turned to look over her shoulder.

'Don't worry. The door's closed. Your sister can't hear us. So they're both lying when they say you and Laquon were making out in the theater – that you were kissing each other and—?'

'I didn't like him like that.'

'Well, how did you like him?'

'Just like a friend. An old friend.'

'What time did the movie end?'

'I don't know.'

'Where did you go when the movie ended?'

'I don't remember.'

'Did you have anything to eat or to drink?'

'Not that I remember.'

Ryan and Stewart exchanged glances. 'I'm telling you,

Alex. She's got total amnesia. She doesn't remember anything else until she was on the subway train,' Ryan said to me. 'We got three hours totally unaccounted for.'

'How did Laquon explain it to the cops?'

'That after the movies, he bought a bottle of wine for eight bucks. It was too cold to hang out on the street, and neither one of them had enough money for a hotel, so they rode around on the subway, drinking and making love – well, having sex – until they got stopped.'

Yolanda seemed entirely disinterested in Ryan's facts, as reported by the police officer. It was as though she had no role in Laquon's arrest and incarceration for a violent felony charge.

'Where were you going when you got on the train?' I asked.

'Home. I was cold and tired. I told him I wanted to go home.'

I looked at the complaint report. 'But you live uptown, Yolanda. Why were you on the downtown train?'

She looked up at the ceiling. 'I'm the victim here. I don't have to be answering all these questions.'

'Actually, Yolanda, you do have to answer these questions. So why don't you tell us when and how you got on the train?'

'We got on right before this happened. Laquon made me get on the subway.'

'What did he do to "make" you?'

'You know, like he dragged me by the arm and pulled me down the steps.'

'Onto the platform? Wasn't anybody else there?'

'I didn't see nobody. And when the train came along,

he just pulled me inside and told me to shut up.' She was swinging her legs back and forth now, staring at a photograph on the wall over my computer.

'And that's when the attack happened, between Lincoln Center and Times Square, just minutes before the officer got on the train?'

'Yeah, that's it.'

'Where's your pocketbook, Yolanda?'

She held up a small bag that was on a long strap, looped around her neck and across her chest.

'Why don't you open that up and empty it out on my desk?'

'Huh?'

I stood up and reached for the bag as she lifted it off.

'Do I have to do this?'

'Yes, I've asked you to empty your purse.'

'First could I go to the bathroom for a minute?'

'Not until we're done.'

She looked to Ryan and Stewart for help, but got none. Reluctantly, she dumped the contents of the small bag onto the desk.

I picked up the three joints that were on top and held them out in my palm.

'Damn,' Yolanda said. 'I bet Laquon put those there. They not mines. I swear I didn't know they was there.'

'Was Laquon smoking that night?'

'Must have been. I – I – uh, I don't do no dope.'

'And the box cutter?' I asked, holding up a slim metal case and pressing the release that popped out a short, lethal blade.

'I got that for protection.'

'You have it with you last Wednesday?'

'Yeah, but I didn't have no time to use it. I was so scared I forget I had it.'

I spread out the small scraps of paper that were wadded together. 'What are these?'

'Friends. Names and numbers of my friends.'

I unfolded each one and read the names of more than a dozen men. 'You got any girl friends, Yolanda, or just guys? You mind if we call some of these guys and ask how you met them?'

She was getting truculent now, defiantly picking glitter off her nails and flicking it on the floor. 'Do what you want. I didn't want to be here anyway.'

'What time was it when you started liking Laquon better? Was it after the movie?'

'I told him,' Yolanda said, pointing to Ryan, 'that I never be liking him. I was afraid of him the whole time after the movie.'

'So when did you stop to write down his beeper number?' I asked. 'When did you draw those little hearts all around it?'

She reached over and tried to grab the paper from my hand. 'That's a different Laquon. That have nothing to do with my rape.'

'Ryan, why don't you ask Wanda to come on back in here?'

'You can't be telling her any of this. This is all privacy between me and the judge.'

'First I'm going to see whether you told your sister the same things you're telling me. Then,' I said, reaching for her MetroCard, which was mixed in with the assorted papers, 'I'm going to give this card to the police, and they're going to check a couple of things for me.'

'It's mines. I bought it last month. It ain't stolen.'

'Even better, Yolanda. Because the police can tell me exactly what time you used it on Wednesday to get into the subway. What time and where.'

'They can't do that,' she said, getting angrier and more defiant.

'It's all computerized. I'll know exactly how long you were on the train. And we'll also be able to find out how many people were on whichever platform you were on when you say Laquon dragged you.'

'Why does that matter?' Her head snapped around when she heard Ryan reenter the room with her sister.

'Because if you don't tell the judge the truth, you're going to be arrested.'

Yolanda was crying now, clearly more afraid of her sister than of me. 'But I told all of you I don't remember what happened.'

'And I'm telling you that I don't believe that. If you weren't drunk or you weren't high or you weren't hit over the head with a baseball bat, you're the only one of us who knows exactly what happened last Wednesday.'

I started to tell Wanda some of the inconsistencies between the story her sister had originally told the police and what she was saying today. I handed her the piece of paper with Laquon's name and beeper number on it, ringed with the hearts that Yolanda had drawn.

Wanda pinched the girl on the shoulder. 'Why you be actin' all "I don't remember this" and "I don't remember that"? Why you be telling me you don't like this boy but you writin' down all his information? Girl, you ain't half as stupid as you pretendin' to be.'

'I'll tell you what, Yolanda. The two of you can go

down to Ryan's office and wait while he sends this MetroCard over to the transit office to be decoded and gets the information about your subway ride last week. I'm going to hang on to your weapon,' I said, holding up the box cutter, 'and we'll just toss your marijuana.'

Wanda smacked her sister on the back of her head. 'What you doing with—'

'Don't hit her again. Don't ever let me hear you laid a hand on her,' I said. 'And, Yolanda, if you decide there's anything about your story you want to change before you meet the judge, you tell Ryan as soon as you get down to his office.'

'If I do, do I have to come back and see you again?' she asked, clearly anxious to avoid that possibility.

'Not if the information Ryan gets from the Transit Authority helps jog your memory.'

'You mean, if I tell him everything I can just go home?'

'If it's the truth, yes.'

Yolanda followed Wanda out the door before I could pick up the file and return it to Stewart. 'I didn't know you could get all that information from MetroCards.'

'That's what you're here to learn,' Ryan said, winking at me. 'Laquon and Yolanda – can't you just feel the love, Alex? I never saw you do the pocketbook trick before.'

'Teenage girls carry half their lives in those things. The older women get, the more you can find in the handbag. Pills, condoms, diaries, weapons, love letters. I've broken more cases with a peek in the purse than everything I learned in law school. I'd guess that little Yolanda's probably half a hooker already.'

'That's what Laquon claims.'

'Well, if the subway records are more consistent with

his story and you can't break her, bring her back up and we'll beep a few of her conquests. See what they can tell us about her.'

Each MetroCard is encoded with a unique ten-digit serial number, which generates a fare-card history report with every use. It would tell me the time Yolanda went through the turnstile in one-tenth-of-an-hour intervals, what train station or bus she used, and even what her remaining balance was. I wouldn't have to be the sole judge of her credibility – the transit records would prove she had lied.

I walked Ryan and Stewart to the door and picked up my messages from Laura. 'These are the only calls?'

'And you just missed an update from Mike. Scotty Taren's still waiting it out on Sixth Avenue. But they think Dr Ichiko pulled a fast one, to avoid the police and save his best stuff for his television debut. He didn't show up for work today.'

Chapter 17

Mercer arrived in my office with Annika Jelt at one, to prepare for the afternoon grand jury. An attendant from the hospital accompanied the young student, who was brought to me in a wheelchair because of her still-fragile physical condition.

He sat beside her and held her hand as she went over all the details of her attack. Her English was excellent as she spoke softly but with determination. Annika described how her assailant had appeared quite suddenly, out of nowhere. Like the others before her, she had no idea whether she had been followed for any distance to the stoop of her building.

It took me the better part of an hour to get from Annika every nuance of the aborted assault, and then another fifteen minutes – once the afternoon grand jurors reconvened – to present her testimony to them. It was clear now that it was only the resistance she mounted at the top of the staircase – unwilling to give her assailant the opportunity to get her alone behind her closed apartment door – that led to the frenzied stabbing.

Mercer wheeled her back to my office to get her coat and turn her over to the attendant from the hospital.

'It's so wonderful to see how much stronger you are, how much you've improved, in just this short time. I know you've got a long way to go, Annika, but you've made a great start. Do you know when you're leaving for Sweden?' I asked.

'As soon as the doctors tell me it's safe for me to fly. The pressurized cabins are not good for my lungs yet, and the flight is so long. But you'll call me there if you catch the man, no?'

'The City of New York will buy you the ticket back here to testify and I'll be your personal escort,' Mercer said.

'The posters – may I ask you a question about them?' Annika said. 'One of the nurses showed me a poster.'

Neighborhood groups had reproduced the composite sketch and circulated it to stores and businesses on the Upper East Side, urging them to hang it in their windows and behind their counters, in case the rapist made an appearance.

'What about it?'

'The poster has one of the drawings on it from the group Detective Wallace showed to me, the one I identified last week. It looks just like him – exactly like the man who did this to me. But what it says on the writing below the picture, well . . .'

'You don't have to be hesitant,' I said. 'If you noticed something different, you can tell us.' Some people were more accurate at estimating height or weight. Some could remember the feel of facial hair rubbing against them that others hadn't even observed, or notice the smallest of scars or blemishes on the skin of a perpetrator.

'The drawing the detective showed me didn't have any writing on it. But the poster does.'

Mercer and I both nodded.

'You know where it says the guy is African-American?' Annika asked.

Mercer seated himself on a chair opposite his witness and let her talk directly to him. 'Yeah, you told me he was a black man.'

'Of course, yes. But, maybe this is because I'm foreign, because English is a second language for me and I hear it differently.'

I didn't know where she was going with this.

'The other women,' she asked, 'were any of them foreign-born?'

Mercer thought for a moment. 'No.'

'Well, I don't think the man is American. That's the word that troubles me. Black, yes. African-American, no.'

'What then? Caribbean?'

'I can't say that. I haven't had much experience with people from the islands. It wasn't all – how you say? – singsong, like a few of the Jamaicans in my class at school. Not like that at all.'

'Can you give me an example?' Mercer said. 'He didn't speak very many words to you.'

'No, no. It's – well, maybe it's not important then,' Annika said, rolling the wheels of her chair backward and averting Mercer's glance, as though she feared wasting his time.

'It's all in the details,' he repeated to her, gripping the arm of the chair. 'What is it you remember? Every bit of it is important.'

'Perhaps it's silly. It's just a single word that I noticed.'

'Which word?'

She looked at Mercer. 'Ass. When he tried to get me to open the door, he told me to get my ass inside.'

'Go on.'

Annika was doing what we had watched hundreds of other victims do. She was putting herself back in the moment, watching a slow-motion replay of the attack in her mind's eye, and fighting the emotions that bubbled to the surface as she did.

'I can hear him say that, just before I braced myself against the wall with my leg,' she said, reminding me of the footprint on her door. 'It's what I believed at the time. I thought he was from England, or that he went to school there.'

'Why?' Mercer asked.

'A lot of my friends in Sweden, they learned their English in boarding school or college. My accent is from speaking it in class, as a second language. But the British pronunciation is different from you Americans'.'

Annika smiled for the first time since I had seen her greet Mercer from her hospital bed. 'My boyfriend? He spent a summer at Oxford. He says the word "ass" exactly the same way. It's silly, no? I didn't think at the time, but whenever that night comes back to me, I realized that's what was so jarring, when I heard the man speak that word.'

Mercer and I both laughed. 'Nothing's silly, Annika,' he said.

One more possible feature for the task force to factor into the investigation. All of the other women had been asked about the perp's speech and none had described it as accented. Unlike many attackers who talk to their victims all through the assault, the Silk Stocking Rapist had not been a man of many words.

We said our good-byes and Mercer took Annika and

her attendant down to help them into the ambulette that had transported them from the hospital. He returned minutes later.

'Back to the drawing board.' He tossed the case folder onto my desk and had an uncharacteristically discouraged frown on his face.

'I'm not exactly convinced that we're looking for an Oxford-educated rapist on the basis of one syllable,' I said.

'Yeah, but we've still got to reanalyze the language in every case and reinterview each victim about every single word the guy said. Annika's too smart to ignore. The list of things to do seems to get longer every day rather than shorter.'

'That's because you two just aren't as efficient as I am,' Mike said, walking into the room and waving his right hand with a flourish. 'Emily Upshaw. Grand larceny in the third degree.'

'Nice work,' I said, clapping my hands in appreciation.

'Bloomingdale's. Men's department. Designer clothes and accessories,' Mike said, as he began to quote from the old complaint report. '"Undersigned did observe above-named defendant conceal three long-sleeved men's shirts, an alligator belt" – there's your felony price tag – "and six pairs of socks in a shopping bag and attempt to leave the store without paying for said items."'

'Who's the guy? Was he locked up, too?'

'Don't jump ahead, Coop. Seems the cowardly weasel waited outside the store and sent Emily in to do the lifting.'

'Well, did the cop see—?'

'Not a cop. Square badge made the collar,' Mike said, referring to a store security guard. 'There's nothing to suggest a codefendant was picked up.'

'Was there any bail set at the arraignment?' I asked.

'Five hundred bucks,' he said, flipping a few sheets of paper. 'What did Emily's sister say about a professor helping her out? The guy who posted bail was named Noah Tormey. Says he taught English at NYU.'

'He put the money up either because he truly wanted to help her or—'

'Or because he was the unapprehended beneficiary of the shirts and belt.'

'Isn't there a detective's name anywhere in the file?' I asked, thinking of Emily's sister's other comments, as I opened the telephone book to see if there was a listing in Manhattan for Tormey.

'Yeah. You'll like this. Emily Upshaw had a change of address on the date the case was dismissed. She had moved out of her apartment on Washington Square and was living on West End Avenue. With a detective named Aaron Kittredge.'

'What? She moved in with a detective?'

'Don't make it sound like drinking poison, Coop. Could be good for you.'

Noah Tormey wasn't in the book. I replaced it on the shelf and logged on to the Internet. 'Kittredge still on the job?'

'Nope. Retired five years ago. Pension bureau still sends his checks to the Upper West Side address. We got places to go and people to see, kid. Saddle up.'

Laura walked in and handed Mike a fax. 'Andy Dorfman called from the medical examiner's office. Wanted you to look at this when you came in.'

'It's the initial report of his exam of some of the things taken out of the basement in the room with the skeleton.

No surprises. First of all, the pathologists agree there's nothing to work with but bones, which don't reveal any gross trauma that could have caused death. Buried alive – entombed in that basement – still seems the most likely way they're going to rule on this one,' Mike said. 'The bricks are a couple of hundred years old. But the sealant is a cement compound that didn't exist until the last fifty years.'

'Those chips Andy pointed out to you, were they really fingernails?'

'Yes, ma'am. And this confirms the nails picked up some of the cement scrapings,' he read to me in a quiet voice. 'That broad wanted *out*.'

He skimmed the rest of the paragraphs. 'What's "vermeil"?'

'Silver, with a gilt finish on top.'

'That's all Andy can tell us about the ring. But he's also picked up something that was scratched into one of the panes of glass on the basement door.'

'What door?' I asked. I had been so absorbed once I saw the skeleton in her coffin I hadn't even noticed much else.

'In the corner of the basement there was a small door with two little windows that looked out onto the yard. Somebody etched this into one of them.' Mike smiled as he read from Dorfman's report.

> 'O Thou timid one, do not let thy
> Form slumber within these unhallowed walls,
> For herein lies—'

I interrupted him to finish the stanza. '. . . *The ghost of an awful crime.*'

Chapter 18

'Trust me. It's not from having my nose in a book.'

'But how'd you know those lines?' Mike asked again. Mercer had returned to his office to go over the casework with another of the task force members. I was riding uptown with Mike to try to find Aaron Kittredge.

'Remember that I told you that Poe was a student at the University of Virginia for a year? He lived on the Lawn, which is still the most magnificent part of the campus, with pavilion homes where professors lived and taught class, and student rooms around a common green, all that Jefferson himself designed. Well, legend has it that he etched those very words into his own window before he left the school, and the original pane of glass with that inscription has been on display in the Rotunda there for as long as I can remember.'

'So maybe the killer was a schoolmate of yours.'

'There were a few sharks in my class but nobody that lethal. I think whoever he is, he's made a life study of Edgar Allan Poe,' I said.

Kittredge's address placed us in front of a small tenement building off West End Avenue in the high Nineties. There was a doorbell with his name on it, but no one answered when Mike rang. It was six-thirty, and the chilled darkness caused us to retreat to the parked car and wait to see whether we'd get lucky.

Within the hour, a stocky man with salt-and-pepper hair turned the corner and walked up the stoop of the building.

'Kittredge!' Mike yelled as he swung open the car door.

The man looked in our direction and squinted, trying to make out whether he knew the person calling his name.

'Chapman. Mike Chapman. On the job.'

'Fuck the job,' Kittredge called out just as quickly, as he stuck his key in the vestibule lock and started inside.

Mike sprinted from the car to the steps and pushed in behind him. 'I just need to talk to you about someone you know – an old friend.'

'Haven't got any of those. Why don't you get lost?'

I was a few feet behind Mike as he tried to talk his way in.

'She thinks you're a friend. She needs your help,' Mike said, pausing before he spoke her name. 'Emily Upshaw.'

Kittredge stopped and pointed at me. 'Who's that?'

'Alexandra Cooper. Manhattan DA's office.'

'I'm out of that game. What's with Emily? Back in her cups again?'

'Look, can you give us twenty minutes? I'm freezing my balls off out here.'

Kittredge unlocked the door and let us trail him up to his apartment on the second floor. He switched on the light and threw his leather jacket on a chair. The charcoal gray walls were hung with paintings of nude women – or rather of one nude woman painted over and over again from different angles.

'They're mine, if that's what you're wondering. I paint. I work out at the gym two hours a day and I don't bother anybody. Next question.'

'Why so hostile, pal?' Mike asked.

The workout time was obvious. Kittredge's five-foot-eight frame was solid and well muscled. His black T-shirt seemed molded to his overdeveloped chest, and tattoos covered his forearms up to the point where the sleeves of his shirt cut off. The wrinkles on his face made him look a decade older than what I guessed was the fifty hard years he had lived.

'You get my address from the department?'

'Yeah.'

'Without the back story?'

'With nothing. I figure you're getting a pension check, so you couldn't have done anything to make yourself a pariah.'

'I got a good lawyer. That's how come they reinstated my pension. Try living six years without one and sweating out a lawsuit.'

Mike sat down on the sofa and I sat beside him. Kittredge stood in the archway between the kitchen and the living area. He took a protein drink from the refrigerator and chugged it from the cardboard container while he waited for Mike to talk.

'Why'd they—?'

'None of your business. What's the problem with Emily?'

'Don't you read the papers?'

'Only the days they got good news.'

'Then you might have missed her obituary yesterday.'

Kittredge took another slug of his protein. 'You here to collect money for the flowers?'

'Emily Upshaw was murdered.'

'And you're the hotshot who's gonna solve the crime? You must have some track record, Chapman, you're wasting time hunting me down. I haven't seen that dame in eighteen, twenty years. Can't even imagine how you hooked me up with her.'

'She must have liked your brushstrokes. Court papers say she was living here when her shoplifting case was dismissed.'

'I bought that sofa you're sitting on so Emily would have a safe place to sleep.'

'Bring your work home with you?' Mike asked.

'It was here or a Bowery flophouse. The poor kid had nowhere to go. Her family didn't want to hear about her, the college wouldn't let her live in the dorms after she got busted, and the guy she'd been living with threw her out on—'

There was the sound of a key turning in the lock and Kittredge walked to the door as it opened. A brunette in her fifties with a well-toned body and a skintight ski outfit entered. She was the model for the paintings and looked as cold and hard in person as she did on every wall surface.

'Anything wrong?' she asked, looking from Kittredge over to Mike and back again.

Mike stood up and extended his hand. 'Hi, I'm Mike Chap—'

'The Duke and Duchess of Windsor will be leaving shortly. Wait in the bedroom,' Kittredge said, jerking his head in the direction of the other door.

The woman took another look at the two of us and patted his arm as she crossed in front of him to leave the room.

'It's the boyfriend we're interested in,' Mike said, although I knew he was now every bit as interested in the disaffected Kittredge as he was in Emily's old beau. 'What can you tell me about him?'

'Nothing. Never met the guy.'

'Well, how'd you get pulled into the case?'

'I wasn't. Had nothing to do with the larceny she got locked up for. I worked in the Sixth Squad at the time,' Kittredge said.

The theft was uptown, we knew from the police report, but Emily had been living in Greenwich Village, in the Sixth Precinct.

'She came to the station house with – well, with a pretty bizarre tale – and I happened to be the schmuck catching cases that day. You know what it's like, don't you, Chapman?'

'What was her story?'

Kittredge crumpled the empty drink container in his fist. 'Poor little Emily was high as a kite. The desk sergeant kicked her upstairs. He wanted one of the women detectives to toss her for drugs 'cause she wasn't making much sense when she talked. Nobody was around but me. The kid said she had information about a murder. She knew a guy who had killed someone.'

'True?'

'I gave it a shot. I asked her to start with the perp. Tell me about him. She was too frightened to do much of that. It was a boyfriend of hers, a guy she'd met in some kind of rehab program.'

'Monty? Was his name Monty?' Mike asked.

'Nope. He may have had a nickname like that, that he called himself, but it's not how Emily knew him,'

Kittredge said, frowning and shaking his head. 'Hey, I haven't thought about this for two decades. I'm supposed to remember the guy's name?'

'Didn't you meet him? Wasn't Emily living with him?'

'She'd moved out by then. Gone off the wagon and moved into the Y to live. She tried to point him out on the street to me one time, but I never got a clear fix on him. Looked like one more Village idiot to me. Doped-up rich kid trying to live like a hippie. Most of 'em outgrow it. I went back to question the guy, but he was gone. I think they had shared a place on Sullivan Street. Couldn't find a trace of him.'

'Was he a student, too?'

'I think he was already out of school. Dropped out or kicked out. His family wouldn't pay the bills, I think she told me. Black sheep syndrome,' Kittredge said, smiling at Mike. 'Been there myself.'

'Who'd he kill?'

Kittredge leaned back against the kitchen table. 'She didn't know that either. Another junkie was all she said.'

'Where'd it happen?'

'Well, if Emily Upshaw had the answer to that, I might have made a case, don't you think? Look, Chapman, here's this sweet kid strung out on dope who kept telling me that her boyfriend had buried someone alive. I didn't know who, I didn't know where, and I didn't even know whether the boyfriend had been one of her delusions. She had those, too, from time to time.'

'Did she tell you why she thought it was true?'

He thought for a minute. 'Yeah. One night, a few weeks after Emily had busted out of the program, the guy came home from a session—'

'You mean an AA meeting – Alcoholics Anonymous?'

'Like that. I think it was called SABA – Student Abusers Anonymous. I think he'd been clean and sober a little longer than Emily. He'd started in the group while he was still enrolled at NYU. Anyway, that night he spun out of control and brought home a few bags of coke. They got high together and that's when he broke down.'

'How do you mean?'

'He wigged out. According to Emily, he was pretty frantic. He told her that he'd been having flashbacks ever since he'd been sober and dried out. He said that during that evening's session he'd admitted to a couple of the guys that he thought he had murdered someone. It was all visions and dreams, mumbo-jumbo, alcoholic blackouts. But as soon as he – what's the bullshit word they use now – shared? As soon as he "shared" his story with his self-help group, he began to worry that one of the other guys would give him up. So he went a little berserk, picked up some drugs to get him through the night, and came home crying to lay it all on Emily's lap.'

'And she came to the station house?' Mike asked.

'You mean did she come that same night, when she should have?' Kittredge sneered. 'Yeah, about four months too late. Not that night, not the next day.'

'Why not?' I asked, speaking for the first time.

'Typical broad bullshit. Emily didn't think it was possible. Such a sensitive soul, the guy was. Good family roots, poetic genius, brilliant student, kind to animals. She laid it off to the white powder he shoved up his nostrils.'

'She stayed with him?'

'Yeah. Then things got more desperate after the

shoplifting. Truth is I never knew whether she was really afraid of him, or he just dumped her and she had nowhere to go.'

'How'd she wind up with you?' Mike asked.

'She told her lawyer – Legal Aid, he was – that she had a friend in the police department. He called and told me that if she had a transient address like the Y, the DA's office wouldn't dismiss the case. He just asked me to let her use my crib for a month.'

'Did you and she—?'

'None of your fucking business, Chapman.'

'But you actually investigated the case?' I asked. 'I mean, did you talk to other people in his SABA group?'

Kittredge looked at Mike while he talked to me. 'Hard to do. By the time Emily got to me, school was out for the summer. The rehab meetings had been confidential – you know the law, drug treatment stuff is privileged – so the college didn't have any record of who attended.'

'All you had was a half-assed confession, fueled by cocaine,' Mike said.

'With no body, no crime scene, and not even a suspect I could put my hands on. I kicked it around for a few months,' Kittredge said.

Probably, I thought, for as long as Emily was putting out for him.

'Then my boss took me off it. He figured that she was just squealing on a guy who had dumped her and we couldn't go digging up ground all over Manhattan unless we had a report of somebody missing.'

'You keep a file on it?' Mike asked.

'There was the usual paperwork I did in the squad, back before we had computers.'

'Take any of your case folders with you? Something that might have names on—'

'For what? My memoirs?' Kittredge laughed as he walked to the front door and put his hand on the knob.

'You mind if we come back to you when we have more information?' Mike said, realizing the opportunity for conversation was about to be over.

'Try not to waste my time. Emily wasn't known for her taste in men. She probably picked up one too many barflys with a rough edge. She just couldn't keep off the juice, I guess.'

We were back out on the stoop, headed for the car, when Mike's cell phone rang. He opened it to say hello, and I could see the condensation of his breath in the air. It made him look as though he was as fired up inside as I figured him to be.

'Where? Does Scotty Taren know?' Mike asked, getting answers that he liked. 'Thanks, Hal. I owe you big-time.'

I waited for him to unlock the car and let me inside. He slammed the door and pursed his lips. 'That was Hal Sherman. Looks like all the pressure of going public with a patient's history may have been too much for Dr Ichiko. He killed himself today. They just found his body up in the Bronx.'

Chapter 19

'Why did Hal call you?' I asked. 'It's Scotty's case now.'

''Cause Scotty's a stand-up guy. When Hal reached out to him, Scotty said to play dumb and give me the first heads-up. After all, I was in the basement after the skeleton was discovered and Hal took the photos. So it would make sense for him to have to call me in order to find out that Taren's got the case now. And why should I know McKinney forbade him to talk to you about it?'

'Don't think you're leaving me behind on this one.'

'McKinney'll go nuts if you show up at the scene, Coop.'

'That fact alone is enough to make me want to go twice as badly. You're always telling me how much I'd love the Bronx. So far I've limited most of my experience to Yankee Stadium. Now's your chance to show me the borough's charms.'

Mike had gone to college at Fordham and loved the rich history of the borough, once the seventeenth-century farmland of Swedish-born Jonas Bronck, the first European settler to live on the mainland northeast of Manhattan.

'Yeah, but a death scene wasn't my vision of an introduction.'

'I guess *Crime Factor* will have to go with a rerun for tonight's show. Dr Ichiko won't be revealing the identity of our skeleton on this episode. C'mon, let's see what happened to this greedy shrink. Where to?'

Mike shifted into gear and pulled out into the traffic. 'The gorge.'

'What?'

'The Bronx River Gorge.'

'Never heard of it,' I said, as he took advantage of the early evening lull in traffic to race across town to the Triborough Bridge, and up the Major Deegan Expressway to wind through what to me was the unfamiliar territory of the Bronx.

'You've never been to the Botanical Gardens?'

'Not since I was a kid.' I had grown up in the suburbs north of the city and remembered visits to the gardens with my mother, who took me there for the brilliant spring displays of roses and the seasonal show of dozens of orchid varieties that she so loved.

'That's where we're headed. The gorge is inside the grounds of the Botanical Gardens. The Fordham campus is right across the street.'

'I know the hothouses and the—'

'No flowerpots, Coop. This is part of the Bronx River. You know that's the only freshwater river in New York City?'

'What about the Hudson, or the East River?'

'They're tidal estuaries, Coop. You got to pay more attention to your surroundings.'

For much of the ride, Mike gave me the early history

of the area. After its discovery by Henry Hudson and its control by the Dutch West India Company as New Netherland, there were frequent and violent clashes with the local Indian tribes.

'You would have had your little prosecutorial hands full here, even in the 1640s.'

'Doing what?'

'Ever hear of Anne Hutchinson?'

'Yes. She was exiled from Massachusetts by the Puritans. Brought a whole little colony somewhere down here because of religious intolerance.'

'This is it. Chief Wampage was a bit peeved about the slaughter of some of his people, so he made his way to Hutchinson's house and whacked her right in the forehead with his tomahawk. Scalped her and her kids.'

By the time we reached Bronx River Park, I had a thumbnail sketch of the county's major military skirmishes, from the revolutionary fortifications at the King's Bridge to the Battle of Pell's Point.

At the entrance to the park, long after closing time, a uniformed officer opened the gate when Mike flashed his badge. He directed us south and told us that the Crime Scene Unit and some groundskeepers were waiting for us there, half a mile inside.

My childhood memories of sun-filled gardens with vividly colored flowers bore no resemblance to the vast, darkened park that we had entered. There were occasional streetlamps along the route, but the roadway was surrounded on both sides by a tall, dense growth of trees. The wind caused tall shadows to dance in front of our headlights, and the sprawling grounds seemed an eerily sinister place.

Some snakelike curves in the road and half a mile later, Hal Sherman waved us down and came over to open my car door.

'I doubt you were ever a Boy Scout, Chapman,' he called out over my head, 'but you might wanna rub a couple of sticks together and start a little fire if you're thinking of keeping me out here any longer. I can't stand much more of this cold.'

'That the doctor?' Mike asked, pointing at an ambulance parked at the curb.

'Not a pretty picture.'

Mike held his arm straight at me, palm out. He walked to the open end, said something to the two EMTs, and they unzipped the black body bag. He leaned in with a flashlight and studied the head and chest of the dead man.

'Looks like he went ten rounds with Mike Tyson,' he said, returning to us. 'Who's calling this a suicide?'

Hal shrugged his shoulders. 'It sure as hell wasn't a mugging. You got enough dark alleys between his house in Riverdale and his office in the Village for someone to do him in. You think a member of the Polar Bear Club brought him up here for a dip in ice water to off him? His wife says he was up all night tearing his hair out because of the bad press over his decision to go on that crappy show and give up a patient's name. Finally was about to get his time in the limelight, but was ready to kill himself once he realized the professional consequences of doing something so stupid.'

'Who found him?'

'We're waiting on a translator,' Hal said. 'That's the head groundskeeper – the tall guy in the khakis. The two others who pulled the body out of the river are the short ones with him. They're Vietnamese.'

I followed Mike over to the trio, who were shielding themselves from the wind against a stand of pine trees.

'You in charge?'

'Phelps. I'm Sinclair Phelps,' the groundskeeper said. 'These men work for me.'

I could see Phelps's profile silhouetted against the light gray rocks lining the riverbed behind me. He was, at about five-eleven, a little shorter than Mike. His hair was long and thick, but flecked with enough silver to suggest that he was in his mid-fifties. His aquiline nose gave him a stern mien, and the years of outdoor labor had lined his face as if it were the hide of a gator.

'You know anything?' Mike asked, after introducing us.

'Only what Trun has told me,' Phelps said, pointing to the slighter of the two men, who were shivering as badly as I was.

'You speak Vietnamese?'

'No, no,' Phelps said, smiling. 'They can manage a few words of English and some fairly effective body language. I can tell you as much as they've told me. Late this afternoon – Miss Cooper, you seem to be uncomfortable. Would you like to move inside?'

'Take us through it once out here, will you?' Mike said, rolling his eyes while Hal Sherman passed me a pair of rubber gloves to put on, this time just for warmth. Phelps had a crew-neck sweater over his uniform and seemed as impervious to the damp wind as Mike did in his navy blazer, collar turned up. The rest of us were miserable.

'Do you know the river?'

I shook my head while both Hal and Mike nodded.

'It's twenty-five miles long, seven in the city and the rest going up through Westchester.'

'It seems bizarre to me for someone to think of killing himself in a river in the wintertime. I'd expect it to be frozen over,' I said, looking at the icy surfaces that gleamed from the rocks in the riverbed and the snow-laden branches overhanging it.

'In the shallow places further north, that's quite true. There are some spots where it's only a few inches deep,' Phelps said. 'But that's not the case here, because of the falls.'

'Waterfalls?' I asked.

'Yes, ma'am. This is a gorge you're looking at. Y'see, there's an ancient fault that was created by the glaciers that moved through here,' he said, turning on the beam of his torch lamp and bending to knock some pine branches out of the way so we could follow him a distance into the woods.

I could hear the sound of water, like a rushing torrent, as we neared the basin at the foot of the falls.

It looked as though we were standing in the Adirondacks, not in the middle of New York City. The frigid water cascaded down an enormous drop from the heavily timbered chasm above us and got caught up in the spinning whirlpools below, which whipped it into a frenzy before whooshing it off downriver.

'Quite spectacular, isn't it? On the more mundane side, once a week,' Phelps said, 'our maintenance men gather trash from the river. Used to be, Detective, that you could find shopping carts, spare parts of automobiles, mattresses, all sorts of flotsam and jetsam in here. We've tried to change that. Today, Trun and Hang were responsible for cleaning up this area.'

The two workers were behind us, dressed in heavy rubber suits – like fishermen – with hip waders and watch caps. Phelps motioned them to stand beside him.

'The man you found,' he said to them, 'where was he?'

'Between rocks,' the one called Trun said. 'There.'

He pointed about fifteen feet out into the water, where two enormous rock formations guarded an eddy of frothy water.

'How'd they get him out?' Mike asked.

'They used a grappling hook,' Phelps said.

Hal whispered in my ear, 'I don't care who does the autopsy. Going over the falls and landing on these rocks would have pummeled the daylights out of anybody. Then these two guys stick a pitchfork in him? Ichiko's a bloody mess and I don't know how the best medical examiner on earth is gonna figure this one out.'

Chapman turned back to the area where we had parked our cars. 'Ask them why they moved him before they called the police,' he said to Phelps.

'They didn't actually. I can answer that. They raised me on the intercom and I raced over,' he said, pointing at a golf cart he obviously used to get around the grounds. 'That couldn't have taken more than three or four minutes. I called nine-one-one at the same time I ordered them to pull the man out.'

'Why'd you do that? I mean, tell them to move the body before we got here?'

Phelps seemed taken aback by the question. 'Well, Detective, just suppose he was alive. Unconscious or, or . . . Well, it seemed to be taking an awful chance to leave him there if he was still breathing. I'm sorry if I did the wrong thing.'

His two workers hung their heads, seeming to understand that Phelps was being blamed for something they did.

'Hey, Hal, you look above for any signs of where the guy went in?'

'Yep. There's a car parked on top, near the head of the falls. It's Ichiko's.'

'Tracks? Any tracks in the snow?'

'Yeah. It looks like Roseland up there. Like people were dancing all over the place. Not to mention the wildlife. You go up there, Mr Phelps?' Hal asked him.

'No, sir. Trun? Hang?' The groundskeeper questioned his men, pointing up at the heights of the gorge.

Both men nodded in the affirmative. 'I go there look for help,' Hang said.

Mike turned to Hal. 'Charlie Chan he's not. What's in the car?'

'Dr Ichiko's wallet. ID, cash, credit cards. None of that touched. We dusted for latents, just in case.'

'Any note? Anything to suggest he was going to end it all?'

'Nope.'

'Signs of a struggle?'

'Nothing like that either.'

'Gentlemen,' Mike said, addressing Trun and Hang, 'you were taking trash out of the river when you saw the body?'

Both men nodded eagerly.

'Where is it now?'

Each pointed at a row of three dark green plastic bags.

'Not much to speak of this time of year,' Phelps said. 'It's the other three seasons we're overloaded with bottles and cans, picnic remains—'

'Get a tarp, Hal,' Mike said.

Sherman walked the few steps to his station wagon and came back with a large canvas that he dropped on the hard ground.

'Dump 'em out.'

'Right here? This is going to be messy,' Phelps said, helping his two workers untie and empty the bags. Food wrappings, wads of paper, empty coffee containers, and several small bird carcasses were spread out on the tarp. Mike ran his flashlight over the day's take, kicking larger items out of his way with his foot.

Something small and silver gleamed amid the rubble. Mike reached for it and threw it back – a crumpled aluminum soda can.

Another shiny object caught the light. I bent over and picked up a small cell phone.

'Way to go, Coop. You guys get this out of the water?'

Hang spoke. 'No,' he said, pointing up at the top of the gorge. 'Snow.'

I flipped it open to see if it was still working and hit the recall button.

'Don't touch it. Let the tech guys figure out what's on it.'

'Sorry. I just wanted to see if it's connected to Ichiko and who the last call went to,' I said, holding the phone to my ear as Mike started to circle around the tarp to take it from me.

It rang four times before rolling over into voice mail and I signaled to Mike to wait a minute.

A deep voice with a heavily accented Southern drawl spoke to me. 'You have reached the office of the Raven Society. Please be so good as to leave a message after the tone.'

Chapter 20

'You gonna tell McKinney you just came from viewing Dr Ichiko?'

'Of course I am,' I said.

'And you're going to tell him about the Raven Society phone call, too?'

'Not until I know what the society is.' By morning, Mike would be able to check the reverse telephone directory and get a name and address for the number that had been displayed in the lighted dial of the cell phone.

We had just reached the Nineteenth Precinct squad room, shortly after nine-thirty Tuesday evening. When Mike had called Scotty Taren earlier to tell him about the scene at the gorge, the cold case detective had a new development to report, too.

Pat McKinney had been contacted late in the day by a man who claimed to have information about the skeleton in the West Third Street basement. He had directed Scotty to set up a meeting with the man, himself, and Scotty at 9 P.M. in the Nineteenth Precinct station house.

Mike knocked on the frosted glass pane of the captain's office. Through it, I could see the outline of McKinney's figure, standing in front of the desk. He walked to the door and opened it, stepping out into the squad room to greet Mike.

'Hey, Chapman. Scotty tells me you've been to the river to—' McKinney said, stopping short when he spotted me over Mike's shoulder. 'I suppose you had to stick your nose in the middle of this, too? Maybe if you concentrated your energy on the Silk Stocking Rapist you could solve that one, Alex.'

A man was seated inside the room with his back to me. I was more curious about the pair of legs sticking out from a chair behind the door – a woman's legs, crossed at the knees, displaying thick ankles planted in cheap black pumps.

Mike saw them, too, and recognized them. McKinney's longtime lover, Ellen Gunsher, was also a prosecutor, but her fear of the courtroom and her lack of any creative investigative ability had landed her a succession of administrative jobs that were nestled under McKinney's protective eye.

'Are those the stumps – I mean stems – of my favorite yellow rose?' Mike asked, pushing back the door and exposing a bit more of Ellen, who played her big-city helplessness against her homespun Texas roots.

She waved at Mike and offered a wan smile.

'Are we interrupting anything personal, Pat?' I asked.

'Ellen and I were working on turning an informant down at the office when I got this call. That's why she's here.'

'Who's the suit? Is that the guy who called with information?'

Pat reached for the doorknob to close it behind him to answer me.

'Just a minute, pal. Don't be leaving any witness on something I'm involved in alone in a room with Ellen,' Mike said, motioning her out of the room while the dark-haired man in the chair turned his head to examine the four of us. 'C'mon, Tex.'

Mike closed the door, leaving the man inside.

Pat was trying to get between Mike and the door. 'Last I knew this was Scotty Taren's investigation, not yours. The skeleton's a Cold Case Squad matter, and Ichiko goes with that.'

'Yeah, well, Lieutenant Peterson changed the rules. He wants all hands on deck – I just got off the phone with him – until we know if any of these things are connected. You heard Ms Cooper. Who's the suit?'

Scotty Taren spoke while McKinney glared at Mike, and Ellen stood frozen like a deer caught in the head-lights. 'His name is Gino Guidi. Fifty-six years old. He's an investment banker with an operation called Providence Partners.'

'Stop right there. I know why four of us are here, but I think it's time for Ellen to hit the road,' Mike said. 'She's got no business with me, and either she packs it in or I make a call to the chief of d's and we go to the mat on this.'

McKinney usually bullied detectives into getting his way, but Mike wouldn't brook it. An assistant who had never handled homicides would not be cutting her teeth on one of his investigations.

Ellen raised a hand at Pat to stop whatever feeble protest he was about to make and put on her coat. As she said good night and walked to the staircase, Mike sang out after her: 'Oh, I've got spurs that jingle, jangle, jingle.'

McKinney was close to boiling point.

'You want me to continue?' Scotty asked Mike.

McKinney slapped his hand against the wall. 'I'm the senior man here. We'll do this the way I say.'

'Look, Pat. I think Mike and I have more information than you do at this point,' I said. 'You can run the show. Just grow up and realize that we're all in it for the same result. I'll take the backseat but you're not doing this without us. Go on, Scotty.'

Taren shook his head. 'You guys ready? Guidi's married with four kids. Lives in Kings Point. The reason he called is that he was treated by Dr Ichiko a long time ago. He was in that same rehab group as Emily Upshaw – SABA. He was an alcoholic who moved into other drugs. He was in business school at the time. Guidi thinks he knows the name of the skeleton – well, the girl whose bones you found.'

'Who is she?' Mike asked.

Scotty looked at his notes. 'Aurora Tait.'

'He's got the initials right,' I said, referring to the ring that we'd found inside her brick coffin. 'Why'd he come forward today?'

'That's what he was telling us when you two interrupted,' Pat said.

'He seems pretty freaked out about Dr Ichiko going on television to name his former patient. He's willing to give us information if we can stop Ichiko,' Scotty said.

'Apparently someone else shared that sentiment. Shall we continue?' Mike opened the door and introduced the two of us, apologizing to Guidi for the commotion and reconfiguring the chairs so that we could all fit in the small office.

Pat McKinney took the captain's seat and picked up his questioning. I was against the back wall, listening to the conversation and looking over Gino Guidi.

The banker was dressed in a well-tailored charcoal gray suit – Brioni, if I had to guess. His shirt was a white-on-white herringbone, with his initials on the barrel cuff. The subtle circular weave on his necktie was perfectly matched to the lavender pocket square, and his fingernails had been recently buffed to a high sheen. His black hair looked like a good dye job, and the only sign of a bump in the road of Gino Guidi's life was a raw scar that ran from the middle of his right cheek down below his shirt collar.

'You were going to give us some background, Mr Guidi,' Pat said.

'I trust this is still confidential?' Guidi said, gesturing at Mike and me.

'My colleagues understand that. You were telling us about Ms Tait. About why you think she's the woman who was found last week.'

'Aurora was what people used to call a free spirit. I was at the B-school when I first met her,' he said, resuming his story.

'Was she an NYU student, too?' Pat asked.

'No. She lived in the Village, so she was always hanging around Washington Square. I think a lot of people assumed she was a student, which gave her entrée to all the kids, but in fact she was just a hanger-on.'

'How did you meet her?'

'At a party. Nothing memorable about the event except Aurora.'

'What about her?'

184

'She was the sexiest woman I'd ever seen, I think. Tall and willowy, moved like a cat, had lots of dark hair that kind of framed her face and made her smile seem even more electric. And mean,' Guidi said, smiling. 'She had a really mean streak.'

'How'd she show that?'

'She had a pretty vicious tongue, Mr McKinney. I guess she'd heard every pickup line in the book so her come-backs were designed to cut through all the crap, separate the men from the boys. She kept me on a tight wire for the first couple of weeks, threatening to destroy anything in my life I cared about.'

'Did you date her?' Pat asked. I knew that Mike was as ready to hijack the questioning and let Guidi tell his story as I was, but Pat plugged ahead.

'Aurora didn't date. She conquered. Took me home with her that night and—'

'Where did she live? On Third Street?'

Let him finish his goddamn sentences, I thought to myself.

'No. No, not where the bones were found. I don't know anything about that place. We went to a pad on Bleecker Street. I thought it was where she lived, but it turned out to be just a place she flopped for the night. Anyway, Aurora showed me some tricks,' Guidi said, looking over his shoulder at me, as though to make sure he wasn't offending me. 'Some experiences that were new to me. And then, of course, there were the drugs.'

'What drugs?'

'Aurora introduced me to crack, Mr McKinney. I was a big drinker at the time. Both my parents were alco-holics, so whatever genetic predisposition there was kind

185

of doubled up in me. But I was in denial, like most alcoholics. I thought everyone in college drank like I did. Then I had my first job on Wall Street and got into the two-martini lunches of the eighties, to get me through the afternoon until I could start drinking in earnest. Went on to business school, where I mixed my liquor with the occasional line of coke.'

'Why crack?'

Guidi leaned in and lighted a cigarette, throwing the match into a half-empty coffee cup. 'Because Aurora Tait lit the pipe and put it in my mouth while she was lying naked next to me in bed. It seemed like a fine idea at the time.'

'And then?'

'I guess you haven't talked with many crack addicts, have you, Mr McKinney?'

McKinney had spent too much time doing administrative work behind his closed office door to know, from witnesses, the things the rest of the line assistants and cops heard firsthand every single day.

'I don't understand, Mr Guidi.'

'The first time I smoked crack I thought I had found nirvana. I wanted to do it again, that night, and every night thereafter. I felt a sense of freedom I'd never known before – no pressure, no anxiety – completely sensual and pleasurable. And like every truly addictive personality, I began by assuming that I could control my reaction to the drug. Denial worked just as well for crack cocaine as it did for alcohol.'

'And Aurora was with you throughout all this?'

Guidi exhaled and laughed at the same time. 'No. She was just the siren, luring me onto the rocks.'

'Excuse me, what siren?'

McKinney was so literal, so rigid, he was undoubtedly thinking of the sound box of a police cruiser, not the legendary women of Greek mythology whose singing was the downfall of unwary sailors.

'She was a stone-cold junkie who supported her habit by selling drugs. She'd found the perfect niche, Mr McKinney. She set herself up in the middle of Greenwich Village, cruising the campus and the bars and the parties to find guys like me – rich boys with generous allowances to spend on books and dates and work clothes. Only, me? I never made it to the bookstore. She had me hooked within two weeks of meeting her. Left me with an expensive habit and moved right on to the next guy.'

'What happened to you?'

'I had a very sobering wake-up call about a year and a half later. I ran into the sharp end of a jackknife at four in the morning on Avenue C, desperate to find some crack. I was admitted to Bellevue Hospital and regained consciousness three days later. While I was convalescing, the shrink on intake was Dr Wo-Jin Ichiko. He worked with me while I was in withdrawal and detoxing. Then he introduced me to SABA, the rehab program at the university.'

Guidi paused and dropped his cigarette butt in the cup. 'The prick probably saved my life. But today, I'll be honest with you, I was ready to kill him.'

'Because?'

'Because I've spent two decades of my life trying to put the pieces back together. I've got a very understanding wife, who met me fifteen years ago. I flunked out of business school while all this drug involvement was going on, so I had to claw my way in by starting from scratch. I worked in the mail room at Credit Suisse until I could make enough money to get back into school. But my kids have no idea that for almost three years I lived like a derelict and came close to throwing every advantage I'd been given to the wind. And I bet they'd understand and accept it a whole helluva lot better than my partners and most of my clients.'

'When's the last time you saw Dr Ichiko?' McKinney asked.

'Eighteen, twenty years ago.'

'And you haven't spoken to him either?'

Guidi tapped another cigarette out of his pack and lit up. 'Yeah, I did. Last night. I called his house.'

'You had his home number?'

'No. I called the office and got his service. I told them I was a patient with an emergency and they patched me through.'

'Did you have a conversation with him?'

'When I stopped cursing at him, I guess you'd call it that.'

'What did you say?'

'I called him every name in the book. I thought there was some kind of privilege between doctors and their patients. I didn't know why the hell he was going to go on television and give out the name of someone he treated years ago. I don't need this kind of shit, this kind of publicity, coming out now – not for my family, not for my clients.'

'Why were you so concerned about Aurora Tait?' McKinney asked.

'I never said I was,' Guidi replied. 'But if a medical doctor could be paid by a television show to make Aurora's name public, what was to stop him from identifying the rest of us?'

'Well, she's dead, so the question of privilege—'

Guidi leaned forward and interrupted McKinney. 'You're damn right she's dead and it doesn't make a bit of difference in her sorry case. Nobody even missed her when she drifted out of our lives, so it's nice to know she can finally be laid to rest. But the last thing I need to see on some tabloid television show is a feature about my own wasted youth and drug addiction.'

'The girl was buried alive, Mr Guidi. Somebody had to hate her awful bad to wish that kind of ending.'

Gino Guidi covered his eyes with his hand and leaned his head back. He actually seemed shocked. 'I saw the news story. I just figured she ran into the wrong junkie, made the same mistakes I did,' he said, now rubbing a finger along the length of his scar. 'That's chilling.'

'Did you threaten Dr Ichiko?' McKinney had to change direction to show his authority.

Guidi tossed his head and took a draw on his cigarette. 'I get it. He taped me. Yeah, I threatened him. So what? I told him I'd nail him, one way or another. I told him I'd sue his Oriental ass from here to Hong Kong.'

Mike spoke for the first time. 'Rugs are Oriental, Mr Guidi. People are Asian. PC enough for you, Coop?'

Guidi snapped his head around to look at Mike. 'I told him he was dead meat if he messed with me.'

A sharp rap on the glass pane startled me. Without waiting for an invitation, someone pushed open the door and walked in.

'Cut it out, McKinney.' The speaker was Roy Kirby, from the white-shoe law firm in which he was a name partner. 'Give me some place to talk to my client. Gino, don't say another word.'

Chapter 21

The four of us stepped out so Kirby and his client could confer.

'Does he know that Dr Ichiko is dead?' Mike asked.

'He didn't seem to when he walked in the door,' McKinney said. 'Unless he came in here to set up the perfect alibi for himself. "Me? I was cooperating with the police when Ichiko went over the falls. Just ask them."'

'Yeah, well, nice job, Pat. You did everything except get what we really need – the name of the guy who killed Aurora. The person who hated her enough to brick her up behind a wall, still breathing. Solve Scotty's case for him.'

'Take your best shot, Mike. Guidi told me before you two showed up, right off the bat, that he didn't know anything definite. All he can do is guess. Everyone in the rehab group was students or had once been enrolled in the university. They were each told to use nicknames so no one could make any official connection between them and the school.'

'You got a nickname?'

McKinney looked at his pad. 'Monty. He told me the guy who might have wanted Aurora dead used the name Monty.'

That fit with the nickname Emily Upshaw's friend, Teddy Kroon, had told us. Mike and I knew that, but McKinney wasn't familiar with the details of the Upshaw investigation, so the name Monty didn't seem to have any significance to him. Mike looked at me and winked.

'What does Guidi know about Monty? Anything else?'

'That he was in a graduate program – something to do with literature. Guidi thinks he was a poet or a writer.'

'And the police – did Guidi ever tell the police about Aurora back then, when she disappeared?' I asked.

'No. He says he was too whacked out on drugs. She vanished and most of the kids figured she just either left town or she got caught up in some drug sweep and went to prison for a while.'

Fifteen minutes later, while Mike worked the phones to set up meetings for the next day, McKinney was summoned into the room by Roy Kirby. Whatever agreement they reached, Scotty, Mike, and I were not privy to it. McKinney came out to ask Taren to set them up in the interrogation room with the two-way glass, so that Taren could watch the rest of the conversation without being seen by Guidi. McKinney's excuse for excluding Mike and me was that Guidi was uncomfortable with so many investigators surrounding him.

After McKinney went inside with the witness, Taren waved both of us into the darkened cubicle so we could observe the interchange alongside him.

Gino Guidi had started to explain what he knew about Aurora Tait and the man known as Monty.

'The program we were in – SABA – was set up on the twelve-step model of Alcoholics Anonymous. You know what that is?' Guidi asked.

'I've got a pretty good idea. Why don't you be specific,' McKinney said.

'The first thing is just to admit that you're powerless over alcohol and can no longer control your life. The second step is to acknowledge your belief in a higher power that can help restore your sanity. Next you agree to turn your life over to God – whatever your understanding of him is – and then to make a soul-searching inventory of yourself,' Guidi said, still smoking as he talked.

'We got to the fifth step and that's where Monty started to choke.'

'What do you mean?' McKinney asked.

'I think the way it goes is that you have to admit to yourself, and to God, and to another human being the exact nature of your wrongs. Most of us had hurt the people we loved, stolen money to buy drugs, hocked the family jewels – that kind of thing,' he said, crushing his cigarette in an ashtray on the bare table in front of him and shaking his head.

'And Monty?'

'I was sitting on a bench in Washington Square Park, waiting for a meeting to begin. I didn't even know the guy except for an hour a week in a church basement, listening to him talk about getting kicked out of boarding school and being an orphan and that kind of shit. Next thing I know, he's telling me he'd been having weird dreams.'

'Dreams?' McKinney asked.

'Yeah, nightmares. Said he had visions that he had killed someone.'

'Did he tell you who?'

'Not by name. I mean, I didn't know it was Aurora Tait. He told me he kept waking up in the middle of the night, thinking he had murdered a girl. Some chick, he told me, who had betrayed him. He said he'd had a summer job doing construction work – this was where he got especially weird – and that he'd used materials from his work to bury her behind a wall.'

'And what did you do about it?'

'Do about it?' Guidi asked, looking puzzled.

'Who'd you tell?'

'I just assumed he was back on the blow, Mr McKinney. Dreams and visions and blackouts were nothing unusual to any of us. I just chalked it up to the fact that he was using crack again, hallucinating and being paranoid. I knew firsthand what that was like.'

'Do you know whether he – this, this Monty – told anyone else?'

'No idea.'

'Can you give me the names – the nicknames, that is – of the other people who were in the SABA group with you?' McKinney asked.

Guidi looked over at Roy Kirby before he answered. 'No. No, I can't.'

'Or won't.'

'I said I can't. Twenty years is a long time.'

Mike whispered to me and Scotty, 'Why's McKinney going soft on him? Give me ten minutes in the room with Gino and I bet we'd have names and social security numbers. He's too smart not to know.'

Scotty agreed. 'Yeah, but he's got too much on the line. I guess Pat'll shake a little more out of him in front of the grand jury.'

194

McKinney stood up and shook Gino Guidi's hand. 'Well, I'll get in touch with Roy if we need anything else from you. A deal's a deal.'

'What's the frigging deal?' Mike asked.

I walked to the door and waited for McKinney to step out of the interrogation room. 'What did I miss? What do you mean by "deal"?'

'The reason Kirby offered to let Guidi talk to me just now is that I agreed not to subpoena him, because of the privileged communication.'

'Privilege?' I asked. 'Are you talking about Dr Ichiko? Doctor-patient?'

'No, no, no. The clerical privilege.'

'I must be confused,' Mike said. 'Where's the priest? Who's got a collar here?'

'Kirby's worked on a case. He just let me read it. Westchester County. He made law in the Second Circuit, getting them to treat Alcoholics Anonymous as a religious entity. There's a cleric-congregant privilege that protects communications made even during unconventional forms of religious expression,' McKinney said, talking down to Mike with his newfound legal knowledge that Roy Kirby had imparted. 'Like disclosing one's "fearless moral inventory" to God and your fellow A.A. members.'

Mike was muttering under his breath and making the sign of the cross. 'Monty didn't confess to a priest, Pat. He was talking to another goddamn junkie on a park bench.'

McKinney called out to Kirby, 'Miss Cooper doesn't trust your interpretation of the law, Roy. Want to show her that copy of the opinion in the Cox matter?'

'I'm going to say this very quietly, Pat, because now

that Roy Kirby has made a fool out of you once tonight, I don't need him to do it again. Just like Monty, Mr Cox – Kirby's client in that Westchester case – didn't make his confession to murder for the purpose of getting spiritual guidance.'

McKinney screwed up his nose. 'So? I don't follow you, Alex.'

'So the decision was reversed by the United States Court of Appeals a year later. It helps, Pat, if you read the slip opinions every now and then.'

McKinney reddened and bit his lip.

'You've just let Gino Guidi off the hook and now we'll never truly find out how much he knows about Monty and any other people who might be able to identify him.' I was steaming. 'You let Guidi bargain to stay out of the grand jury when he might also have the names of disgruntled group members or former patients who didn't want Dr Ichiko to go public tonight. Way to go, McKinney. Way to go.'

Chapter 22

Mercer, Mike, and I were sitting in my living room eating takeout from Shun Lee Palace at midnight. I had kicked off my boots, still damp from my trek through the snow-covered ground at the gorge, and was curled up on the sofa working the crispy sea bass with my chopsticks.

Mike poured us a second round of drinks as we tried to figure out the next day's plan of attack.

'The computer guys promised me answers from Emily Upshaw's hard drive,' Mercer said. 'I'd like to revisit Teddy Kroon to confront him about his DNA on the mouse, if they've figured out what files he tried to get into.'

Mike eschewed chopsticks in favor of dipping his spring rolls into the duck sauce and popping them into his mouth. 'I located Noah Tormey, the professor who bailed Emily out.'

'I looked in the phone book this afternoon and couldn't find him.'

'That's why I've got a gold shield, kid, and you've got a desk job. I guess he got flopped. I had somebody back in the office Google him while we were at the precinct. He's teaching now at Bronx Community College.'

'Where's that?' I asked.

'And she thought I'd never be so useful, Mercer. Isn't that right? Coop's own little outer-boroughs guy. Your second Bronx geography lesson in one day. Till 1973, NYU used to have a campus in the Bronx. It was called the Heights – all male, very prestigious – much more so in those days than the one in the Village. They sold it to the City University in the Bronx, once all of NYU's focus shifted to its Washington Square facility.'

'You want to drop in on Professor Tormey in the morning? I'm with you.'

'Yeah. Scotty's going to attend at the Ichiko autopsy. Will you be in the office or you want me to pick you up here at nine?' Mike asked, trying to keep the honeyed baby spareribs from dripping onto my rug.

'Here is good. How about the Raven Society?'

'No listing under that name in the Manhattan directory. And no individual's name associated with the number we have came up in the Coles directory. Just an address in the East Fifties that's linked to the phone listing. We can rendezvous with Mercer and check it out tomorrow afternoon. You didn't mention it to McKinney, did you?'

'Not once he screwed up the chance to get Gino Guidi to cooperate,' I said. 'It just slipped my mind.'

Mike tossed each of us a fortune cookie and I tore open the plastic wrapper to break it in half and read mine. '"Happiness returns when black cloud departs,"' I said aloud.

'I hope the weather pattern doesn't stall over Manhattan. She's always more cheery when she's getting some. What's yours?'

Mike ripped his open while Mercer answered, '"Avoid temptation. Tastiest dishes in your own kitchen."' He smiled as he stood and carried his dishes to the sink. 'I'm afraid the kitchen will be closed by the time I get home tonight.'

Mike tossed the little slip of paper onto his empty plate. '"Bad news travels faster than lightning."'

'I thought I paid Patrick extra for good fortunes,' I said, referring to our favorite maître d' at Shun Lee. 'These are as gloomy as this week's forecast. I'll pick up the rest of the mess. Why don't you guys get going?'

The alarm went off at seven and was followed immediately after by the ringing telephone. 'You up?'

'Thinking about it, anyway.' It was Joan Stafford, one of my best girlfriends, calling from Washington. 'It's too cold and gray to get out of bed.'

'What are you doing next weekend?'

'Saturday? I'm right in the middle of a very complex investigation. I can't—'

'No, not this one. The one after?'

'I don't know how this thing is going to break, Joanie. I think I'm grounded for the foreseeable future.'

'We'll come to you. I've got a guy I want you to meet.'

I groaned and threw back the covers. Joan had kept her apartment in New York despite her engagement to a Washington foreign affairs columnist. 'I'm through with reporters. And none of your foreign diplomats. I don't even want to talk to any man who has a valid passport. I'm thinking local talent only.'

'He is local. You have to do me a favor, Alex. Just this once. It's one evening, one night of your life – it's not like I'm asking you to marry him. Pick a restaurant and we'll just have a quiet dinner for four.'

'Maybe in a couple of weeks, when this settles down,' I said, in an obvious effort to stall her well-intentioned matchmaking. 'What are you two doing for Valentine's Day?'

'We'll be in the city. I took a table for the museum benefit.'

'Count me in. Chapman's betting me I can't get a date.'

'That'll work fine. I'll see if I can put this together for the fourteenth.'

'Who is he, Joanie?' I could lose him at a group event. The benefit would actually be an easier setting than an intimate dinner for four.

'No names. You're not going to check him out with anyone. He's a writer. He came to one of my readings last month and Jim and I have had him for dinner three times. He'd be perfect for you. Completely available, no professional competition, very dishy.'

'Well, it's a great big "if" until the cases are solved. But in case Chapman asks you, tell him I jumped at the offer.'

I showered, dressed warmly, and caught up on the news until the doorman buzzed to announce that Mike was waiting for me in the driveway. We sipped coffee on our way up the Major Deegan Expressway until we exited at West 183rd Street. The old NYU uptown campus had been purchased, Mike told me, in the late 1890s, and the great architect Stanford White had been commissioned to build a Beaux Arts complex on a grand scale.

We drove through the makeshift guard station where a young woman handling security directed us to the administration building. From blocks away I could see the monumental dome of the Gould Memorial Library with its distinctive green copper patina, clearly a copy of the Roman Pantheon.

As we pulled up in front of the entrance, another guard directed us to a parking area on the far side of the steps. Mike decided not to put the police parking plaque on the dashboard, as there was no need yet to declare our presence on the small campus.

Students milled inside the lobby of the old great hall. No one was dawdling on the cold, windswept grounds between the buildings that towered over University Park and the highway below. Somehow, the massive interior columns of verdigris Connemara marble, the Tiffany stained-glass windows, and the fourteen-karat gold-leaf coffered dome that once had graced this scholarly outpost seemed terribly inconsistent with the poorly funded community college population the institution now serviced.

The faculty listings and campus map were tacked to a board inside a display case with a cracked glass door. Noah Tormey was listed as a member of the English department, with an office on the third floor of the old library.

'How are you going to start this off?' I asked as we climbed the dark staircase.

'Just follow my lead. It's a work in progress.'

Adjacent to Tormey's empty room – number 326 – was a small lecture hall. An instructor's voice carried into the corridor and I motioned to Mike to stop and listen. The schedule posted on the wall next to the door had the week's classes listed, and this was one of Professor Tormey's. I could see some of his thirty or so students slumped in their chairs, while a handful were furiously taking notes as the lecturer spoke.

'Coleridge's *Biographia Literaria* is the greatest single book of literary criticism ever written. It suggests to you all the things you must consider to discuss a poem, it clears out whatever gets in the way of your understanding of reading poetry. It was written, of course, because he believed the work of his dear friend William Wordsworth was the greatest poetic achievement of his time.'

Mike looked at me and whispered, 'Is the dude on target?'

'Bull's-eye.'

I looked back into the room and could see that the speaker had lost the better part of his audience, if he'd ever held their attention.

'Coleridge uses the word "fancy" to describe the mode of memory. A poet needs fancy, of course, but it's just his storehouse of images, as memory is for all of us. Now, imagination – well, that's the higher power, the creative form. It's inherent in the words and possessed in the mind of great poets, adding pleasure to—'

The end-of-period bell rang and all but two young women, hanging on to the speaker's every word, clapped their notebooks shut and emptied into the hallway.

The professor, a bespectacled man in his mid-fifties, with a sizable paunch and dull brown hair in need of shaping, walked out explaining Coleridge's primary and secondary imaginative degrees to his young disciples.

'Excuse me, sir, but are you Professor Tormey?' Mike asked.

The man nodded.

'Could you give us a few minutes to chat? Maybe in your office?'

He cocked his head, no doubt trying to figure, unsuccessfully, who we were. Police were probably the farthest thing from his mind. 'From administration?'

Mike waited until the young women crammed their notebooks into their backpacks and lumbered off. 'NYPD.'

Tormey frowned and led us into his small office. He turned on the light, closed the door behind him, and offered us two seats. Walking around his desk, he picked up the three yellow roses that were on his blotter and moved them to the side, putting his lecture notes squarely in front of him. 'What's this about?'

Mike told him our names. 'We're handling a missing persons case.' Anything worked better in eliciting information from people than telling them they might be involved in a murder investigation. Or two.

'A student?' he said, the right side of his mouth pulling back in a twitch.

'An NYU student, actually.'

'Well, I haven't had anything to do with NYU in more than a decade.'

'Tait. Aurora Tait. Does that name mean anything to you?'

'No. No, it doesn't.' The twitch was either a preexisting condition or something with an immediate onset caused by Mike's questions.

'She disappeared from the Washington Square area more than twenty years ago.'

'What has that got to do with me?' He looked back and forth between us.

'Maybe you can tell us why you chose to leave NYU for Bronx Community College?' Mike asked.

Tormey twitched and laughed at the same time. 'I

suppose even a rookie cop would be smart enough to know it wasn't entirely my choice. I crossed boundaries, Mr Chapman. I believe that's what the dean called it.'

'With a student?'

'With – with a couple of students,' Tormey said, playing with the edge of his papers.

'It happened more than once, which was more than the school was willing to tolerate.'

'Were you tenured?' I asked.

'Painfully close, Miss Cooper. I went from a position teaching some of the most eager, brilliant students you can imagine to – well, I've got a few dreamers here who are motivated to get themselves out of the Bronx, but for most of them, English is a second language, and a very foreign one at that.'

'You still teach English literature?'

'English and American. Lucky for me I like the sound of my own voice. I try to teach them, that's all I can do.'

'You had a full class today.'

'First week of the new term. Attendance is required for at least six classes. I think some of them have hit bottom already.'

'But why BCC, after you had to leave NYU?' I asked.

'I couldn't get myself looked at by another institution of that quality here in the city, and my entire family is around this area now. I didn't want to leave. I assumed I'd do my penance for a while and work my way back into a better academic environment,' Tormey said, looking somewhat embarrassed. 'I just haven't been able to do that.'

'You want to try some name associations, Professor?' Mike asked.

A single twitch. 'Certainly, if that would help.'

'Guidi. Gino Guidi.'

Tormey shook his head.

'Ichiko. Dr Wo-Jin Ichiko.'

The corner of Tormey's mouth danced with tension. 'Familiar, that one.'

'How is that? You know him?'

'Wasn't that the man whose body was found in the river last night? I heard that on the news this morning, before I left home.'

'Did you know him? That's what I asked,' Mike said.

'No, no, I don't.'

'Were you teaching yesterday, Professor?'

'Actually not. Monday, Wednesday, Friday. I spent all of yesterday afternoon at my home.'

'With anyone?'

'Afraid not. My wife was a lot less tolerant than the head of the department at NYU. She left after the first time I was caught up in a relationship with a student.'

'How about the name Emily Upshaw?'

The twitching was off the charts. 'I saw that story on the news, too. Such a tragic case, that one. Yes, yes, I knew Emily.'

'Intimately?'

'No, Mr Chapman. Emily was a student of mine – I'd say, Lord, it must have been almost twenty-five years ago. She was very smart, but a girl with more problems than anyone that age should have had to handle. No, no – nothing went on between us. We weren't even close.'

Mike sat forward in his chair and stared into Tormey's face. 'How many times in your life have you gone to court and posted bail for someone?'

'What do you mean?'

'Emily Upshaw's arraignment. It's all over the court papers that you bailed her out.'

Tormey sat up, tapping his fingers on his desktop while he regrouped his thoughts before speaking again. 'I'd actually forgotten about that.'

'Like I forgot Mariano Rivera blowing the save against the Diamondbacks in the last game of the 2001 World Series. I don't think so. Your lip is moving like it's a 7.0 on the Richter scale.'

'There are some things I can't control, Detective. You don't have to mock—'

'Yeah, but *you* can sure as hell control what you want to tell me, can't you? Think about it for a minute or two. Ever been to court any other time?'

Tormey shook his head.

'It usually makes an impression. You the guy she was stealing the shirts for?'

'Of course not.'

'But Emily Upshaw was allowed to make one phone call and you're the jerk she decided to lean on. Why?'

He spoke softly. 'I think she trusted me. She'd been working as my research assistant. She'd been spending a lot of time in my office. I'd been trying to convince her that she had some real potential as a writer, if she could get herself cleaned up and get off the drugs.'

'Nothing physical between you?'

'I was happily married then, Mr Chapman. I was thirty years old with a wife and two babies. I hadn't started looking for trouble yet.'

'Tell me about the research Emily was doing for you,' I asked. 'What were you working on?'

206

'Samuel Taylor Coleridge. Not very titillating, Miss Cooper.'

'We heard you talking about him today, from the hallway.'

'Well, I've written three books about him and God knows how many articles for academic journals,' Tormey said, checking his watch. 'Will we go much longer, Detective?'

'Why, you got other plans?'

'There's actually a little ceremony I have to perform outside at eleven o'clock.'

'A ceremony? We're here to talk about murder.'

Tormey looked to me for help. 'I'm not planning to abscond, Miss Cooper. I'll be back up here in half an hour,' he said, picking up the three long-stemmed roses as though they explained something. 'Or perhaps you'd like to come along. I've just got to put these next to Poe's bust. The students are expecting me.'

The professor must have seen me look at Mike when he mentioned the great poet's name. It had figured too prominently in this case to be a coincidence. First Aurora Tait's place of entombment, and then Emily Upshaw's preoccupation with premature burial.

'What bust? What's this about?' I asked.

'February second,' he said. 'The anniversary of the funeral of Poe's wife, Virginia. There's an old tradition in Baltimore, where the Poes are buried, that some mysterious stranger places roses on his grave every year on his birthday. That fell on January nineteenth, during the winter break, so I couldn't observe that event this time. But this particular memorial fits the school schedule, so we'll have a little ceremony out at the statue today.'

'What statue are you talking about?' I asked again.

'The Hall of Fame.'

'Button up, Coop. Let's take a walk.'

Professor Tormey looked relieved for the first time since we started talking. 'You know it, Mr Chapman?'

'I went to Fordham,' Mike said, standing and opening the door for the three of us.

'Then you're acquainted with the neighborhood?'

'Used to be. Hall of Fame for Great Americans, right?'

Tormey led us to a rear stairwell and down, out the side door and along a walkway behind the library and the Hall of Philosophy. Fifty or sixty students lined the path, oblivious to the cold as they stood with cameras and coffee cups, calling out to Tormey as we passed by.

'Today, of course, there are halls of fame for athletes and singers, cowboys and country music stars. But this was the very first one in the country.'

'Built when?' I asked.

'Nineteen oh one. I guess you knew that – ironically, I must add – this campus was once NYU. There was the downtown campus that's still thriving today, and this one was the uptown part of the school. The man who was then president of the college had this fabulous colonnade built just to conceal the unsightly foundation of these great buildings up on the heights. You remember *The Wizard of Oz*, don't you?'

'Sure,' I said.

Tormey was alive now, warm and engaging. 'Well, in the movie, when Dorothy dissolves the Wicked Witch of the East, don't you remember the Munchkins singing to her? "You'll be a bust, be a bust, be a bust in the Hall of Fame"? This is the very place they were singing about. It really used to be famous all over the country.'

I looked around as we walked toward the entrance, paved with red bricks rather than the yellow ones of Oz. We were high on a promontory over the expressway below, the bare trees covering the steep slope beneath us. I had assumed a 'hall' would be the interior of a dusty old building, but this was an outdoor vista with sweeping views to the Harlem River, less than a mile away.

'What's here now?' I asked.

'Ninety-eight bronze busts, commissioned by prominent sculptors and artists. The project was abandoned in the 1970s, but it used to be quite grand in the first half of the last century.'

'What's your interest in Poe?' Mike asked, as we both tried to keep pace with Tormey, who moved with greater speed than I expected of a man of his girth.

'A genius, Mr Chapman. Possibly the greatest American writer ever to have lived. And despite the fact that he borrowed a bit too liberally from my man Coleridge, the kids here get him in a way they don't get the Brits and the Romantic poets.'

I nodded at his enthusiasm for the macabre storyteller.

'They love the bizarre, the ghastly, the obsession with mortality,' Tormey said. 'The dean wanted me to find some way to put this wonderful landmark to work – the Hall of Fame, that is – so here you have it. I've created these little ceremonies, if you will, for many of the grand old gentlemen who still sit vigil here in the Bronx. Anything I do with Poe is especially popular with the students, as you can see. His death obsessions are so classically timeless.'

Tormey pointed up at the words carved into the stone

arch over the entrance, directly behind one of the original campus buildings on the quadrangle. "'Mighty Men Which Were of Old – Men of Renown.'" He held the elaborately filigreed iron gate open for me and I entered, staring off between the columns at the sharp precipice to the highway below.

This alfresco hall was, in fact, a series of more than ten connected serpentine paths. They were open and airy, high on this lofty point, twisting and winding with busts on both sides of the walkway and bronze plaques beneath them identifying the subjects, who were separated from one another by tall white columns supporting an arched ceiling.

Names familiar to every schoolchild were mixed with those of long-forgotten heroes. Walter Reed, Robert Fulton, and Eli Whitney peopled the first long crescent, with several hundred feet of turf dedicated to their great accomplishments. Beside and between them were others whose deeds were little known today. I squinted at the chiseled descriptions of Matthew Fontaine Maury, pathfinder of the seas, and James Buchanan Eads, who built the first submarine before the Civil War.

The walk curved, abutting the solid wall of the building on its interior side. The second series of busts arched ahead of us. Tormey moved briskly, pointing his small bouquet of roses at figures along the way. The Wright Brothers stood opposite Thomas Edison and beside a mathematical physicist named Josiah Willard Gibbs. 'George Washington,' Tormey said. 'He's the only one ever elected unanimously to rest here.'

'An hour or two,' Mike said, stopping to read the descriptions on some of the plaques, 'and I'd be set with *Jeopardy!* questions for the next couple of years.'

Around another corner and the building behind us – to our east – gave way to a courtyard, where we could see the students waiting for Tormey at the far end of the walkway. Framed against the bare gray branches that faced out over the western view were Abe Lincoln and Henry Clay, stuck for eternity opposite Thomas Jefferson and Daniel Webster.

The redbrick path wound around another corner, where jurists like John Marshall and Oliver Wendell Holmes presided over the distant view, and then a further stretch of columns positioned with soldier heroes – John Paul Jones, the Marquis de Lafayette – the only non-American I spotted in the lineup – Robert E. Lee, and Ulysses Grant. Mike lingered to study the notations beneath them.

'This is quite a stretch.'

'Typical, isn't it?' Tormey said to me. 'Writers and artists come at the very end. Even teachers and scholars get their due here first.'

We passed educators like Maria Mitchell, James Kent, Horace Mann, and Mary Lyon before turning to the final row of great wordsmiths. James Fenimore Cooper and Harriet Beecher Stowe were the first pair, gazing blankly into each other's eyes across the windy corridor.

'There's your Mr Poe,' Tormey said, pointing to a solemn figure perched several hundred feet above the roadway, situated between Samuel Clemens and William Cullen Bryant.

'Who was the sculptor?' I asked.

'The great Daniel Chester French.'

The man best known for the massive monument to Abraham Lincoln on the Mall in Washington, D.C., had also crafted this smaller tribute to the dark poet – a solemn visage capped by thick wavy hair, with the bow of his waistcoat tied beneath his chin.

Noah Tormey lifted his arm over his head, waving to the students with his three roses to get their attention. He checked his watch and I looked at my own. We had caused him to be only a few minutes late for his eleven o'clock ceremony.

With a bit of a flourish, evident to those who were watching him from the courtyard, Tormey bowed to the bust of Poe and laid the flowers at the base of the granite pedestal on which it was mounted. The kids laughed and clapped and camera flashes lightened the gloomy morning sky.

As the professor straightened up and took my arm, the blast of gunshots repeating from a high-powered rifle sounded from directly below us on the wooded slope. The third one ricocheted off the head of Samuel Clemens and slammed into Noah Tormey's shoulder. He fell to the ground and I dropped to my knees beside him.

Chapter 23

Mike Chapman screamed my name and came running around the last curve.

Tormey was crawling to me on his left elbow, his right arm hanging limp beside him.

Mike's gun was drawn, and with his other hand he flattened Tormey on the cold brick pavement. 'Get down, both of you.'

I couldn't see where the students had scattered but I could hear them shouting in the background.

Mike positioned himself in front of Poe, face-to-face with the bronze head, rising to his full height and peering around the writer's brow at the steep hill below.

I tried to dislodge myself from beneath Tormey's arm. Blood was seeping through the sleeve of his jacket onto my leg and he was groaning in pain. I tried to sit up.

'Down, dammit,' Mike said.

He waited a second until I lowered my head again and let off two shots. Again I heard the sound of the rifle as it returned fire, bullets wildly hitting pillars and pedestals and poets before bouncing onto the floor. Beneath the canopy of the brick ceiling, each volley sounded magnified, like rounds from a cannon.

'You – Tormey – you okay?'

He was lying on his stomach now, his left hand covering the top of his head. Mike ducked and pulled him flush up against the front part of the wall.

'I'm gonna stand up and throw off a shot, Coop. I want you to get on all fours and retrace your steps back to the entrance as fast as you can.'

I turned my head to the side as I squatted behind Mike and looked up at him.

'Don't fuck with me, kid. Target practice isn't my strong suit. Move!'

All my attention was on moving forward. I tried to do it as quickly as possible, knowing that Mike was exposed to the shooter while he was trying to cover my back. I doubted there would be enough bullets left in his gun to get us to the iron entrance gate if the assassin was tracking our retreat.

I could hear the sound of sirens coming closer. I was hoping the gunman could hear them, too.

More shots echoed around my head. I couldn't tell how many had actually been fired and how many were simply resounding off the various surfaces. I looked back and saw that Mike was still standing, just a few feet behind me, shielded by the statue of David Farragut.

I was as low to the ground as I could manage to be and still propel myself forward, passing Henry Ward Beecher and John James Audubon. I hadn't heard Louis Agassiz's name since I left Wellesley and didn't stop to make note of his many accomplishments.

I took another corner and Mike let go with another round. I glanced back again to make sure he hadn't been hurt. 'Keep going, Coop. You're almost there.'

Pushing along the rough surface of the bricks had worn back the tops of my gloves. My wrists were raw from rubbing against the ground as I tried to scoot along.

Now I could hear what seemed like a small army of footsteps pounding toward us. 'Stay back. Someone's shooting at us,' I yelled, as I saw a guard dressed in the uniform of the campus police coming toward me. I pointed at Mike. 'He's a cop!'

Mike was too engaged to pull out his gold badge. The danger was off to the side and below him, not in the form of bewildered and unarmed security guards.

He took one look at the startled officers, called out to them to watch me, and vaulted over the two-foot-high balcony that bordered the hilltop. In that split second given me to decide what to do, I knew that if I made the mistake of calling out his name, it would cause him to look back and think I needed help.

I picked my head up and watched him slide down the embankment, rolling only ten or twelve feet until he crashed into a tree trunk. Everything down there was silent now, with no sign of an attacker.

'The professor's been shot,' I said to the officer who reached me first. 'He needs an ambulance.'

'Who's the . . . ?' one guard asked, while I directed two others down to the far end to tend to Tormey.

I looked over the side of the wall. Mike was sitting with his back against the large tree trunk. The guards glanced back and forth at each other, uncertain about what lay below.

'Can you help him, please? He's a detective – NYPD – Homicide.'

'He do the shooting?'

'No, we were fired at,' I said. 'From somewhere down there.'

I had just killed their enthusiasm for climbing down to help Mike. One of the men leaned over and picked up a bullet.

'Looks like a twenty-two-caliber—'

'Please don't touch anything. We'll have to get the Crime Scene Unit here.'

I could hear more sirens. Guards checked on Tormey and assured me that he was conscious and coherent, and that an ambulance had been called. I stood up, and ignoring Mike's gestures for me to stay with the men from security, I swung my legs over the balcony and lowered myself onto the densely wooded hillside.

'Graceful, huh?' Mike asked as I made my way down the slope to him, bracing myself against trees along the way, and helped him to his feet. 'How's Tormey?'

'Looks like he's hit in his upper arm, from the way he's just dragging it and the amount of blood soaking through his jacket. They've got a bus on the way. D'you see anything?'

'Somebody knew exactly what he was doing. Had Tormey's arrival timed to the minute, didn't he? And wouldn't have minded shaving some peroxide off the top of your scalp, either. He was comfortable in these woods,' Mike said, looking around at the rough terrain.

'Unless he was over there,' I said, pointing at the railroad tracks on the far side of the highway. 'There's enough scrub to conceal yourself, especially if he was shooting with a scope. Did you fire down because you saw someone?'

Mike started to walk back up to the colonnade.

216

'Nothing. Nada. I just wanted to draw the guy out if he was still around.'

'Hey, Chapman. Clara Barton's down the hall, if you need a hand,' a uniformed cop called out, clearly delighted to have seen Mike on his ass, then being guided back up the hill by a woman Sherpa.

Mike scrambled over the metal railing behind the entrance gate, while I stretched my arms out overhead so two cops could hoist me up onto the balcony next to a stone-faced Elias Howe.

Medics were loading Noah Tormey into the rear of the ambulance and I followed Mike over to check on him.

One of the EMTs spoke first, shaking his finger at us. 'Sorry. You'll have to question him at the hospital. We can't hang out here with a gunshot wound.'

Mike boosted me up into the rear of the van. 'We're going with you. We need medical attention, too. I'm full of cuts and scrapes.' He stepped up and swung the door closed behind him. 'We're going to Columbia Presbyterian,' he said, flashing his badge.

'This ain't a taxi service, boss. We're a Bronx unit.'

'And I think too much of the professor's life to go to an emergency room in the Bronx, okay? Right across the river and you're practically there.'

The medic chose the path of least resistance. He told his partner to go across the University Heights Bridge to one of Manhattan's premier medical facilities, near the northern tip of the island, which was actually the closest hospital.

We watched while the serious young EMT stabilized Noah Tormey, removing his jacket, ripping off the sleeve of his shirt to examine the wound in the fleshy part of the

217

upper arm, and starting an intravenous drip so that he could go straight from the ER into surgery, if that was necessary.

My wrists were bleeding, and there was a long scrape on the side of my chin from the moment Mike directed me to flatten out on the pavement. I rested my head on his shoulder and could feel the rapid beating of his heart.

Mike's face was cut in several places from the tree branches that had whipped against him as he rolled down the incline. I dabbed at the marks on his forehead with some tissues until he pushed my hand away.

'How are you feeling, Professor?' Mike asked.

The twitch was less pronounced than earlier. 'I've never been so frightened in my life. Why was that person shooting at you?'

'You got that wrong, pal. Why was he shooting at *you*? That's what we'd like to know. You got any problems you want to tell us about?'

The medic was monitoring Tormey's vital signs. 'How about you take it easy on the guy's blood pressure, Chapman?'

Tormey whispered the word no.

'This little ceremony, did anyone know about it besides your students?'

'It was in the college paper, of course. I think the Bronx Historical Society writes up all the events, too. I simply can't imagine—'

'Think about it, Professor. You'll have a couple of days in your hospital bed to concentrate on nothing else but today's riflery exhibition. Your old friend Emily Upshaw was killed. Stabbed to death in a particularly vicious attack, right in her own home.'

Tormey cringed and closed his eyes.

'That probably has something to do with the skeleton that was found in a basement in a Greenwich Village tenement last week. In fact, inside Mr Poe's house.'

The twitch was back in full force and his eyes were shut tight.

'Dr Ichiko finds the only waterfall in the city of New York to throw himself over – or get pushed into – and crushes his skull in so many pieces you could play Chinese checkers with the chips. And you, you're somebody's idea of a bull's-eye.'

Tormey opened his eyes and looked for me. 'Miss Cooper, will there be protection for me while I'm in the hospital? I mean, you don't suppose this was just some drive-by shooting from the highway?'

'The shots didn't come from a car, Professor. Detectives will analyze the scene, but there's little doubt someone was positioned in place, waiting for you to appear. And yes, the NYPD will have someone with you the entire time you're in the hospital.'

His eyes shifted in Mike's direction. 'Not—?'

'Not him.' It seemed to be Tormey's worst fear. Wounded, bedridden, and attached to an IV tube with Chapman at his side, relentlessly asking questions.

'I haven't given any thought to Emily Upshaw in years, Miss Cooper. Do you really believe this could have something to do with her?' Tormey asked.

Mike sensed that the professor wasn't comfortable talking to him and turned his back, pretending to busy himself making notes about the day's events.

'It's hard to think otherwise,' I said.

'The incident with the bail? It's coming back to me a bit,' Tormey said.

Funny how a good scare can improve the memory of almost every witness.

'Emily was working as my research assistant that semester. She was desperate for money – not that I realized at the time how much of it was going to support her drug habit. Two or three times she actually wrote articles for me, ones that were published under my name. I needed those credits for the tenure process.'

'Okay.'

'When she was arrested, she called me because I owed her money. Several hundred dollars, if I'm not mistaken. I don't imagine there was anyone else she could have called who'd give her money.'

Tormey's mind was drifting in another direction. He turned his head to the other side, but before he did I thought I saw tears forming in the corners of his eyes.

'I'll be looking at Emily's college records tomorrow,' I said, a bluff that I hoped to make good on before too long. 'What class did she take with you?'

He seemed unable or unwilling to speak.

'Professor Tormey?'

'Emily wasn't in any of my classes. You'll see that in her transcript.'

'But she did research for you?'

His head moved slowly up and down.

'How did she find you? How did you two get together?'

'Before . . .' he said, choking on the words that followed.

'Before college?' I asked.

Tormey's words were muffled but I held my head close to his mouth and made them out. 'I'm the reason Emily came to New York to go to college. I don't know what her family has told you about her background, Miss

Cooper. I was her faculty interviewer the week she came to the city to visit NYU at the start of her senior year of high school. She was alone here – and, well – we spent some time together.'

The story Emily's sister had told us took on a new significance as Tormey finished his explanation. 'I'm the guy who got her pregnant.'

Chapter 24

I knew the triage process would begin the moment we hit the entrance to the ambulance bay at Presbyterian. A medical team would be waiting for us, Tormey would be evaluated for surgery, and if they put him under with anesthesia, we'd be lucky if we could get back at him within the next forty-eight hours.

'There's no time for bullshit now, Professor. I need more honest answers or I can't protect you from whatever's going on.'

'But I thought Emily's attack was a random one – a man who followed her in off the street.'

'Maybe it is that. I happen not to think so. Too many things are going on that seem to be related. The child you fathered with Emily, have you ever tried to have any contact with her?'

Tormey looked directly at me. 'The baby died, Miss Cooper. She was stillborn.'

'That's what Emily told you?'

'Yes. And that's what her mother told me, in the one or two conversations we had together. I felt responsible for the fact that her family disowned Emily. Then how ironic it was that she lost the baby after all.'

The truth about the child and the fact that she had been raised by Emily's sister could wait a day or two.

'But your relationship with Emily, that continued?'

'Sexually? No, not after she came back to New York and started at the college. She had visions of setting up house together, of me replacing the family she thought she had lost. Getting her pregnant had been a pretty sobering experience for both of us – well, that's a particularly bad expression for me to use. I was a few years older than she, and by the time that year had passed, I was involved with someone else. Someone more appropriate. The woman I married, actually.'

The medic signaled me to get out of his way as we turned onto 168th Street.

'We're almost there, Professor. Those names Detective Chapman was asking you about? You know he didn't finish.'

Tormey sighed.

'Did you ever meet Monty?'

'Who?' he asked. He seemed weary from the pain and apprehension.

'A guy Emily lived with before she was arrested. Someone who may have done something that frightened her.'

'It doesn't sound familiar.'

'This ceremony about Edgar Allan Poe today, what's your interest in him?'

Tormey smiled and closed his eyes. 'I told you earlier, I think the man was a genius.'

'And Emily, did she agree?'

'I don't know what she thought, Miss Cooper. She worked on projects for me. She did what I asked her to do.'

The ambulance lurched as the driver stopped short and backed it into a bay. The men who were standing by to receive Noah Tormey lifted the gurney out of the rear and placed it on a set of metal wheels, rushing it into the doors that opened automatically as they approached.

'Hey, loo, you got nothing better to do than make house calls?' Mike asked. Raymond Peterson, the lieutenant of the homicide squad, was standing with a nurse at the ER entrance. He held out a hand and helped me step down.

'I was on my way in when I got the call. Thought I'd stop by and check the damage. You all right, Alex?'

'No worse than falling off a bicycle. May I wash up inside?' I asked the nurse.

'I'll have someone look you both over right away. You just need to go sign in at the desk. They'll give each of you an examination cubicle and—'

'I really don't need to waste anyone's time. I've just skinned my hands a bit.'

'C'mon, Coop. We can share a cubicle, put on those cute little gowns.'

'It's policy, ma'am. You came in in an ambulance and we can't let you go without an examination.'

'Go ahead, Alex. I've got to make sure Mike doesn't claim any injuries that would get him out on three-quarters,' the lieutenant said, referring to the department's generous retirement pension for injured cops.

It didn't take long to determine that neither one of us had anything more serious than cuts and scrapes. Noah Tormey was taken into surgery to remove the bullet in his shoulder, and we described the morning's events to Peterson.

'You hear anything yet about Dr Ichiko from the autopsy?' Mike asked.

We both knew that no reliable tests existed to permit forensic pathologists to make an unequivocal diagnosis of drowning. Instead, that conclusion is usually reached by the circumstances of the person's death.

'Water in the lungs?' I asked.

'Yeah, but Dr Kirschner says it's not significant. When there's as much turbulence as there is at those falls, water gets forced into the organs even after death. There's a fracture to the skull—'

'And that doesn't give us a homicide?' Mike asked. 'Somebody splitting his head open before he jumped in for a whirlpool spin?'

'Kirschner's not ready to declare,' Peterson said. 'He wouldn't expect someone to go over those falls and hit the rocks below – voluntarily or not – without cracking his head fatally.'

'But the wound,' I asked, 'wouldn't the antemortem injury look different than the postmortem?'

'The doc says no. The water causes more profuse bleeding, Alex, and it prevents clotting. So the blood leaches out and makes it impossible to differentiate.'

'Anything on time of death?' Mike asked.

'Ichiko had washerwoman skin,' Peterson said, referring to the profound wrinkling that occurs after long immersion. 'But the doc tells me that can set in earlier than I thought – maybe within half an hour – when the water temperature is as frigid as the river is right now. This one's dicey. On the good-news front, we may be able to lay Aurora Tait to rest.'

'What happened?'

'Missing Persons found an FBI report that's about twenty-five years old with that name on it. They're sending the dental records out today.'

'Is there any family?' I asked. 'Where's she from?'

'Parents are dead. There's a brother back home. Outside of Minneapolis.'

That hometown location wouldn't surprise any old-timers in law enforcement. Before the 1990s' cleanup and Disneyfication of midtown Manhattan at Forty-second Street and Eighth Avenue, the area was known as the Minnesota Strip. Unhappy teens from all over the Midwest would make their way to the big city, most often by buses that disgorged them at the Port Authority building, where seasoned pimps – acting as Good Samaritans – would embrace them, offering to feed and shelter them until they found jobs and lodging. Within weeks, those too weak to escape the grasp of these men would be addicted to some form of drug and selling their bodies to pay the price. Aurora Tait may well have been one of those girls.

'Look, Coop and I have some things to take care—'

'First stop is a change of clothes, and then you're taking her down there to see the district attorney. He hates to be last to know about capers like these.'

'You've spoken with him?' I asked.

'Let's just say he prefers it when he thinks you're sitting safely behind your desk. I told him this shooter wasn't aiming for you,' Peterson said. 'Nobody – not even Tormey – knew you were going to be at the college today, did they?'

'That's right.'

'Okay, Chapman. Take her downtown before you do anything else.'

'We need a lift back to the Bronx so I can pick up my car.'

Peterson sent us off in an RMP – radio motor patrol car – and by two-thirty we were standing at Rose Malone's desk, waiting for Battaglia to call us in.

'Hey, Mr B,' Mike said, 'how come you always miss the fireworks? You think all the action's in the white-collar crap, while Coop and me are busy cleaning up the mean streets. Well, howdy, Miss Gunsher. How'd you find your way in here without holding on to McKinney's hand? I didn't know your sense of direction was that sharp.'

Of course Ellen would be here for this. McKinney had to dump her somewhere once her lack of courtroom ability had been memorialized in some lousy trial results a few years back. He had created GRIP – the Gun Recovery Information Project – a useless little unit that tried to imitate the feds' successful efforts to track the illegal hand-guns that flooded the city and were used to commit violent felonies.

'Good afternoon, Mike. Alex,' Ellen said, with undisguised gloating. She had undoubtedly told Battaglia that we had ejected her from last evening's proceedings. He continued to tolerate her as a staff member rather than acknowledge that she had been one of his rare hiring errors – a 'celebrity scion,' as we called them, whose mother had been a prominent reporter useful to Battaglia in Ellen's early days, but of doubtful worth now since she'd been fired from the network.

'I guess it would have been stupid of me to think you might have been in court this morning, Alex,' Battaglia said. 'Who's this professor you went to see?'

'His name is Noah Tormey.' Ellen was taking notes as

I spoke. 'I think Mike and I have begun to make some serious progress on the investigation, Paul. My next trial isn't scheduled until the first week of March. I'd like to stay on this, if you don't mind.'

'What kind of gun was it, do you know?' Ellen asked Mike.

'It wasn't a handgun.'

'Well, we're not limited to tracing just those. My people can still be helpful.'

'Can't you cooperate with GRIP on this?' Battaglia asked. 'I'm trying to get them on the map so we can grab some federal funding for the program. Put the damn personalities aside, stop sniping at each other and work together for once. Alex, you're in charge.'

'Sure. Let's go over to my office.'

Mike grabbed a Cohiba from Battaglia's humidor. 'Wish you'd been with us this morning, Ellen. You'd probably have known whose rifle it was just by the sound of the whoosh as it went by your ear. Thanks, Mr B.'

I knew McKinney was determined to stay inside our operation and had engineered Ellen's involvement as a backdoor move. He must have appealed to the district attorney's tireless desire to get government money for prosecutorial projects.

Mercer was waiting for us inside my office. He lifted an eyebrow when Ellen trailed in behind me. 'So rumor has it the morning held some surprises. You guys okay?'

'Still standing, m' man,' Mike said.

'What's all the paper?' I asked.

'Property records for Third Street, and some university housing listings. It's going to be tedious, but—'

'Ellen can start going through those,' I said, turning

to her. 'Pat and Scotty Taren know what we're looking for. That's the part of the investigation Pat is so keenly interested in, so he can fill you in. And your other assignment is to work on Gino Guidi's lawyer. Pat made that stupid deal with him last night and we need to undo it.'

She started to protest.

'People are dying, Ellen. D'you get it? You and Pat need to make it clear to Roy Kirby that we can only protect his client if he helps us. Do it the easy way or I hand him a subpoena and let him go to court to quash it.'

'I'll talk to Pat,' she said, picking up the stacks of files that Mercer had brought and walking out of my office.

'What else?' Mike asked Mercer.

'According to the computer squad, if that was Teddy Kroon at the keyboard deleting information from Emily Upshaw's machine before he called nine-one-one, he managed to get a few files cleaned out. Whether he printed them out for himself or just tried to erase any record of them is what we'll have to ask,' Mercer said.

He handed me a sheaf of papers. Several seemed to be articles that Emily had been working on at the time of her death. Mike and I could read those later.

The last page was a draft of a letter to Sally Brandon – still incomplete – dated just days before Upshaw's murder. Emily's daughter, given up at birth and raised by Sally, had recently sent for her original birth certificate in order to apply for a passport. From that, the girl learned the truth – that Emily was her mother. She had called to ask if she could come to New York, on her own, so they could meet.

In the letter, Emily Upshaw revealed this startling new development to her sister, and also said that she had called Noah Tormey a week earlier, to tell him that she needed to see him.

Chapter 25

The man who opened the door at the East Fifty-fifth Street brownstone to Mike, Mercer, and me later that afternoon was seated in a wheelchair. Mercer identified himself and asked if we could step inside.

'And who might you be looking for, Detective?'

'I'm not certain of that, but we'd like to start with you.'

The man pushed back from the door and admitted us. 'I'm Zeldin. Does that help the three of you?'

'Actually,' Mike said, 'we're interested in something called the Raven Society. Do you know it?'

Zeldin smiled broadly. 'Please come in and sit down. I'm always happy to talk about that.'

I recognized the Southern accent that I had heard on the answering machine message when I pressed the recall button on Dr Ichiko's phone the night of his death.

He swiveled the chair and led us into a room that had been rebuilt in the old town house space to accommodate an enormous library. Hundreds of leather-bound books and modern first editions in plastic-covered dust jackets lined the walls. We drew three of the chairs together so that we were close to our host.

'Mr Zeldin,' Mike started, 'is that a surname or—'

'It's just what it is. Zeldin. No "mister," no other name.'

There was no question this man would be quirky. He was dressed in a dark burgundy smoking jacket over a pair of nicely tailored gray slacks. The expensive hairpiece had been purchased long enough ago that it didn't match the new patch of gray growth coming in around its owner's ears. Zeldin was probably close to sixty, but had fine skin that gave him a more youthful appearance. The Beatles' *Sgt Pepper* album was playing on his sound system and there was a strong scent of burning incense overlaying what I guessed were the remains of a sweet-smelling marijuana cigarette.

'We have some questions about the society. In fact, we don't know anything at all about it.'

'I should hope not. We're not known for our inclusivity, Detective.' He looked at each of our faces. 'Am I allowed to ask what brings you here?'

'A phone call from a dead man,' Mike said.

Zeldin was no longer smiling. 'Who do you mean?'

'What's your telephone number?'

Zeldin's answer was the number Mike had taken off the cell phone.

'Who is it that called you yesterday? Probably late afternoon, maybe a bit earlier.'

'I wasn't at home, Detective. I spent the day in my office. I've taken an early retirement, but I've kept an office and I go in to it from time to time.'

'Do you have an answering machine here?'

'Indeed. You can check it yourself. The only messages yesterday were from my rare book dealer and one hangup call. Perhaps it's the latter you're referring to. Perhaps it was a wrong number.'

232

We could check the length of the call from telephone records to determine whether it was true that the call was a hang-up, by its short duration.

'What's the name of the dead man?'

'He was a doctor,' Mike said. 'Wo-Jin Ichiko.'

Zeldin scratched his head, gently enough not to shift the position of the rug. 'I don't know that name.'

'The news story today – the one about the man who died in the Bronx River?'

'Yes, I heard about that, but I didn't know the fellow. My office, in fact, is in the Bronx.'

I hesitated asking what condition confined Zeldin to a wheelchair and wondered whether he was remotely capable of sending someone to his death at a rugged crime scene. But there would be time for Mike and Mercer to come back to that.

'Why don't we start at the beginning. What is the Raven Society?' I asked.

Zeldin wheeled himself to a cabinet and opened the door to reveal a wet bar, constructed at the height of his chair. 'A glass of wine, anyone?'

We all declined and waited while he poured himself some Burgundy.

'The society was formed a century ago to honor Edgar Allan Poe on the fiftieth anniversary of his death. It was conceived as a secret society, membership by invitation only – just a scholarly tribute to the great poet. It was limited to five members.'

'Five? That's a pretty minuscule society,' Mike said.

'Unlike many writers of that period, who never achieved fame until long after their deaths, Poe was recognized for his genius during his lifetime, here and abroad. But he suffered so many tragedies during his short time on this earth – so many personal indignities – that when he died, there were only five men to take him to his grave. Five – including the minister who presided over the burial. It seemed, at the time, a fitting number to honor him.'

'And now?' I asked.

'Still by invitation only, Miss Cooper. Now there are twenty-five.'

'All in New York?'

'Oh, no. But about two-thirds of them are here.'

'What are the criteria for membership?'

'We look for scholars, Detective. Not necessarily academics, but people who have immersed themselves in Poe and know his body of work. The poems, the stories, the literary criticism. Aficionados of the master.'

'And do you meet?'

'From time to time, certainly. Dinners for the most part. Lectures and other events marking significant dates or new research.'

'Would you be willing to give us a list of your members' names?' I asked.

Zeldin hesitated. 'That would not be my decision to make. I'm merely the secretary of the society at the moment. I would have to ask—'

Mike interrupted him. 'You're right that it's not your decision to make. We're in the middle of a murder investigation. I think it's gonna be Ms Cooper who decides. Along with the grand jury.'

Zeldin sipped his wine. 'I don't mean to be obstreperous, Mr Chapman. We shy away from publicity. Of course we'd be only too keen to help with your work, but I'd like some assurance that all this won't be material for the headlines.'

'It's not likely that any of it will be made public,' I said.

'I don't suppose you're going to tell me what you know about the skeleton at Poe House,' Zeldin said, smiling as he drew a reaction from each of us, 'and whether this man's death – Ichiko, is that his name? – is connected to the finding of those bones?'

'How about you go first?' Mike said. 'What do you know about the skeleton?'

'I told you, Detective. Poe is our life's work. The society was part of – how do you say it in the law, Ms Cooper? – part of the amicus brief to oppose the destruction of the old building by the university. I was naturally very interested to read that someone's remains had been discovered there.'

'Why is that site so important to you?' Mercer asked.

Zeldin sighed. 'From a historical point of view, and a cultural one, the places any great man lived should be preserved. In January of 1845, "The Raven" was published. It brought Poe enormous acclaim, of course, and the fame he'd been longing for. It was that very same year he moved into the building on Third Street from uptown – from Brennan's farm in the West Eighties.

'You've seen that place? Can you imagine what works, what brilliant writings were created in those tiny, inhospitable rooms he rented?' Zeldin paused. 'But then I suppose you care nothing about that. It's what keeps you in business.'

'What do you mean?' I asked.

'If the lawsuit had not been lost, if the building had

235

not been demolished, well – you'd never have come upon that skeleton. It would have been interred behind the brick wall forever, as its killer intended.'

'And what do you know about the bones? About those intentions?'

'Nothing more than what I've read in the newspaper and discussed with some of the society's members. We're interested, obviously,' Zeldin said, gesturing at Mike with his glass.

'Poe only lived there for one year. What's your interest in that particular place?'

'Yes, Mr Chapman, just a year. But do you know what he wrote in that house on Third Street?'

We each shook our heads.

'The most exquisite meditation on passion and revenge ever created. A tale called "The Cask of Amontillado."'

'Of course,' I said. It was one of the most famous of Poe's tales, and I had studied it in a literature course at college. 'The narrator entombs someone who has betrayed him behind a brick wall. Buries him alive, laughing while the man screams to be freed. Why is it he did that to his victim?'

Now my mind flashed to images of the young Aurora Tait, left to die inside the very same place where that story was created.

Zeldin's Latin was perfect. 'The family motto, Miss Cooper. *Nemo me impune lacessit.* "No one insults me with impunity."'

'Maybe we're on the same page,' Mike said. 'Is there anyone associated with the society whose name or nick-name is Monty? Maybe going back twenty or thirty years?'

'Why do you ask?'

236

'One of the victims involved may have had a boyfriend named Monty.'

'I would guess he was pulling her leg, Detective. It would be a wonderful joke for the killer to take that name, for either of two reasons. There's amontillado itself.'

'Sherry?' I asked.

'Exactly. A blend of pale, dry sherry from the Montilla region of Spain. It was casks of this wonderful rare drink that the storyteller invited his prey down into the catacombs to sample. He wanted to get his victim intoxicated enough to pass out, but then have him come around in time to see that the last bricks were about to seal him in forever.'

I could imagine Aurora Tait, being lured into the basement on Third Street by someone she had betrayed, with the promise of some pure smack or a stash of high-grade cocaine.

'And then there's the name of the killer himself,' Zeldin said. 'Don't you remember, Ms Cooper? Montresor. Poe called him Montresor.'

'Monty,' Mike whispered. 'All the time I'm looking for a guy called Monty, like that was really his given name. If he was Emily's boyfriend, and if he did kill Aurora Tait, he was probably just playing with people's heads, counting on the fact that the junkies in his little self-help group wouldn't have a clue about the stories of Edgar Allan Poe.'

'I'm just commenting on the irony of finding the poor woman in that particular location,' Zeldin said, backing off a bit, 'and here you people are trying to connect it with someone named Monty.'

'I got to catch up on my reading,' Mike said. 'Meantime, if you come across any tales by Poe where someone is killed going over a gorge and pummeled to death in a vortex, be sure and let me know. Once might be a coincidence, twice could be a plan.'

'Sounds more Sherlockian than Poe, doesn't it? Professor Moriarity and the great Holmes, struggling with each other at the Reichenbach Falls,' Zeldin said. 'But then you'll want to move my crutches out of the corner, take down that slim lavender volume of Poeiana on the end of the third shelf and read a bit of it, Mr Chapman. The story you're looking for is in that collection.'

Chapter 26

I had never read 'A Descent into the Maelstrom,' but a scan of the ten pages in one of Zeldin's leather-bound first editions revealed a scene eerily similar to Dr Ichiko's last minutes on earth. It seemed characteristically Poe to describe 'how magnificent a thing it was to die in such a manner,' and then have the narrator watch his own brother disappear into the vast funnel and gyrations of the whirling water below.

At exactly 6 P.M., a housekeeper in a gray uniform knocked on the library door. She announced to Zeldin that his physical therapist had arrived and was awaiting him in the exercise room. He looked at us and asked what we wanted him to do.

'Most people I know start their drinking after they work out,' Mike said, with his usual skepticism.

'I've got a degenerative nerve condition, Detective. It actually relaxes me to sip on some wine before we go do the therapy.'

'May we continue this conversation tomorrow?' I asked.

'Of course, Ms Cooper. In the meantime I shall inquire about the release of the list of society members' names. And you three should brush up on your Poe.'

'Here, at nine o'clock?'

'Actually, I had planned to spend the day at my office tomorrow,' he said, as the attendant wheeled him to the door of the spacious room. 'You'll find that quite interesting, in light of the death of Dr Ichiko.'

'Why's that?' Mike asked.

'For years until I retired I was the head librarian in the rare books department at the Botanical Gardens,' Zeldin said.

Mike was on his way to the door to put the brakes on the wheelchair. 'You were at the gardens and yet you didn't know anything about Ichiko's death until you read it in the newspaper?'

'Mr Chapman, I was in the Mertz Library at an acquisitions meeting all afternoon. By the time my driver came to take me home at four o'clock in the afternoon, according to the published accounts, the poor man's body hadn't even been discovered. The first I knew of it was the morning papers. Julia, please – let's show these people out and get on with my session.'

'And this morning,' I asked, thinking of our near-miss at the Hall of Fame, 'were you in the Bronx again today?'

'Alone here with my books all day. Julia will be only too happy to confirm that.'

The housekeeper nodded as she held the door open for us.

'Nine o'clock?' I repeated.

'At the library, inside the Mosholu Parkway gate and turn left.'

Once again we were out on a stoop in the cold. 'I'm hungry,' Mike said, 'and everything aches. My tailbone, my pride, my stomach. I need a good steak.'

We split up in two cars and met a few blocks away, on Forty-sixth Street, to have dinner at Patroon. This mecca for power business diners and elegant parties had long been a favorite. The waiting area was packed and the hostess was alarmed that we had no reservation.

'Hey, Mike, c'mon upstairs for a drink.' The owner, Ken Aretsky, was waving to us from the staircase. We squeezed in through the crowd and walked one flight up to the lounge, past the stunning collection of elegant black-and-white photographs of Manhattan from the forties and fifties.

No matter how packed with tycoons and traders the restaurant was, Ken always made us feel welcome. Within minutes, we each had a drink and a quiet corner in which to catch up on our thoughts.

'Salut,' Mike said, clicking our glasses together. 'To a peaceful end of a busy day.'

'Now how are we going to figure out how to put all these pieces together?' I asked.

'You're the literature major. What do you know about Poe? There's too strong a connection here among Aurora Tait, Emily Upshaw, and Dr Ichiko to ignore it.'

'I know the obvious – a lot of the poetry, some of the stories. I know he was born in Boston, and that his father's family was from Baltimore – which is where he died and was buried. There's a Poe museum in Richmond, where he was raised, before he went to school in Charlottesville.'

'Did you ever know about the New York City connection?' Mercer asked.

Mike answered, 'There's the place he once lived on West Eighty-fourth Street that Zeldin mentioned. I handled a burglary on the block. Back in the 1840s it

241

was all a farm belonging to the Brennan family, like he said. I think it's even called Poe Alley.'

'It seems to me it's worth letting Zeldin give us as much detail about the man as he can,' Mercer said. 'Maybe something, some little fact he suggests, will pull things together for us. If it turns out Zeldin himself is in the mix, all it does is give him more time to sink himself. I say we take advantage of the fact that he likes to talk.'

'You believe his bullshit?' Mike asked.

'D'you see those crutches in the library? They wouldn't be there if he wasn't capable of getting out of the wheelchair. I want to know if he really can walk and just how well, and what route his driver took home from the Botanical Gardens office yesterday afternoon. The gorge isn't very far from where he worked.'

'Man, I'm looking for the exercise routine that starts with marijuana and red wine.'

'There are too many links here to ignore,' I said. 'I agree – let him explain what he can about Poe's life. Keep in mind that lots of great artists have their clubs and cabals – the Baker Street Irregulars, the Wolfe Pack, Poirot's Peers. I'm sure Tolstoy and Trollope, Mozart and Mahler, all have followings.'

'They don't necessarily kill each other,' Mike said.

'You guys need the television?' Ken asked, coming through to check on us.

'Hey, we skipped it last night. Check *Jeopardy!* and then we can order,' Mike said.

By the time the final category was announced, we had downed our first drinks and paused in front of the large screen in the lounge.

'Scientific Theories,' Alex Trebek announced.

Two of the three contestants groaned along with each of us.

'I'll pass,' I said. 'My weakest link.'

'Nothing worse than a coward,' Mike said. 'Ten each. That won't get us a bottle of water in this joint.'

The answer displayed read that the Big Bang theory, accepted in the 1960s, was first described in this prophetic work a century earlier.

'I'll take another Grey Goose,' Mike said. 'Let's order some grub.'

None of us even took a guess as we watched all three players lose their bundles.

'No,' Trebek told the anthropology graduate student, who was the only one to venture a guess. 'Hubble came along a little later.'

'This one surprised me, too, gentlemen. What is "Eureka"? "Eureka," remember that? In a work called "Eureka," Edgar Allan Poe insisted that the universe exploded into existence in "one instantaneous flash" from a single primordial particle.' Trebek went on reading from his note cards. 'Amazing, folks, that this amateur stargazer – back in 1848 – came up with the version of the Big Bang that is still the best guess of contemporary scientists.'

'Ever get the feeling that something was meant to be?' Mike asked. 'It's frigging creepy to be surrounded by this guy Poe – he's everywhere.'

We had a table in the back of the room on the first floor, near the kitchen. I sat by myself while Mercer went to call Vickee to tell her he'd be home late, and Mike tried to find Valerie on the Western ski slopes.

We each ordered New York strip sirloins – the

sixteen-ouncers for the guys and the twelve-ounce for me. Mike piled on onion rings and cottage fries, and Ken spoiled us by sending over a superb Bordeaux from his fabulous cellar.

'Who's going to call Sally Brandon and break the news to her that Emily's kid knows that Sally's not her birth mother?' Mercer asked.

'Sounds like woman's work to me.'

'I'll do it tomorrow afternoon. When Tormey is cleared medically, we've got to see if Emily really called him, like her letter says,' I said, then shifted gears. 'What's with Val?'

'She's over-the-top. The family's all up in Canada, doing that heli-skiing stuff.'

I laughed. 'Guess that's why you got left behind. Do they know her super-macho RoboCop is afraid of flying in choppers?'

'Hey, I did it for you once, didn't I?'

'Yeah, but that's because I didn't ask you to jump out.'

'Last year, Val was so sick from the chemo that she couldn't make the trip with the rest of them. That's why her father thought it was such a special gift for her this time. She and her brother are like cowboys – you oughta see their videos.'

The fancy dinner was a nice end to a day that had taken such an odd twist. We walked out of the restaurant, the guys agreed to pick me up at eight-thirty as Mercer got in his car, and Mike drove me up Third Avenue to drop me in front of my door shortly before ten o'clock.

I hadn't been asleep long when the telephone rang.

'I know you wouldn't be happy if you heard this on the morning news,' Mercer said.

I cocked an eye and looked at the dial on the clock radio. One thirty-five A.M.

'I guess you're not calling to tell me you didn't enjoy dinner.'

'I'm back in your 'hood. Our Silk Stocking Rapist tried again. East Eighty-first Street, just off York. The girl Maced him, though, and he ran off.'

'Good for her. She's okay?'

'Hanging tough. I'm doing the interview now. When he reached up to cover his eyes, he dropped the knife. She picked it up and tried to slash at him.'

'Well, so much for fingerprints.'

'Everything's a trade-off. She slit open his jacket pocket and a few things fell out.'

'Driver's license?' I asked, shifting beneath the warm blanket.

'You wouldn't like it if it came that easy. Nope, no ID. Just a MetroCard.'

I smiled, thinking of the interview I did yesterday with the witness whose card had broken her story. 'That's a fine place to start, Mr Wallace. We know what part of the silk stocking district he frequents. Let's see where else he likes to travel.'

Chapter 27

Zeldin's fifth-story office window in the magnificent Beaux Arts building known as the Mertz Library looked out over a snow-covered expanse that stretched as far as I could see.

'Would you imagine it, Miss Cooper? Two-hundred-fifty spectacular acres of gardens and greenery in the middle of New York City. It's extraordinary, isn't it, and so magical in the middle of winter with this lovely dusting of snow?'

'I'm ashamed to say I'd forgotten quite how beautiful it is, and how grand.'

'It was the vision of an American couple named Britton, you know. They were philanthropists who had a great interest in botany. She was just overwhelmed by a visit to the Royal Gardens at Kew, back in the 1880s and returned home insisting that her husband try to replicate it in America. Re-creating Eden, that's what these gardens are all about.'

'The Garden of Eden – set the backstory for the first homicide, too, if I remember correctly,' Mike said. 'How we doing on that list of Raven Society members I asked about?'

'You shall have them, of course,' Zeldin said, surprising me as well as Mike. He gestured around the room, packed full of botanical prints and books on plants and trees. 'I have someone picking us up in an hour to take us over to the building where I keep the society records. I've never mixed my hobby with the garden's business.'

'How long did you work here in the library?' I asked.

'Nearly thirty-five years.'

'And which came first, your interest in plants or in Poe?'

'It's sort of a chicken-and-egg thing, if you know what I mean. I've always loved both,' he said, wheeling himself to a shelf near his desk and handing me a book from it. 'My first published work, and it's still a classic in the field.'

I examined the well-worn volume and opened it to its title page. '"Flora and Fauna in the Poetry and Prose of Edgar Allan Poe – An Illustrated Guide."'

'So, if I say "buttercup," you can tell me if Poe used it in his work?' Mike asked.

'Precisely, Detective. Buttercup, better known by its Latin name *Ranunculus*, is used only once, in the story "Eleonora" – "so besprinkled through with the yellow buttercup."'

'Must be a huge audience for this stuff I just don't know about.'

'Or shall we try something like "jackass," Mr Chapman? Both in "Marginalia" and in "Politian." You'd be surprised at how many scholars rely on this kind of thing. The book is in its twelfth printing.'

Like every other author I'd ever met, Zeldin neglected to mention the size of each printing. I didn't expect they were large.

'As much as I've admired Poe's work,' I said, 'I certainly know very little about his life. Perhaps it would be useful if you would spend some time telling us about him.'

'It's Edgar Allan Poe who brought me here, to this very place,' Zeldin said, spinning his chair around to face the three of us.

'To New York?' Mercer asked.

'To the Bronx. To these Botanical Gardens.'

'We knew he lived in Manhattan,' I said. Recently acquired knowledge, for me, but the skeleton had made an indelible impression.

'But his last home, Miss Cooper – in fact, the longest residence of his adult life – was here in the Bronx.'

I looked to Mike, my outer-borough expert, for confirmation. He shook his head.

'Poe Cottage. You don't know it? You'll enjoy seeing it,' he said, explaining to Mike that it still stood on Kingsbridge Road, in a small park dedicated to the poet. 'It was not only his last real residence, poor soul, but the only one still standing. They'd best not tear that one down or every writer in America will be up in arms.'

'And these gardens?' I asked.

'Well, they hadn't been created as a formal botanical sanctuary then. In fact, this whole area wasn't even considered to be the Bronx in those days. It was a very rural village, part of Westchester County, known as Fordham. The building in which the skeleton was found in Greenwich Village? Poe had to leave that house because his wife was suffering from tuberculosis. The doctors insisted that she could only survive with the help of fresh country air.'

'So they moved out here?'

'Yes, ma'am. To the little farmhouse on Kingsbridge Road, near One Hundred Ninety-second Street and the Grand Concourse. He loved to walk, Poe did. He spent long days traversing the farmlands in this Fordham area, much of it here in these very woods that make up part of our Botanical Gardens property. Even to the gorge at the river, where that accident occurred this week. The waterfalls fascinated him.'

'You sure he walked right here?' Mike asked.

'Would you like to read his letters, Mr Chapman? He describes the area in exquisite detail, from the cottage to this forest to the High Bridge that carried water from the Croton Aqueduct over the Harlem River to Manhattan.'

'His story called "Landor's Cottage"?' I asked tentatively.

'Now you're onto it, Miss Cooper. That describes the little house he rented for his family, the one that still stands in Poe Park. One hundred dollars a year. He used to find great tranquillity in walking the heights, looking out over Long Island Sound. You could see it then from his doorstep, before all the high-rise buildings went up and got in the way of the view. There was a group of Jesuits at something called St John's, not too far away—'

Mike interrupted. 'Yeah. They're the ones who founded Fordham College.'

'Well, there you go, Mr Chapman. He used to love to walk over to have discourse with the Jesuit scholars and use the books in their library. We'll get you into this, too.'

'I'm about as deep in as I want to get, thanks. But now I understand why he named a character Montresor,' Mike said.

Zeldin expected another wisecrack.

'That name doesn't mean anything to you?' Mike asked. 'You know Randall's Island?'

We all did. It sat in the East River, between Manhattan and the Bronx.

'John Montresor was a British captain during the Revolutionary War. He bought that island and moved his family there, spying for the Brits and advising them where to base invasions in New York Harbor. He's the guy who witnessed Nathan Hale's execution, the reason we know Hale's last words.'

'"I only regret,"' Zeldin said, '"that I have but one life to give for my country." I'm impressed, Mr Chapman. I guess Poe didn't have to look much further than his back-yard to dig up some names for his tales.'

'You talked about the tragic circumstances of Poe's life yesterday,' I said. 'Would you mind telling us what they were?'

I had a notepad ready. I was hoping the salient facts would be things I could later compare against the life of a vengeful killer who may have been identifying too closely with the great writer.

'Poe's grandfather was a Revolutionary War hero. Somewhat celebrated in Maryland, where the family had settled. His father, David, was the typical black sheep, even back then.'

'In what way?'

'Defied the general's wishes by dropping the study of law to become an actor. And a drunk. And married beneath his class, to a woman of no pedigree. An all-round ne'er-do-well,' Zeldin said.

'Whom did he marry?' I asked.

'An itinerant actress named Eliza. A young woman who toured with small companies playing comic juvenile roles and ingénues. Edgar was their second child, born while Eliza was performing in Boston in 1809.'

I had to remind myself, now that the events of Poe's life seemed to be responsible in some way for the recent deaths, that Poe himself had lived two hundred years ago.

'A daughter came along two years later, and by the time of her birth, David Poe had disappeared. He was only twenty-five years old.'

'What do you mean, disappeared?'

'Exactly that. He was never heard from again. I can't tell you what became of him, where he lived thereafter or when he died. He simply vanished from their lives. Estranged from his parents in Baltimore, already deeply in debt with three babies to support, lousy reviews for his stagecraft, and a serious alcohol problem, he simply abandoned Eliza and the children.'

'So Poe never knew his father?' I asked. 'Eliza raised the children alone?'

Zeldin shook his head. 'She didn't have the chance. The local newspapers wrote of her "private misfortunes." The baby girl was rumored not to be David Poe's child, and within months Eliza had moved her little family to Richmond to try to make a new life for them. She had a catastrophic health failure and become a bedridden charity case shortly after she arrived. Before Edgar was three, his beloved mother had died.'

A broken home, illegitimacy, alcohol abuse, and now three orphaned children – it all sounded like an overwhelmingly dismal start to the boy's life.

'Who raised them?'

'Another emotional blow to the young trio. They were separated from each other. David Poe, senior – the parental grandfather who lived in Baltimore – agreed to take in the oldest child, whose name was William Henry. And a local family named Mackenzie took in the infant girl, Rosalie. It was Edgar who was the hardest to place.'

'At the age of three?'

'Yes, Miss Cooper. As it happened, a well-to-do merchant in Richmond was convinced by his wife – they were childless – to raise young Edgar. He became a ward of John and Frances Allan—'

'So that's where the name Allan comes from,' Mike said. 'I just assumed it was his given middle name. I didn't know he'd been adopted.'

'Adoption might have been an easier path for him, Mr Chapman. John Allan was a tough taskmaster. He refused to adopt the boy. Allan was entirely self-made and used his own childhood deprivation to try and instill in young Edgar that kind of school-of-hard-knocks experience. Sort of "Why should I hand you anything that I had to work hard for?" So the only promise he made the Poe family was that he would provide the boy with a liberal education.'

'I take it the Allans held up that part of the bargain,' Mercer said.

'Yes, they actually moved to England for a time, where Edgar's first serious schooling began. They sent him from there to Scotland to board for a year when he was only seven, where he was quite lonely. Five years later, when John Allan's business failed, the family returned to Richmond. You know about his stay at university?'

'A bit,' I said. 'In Charlottesville.'

'Mr Jefferson's great university had just been in existence for one year. Edgar was only seventeen when he entered, living in a room on the Lawn that you can still see today.'

'Yes, I know. The unlucky number thirteen.'

'Superstitious, Miss Cooper? Well, maybe his stay there would have been cursed anyway. Poe loved language. He studied French and Italian and Latin. He was a debater and a great swimmer. He wrote verse and sketched charcoals. That was the good side of student life at Virginia. But there was a dark side as well.'

'In what sense?'

'Virginia was the most expensive college in the country at that time, but in addition to the usual costs he ran up, Edgar Poe developed a serious gambling habit, falling several thousand dollars in debt. And alcohol was already becoming a problem for him, as it had been for his father. He gambled and drank, drank and desperately gambled at cards.'

'Did he finish college?' I asked.

'It was a two-year course at the time. He left after the first year, and that marked his major rift with John Allan, who refused to pay the boy's debts and wouldn't let him return to school. They quarreled more vociferously than ever before, and as Poe frequently wrote in his letters, he was keenly aware that this surrogate father who had raised him had absolutely no affection for him.'

'How painful for a young man who had no family to speak of. It's so odd then, that Poe used his name.'

'You're wrong, Miss Cooper. *We* use his name – Edgar rarely did.'

'I don't understand.'

'So far as we know, the first time Poe signed his name using Allan as part of the signature was years later, after John Allan's death. He often used the initial *A* when he published works, but he rarely used the name *Allan*, the way we do today. I truly think he hated that man.'

I thought of the signature that was so familiar from reproductions of books and manuscripts. Zeldin was right, of course. It was Edgar A. Poe – the name Allan was never spelled out in the writer's own hand. 'So Poe left Richmond?'

'At the age of eighteen he was alone in the world again, and restless. He struck out for Boston – probably because his mother had written of loving the city so much. That's where a forty-page volume of poetry called *Tamerlane* first appeared in 1827, wrapped in plain brown paper and distributed around town by an anonymous author.'

'Poe's first publication?'

'Indeed, Miss Cooper. He never signed any of the copies, nor did he even keep one for himself. Only a handful exist at this point in time. It's no secret that one of our members bought one at auction last year for six hundred thousand dollars. But that's today. As you know, poetry has never been the means to support many young men or women. So Poe took another route – he lied about his age and enlisted in the army. Claimed to be twenty-two years old and said his name was Edgar Perry.'

Mike hadn't known about the military piece. 'Didn't that commit him to five years? Wasn't that pretty standard back then?'

'You're right, Detective. But life as a private wasn't all he had imagined, and he wanted out after two. He actually created an entirely false pedigree – you people would call it perjury – just so he could gain admission to West Point and become an officer.'

'Poe actually entered the Academy?' Mike asked.

'He was a cadet for a year and a half. Until he was court-martialed for gross neglect of duties and failure to obey orders. He left in disgrace, and again in debt.'

'What then?' I asked.

'He was like a lost soul. He wandered a bit writing poetry, and finally wound up in Baltimore, where his father's family lived.'

'Was his older brother still in residence there?'

'That was a brief reunion. Shortly after Edgar reached Baltimore, his brother died – of intemperance, it was called at the time.'

'Intemperance?' I asked.

'Alcohol, Miss Cooper. William Henry Poe drank himself to death by the age of twenty-four.'

'What a ghastly series of events. Did Edgar reconnect with any other family members?' Mercer asked.

'Some might call the word "reconnection" an understatement, Mr Wallace,' Zeldin said. 'Edgar's father, David, had a widowed sister named Maria Poe Clemm living there in Baltimore with her two children – her son, Henry, and a nine-year-old daughter named Virginia. So Edgar moved in with his poor widowed aunt Maria and his little first cousins – the only real family he had known in a lifetime.'

'Seems like finally it might have provided some stability,' I said. 'Was it a productive period for him?'

'In a literary sense, it was quite so. He was writing stories and getting them published in the *Southern Literary Messenger*. Gothic tales of premature burial, physical decay and putrescence, addiction to alcohol, questions about the finality of death. You can only imagine how the tragic events of his youth had fueled his imagination,' Zeldin said, pausing for a moment. 'On the personal side, he had fallen in love.'

'Against that cheerful background? Who's the lucky woman?' Mike asked.

'Girl, actually. Hard to call her anything else. His first cousin, Detective. Little Virginia Clemm.'

Mike slapped his knee. 'The friggin' nine-year-old?'

'He waited, Mr Chapman,' Zeldin said, wagging a finger and smiling wryly. 'He didn't marry her until she was older – until she turned thirteen.'

'And Poe himself?'

'Twenty-seven years of age.'

'Goodness gracious, great balls of fire!' Mike said, blushing. 'People used to think Jerry Lee Lewis was a pervert. Roman Polanski had to become a fugitive for the rest of his adult life 'cause he'd had sex with a teenager. Listen to this shit, will you? Poe was a pedophile. An incestuous pedophile. Coop would have probably thrown his ass in jail for statutory rape as well as incest.'

'You're speaking of the poet's muse, Mr Chapman. My cohorts in the Raven Society believe in giving great latitude to someone of such unusual creativity. We don't dwell on his peccadillos,' Zeldin said, amused by Mike's reaction to Virginia's age.

'I'm speaking of something that would shock just about anybody I can think of. And was he a drunken pedophile, too?'

'Yes, Detective, there are letters from his publisher at the very time despairing of the fact that he was already an alcoholic. And suggestions of a worse addiction.'

'What's that?' I asked, reminded of the involvement of substance abuse in the lives of Aurora Tait, Emily Upshaw, Gino Guidi, and some of the other names that had surfaced in our case. I wondered if there was any relevance to the connection.

'Our members divide on this issue,' Zeldin said. 'Some don't like to attribute more faults to the master than are well documented. But most of us are convinced that Poe was addicted to opium as well as alcohol. There are even letters from the period that suggest he used laudanum.'

'How was he able to write?' I asked. 'How was he able to leave us this brilliant body of work?'

'Poe suffered all the demons, Miss Cooper. Every one of them. Start with his fractured, loveless childhood. Then, for almost all of his adult life, he was impoverished – even though his work was known and acclaimed both in America and Europe. Add to poverty his constant despair over his wife's chronic, debilitating illness, his lifelong battle with alcohol and opiates, and what he himself described as his insanity after Virginia's death.'

The three of us were quiet.

'He died alone?' Mercer asked.

'His final weeks are somewhat of a mystery, Mr Wallace. He left the Bronx for Philadelphia, then on to Richmond, then back to Baltimore. He was found at a rum shop, greatly intoxicated and incoherent, the story goes. Friends took him to a hospital where he spent the night, with terrible tremors and sweats, addressing and having conversation with spectral images on the walls of his room. Within days, young Edgar Poe – forty years of age – was dead. "Lord help my poor soul" were the last words he spoke.'

'And in between all these aspects of profound dysfunction,' I said, 'he wrote some of the most remarkable poetry – and prose – in the English language. It's quite extraordinary.'

'Pure genius. Tortured, tormented genius, Miss Cooper,' Zeldin said. 'If he hadn't been a successful poet, Edgar Allan Poe had all the makings of a serial killer.'

Chapter 28

'Our head groundskeeper, Mr Phelps, tells me you made his acquaintance at the gorge the other evening, is that right?' Zeldin asked.

At the prearranged time, Sinclair Phelps had knocked on the door of Zeldin's office to take him down to a minivan that had been specially fitted with a ramp for his wheelchair.

'Yes, we've met,' I said, greeting the groundskeeper and introducing him to Mercer.

'Tell them, Sinclair. They don't seem to believe I hadn't heard of the doctor's unfortunate drowning by the time I left my office on Tuesday.'

'If there's any question of that, Mr Chapman, I'm the one who made the notifications,' Phelps said. 'The only call I made, other than to nine-one-one, was to the director of the gardens. He cautioned me himself not to tell any of the staff until the police investigators left the park.'

Phelps was wheeling Zeldin to a large elevator, which delivered us all to the ground floor. 'You're welcome to leave your car here and drive with us in the van.'

'Where are we going?' Mike asked.

'To the snuff mill, Detective,' Zeldin said, laughing.

'It's the unofficial headquarters of the Raven Society, for the time being.'

The wheelchair locked in place in the rear of the van. Mike sat in the front passenger seat with Mercer and me behind him. 'Snuff what?'

'If you go back to the seventeen-forties, Detective, six hundred acres of this prime country real estate was owned by the Lorillard family. Pierre Lorillard was a French Huguenot who settled in this part of Westchester and began his tobacco industry in Lower Manhattan. But he moved it here, to this very site, to take advantage of the swift flow of the river just below the gorge.

'Yes, this was all Lorillard land when Poe came here on his peregrinations, isn't that right, Phelps?'

'Yes, sir.'

'Sinclair's been here about as long as I have. It's thanks to his conspiratorial nature that I've been able to give a home to the society's papers.'

'You like Poe, too?' Mike asked.

'No, sir. Not particularly. I like Zeldin, though. And the mill is too handsome not to put to some use.' Phelps didn't smile. I figured that was a good thing because the cracks in his weathered skin looked as though they would split open like an eggshell if they moved at all.

'Tobacco was actually milled here?' I asked.

'Yes,' Phelps said. 'The waterfalls you saw the other night, they're what powered the tobacco mill in the eighteenth century. That's the only reason the Lorillards' business could thrive here. There are no other falls in New York City. The first botanical plantings in this area were rose gardens. That was purposely so the rose petals could be used to add scent to the snuff.'

'And to think the Bronx always gets such a bum rap,' Mike said. 'What's over there?'

The road curved and on our right was an enormous Victorian structure, crisp white paint outlining its form against the powder blue sky, countless glass windowpanes reflecting the rare February sun.

'That's our conservatory,' Zeldin said. 'It's the largest crystal palace in America. You must come back and allow us to guide you through it. It's full of the world's most exotic plants, set out like an ecotour in its eleven galleries.'

'Pretty spectacular greenhouse,' Mike said.

'The first one was built in London – Palm House, at Kew, Detective – for Queen Victoria and her royal gardens. The idea was to construct these enormous, shimmering structures, allowing all sorts of tropical and rare gardens to be under one roof, exposed to the sunlight. Remarkable sight, isn't it?'

'I remember coming here as a child, but I thought it had been closed,' I said.

'Just reopened a few years back, with twenty-five million dollars worth of improvements. This treasure was built in 1901. In fact, a few of them were erected – I guess the most famous was at the Chicago World's Fair. But as large as they seem, they're extremely fragile.'

The gleaming cupola of the rotunda was the center-piece of the structure, with long transparent arms stretching out on both sides.

'That's one entire acre beneath that roof,' Zeldin said. 'Seventeen thousand panes of glass hold it together, each one specially made to fit in the curves of the old iron frame.'

The van wound around the vast grounds of the gardens,

stripped now of all the colorful flowers and plants that would blossom again in another couple of months. Within minutes, we had left all the buildings behind and appeared to be driving through a rambling countryside that more closely resembled the foothills of the Berkshires than an urban park. Ahead for as far as I could see were thick stands of trees, which looked as chillingly foreboding as they had when we drove in a couple nights back to visit the scene of Ichiko's death.

'Into the woods?' Mike asked.

'This is the only remaining native forest in New York City,' Phelps said.

'I didn't even know there was one.'

'Fifty acres' worth. It's a first-growth, mixed-hardwood forest. This is what most of the Bronx looked like when the Europeans arrived,' he said.

'What are the trees?'

'Hiawatha and his hemlocks,' Zeldin said. 'Don't you remember your Longfellow poems, Miss Cooper? The most common tree throughout these low hills of the Bronx is hemlock, and we've got all that's left of them.'

'Did Poe use . . . ?' Mercer began.

Zeldin interrupted before he could finish. He delighted in showing off his unique mastery of Poe and the local flora. 'Hemlock appears in only one story. It's called "Morella." But in his letters, as I told you, he wrote often about walking in this very forest.'

We crossed over a bridge and stopped before a hand-some stone building, two stories high and covered with ivy, which appeared to be a meticulously restored structure from the early nineteenth century.

I stepped out of the car and the only thing I heard to

break the silence in the snow-carpeted forest was the running water of the river directly below us.

Phelps opened the rear of the van and lowered Zeldin's wheelchair down the ramp. We followed them to a dark green wooden door of the old mill at the back of the building, fronting the river. This was a third floor, below ground level, which wasn't visible from the approach on the roadway. Phelps unlocked the combination that hung on the hinge and turned on the lights as we entered.

'The administration hasn't really figured out how to use this building,' Zeldin said. 'Frankly, after the Palace, I think it's the structural gem of the whole institution. So for the meantime, the upstairs is almost like storage space for the garden's library, but Phelps has helped me outfit this area for the Raven Society.'

One-half of the basement was a large open space. It was furnished with several oversized sofas and armchairs that looked as though they had come from the Salvation Army. The other side was a series of small rooms set up like a small office suite. The entire wall was ringed with bookshelves. An assortment of ravens in all shapes and sizes – stuffed birds, porcelain ones, and carved ebony figures – were mounted on every flat surface.

'Is this where you meet?' I asked.

'Rarely. But this is the repository for all our documents and research. Some members just enjoy coming here for the ambiance. Sitting in a comfortable chair, gazing out at the forest, and reading a good book.'

'And the members just come and go as they like? They all have the combination to this lock?' Mercer asked.

'We're fortunate that Phelps lives here.'

'Here, in the snuff mill?' Mike asked.

'No, no,' the groundskeeper said. 'Did you see the carriage houses we passed before we reached this building? I live in one of those.'

I had noticed three buildings, smaller than the mill but in the same old style with wooden gables over the door and windows.

'Obviously, people can only come here to the mill on the days the gardens are open,' Zeldin said, 'because the entire perimeter of the park is gated, of course. But that's most of the year, except for major holidays. And yes, members are free to come and go from these rooms as they please.'

He rolled into the first alcove and beckoned us to follow. Once inside the office, Zeldin steadied himself on the edge of the desk and hoisted his body out of the wheelchair. For the several minutes it took him to open a file cabinet and remove the papers we had asked for, he balanced against the desktop.

I watched Mercer and Mike staring at him, knowing they were trying to determine the strength of his legs and the extent of his movement to figure whether he was capable of playing a role in any of the recent crimes. But Zeldin lowered himself back into the chair before any of us could gauge his mobility.

'Here's what you've asked for, Detective. The list of our members,' he said. 'You may have that copy, and I trust you'll treat them kindly.'

Mike put the papers on the desk and I leaned in next to him to read with him. The pages were divided by cities, and I quickly scanned the out-of-towners for familiar surnames, finding none. Baltimore, Boston, Philadelphia, Richmond – most of them lived in places where Poe had also spent time. The rest of the members lived in New York City. Other than Zeldin, I was disappointed to see that there was not a name I recognized.

Mike turned to the last paper, which was headed with the initials *PNG*. We both stared at one of the names that jumped out at us. 'Help me here,' Mike said to Zeldin. 'Who are these guys?'

'*PNG*? Personae non grata, Mr Chapman. Not everyone in the group knows the institutional history as well as I do, Detective. There are some people who might try to reapply to the society after old-timers like myself are no longer alive. This is to make sure certain people never enter our fold.'

Mike pulled out the desk chair and sat down. 'I'd like to start right here, if you don't mind. Why is Noah Tormey on this list?'

Chapter 29

'I suppose I first met Noah Tormey about twenty-five years ago,' Zeldin said. 'Maybe longer. Quite an intelligent young man, fancied himself a scholar although I'm not sure I'd be that generous. He had just graduated from New York University and was an instructor in the English department. He came to me to borrow some books – they were out-of-print volumes – to do some research for a dissertation.'

'Came to you here, at the Botanical Gardens?'

'Heavens, no. I was just a lowly librarian then. Well-known in literary circles for my collection of Poe – his works, as well as biography and criticism. He came to my home, where you were yesterday.'

Not bad digs for a 'lowly librarian,' as Zeldin described himself, is what I was thinking. Perhaps he sensed that and decided to explain.

'My mother had owned that apartment, Ms Cooper. I inherited it upon her death. She had been collecting rare books most of her life, including Poe. It's thanks to her family fortune – sewing thread, simple cotton sewing thread that my great-grandfather manufactured – that I've been able to indulge myself in my two passions, horticulture and literature.'

'So you and Tormey struck up a friendship?' Mike asked.

'He was an interesting fellow. I wouldn't say we became close, but he'd call when he needed something and if it was a volume I owned, I was happy to loan it to him.'

'Did the two of you talk? Socially, I mean.'

'Our conversation was always about the nineteenth century, Detective. Not women, not current events, not our personal lives, if that's what you mean.'

'And the Raven Society?'

'I suppose that came up. In fact I'm sure it did. Tormey eventually got around to asking me about joining, I'm quite sure of it.'

'Were you already a member?' Mike asked.

'Yes, I was admitted rather early. I had come along at the moment the group was trying to expand a bit, and my scholarship in the field was well documented. I think I was in my mid-twenties when I was accepted.'

'Secret handshake? Flap your elbows like a bird? Swear you'll never watch *The Maltese Falcon* or read Rex Stout again?'

Zeldin wasn't amused. 'I submitted some of the papers I had written and demonstrated, at meetings with some of the members, that I was intimate with the body of work. I'm sure my collection of first editions made me an attractive candidate.'

'So what happened to Noah Tormey? Why'd he get blackballed?'

'There was no question that he knew Poe's writings as well as most of us. But then he published a paper in one of the literary reviews. It was brilliantly researched and quite well written,' Zeldin said.

I thought immediately of Emily Upshaw, who had done some of Tormey's writing for him.

'The problem was,' he went on, 'the piece dredged up all the petty old claims, with impressive documentation.'

'The personal foibles you just described to us?' I asked, wondering why they would matter to scholars.

'No, no, Miss Cooper. Poe's plagiarism.'

'His what?' Mike asked. 'What did he plagiarize?'

Zeldin sighed. Then he called out the groundskeeper's name. 'Phelps?'

Sinclair Phelps came back into the little office from the other room. 'Yes?'

'Against that wall, third drawer down, would you mind fetching me a folder labeled "Tormey"?'

Phelps retrieved the document and left the room. 'We're talking about a young man hoping to establish himself in academia,' Zeldin said, opening the file and passing an issue of the review to Mike. 'Naturally, the immature Poe he wrote about was struggling to find his voice. You'll see some examples in this study.'

We took a few minutes and read the first several pages. There were lines that appeared to be lightly lifted from obscure poets I'd never read. Here was Poe's 'Song':

> *I saw thee on the bridal day –*
> *When a burning blush came o'er thee . . .*

And below it a poem by John Lofland, published a year earlier:

> *I saw her on the bridal day*
> *In blushing beauty blest . . .*

I had just heard Tormey yesterday, teaching his class *Biographia Literaria*. Now here in the paper Zeldin gave me to look at, he was quoting Coleridge and his classic description of poetry as a kind of composition 'which is opposed to works of science, by proposing for its immediate object pleasure, not truth.'

Next to Coleridge he interposed the words of Poe, who wrote that 'a poem, in my opinion, is opposed to a work of science by having, for its immediate object, pleasure, not truth.'

Least welcome to Zeldin and his cohorts must have been the lines referred to in the masterwork, 'The Raven.' Here was Elizabeth Barrett Browning first, hardly an obscure poet if one was to be borrowing phrases: 'With a murmurous stir uncertain in the air the purple curtain . . .' And then Poe's famous line: 'And the silken, sad, uncertain rustling of each purple curtain . . .'

I handed Tormey's essay back to Zeldin.

'Mr Tormey took Poe apart, as the two of you can see. Most of my colleagues didn't treat that lightly. He was even anxious to show off his own skill at researching, noting how Edgar had taken commentary for many of his treatises practically verbatim from secondary sources, sometimes right out of the encyclopedia – like a schoolchild might do.'

'Had Poe ever been exposed to this kind of claim in his lifetime?' I asked.

'Attacked for his lack of literary morals? Indeed he was,' Zeldin said. 'It was another source of his great despair. When Poe's critics accused him of plagiarism, he was barred from some of New York's most important literary salons.'

'No wonder his characters so often resort to revenge in his stories,' I said. 'Poor Mr Poe must have dreamed about it often.'

'You've got that right. Of course, he took it out on other writers, Miss Cooper. He viewed everything as a personal wound. Have you ever read his volumes of literary criticism?'

'No, I haven't.'

'He published quite a lot of it, and went after many of his contemporaries – quite mercilessly.'

'Which ones?' I asked.

'He had absolute contempt for Longfellow. Hated him as much for the heiress he married and all the private volumes of work that her wealth enabled him to get published as for his derivative and mediocre poetry. Then there was William Cullen Bryant and Washington Irving. I could go on and on.'

I thought of the Hall of Fame. Poe might have used the surrounding busts as a shooting gallery himself – taking potshots at his rivals – had it existed in his day.

'So what's the big deal to the Raven Society?' Mike asked. 'People had heard this criticism before.'

'Our members come to praise Caesar, not to bury him, if you will. We gather to celebrate the genius and originality of Poe, which is far outweighed by a few youthful indiscretions. We're very collegial and quite admiring of the master. We didn't need Mr Tormey to put a spotlight on these things again. I don't know that anyone was ready to kill the young professor for that sort—'

Zeldin stopped himself with that thought. 'Sorry, I shouldn't use language like that around the three of you. You might take me seriously. They just didn't want Tormey in their mix. He knew the poetry, but he didn't love the poet quite as unequivocally as the rest of us do.'

'Talk about holding a grudge,' Mike said. 'You guys are tough. You hear anything lately from Mr Tormey?'

The morning papers had lowballed yesterday's shooting at the Hall of Fame. It took place in the Bronx, after all, and to crime reporters, that might as well have been Siberia. An outer-borough triple homicide might earn a paragraph in the *Times* and space within the first ten pages of the tabloids. But there was no reason Zeldin would have heard about this assault.

'Nothing. Nothing at all.'

'So the people on this last page – the ones you've black-balled – are they all here for reasons like this?' Mercer asked.

'More or less, Detective. Some aren't really committed to serious scholarship, some can't afford the dues. Why? What did you think?'

Mercer hesitated.

'Ah, were they dangerous? Is that what you mean? You're thinking that whoever killed the woman in Greenwich Village might be one of us?' Zeldin said. 'Not very likely. The closest we've ever come to an actual crime was – Phelps, are you there? When was that shooting?'

The groundskeeper reappeared and leaned on the door-frame. 'Outside the main gate? It must be almost ten years now.'

'What did it have to do with the society?' Mike asked.

'There was a detective with whom I'd spoken on the phone several times. I don't recall his name. He was quite interested in meeting with me.'

'About the Raven Society?'

'Oh, no. I doubt he knew of its existence. Ratiocination it was. He was quite intrigued with ratiocination.'

'What?' Mike asked.

'The process of deductive reasoning. Old hat to you and Mr Wallace, perhaps, but when Poe wrote his first tale of ratiocination – "The Murders in the Rue Morgue" – the word "detective" had not yet been used in the English language. The first professional police department in the world had only been set up in London twelve years earlier.'

'What did this cop want?'

'He wanted to talk to me about Poe's detective stories, he told me. Use the archives for some research, I assumed. And I thought, in return, that it might be interesting to have him address the society, with these tales as background to the work that police detectives do today. After all, Poe's works are the first time in literature that you see some of these techniques used – postmortem examinations, ballistics discussions, locked-room mysteries.'

'And there was a shooting near the gardens, you say?'

'Yes. Really dreadful. The officer claimed some kids tried to rob him right outside the main gate, on his way in to meet with me. Turned out one of them was a young fellow who had done some part-time work here on the grounds. Phelps, you remember any of the details?'

'Just like you said, sir. The boy who was killed was a pretty decent kid, according to everyone who knew him. Shot in the back, from quite a fair distance away. That's the main thing I remember.'

'That's why we screen everyone who approaches the society so carefully now. The last thing we need is to attract any attention to ourselves – certainly not any scandal. I never returned the officer's calls after that. He was a damn good shot, I'll tell you that.'

'Well,' Mike said, standing and reaching for Zeldin's hand, 'thanks for your time. We'll let you know if we need to speak with you again.'

'Wouldn't you like me to arrange for you to see Poe's cottage, as long as you're so close?' he asked.

'Yes, of course,' I said, at the exact moment Mike answered with a 'No thanks.'

'We really got some ground to cover, Coop,' Mike said to me. 'Another time.'

Zeldin wheeled himself out to the main room. 'Phelps will drive you back to your car. You just let me know when it would be convenient for you to stop by. The cottage is open five days a week, or if you'd prefer a private tour, I'll just call Mr Guidi's office and they'll accommodate you.'

Mike was as startled as I. 'Guidi? Gino Guidi?'

'You know him?'

'I've heard the name,' Mike said. 'Investment banker – is that the one?'

'Bronx boy makes good, Mr Chapman. That's our Gino Guidi.'

Chapter 30

'I didn't see his name on the list,' Mike said, unfolding the copy of the Raven Society membership for a second look.

'No. You won't find it there,' Zeldin said. 'You probably know him from the business pages of the newspapers. He's made a fortune on Wall Street, but luckily for us he chairs the board of the Bronx Historical Society. They oversee the management of the cottage.'

'He's into Poe, too?'

'Not that I'm aware of, Detective. I've met him at a few fund-raising events here at the conservatory, but we've never talked about literature.'

Mike winked at me. 'On second thought, what's half an hour? You wanna see the place?'

If a visit to Poe's home hadn't whetted his appetite, the Guidi connection had.

'Why don't you stop for some coffee in our cafeteria? Your car is parked right near there. The cottage isn't normally open for tours until one o'clock on weekdays. I'll make sure they send someone over to show you around. Mind you, Mr Chapman, it's a tiny, little place – I don't imagine it would take you five minutes to walk through, even if you tried to stretch it.'

Phelps dropped us in front of the Garden Café and the three of us went in to nurse a cup of coffee, chart the next few days' work, and await Zeldin's call. Fifty minutes later he rang me on my cell to say that we were expected.

At eleven-thirty, we drove away from the Botanical Gardens and headed to the intersection of the Grand Concourse and Kingsbridge Road. The eighteenth-century farms that once graced the area had given way to elegant apartment buildings in the early twentieth century, and were now replaced by grim-looking tenements whose doors and windows were covered with the roll-down metal gratings so omnipresent in Third World countries. Waves of immigrants had peopled this neighborhood on their way to more successful, suburban lives. Now all the printed signs were written in Spanish, from PEPITO'S PAYAYAS to MIGUEL'S FRITAS, and watched over by a giant billboard with the beaming smile of J. Lo in her latest, tightest jeans.

Just off the Concourse, completely surrounded by wrought-iron fencing, was a small oasis about the length of two city blocks. At the far end was a round gazebo and an attractive open bandshell with eight tall columns supporting a green copper roof. Next to that was a playground, with slides and structures for kids to climb on, painted a bright scarlet, cheerful against the dull gray facade of the buildings across the way.

We left the car at a meter, next to an opening in the gate. A square city plaque labeled the landmark, with the familiar maple leaf logo of the Parks Department below the words: POE PARK. Beside it hung a frame with the enlarged script signature of the writer.

I walked ahead of Mike and stood on the blacktop path. I was face-to-face with a building that was a complete anachronism in the middle of this urban jungle. It was a tiny white cottage that had once stood here alone as a farmhouse. Now its simple wooden frame, slim porch, dark green shutters, and the little shed that was attached to its side looked lost in time among the asphalt and brick of the surrounding streets.

The door opened and a young woman waved to us from the top of the steps. 'Welcome to Poe Cottage,' she said, introducing herself as Kathleen Bailey as we approached and greeted her. 'C'mon inside.'

I entered directly into the first room, which was the kitchen, no bigger than ten feet square. Restored to appear as it did at the time Poe lived here, the cramped space held a cupboard and wood-burning stove, an antique wall clock, and chairs with a table set for a meal – as though we might be joined by the poet any minute.

'Make yourselves comfortable,' she said, as I unzipped my jacket and unwrapped the heavy scarf that was around my neck.

Bailey began her story. 'This is the house that Edgar Poe rented in 1846, so that he could bring his wife, Virginia, here, in hopes the fresh country air would improve her health. It's actually thirteen miles north of what was considered New York City then, in the village of Fordham, and all the surrounding land was an apple orchard.'

'The house was built on this spot?' Mike asked.

'At the time the house was across the street, down near the bandshell, on the far side of the avenue. It was the former police commissioner of New York – Teddy

Roosevelt – who decided to preserve Poe's home and move it to this site in 1913. It was the place Poe lived in for three years, and when he died later on, in Baltimore, he was on his way back here to this cottage.'

I ducked my head and followed Kathleen Bailey to the next room, slightly larger and a bit more formal. It had a great hearth, bordered in a colonial blue paint, with a gilded mirror hanging beside the window and a rocking chair in front of the fireplace. Against the wall was a small desk with two candles on top of it along with an open book.

'This is obviously the parlor, and the room in which Poe worked.'

'Do you know what he wrote while he lived here?' I asked.

'Many of the things, yes,' she said. 'I suppose you know that Virginia died here, quite tragically, within the first year after they arrived.'

Mike whispered in my ear, 'She would have been better off in a pediatric hospital.'

Mercer asked Bailey, 'How old was she?'

'Only twenty-five. Pulmonary consumption is what they called it then. Tuberculosis. Some of Poe's most famous poems were crafted at that very desk in front of you – "Annabel Lee," "Ulalume," "The Bells."'

I thought of these familiar rhymes, each portraying themes of a man's enduring love for a woman who had died.

She was a child and I was a child,
In this kingdom by the sea . . .
The wind came out of a cloud, chilling and
Killing my Annabel Lee.

'And this,' she said, stepping back so I could look over the half-door that opened into a tiny room that held only a single bed, with a small round table and chair beside it, 'this is actually the bedroom in which Virginia died.'

Stark and almost bare, the room was smaller than any jail cell I had ever seen. It was depressing to contemplate the last days of Virginia's young life, and far easier to understand the great melancholy that enveloped the poet while she lay dying.

'There's not even a fireplace,' I said. 'How could she have possibly made it through the winter in here?'

'There are letters from friends who visited the Poes during those months. Edgar used to wrap her in his coat under the thin coverlet and sheets. The bitter cold certainly must have hastened her death.'

Behind me, in a corner, was a duplicate of the bronze bust of Poe that stood in the Hall of Fame. Mike pointed to a scroll on the wall next to the statue that listed the names of the Bronx natives who supported the preservation of the cottage. Gino Guidi's was at the top in bold letters. There were only several others I recognized who had achieved prominence beyond the neighborhood: from fashionistas like Ralph Lauren and Calvin Klein to leaders of the bench and bar, like Justin Feldman, Roger Hayes, and the Roberts brothers – George and Burton.

Opposite the half-door was a very narrow staircase that wound up to the second floor.

'You'll have to go up one at a time,' Bailey said. 'Three of you won't fit there.'

I ascended first, to see two more little rooms – one in which Poe slept when he wasn't keeping vigil by his bride's bed, and the other in which Virginia's mother lived, first with the couple, and then after both had died. These quarters had low, sloping ceilings and only the light from an eyebrow window that looked out to the park. I held on to the railing and backed down the stairs. Mike and Mercer were waiting at the front door, and I walked toward them behind our knowledgeable guide.

'So despite his success,' I asked Bailey, 'they were still quite poor, weren't they?'

'Desperately poor,' she said. 'There's a letter he wrote to a friend in which he complained of living in such dreadful poverty here that he had no money for shoes or—'

Her words were cut short by a bloodcurdling scream that seemed to come from the far end of the park.

'Help me! Help!' I heard. The voice sounded like that of a child or adolescent.

Mike and Mercer stepped outside and Kathleen Bailey was down the steps immediately behind them, running toward the playground, where four or five people were gathering at the scene of the commotion. I stopped on the porch for a few seconds, debating whether or not to leave the cottage open and unguarded.

Passersby clustered on the sidewalk, some moving in the same direction as Mike and Mercer, while others withdrew with their children, disappearing down the side streets.

I walked several more steps down the path and fixed myself at the gate, so that I could keep one eye on the house while watching the melee, still available if the guys wanted my help.

Suddenly, before Mercer got to the playground, I saw an older kid dash from behind the swings, race around the bandshell, and cut out across Kingsbridge Road into the traffic.

'Get him!' the voice screamed again.

I stood on my tiptoes to see whether Mike and Mercer had reached the small crowd at the far end of the park. It was too late for me to turn and look when I finally heard the noise behind me. Everything went black as I felt a crushing blow against the back of my head.

Chapter 31

The pain was so intense that when I regained consciousness, I couldn't bear to open my eyes. I tried to inhale and give air to my aching brain, but there was something in my mouth that I gagged on as soon as I drew breath.

My pain was dwarfed by fear. I was in a box, smaller than a coffin. I didn't need to look. I could feel the wooden boards beneath my back, close to my arms on each side, and knew there was not enough space above me to allow me to pick up my head.

Panic prevented me from doing what I needed to do most – regulate my breathing and conserve whatever oxygen there was available.

Slowly, I opened one eye. A sharp pang sliced across my forehead, forging little lightning streaks in my line of sight. There was a board above me – several boards – and between them were slats through which the gray daylight filtered in.

I wasn't underground. I wasn't buried in the earth. I tried to eliminate those two horrors that had frightened me the most.

I sniffed the air as I breathed in. The odor was dank and moist and the wood beneath me was wet and cold.

I closed my eyes again and watched as the lightning streaks dissolved into yellowish blobs that floated back and forth across my eyelids.

Ordinary street noises seemed close by. Automobile traffic and honking horns, then police sirens too far away to be useful to me. I could hear voices of women – a group of women – speaking in Spanish but walking away from whatever sidewalk was near my temporary coffin.

Voices again. This time it sounded like men, coming from the opposite direction. It was Mercer Wallace, calling my name, opening and closing doors as he did. I must still be somewhere within Poe Cottage.

Surely he and Mike would think of the poet's bizarre tales of premature burial, one of which had launched us on this hunt for a killer. The 'dull, quick sound' of my own heart beating – like that of the telltale one – seemed deafening to me. Surely they would figure to look everywhere for me before leaving and locking up the sad little house. How did Poe describe that telltale noise that haunted the murderer? Like the 'sound a watch makes when enveloped in cotton.'

Voices came closer, and footsteps on pavement, too. I was on my back; my arms had been folded behind me and loosely restrained – probably with my woolen scarf – my hands beneath my thighs. The walls of my confinement restricted me, and I couldn't free my hands, which were tingling from the lack of circulation. I moved my right leg to try to bring my knee up to knock against the floorboard above me. But the space was tight and I could only lift it an inch or two. It rubbed against the wood but made no noise.

The pounding on the back of my brain was intense.

My neck strained as I raised my head, knocking the crown of it against the boards. My hair cushioned the contact and it seemed to me even less audible than my heartbeat.

'What's in here?'

It was Mike's voice, and I almost laughed with relief at how ridiculous I had been to panic with my two friends only yards away.

'Just the root cellar,' Kathleen Bailey answered. 'Nothing.'

Of course I had noticed the slanted roof of the small addition that was off to the right of the cottage entrance. It had a door that faced the rear street, where we had circled around before parking the car. It seemed no larger than a dollhouse. No wonder there were boards on either side of me, too. They supported the uneven flooring as the ground beneath sloped down the short incline.

I saw more light as a door opened above me and to the side. I grunted and groaned against my gag but the sound was too muffled and the voices of Mike and Kathleen masked my own weak effort to be heard. Whoever had opened the door and looked in for a brief moment had closed it again and turned the latch.

'She's just dumb enough to have taken off after that kid if she saw him running out of the park,' Mike said. 'Let me talk to the guy in the RMP and see if they have her at the station house.'

The sets of footsteps walked away, with Mike going to ask the cops in the radio motor patrol car if they could phone in to locate me.

'I thought she was coming out of the cottage right behind me,' Bailey said. 'She might have just dashed out the gate. I – I just didn't see.'

Mercer's deep voice was still in range, calling after Mike, 'Alex may swim fast, but I wouldn't bet on her in a sprint through the side streets. It's not like her to take off on a footrace like that.'

Don't leave me, Mercer, I prayed silently. How ironic that this was like Poe's classic, the officers standing right over the buried body, chatting pleasantly, making a mockery of my horror but hearing nothing.

I writhed and wriggled in my box. The noise of my clothes rustling against the old boards as I moved sounded as loud as thunder to me. Why couldn't anyone outside hear it? I gnawed on the gag, but quickly grew dizzy from the shortness of breath. I urged myself to lie still until someone returned to the cellar door. I urged myself to believe that someone would.

The dampness seeped through the back of my pants legs and I realized I was shivering. I moved my body again and struggled to pull my left hand free from under my thigh. It slid an inch or so, coming to rest against something slimy and fat and cold. Something that crawled.

This was a root cellar, I reminded myself. The thing I touched was probably a slug. It was Poe's root cellar, so most likely it was what he called a conqueror worm, waiting for me in my burial plot.

Why had I been stored here in this hole? What would my captors do to me when they returned, once the police moved their search away from this dank prison?

Now there were noises in an adjacent room above. 'Everything,' I heard Mercer say. 'Open everything.'

Lots of pairs of feet were traipsing through the tiny cottage, banging doors and moving furniture. There was a cupboard in the kitchen, I thought as I closed my eyes and tried to visualize the rooms we had seen earlier, but not even a closet in the parlor or bedroom.

'The fireplace,' Mike said, 'any trapdoors in there, at the back?'

Somebody was pounding up the narrow steps to the second floor. I could have saved them the time. There was nowhere to conceal anything upstairs.

Kathleen Bailey was trying to help them, answering someone's question about whether anything like this had ever happened here before. 'Never. Nothing like this.'

'How about the building foundation?' Mike said. It sounded like he was outside, at the top of the steps near the entrance.

'This side is solid rock,' Mercer said. 'I'll try the lattice-work on the left.'

I heard several thuds and then the sound of splintering wood. Mercer had probably kicked through the decora-tively carved front below the old porch.

'You been in here?'

An unfamiliar but welcome voice was close to me, unlatching the cellar door. I twisted around again, undoubtedly crushing the worm as I shimmied back and forth on top of it and grunted as I moved.

'They checked that already,' someone answered. 'It's empty.'

The door that had been cracked open slammed shut again.

The entire inside of my mouth was chewed up by my efforts to loosen the gag. I could taste the blood as I swallowed.

Mike and Mercer were on my other side now, near the front steps of the cottage. 'I'll take a ride around the 'hood. She's obviously not here,' Mike said. 'She's probably doing social work for the little bastard who punched out the kid on the playground.'

'I'm not leaving,' Mercer said. 'I'd rather pull this damn park apart. She doesn't know the Bronx. I'm telling you she didn't run off anywhere.'

'What coulda happened to her?' Mike asked. 'We weren't out of sight for ten minutes. She's got a short fuse but I didn't think she was so impatient that—'

'Do it your way. Just leave a couple of uniformed guys here.'

Stay with me, Mercer. Please just stay here with me.

I could hear Mike walk away from the building. 'If you need a bloodhound, let me know. Or just sniff the floorboards for that Chanel shit she wears.'

Floorboards. That's exactly what you need to think about. Stop your goddamn joking and come and get me.

I counted the five steps as Mercer walked up to the front door and reentered the cottage. Maybe it was my imagination but it seemed as though worms or spiders were crawling up the leg of my pants.

Minutes elapsed, and the frigid dampness continued to work its way into my bones. Now several people emerged from the house and stood on the porch, talking to one another before I heard one of them start down the steps.

Kathleen Bailey called out, 'We don't use it, actually. It's too damp to store things in. It's been empty for years.'

Footsteps rounded the far end of the cellar and stopped in front of the old entrance.

There were no voices this time. The latch was lifted and the door opened.

A man bent his shoulders to duck into the room. I tried to make sure it was Mercer but the slats were so narrow that all I could see was the sole of a large shoe and the dark leg of his trousers.

I braced my shoulders against the floor and pushed up with my hips. I knew that I had pulled the metal zipper of my ski jacket down to waist level when we had gone inside the cottage. I rubbed it as hard as I could against the plank above my stomach, creating the faint sound of a scratch. I whimpered through my gag.

The man standing over my head stopped and listened. He turned in place and kneeled, his ear placed against the boards beside me. I twisted again and gurgled a mixture of saliva and blood.

'I got you, Alex,' Mercer said. 'Hang tough, I'll get you out.'

Chapter 32

The technician pushed back the enormous shell of the MRI machine that had swallowed my entire body to take the images of my head and chest. 'You can open your eyes now. Was that okay for you?'

I had balked at the idea of going back inside such a confining enclosure, the sense of claustrophobia still over-whelming me after the morning's experience. I nodded without enthusiasm.

'What time is it now?' I asked, having spent a long afternoon in the emergency room, being examined and completing a battery of X-rays before this scan was ordered.

'Almost six o'clock.'

'Will I be discharged now that you're done?'

'Dr Schrem has admitted you, Miss Cooper.'

I sat up and retied the hospital gown. 'I'm really fine. The headache is practically—'

'It wouldn't be smart to let you go without observing you overnight,' he said, motioning me to sit in the wheelchair. 'You don't even know what the object was that hit you on the head. A mild concussion alone would bear watching.'

This was the wrong guy with whom to argue. He handed my record to an older gentleman whose sole job appeared to be to escort me from waiting area to waiting area within New York University's massive medical center. My driver took control of the handles and backed me through the double doors.

When they closed behind me and we started rolling down the corridor, Mike jumped off a gurney he'd been sitting on and grabbed the wheelchair handles.

'Look, I'm sorry I—'

'I don't even want to see you tonight, Mr Chapman. Get your hands off my wheels – I wouldn't trust you to drive me from here to the cafeteria. I can't believe that you went off and left me for dead. What were you thinking? Where's Mercer?'

'Right here, Alex,' he said, walking beside me and taking my hand in his. 'You know Mike isn't really a heartless son of a bitch. He's just not a first-grader like I am. Might need to send him back to the Academy for a refresher course in detection. Nobody was going to leave that park on my watch.'

'What's the room number, Pops?' Mike asked.

'Six-thirty. Elevator straight ahead.'

'I want a drink.'

'Not yet, kid. Doesn't mix with those painkillers the doc's got you on.'

'Why can't I just take the medications and go home?'

''Cause whoever tried to put a hole in that thick skull,' Mike said, 'left a sizable little lump that might have to be coated with peroxide if it sticks out any farther on your scalp. I just knew we'd get to play doctor together eventually.'

I looked up at Mercer. 'I'm not kidding. I really don't want him in my face all night. I don't want him anywhere near me. He's bad for my blood pressure.'

'You want an apology, blondie? That's what you want?'

'I want to be alone,' I said, Garbo accent and all.

We got on the elevator and rode it up to six while Mike chattered. 'You want me to flog myself and put on a hair shirt for not having had the good sense to think you were walled up behind a door or buried alive with a black cat. Right? It just goes to prove my theory that this would never have happened if you put on a little weight.'

'Shut him up, Mercer.'

'Fat people are harder to kidnap. Wouldn't you agree, Mr Wallace? You never read in the paper that the victim of an abduction weighed in at three-fifty. They're always skinny broads like you who get carted away. It's simply a fact, and you can do something about it for the future, young lady.'

We wheeled in front of the nurses' station and Mike put the brakes on the chair. He lifted a bouquet of flowers from the top of the desk and dropped to his knees in front of several doctors, nurses, and visitors who were passing by.

'Coop, as long as I live I swear I'll never walk out on you again. I'll never criticize your perfume or your heels or your hair color or your temper or—'

I unhitched the brake and pushed myself away from the onlookers toward the wing that corresponded to the room number I had been assigned.

'I'll stop to look under the bed and inside the closet and even rip up the floorboards next time I can't find you.'

'So much for my anonymity,' I said to Mercer, who

had taken charge of pushing me. 'If they didn't know who I was before I got up here, I guess they'll figure it out.'

A nurse followed us into the room. 'Need any help getting into the bed?' she asked, taking my chart from the bewildered escort. 'Stanley Schrem called. He'll be by for rounds later this evening.'

She waited until I settled back against the pillow and raised the bed's metal railing before she and the escort left the room.

'Feel good?' Mercer asked.

'Safe and soft and clean and better. I would not say that "good" is a word that comes to mind tonight.'

Mike was in the doorway. He must have stopped in every room along the way and cajoled patients out of their flowers. His arms were loaded with assortments — ten or twelve of them in a wild variety of colors — pulled from their vases and dripping water down the front of his clothes and onto the floor.

'I'm just a fool whose intentions are good,' he sang to me, crossing the room and laying the dozens of wet flowers across the crisp white sheets that covered my legs. 'Oh, Lord, please don't let me be misunderstood.'

'Misbegotten, misguided, misogynistic, misinformed,' I said. 'Just add misunderstood to your long list of "mis"es.'

I looked over at Mercer, who was leaning against the windowsill. 'So, the only person who knew we were going to be at the cottage was Zeldin. And I guess Phelps, the groundskeeper, must have heard him suggest it. And Gino Guidi. Maybe three people in the world. Doesn't that give you a head start?'

'Don't make yourself crazy tonight, Alex. We're working on it.'

'I've been inside that torture chamber, with clanging noises pounding at my aching head, pinched and prodded and observed by the entire ER staff. What else have I got to think about but who clobbered me and why? And what they were going to do when they came back for round two?'

'Zeldin and Phelps were in a meeting with a dozen other staffers from the time we left the gardens. Guidi's secretary is the one who dispatched Kathleen Bailey to be our guide. He was downtown all morning. She's not even sure she told him about it when he called in.'

'Well, is anybody going to tell me what happened to me?' I asked. 'And would you please take these back to the other patients, Mike? It smells like a funeral parlor in here.'

'I got a pizza on the way. Extra pepperoni, extra mushrooms, no anchovies. No worms, either. Special delivery. You'll be like new in no time,' he said, scooping the flowers off my legs and walking to the hallway.

'Soup,' I said to Mercer. 'A hot bowl of soup is all I want. And a drink.'

NYU Hospital was next door to the medical examiner's office. We had tested every deli and restaurant within sight of the morgue and I knew where the best chicken soup and the closest Dewar's could be found.

'The soup we can do. I think you're grounded on the alcohol.'

'I suppose they have to put a cop on my door, too?'

Mercer laughed. 'We're camping out with you.'

'You can't do that. It's ridiculous. I understand they have to station someone outside the room, but you guys can go home and get a good night's sleep.'

'Hush, Miss Cooper.'

'Now you'll make me feel guilty on top of feeling stupid.'

'Battaglia made a few calls. The room next door is empty. One of us will snooze in this chair and the other can stretch out in the bed. We'll take turns. Better us than some guy from the Thirteenth who doesn't know your favorite lullabies like we do.'

'Yeah, we get demerits when bad things happen on our shift,' Mike said, as he came back into the room. 'I'm already down points 'cause of your antics today.'

'I'm going to ask you again. What happened?'

Mike and Mercer looked at each other.

Mercer spoke first. 'The cops in the precinct think it was a prank. They—'

'A prank? Are they nuts? Haven't they ever read Poe?'

'Hear me out.' He stood up and walked to my bed, lowered the rail and sat beside me. 'There was a mugging down at the end of the park, in the playground behind the bandshell. A fifteen-year-old girl was watching over her kid brother and she got roughed up by some homies. Threw her down, snatched her wallet, touched some body parts they shouldn't have.'

'I heard the screams. I remember that much.'

'It was three guys, part of a gang. Wannabe baby Bloods. Punks from the 'hood who were just running around roughing folks up.'

'Were they caught?'

'Not yet. They scattered in different directions.'

'I saw one run across the street.'

'Yeah,' Mike said. 'He's the one I figured maybe you tried to follow.'

'The girl who was mugged – she knows who they are?'

Mercer smoothed the bedcover. 'She's not saying yet. She's got to live there on One Hundred Ninety-second Street without any protection – and she's smart enough to know that.'

'And what does that have to do with me?'

'The cops figure the gang was just wilding. While a few of them were causing trouble at the south end of the park, a couple of them saw you standing alone and—'

'I was alone for maybe sixty seconds.'

'It only took two to smack you over the head with a two-by-four.'

'Is that what it was?'

'There was one at the bottom of the front steps. It's at the lab now, being tested for blood and hair,' Mercer said. 'Then they carried you into the root cellar, tied your hands with your own scarf, gagged you, and tucked you under the boards.'

'How could they know? Why would they—'

'Trust me, Coop,' Mike said. 'It ain't nothin' they picked up spending time at the local library reading short stories. Ms Bailey says that root cellar is just an empty little room that's been an attractive local nuisance for ages. It's too damp to keep any of their supplies in, it's got no security, except when the entire park is locked at night. All those floorboards are loose – it's not like they were nailed down or anything. Hoodlums break in all the time to sit there and smoke dope. These kids just picked up a few planks and dropped you in to scare you to death.'

'And that part of it worked just fine. Tell them for me when you find them. What was I gagged with? And tied?'

'The gag was a sock,' Mike said.

'Just like Aurora Tait,' I said, thinking of our skeleton in the basement.

'Your scarf was around your hands. Really loose.'

'Loose to you, maybe. I'm telling you I couldn't move a muscle. Somebody put me in there to kill me.'

Mike looked at Mercer again.

'Don't treat me like a psycho, like I'm exaggerating this. Have they ever found anything under the floorboards there before?'

'Yeah. Dead animals. Half-eaten sandwiches. Weapons. It's a natural. It's like the local haunted house.'

'And you're going to tell me no one saw anybody lurking around the cottage before this happened, or running away from it afterwards?'

Mercer hesitated. 'We've got a 'scrip, actually. Two kids, probably part of the same gang that worked over the teenager.'

'Well, what's the description?'

'What's the difference if you never got a look at them?' Mike asked. 'You're not the one who's going to make an ID. The docs tell us even if you'd seen someone or heard them coming right before you got whacked on the head, the blow would have wiped out the short-term memory. You'd never call it up.'

'Who's the witness?' I asked.

'You know the rules.'

'Well, I can only hope it's not you,' I said to Mike. 'After today I would hate to have to rely on you for anything. And just for the record, I want the police reports to say that whoever stored me in that – that hole in the ground – was either leaving me there to die—'

'Yeah, right. With visiting hours just about to begin.'

'Or planning to come back and get me after dark and then take me somewhere to finish me off.'

'These kids wanted you to wiggle loose and pop out of your box right in the middle of some school tour and give the third-graders from the suburbs an urban legend to take home with them,' Mike said.

The phone rang. I stared at it and inched farther down in the bed. 'Who knows I'm here? I don't want to talk to anyone.'

'That's gonna be Sarah,' Mercer said. 'She's been concerned about you all day. I told her to wait until they got you into a room this evening before she called.'

I took the receiver after he answered for me. 'Do I still have a job?'

My loyal deputy had held down the fort for me through protracted trials, complicated investigations, and personal turmoil – or mental health days, as we liked to call them.

'How's the head?' It was good to hear the normalcy of Sarah's voice. 'You know I wouldn't get to throw my weight around at all if you were here at your desk every day. I'd written you off for the course of the Upshaw matter anyway. The boss wants you to stay out for another week, and I'm just adding my vote to his.'

We chatted for a few minutes, while Sarah assured me she was on top of everything that was pending. I thanked her for her friendship and hung up the phone.

By the time my doctor arrived, he had studied the test results and confirmed that I had neither fractures nor a concussion. If I was stable throughout the night, he would sign the release forms on his morning rounds.

Mercer called out for my soup while he and Mike were eating their pizza. We were waiting for the delivery when Mike turned the television on to catch the end of *Jeopardy!*

Trebek told us the final category was Famous Names.

'Level playing field,' Mike said. 'Twenty each?'

Mercer agreed.

'I'm not interested,' I said. Then I thought of my handbag. 'Did they get my pocketbook?'

'You left it locked in the car when we went into the cottage. Don't you remember?'

'Not really. I feel a little disoriented.'

'It's still there. How do you think I paid for dinner?' Mike asked.

'Great cartographer, born Gerhard Kremer in 1512, who coined the word "atlas" – after the mythical Titan he idolized – for his collection of world maps, renamed himself this,' Trebek said.

'Help yourself to another twenty. I'm out,' I said.

The three contestants drew the same blank I did.

'I guess Rand and McNally weren't born in 1512,' Mike said.

'Baby needs new shoes,' Mercer said, holding out his hand to Mike. 'Who was Mercator? Gerardus Mercator.'

'Sometimes you surprise me,' Mike said. 'The old man?'

Mercer's father had been a mechanic for Delta Airlines. 'He used to bring home maps all the time, so I could study the pilot's routes. Don't you guys remember Mercator's projections, with those rectilinear rhumb lines?'

'Sorry, Mercer. I'm fading on you.'

'I have one little present I've been saving,' Mercer said. 'Transit's got the MetroCard decoded – the one from the pocket of the Silk Stocking Rapist. They faxed it up to the office this afternoon. You'll have it tomorrow.'

'Any surprises?'

'Lexington Avenue subway. Seventy-seventh Street mostly. Just where we figured he was living or working. You can grid it out yourself when you get home. See if it tells you anything.'

By nine o'clock, I could barely hold my eyes open. The guys were playing gin at my bedside.

'Give in to it, Coop. You're whipped,' Mike said. He put down his hand and walked out to ask the nurse for my medications.

I was fighting sleep because I was terrified of my dreams. The pain had subsided but the feeling of being entombed infused every one of my senses. I ached to shut down my body and brain, but dreaded the nightmares to come.

The nurse came in with the white paper cup and dumped some pills into my hand. I didn't even ask what they were before I swallowed them.

Mercer stood up to pull the chain that turned off the light over my pillow.

'Leave it on, please,' I said.

He kissed the tip of my nose. 'I'll keep the one next to my chair on all night. I'm not going anywhere, Alex.'

I turned on my side and tried to get comfortable. Think wonderful thoughts, happy thoughts, my mother used to tell me as a child, when I awakened during the night. Then I would close my eyes and imagine myself walking on the beach with my father, holding his hand while he told me stories about his youth and his romance with my mother, or think of my last trip to my grandmother's farm, and how she indulged me whenever I visited there. Now I called up memories of the happiest events I could conjure, but they were interrupted by dark visions of the day barely over.

I remember opening my eyes, seeing Mike and Mercer engrossed in their card game, and closing them again. I felt the pills start to do their magic. I fell asleep.

It must have been seven o'clock when I awakened. The morning routine in a hospital never allows sleeping in. Nurses and aides changing shifts, meal trolleys carting forty trays down the hall, and janitors mopping floors overcame the strongest sleeping potions.

I stirred and looked up. Mercer and Mike were gone, but the deck of cards was on the table next to my water pitcher.

I sat up and outside the door of my room saw the back of a cop's uniform. The officer seemed to be dozing in his chair, his head hanging forward. I pushed down the bed railing and started toward him. He must have heard the noise and stood up immediately, walking into the room.

'Miss Cooper? Morning. I'm Gerry McCallion, from the Thirteenth—'

'Where's Wallace? Where's Chapman?'

'They were gone when I got here, about one A.M. Don't worry, ma'am. You were never alone. There was an interim shift—'

'I'm not worried about that. It's not like them to leave once they told me they'd be here.'

'It's the one from Homicide, Miss Cooper. Around midnight, he got a call with some bad news.'

'What—?'

McCallion spoke over me. 'His ladyfriend was in some kind of accident up in Canada. Broke her neck in a fall is what I was told. The girl is dead.'

Chapter 33

'Where are you?' I asked Mercer. 'Can you talk?'

'Yeah. I just stepped out of the car when my phone rang. Mike's out cold. He fell asleep about fifteen minutes ago. What time is it?'

'Almost eight o'clock. What happened? Where—'

'Val's brother called Mike on his cell phone. I had gone to the other room to put my head down for an hour or so – must have come in around twelve. This ski business, you know about it?'

'Val talked about it a bit. A helicopter flies them out somewhere in the wilderness, drops them on top of a mountain. Pure powder, that kind of thing. Experts only.'

'Yeah, well, one of the dangers is that those uncharted runs can be pretty unstable,' Mercer said, pausing. 'The group of them jumping, or something the chopper did letting them down, set off some kind of cataclysmic reaction.'

'She fell, is that what did it?'

'Three of them, Alex, they went off into a crevasse. The snow shifted and exposed an enormous break in the surface. Val and two others just – just went over the edge. Her brother was in the pack behind them. He watched it happen.'

I thought of the courage with which Valerie Jacobsen had fought to conquer the cancer that had ravaged her body, only to lose her life to a treacherous sport.

'This happened yesterday?'

'The day before. It took them twenty-four hours to recover the bodies.'

'And Mike only got the call last night? What are those people thinking? Don't they have any idea how much he loves her?'

'His fix on it? He's sure Val's parents didn't want him out there. I don't think they knew how serious the relationship was. He thinks they just didn't want to know.'

'The funeral?'

'First thing this morning. Nine o'clock, in Palo Alto. Family only. He couldn't have gotten there in time if he wanted to. Maybe they planned it that way.'

I always thought it was one of the things the Jewish religion dealt with best. Don't sit with the body in a room for a week. Get the burial done before the next day's sundown and then get on with the grieving. It was so at odds with the practices Mike had grown up with in the Catholic Church, and so foreign to his personal experience.

'There's going to be a memorial service in two weeks, according to the brother,' Mercer said. 'I'm telling you, Alex, Mike's in a blind rage. He doesn't know who to lash out at.'

'Where are you?'

'That's a good question,' Mercer said. 'Ever hear of Jamestown, Rhode Island?'

'Sure, right over the bridge from Newport. Why?'

'We're parked behind a gas station here,' Mercer

answered softly. 'We've been jackassing all over the place since we left Manhattan. It's like he's trying to find a piece of Val, something concrete to hang on to. I can't explain it any better than that.'

'But there?'

'When his phone vibrated, he left your room so he wouldn't wake you up. Of course, he had no idea who was calling or why. He came in and woke me up – must have been just after he got the news.'

'What'd he do?'

'He – he was just out of control. He was angry – he knew he had to get out of the hospital before he turned the place upside down. I'd say he was more furious than he was sad.'

'Mike will have all the time in the world to be sad.'

'Then he started calling the airlines. See what time he could get a flight. Val's brother called back to talk him out of that.'

'Have you stayed with him the whole time?'

'Most of it. He needed to go to Val's place. That's the first thing he wanted to do. And he wanted to go there alone. I thought he needed that.'

'I'm sure he did.'

'He was up there about an hour. When he came downstairs he told me he wanted to take a ride, to drive somewhere. He's got a pocketful of pictures of her and an armful of her favorite books. I told him he wasn't going anywhere without me.'

'Thank goodness.'

'Mike insisted on taking the wheel and I just let him do it. He went north up the Taconic Parkway for about an hour and a half, to some little inn where they'd spent the night once. Just parked in front, got out and walked around the grounds, without saying a word to me. Then he cut back across upstate New York to Connecticut, over to New Haven.'

Val's architectural firm had been working on Yale's master plan. He loved to look at the buildings, the physical structures she had envisioned and created. 'Yeah, they'd been up to the campus together a number of times.'

'When we hit I-95 at five this morning, I assumed we'd be headed south, back to the city. But he came up this way. They spent a weekend together here, at the wedding of one of Val's friends, last fall.'

'Mercer, I've got an idea. Jamestown isn't much more than an hour from the ferry. Take him to the Vineyard. I'll call my caretaker and he can run over and open the house by the time you get there,' I said, calculating the driving time plus the forty-five-minute boat ride from Woods Hole.

'I don't know, Alex. He's kind of flailing about. He doesn't know what—'

'Mike loves it there. And Val liked being there, too. There's a wonderful photograph of her in one of the guest rooms, from a day we spent at the beach. It's deserted this time of year. It's the most peaceful place on the face of the earth – and, well, there's something so spiritual about it. Besides, he can grieve any way he needs to without anybody getting in his way.'

'He doesn't know what he wants. He's just paralyzed with pain.'

I didn't speak for almost a minute. 'I know exactly how he feels, Mercer. You tell him I said that this is one thing I can help him with.'

Mercer and Mike knew all about Adam Nyman, my fiancé who had died the day before our Vineyard wedding, driving to reach the island.

'Yeah, but—'

'I can fly up through Boston and be there by early afternoon. I'm not supposed to be working today anyway, am I? It would be the perfect medicine for me, too.'

'He may fight me on this, Alex. All I can do is try.'

My suit was dirty and musty, but dry. I was dressed by the time Dr Schrem arrived and approved my release. 'Give it a few days before you go back to work,' he said. 'Bed rest, plenty of fluids, don't use the painkillers unless you absolutely need to. Going directly home?'

'Right now,' I said. He didn't know I meant Martha's Vineyard when I said 'home.'

Officer McCallion had orders to get an RMP to take me uptown to my apartment. On the way there, Mercer called to tell me that Mike agreed that some time on my secluded hilltop in Chilmark might help him deal with the tragedy that had taken Val's life and so violently disrupted his own.

I changed into jeans and a sweatshirt. I scrounged around in my dresser drawer for some cash, ID, and a credit card and called a car service to take me to La Guardia to catch the shuttle. I made the ten-thirty, landed at Logan within the hour, and was on a nine-seater Cape Air at noon. There were only two other passengers on the twin-engine prop plane, and the February headwinds tossed us around above the low clouds, slowing our speed so the trip across to the islands took almost fifty minutes.

Unlike the line of minivans that greeted planeloads of summer commuters, there was only one taxi awaiting incoming flights from Boston, New Bedford, and Hyannis. The driver agreed to make a stop while I ran into the up-island supermarket for some staples, then took me to my home, ten miles farther west to the most glorious part of the tranquil island.

Mercer heard the van pull in and came out to meet me.

'Where's Mike?'

'He can't be still. Got back in the car and drove up to the cliffs, I think. All he's had in the way of sleep was a twenty-minute nap after we gassed up this morning.'

The red cliffs of Aquinnah formed the most dramatic vista, high above the western tip of the island, overlooking the point where the Atlantic Ocean crashed against the Vineyard Sound. The ancient tribal home of the Wampanoag Indians, the open land and seemingly endless dunes stretched out to where the sea met the sky. I knew Mike would find his way up there, probably trespassing out onto the heights of the fragile clay, to sit and talk to Val.

'Let's go inside. The wind is vicious,' I said. 'Is Vickee okay with this?'

'You have to ask? Whatever Mike needs – those are my orders.'

'I'll just put my stuff away. Give me five.'

I closed the door behind me in the master bedroom and walked across the room to stare out at the view. The French doors look out over several acres of gently rolling hills, bordered by the handsome stone walls that ringed the entire property. Thick trunks of the sturdy bare trees dotted the horizon, all the way down to the bright blue choppy waters of Quitsa Pond and the sandy outline of the Elizabeth Islands' shore.

I had been standing here when my best friend and my mother broke the news of Adam's death to me, more than a decade ago. That moment had changed the island for me forever, and at the very same time made it even more important for me to savor its unique beauty and restorative power.

I freshened up, put the groceries away, and helped Mercer stack the logs to start a fire. It was three in the afternoon when Mike came back to the house.

I waited for him at the front door and held it open for him.

Mike walked past me, his jaw clenched and his face drained of all emotion. He touched my forearm as he whispered the word 'Thanks.' He had a terrible pallor, with patches of color only where the wind had whipped his cheeks and bitten at the surface of his hands for the last couple of hours. His thick, straight black hair was blown all over his head, and even when he ran his fingers to smooth it down, it remained out of place.

I followed him into the kitchen, where he helped himself to a can of soda from the refrigerator and held one out to me.

'Do you want to talk?'

'Not really,' he said. 'There isn't very much anybody can say that I want to hear.'

'You know that I adored—'

'I know.'

He walked into the living room, leaving me leaning against the counter. I went to my bedroom and made some calls – first to one of Mike's sisters to make sure the family knew what had happened, then to my friends – in the office and out – who had come to treasure his friendship.

I grabbed a pair of gloves for myself and a couple of Yankees caps that were in my closet and went into the living room, where the guys were sitting.

'Keep the fire burning, will you, please, Mercer? I'm going to Black Point, Mike. I'd like you to come with me.'

He looked up at the solid wooden beams in the tall ceiling. Anything to avoid me.

'C'mon. Let's take a walk.' I tossed one of the hats in Mike's lap.

He played with its brim without saying a word, then lifted it to his head and pulled it down, dipping it so that he didn't have to make eye contact with me.

'I'll drive,' he said.

'Can't do it except in my old Jeep.' He had been with me before to the private beach, more than a mile off the paved roadway, down a rutted dirt path that was inaccessible by sedans or sports cars. 'My wheels this time.'

We drove along South Road for miles – past sheep farms, a cemetery, and horse pastures – until we came to the turnoff to Black Point. Mike's head rested against the window, oblivious to the landscape around him.

There was nothing to mark the entrance, but I could have found the well-hidden access in my sleep. I had come here for solace whenever I needed some kind of comfort. I drove down the quiet road, kicking up dust all the way, finally reaching the old gate and stepping out to unlock it. I rounded the bend, scrubby brush giving way to the great expanse of wetlands. Tall brown grasses waved on the edges of the ice blue pond, backing up against the dunes, which dropped away to the fierce surf of the Atlantic.

I got out of the car and hiked the path alone, climbing the cut to the highest peak and sitting there, surveying the miles of clean white sand that reached out in both directions, as far as I could see. The whitecaps on the waves reminded me how rough the ocean could be, how its angry pounding against the shoreline seemed almost a reflection of Mike's mood.

The late-afternoon sun cast my shadow far out onto the sand. When Mike came up behind me minutes later, it threw his tall outline even farther toward the water than mine – two long black figures alone in their mourning on an isolated piece of one of the most beautiful beaches in the world.

I had come here with Nina the day that Adam died – to rage against his loss and to be in a place where we had always found serenity. With his family, soon after, I had scattered his ashes offshore at this very spot.

Mike stepped out of his loafers, took off his socks, and rolled up the legs of his jeans. The water was colder than I dared think, but I knew he wasn't feeling very much. For half an hour, he walked the shoreline until he was out of my sight and when he returned, his eyes were rimmed with red and swollen with tears.

He stood at the edge of the tide as it ran out and spoke to me for the first time since we left the house.

'She never caught a break. You know how it is? How certain people just carry some kind of curse with them from the moment they're born? They've got everything to live for but there's some relentless black cloud hanging right overhead? That was Val.'

'Think what she had with you this last year. Think what happiness you gave her.' I kicked off my moccasins and walked down to be next to him.

'Happiness? You know what a struggle it was for her to smile sometimes? You know what a triumph it was for her to be healthy again? You're sounding like her father – like all I was to her was the court jester, making sure she had a reason to laugh every single day she was alive.'

'Don't put me in his category. She told me what you meant to her on every level, and I know how very much she wanted to marry you.'

'I didn't realize she was that open about it,' Mike said, reaching down to pick up a rock. He pulled back his arm and heaved it into the ocean. 'And it was actually gonna happen, if you can believe it.'

'Val used to—'

'Don't say it. I don't want to talk about her now.'

'You *have* to talk about her, Mike. That's one thing you can still do for her. Talk about her and think about her every day of your life, from now on for as long as you live.'

He turned and started walking back down the beach away from me, weaving from exhaustion as he moved. 'It's too rough. I'd rather—'

'Of course it's rough. That's why you have to make yourself do it. Out loud – to people like me and like Mercer, who know what you meant to her.'

'I think of the fucking mutts I have to deal with every day of the week. People who kill and steal and maim for no reason at all. Scumbags who'd just as soon shoot you between the eyes as turn the other cheek. Bastards who'd rob and rape their own mothers without thinking twice. Assholes who skin cats and shoot dogs for sport. Any of them ever die young, Coop?' Mike was shouting now, trying to make himself heard over the breaking surf. 'Nope.

They'll outlive every guy you ever met in a white hat, every living soul who ever did a good deed for someone else. They've got something in their genes that not only produces an absolutely pure strain of evil, but also lets 'em thrive till they're a hundred and fifty.'

Mike stood in frigid water up to his ankles and threw another couple of rocks far out into the waves. 'That's what consumes me sometimes. All of these shitbirds who don't deserve to live, they're gonna be here long after we're gone. And that sweet, smart, strong kid I fell in love with didn't stand a fucking chance from the get-go.'

'You can't—'

'If you're gonna give me "life isn't fair," Coop, don't even open your mouth,' he said, reversing his trail. 'They're giving heart transplants to prison inmates now, you know that? Did you ever hear of anything more fucking stupid than that? You need a liver or a kidney or a new pair of eyeballs, you could be up for sainthood alongside Mother Teresa but you still gotta get in line behind some serial killer in San Quentin or a pedophile up in Attica.'

He leaned over to pick up a piece of driftwood and began to trace something in the sand. It was a building, a childlike imitation of a skyscraper. 'Can you imagine what it is to leave a legacy like that, something that you've built from nothing but your imagination and raw talent? I'd stand in front of these – these magnificent structures – things that Val had conceived from a drawing on a piece of paper and then seen through to the final construction. Do you know how much joy it gave her to create things like that, things that people will look at and live in and enjoy for generations?

'Me? I run around locking up bad guys like it makes

a difference to anybody. Like there isn't gonna be another son of a bitch to come along to fill the vacuum before I even have the cuffs on tight. Then one of your cowardly colleagues gives 'em cheap pleas and they're back on the sidewalk a few years later, sticking needles in their arms and killing anybody that looks at 'em cross-eyed. Why do we bother? Why do we keep on doing it?'

He knew the answers as well as I did. There was no reason for me to speak.

Mike turned and climbed up to the top of the dune, sitting down in the middle of the path that led down the other side. He stared out at the distant horizon, the seamless line between the ocean and the sky. 'I understand why you come back to this place.'

I slowly moved up toward him, trying to get a foothold in the shifting sand.

'I used to look at you, back when we first started working together,' Mike said. 'I'd heard about – about what happened to Adam from the guy you shared an office with. I used to look at you and wonder how you handled the grief at that young age, when you seemed to have everything else going for you. I used to try to figure out how you got up in the morning and got on with your life. I didn't know why you gave a damn about all the needy derelicts who showed up on your doorstep, why you cared about helping any of them when you could have slammed the door behind you and walked away from it all.'

'You think I didn't wallow in my own self-pity for months? You think the thoughts I had were any different than what you're going through this very minute?'

I reached out my hand and Mike extended his, to pull me up next to him.

'You didn't want to close your eyes in the hospital because you were afraid of your dreams, your nightmares,' he said. 'Me? I wouldn't mind dreaming. The dreaming's gonna be all I have left. It's knowing that every time I wake up and open my eyes, my first thought will be Val, my first image will be that broken little body that fought so hard to make it.'

I stood behind him, my hands on his shoulders. He didn't brush them away, so I squatted and began to gently knead them.

'How long, Coop? You got a smart answer for everything. You got an answer for that, for how long it takes?'

'Longer than you can even begin to imagine,' I said. I talked to him about emptiness and unfairness and profound unhappiness. I told him about the darkest thoughts I had confronted and the hardest things I ever had to do in the face of my despair.

'And it stops? You're gonna tell me that someday this pain just stops?'

'It's going to be with you forever, Mike. Just like you said. Before your eyes open in the morning – every single morning – you'll be stabbed in the heart by some memory of Val the second you're even conscious. The first moment you have a thought, it's going to be Val,' I said, pausing and backing away a bit. 'And then one day – maybe eight months, maybe a year from now – you'll wake up one day and you'll think of something you forgot to do the night before, someone you have to call about a case, some problem you promised to take care of for your mother. Some really trivial thing.'

I stood up, ready to turn and go. The sun had almost disappeared and the temperature was dropping.

'That's the day you're going to hate yourself most – the first time something sneaks into your consciousness before Val does. You'll be angrier at the world than you are right now. Mad at yourself, too, for letting it creep in there. But then it will happen again, more and more often. And each time it does you'll despise yourself for betraying Val's memory with such insignificant thoughts. Until some very distant day, inconceivable now, when the memories assume a balance of some kind, when they bring pleasure with them almost as often as they cause pain.'

'That doesn't seem possible to me,' Mike said, standing and brushing the sand off the seat of his jeans. 'I don't think I can deal with it.'

'Nobody does. Nobody wants to.'

'You come out here to be near him, don't you? You feel closer to Adam when you're here.'

I didn't answer.

'The heavens, the ocean, sand for as far as the eye can see – and not another person around,' he said. 'Makes you pretty conscious of your own mortality.'

He reached into his pocket, removed a black velvet pouch, and handed it to me.

'Open it. Go ahead.'

I untied the drawstring and turned it upside down in my hand. Out slipped a diamond ring – a slim gold band with a small brilliant stone in a classic round setting.

'It's very beautiful,' I said, holding it up and watching the gem sparkle, reflecting against the shimmering surface of the water. 'Did Val—?'

'Nope. A surprise,' Mike said. 'Valentine's Day. I had it up on a shelf in her bedroom closet that she couldn't reach.'

No wonder he'd been so short of money these past two months.

He took the ring from me and loped down the dune toward the edge of the water. I called out after him but I knew there was no way to stop him. I watched as Mike waded into the frigid surf, drew back his arm, and hurled Val's ring into the riptide that was sucking the waves out to sea.

Chapter 34

None of us felt much like eating dinner.

More than the landscape and the foliage change when winter comes to Chilmark. Not only the general store closes, but so does every up-island restaurant and inn. No fried clams at The Bite, no lobster rolls at The Galley, no shore dinners at The Homeport, no conch fritters at Cornerway, and no harpooned sword from Larsen's. There was always some clam chowder in the freezer, and I defrosted it for the three of us. Mike barely played with it while we tried to distract him with memories of weekends and evenings that all of us had spent together.

Mike stood up from the table, walked to the bar, and opened the liquor cabinet. He closed it and turned to Mercer. 'I'm not gonna drink. It's too easy to get through it that way. Feel like a walk?'

They let themselves out the back door and went off in the dark. I took a book into the living room, added some logs to the fire, and poured myself the drink that Mike had rejected. It was almost ten o'clock by the time they returned.

Mike warmed himself in front of the fireplace for a few minutes before telling us he was going to try to get some rest. He and Mercer clasped each other in an embrace and then Mike grabbed the banister and pulled himself up the stairs.

'I think he's worn himself out enough so that he may actually sleep a few hours,' Mercer said, joining me with a glass of vodka.

'Did he talk?'

'Enough. You know he was prepared for, well – the worst – a year ago, when Val's treatments weren't going well. With the cancer in remission, this hit him like such a bolt of lightning I'm afraid it's going to set him back twice as hard.'

'What time do you want to head home?' I asked.

'Grab a ferry late morning, if we can. Be in the city by six.'

'Did you reach Lieutenant Peterson this afternoon?'

'Yeah. You and I have some catching up to do this weekend. We've lost Mike for the rest of this one.'

'I've been making a list,' I said, ticking off names with each finger of my left hand. 'I'm sure Peterson has, too. We've got to sit down with Professor Tormey, now that we know what the Raven Society is. I'm going back at Gino Guidi, whether or not Ellen Gunsher has been able to rework a deal with his lawyer.'

'You guys never got to talk to him about Poe, and there he is, a major benefactor of the cottage.'

'Well, we didn't know it at the time. And Emily's pal Teddy Kroon still has questions to answer, as far as I'm concerned.'

'It's not the right moment to bring this up with Mike,' Mercer said, 'but you were with him when he went to that retired cop's apartment, weren't you?'

'Aaron Kittredge? Yeah.'

'Mike had asked the lieutenant to get his departmental file. The loo filled me in on that today. Kittredge is my first priority when we get back.'

'Why?'

'He left the department without a pension. Had to sue to get it reinstated.'

'He told us that. You got the back story?'

'Rubber gun squad,' Mercer said. 'Got dumped to Central Park.'

Trigger-happy cops were relieved of their weapons while the shootings they were involved in were investigated. Those who weren't indicted, but who weren't completely exonerated either, wound up flopped into some uniformed assignment where little harm could come to people in their way. Central Park was one such holding zone – very few human residents, with only squirrels and pigeons to endanger.

'Who'd he shoot?' I asked.

'Think of the story that Zeldin and Phelps told us.'

'Of course,' I said, closing my book. 'Ten years ago – the cop on his way into the Botanical Gardens to talk to Zeldin. Shot a neighborhood kid in the back. Why the hell was he going to see Zeldin in the first place? That had to be at least ten years after Kittredge met Emily Upshaw, so what's the connection? What's the renewed interest in Poe, assuming that's what he was going to Zeldin's about?'

'I've been spinning with that one all afternoon. You with me? We'll get to Kittredge first thing Sunday morning.'

Mercer said good night and went upstairs to his room.

I turned on the television to watch the late news before going to sleep. Mike's devastating loss had taken my mind off what had happened to me yesterday. My headache had been replaced by a dull throb.

I could smell the coffee brewing shortly before 7 A.M. I asked Mercer to have the transit department's report from the rapist's MetroCard faxed to the house, so I could play with it on the long car ride home. The three of us moped around before driving to Vineyard Haven to get on the short standby line for the ferry. By one-fifteen, we were on Route 8, headed for I-95.

Stretched out on the rear seat, my ski jacket pillowed under my head, I unfolded the papers from Transit SIB – the Special Investigations Bureau – and began to scan the report.

The MetroCard had been purchased on January 3, a little over a month ago. It was sold at a newsstand on Fifty-ninth Street. Unfortunately for us the buyer paid cash. A credit card imprint might have solved the case nicely.

I leaned a pad against my right knee, to chart the man's movements. Between eight and eight-thirty every weekday morning, he boarded the downtown Lex at Seventy-seventh Street. I drew a star at that intersection, just a few blocks west of the location of all the attacks. In the evenings between six-thirty and seven o'clock, most of the return trips were from the East Fifty-first Street station, a commercial area surrounded by financial institutions as well as offices and stores of every kind.

There were several random rides, some late-evening trips home, where he boarded the train close to midnight. I would have to compare these dates against the crime occurrences, to see whether he was prowling the neighborhood close to the times of the attacks.

There was only one anomaly.

'Hey, Mercer. The snowstorm two weeks ago, do you remember what night it was?'

'It was a Monday. I don't remember the date but it was my RDO' – police jargon for regular day off – 'and I was home after the weekend. Why?'

'Give me a minute.'

Mercer's Metro man had followed his usual route in the morning, going back uptown from Fifty-first Street a bit earlier than usual, at five-thirty in the afternoon. An hour later, he got on the southbound train again at Seventy-seventh Street.

At ten that same evening, the rider took his first bus ride using this pass. All his other travel had been in the tube. He boarded the M2 on First Avenue, scanning the MetroCard in at the Forty-fourth Street stop.

All the details began to click into place. The secure residence on the Upper East Side; the physical description of the clean-cut, well-spoken assailant; Annika's good ear – picking out a single word that sounded like the accent of an upper-class British student; a rapist who disappeared from the city – perhaps the country – for four years before returning; a compulsive criminal whose DNA didn't seem to be in any data bank in America; and a MetroCard from the perp's pocket that suggested he entered a bus in front of the only buildings that stand on the east side of First Avenue and Forty-fourth Street.

'John frigging Doe. You want to nail the bastard, Mercer? Call the squad and get somebody over to the United Nations stat. Find out whether there was a reception, a speech, a party – whatever was going on the night of that storm. Get the list of whoever attended – spouses, children, staff. Get the address of every ambassador and delegate who lives in Manhattan.'

Mercer was watching me in the rearview mirror, smiling for the first time in two days.

'Take it to the bank, gentlemen. John Doe is the son of an African diplomat.'

Chapter 35

Mike didn't even seem to be listening to me.

Mercer was interested in my idea. 'Break it down for me, Alex.'

'We're talking about the comfort zone of the perp, right? We've been looking at black men who work on the Upper East Side – restaurants, hospitals, high-rise buildings. Clerical jobs, dishwashers, janitorial staff, and all the other menial positions. Now think about how many of the diplomatic corps and consulate employees associated with the United Nations live in town houses in the exact same neighborhood. Do you have any idea how many African diplomats and their families are living there?'

'The map has changed so many times since I was in college, I'm embarrassed to say I can't even tell you how many countries are in the UN.'

'Coop's stretching on this one,' Mike said.

'Maybe so. Maybe I'm too high up the ladder, but these missions all have big staffs, and most staff members have families here, even U.S. nationals who live in the zone.'

'What else?' Mercer said. 'I better give our profiler a nudge. See if he's ready with his geographic jeopardy spot, and if your theory works with it.'

'This guy is well dressed and carefully groomed. If you trust Annika, he may even have been educated in England, like so many families from the territories of the former British Empire,' I said. 'That one little word she picked up had me thinking this guy didn't learn English in America. It fits so well with a connection to the UN.'

'That could be why his DNA isn't in any data bank in the States.'

'I'm figuring it can't be an ambassador or high-ranking diplomat himself, just 'cause the age we're going for is too young for that,' I said. 'But suppose his father is posted here. The son gets a job as an investment banker – an office on Park that fits with the subway stop on East Fifty-first Street and with hanging out at the bar at Primola with a handful of yuppies, yapping on their cell phones the night Giuliano made him.'

Mercer picked up the thread. 'Maybe someone on the father's staff got wise to the fact that the kid's got a problem. Maybe even tags his comings and goings to the nights of the attacks, back four years ago when the newspaper coverage was saturating the city. Shows Papa the sketch that was plastered all over the East Side and that convinces the father to send him back to the mother country.'

'The rapes stop happening for a few years. The father doesn't have any reason to know the pathology of a rapist. Figures his son has outgrown the problem and decides it's time to ease his way back into town,' I said.

'That's a lot of data to read into a few MetroCard entries, but it makes as much sense as every other shadow we've been chasing. I'll get on it tomorrow.'

It was after 7 P.M. when the guys dropped me at my

apartment. We had talked Mike into taking time off, spending a few days with Val's brother when he came into town to close up her apartment at the end of the week. I had never seen him look as lost as he did when the car pulled away from my building, and I wondered when I would hear from him again.

There were so many messages of concern about Mike on my answering machine that it had run out of space. I played them all back and settled in to return some of the calls.

The last conversation was with Joan Stafford, who adored Mike and spent some portion of each of our daily phone calls inquiring about him. I didn't repeat everything that had happened during the last few days, but I confided in her about the engagement band that Mike had heaved into the ocean.

'Did you know he had bought Val a ring?'

'Not until he put it in my hand. I – uh, I hadn't really thought he was that close to a proposal. He seemed like the last guy in the world to make that kind of commitment.'

'Yeah, it would have changed everything between the two of you. The way you work together, the way he protects you, the joking—'

'That's just ridiculous. His marriage was bound to have happened sooner or later. It wouldn't have made the least bit of difference on the job. Look at the way Mercer and Vickee have got it together. We're still—'

'It's me you're talking to, sweetie. Didn't the sight of that ring make you just a little bit jealous?'

'Jealous? Are you crazy, Joan? My heart just breaks for Mike, seeing him like this.' I tried to sort through my

323

emotions and reassure myself that one of my very closest girlfriends hadn't seen something more clearly than I had.

'He's going to need you to get him through this.'

'Right now he's pushing everyone away. I don't even know how to begin to help him.'

'Trust me, Alex. When he's ready for a shoulder to lean on, it's going to be yours.'

I called P. J. Bernstein's deli to get the last delivery at nine o'clock, and ate half a turkey sandwich before abandoning it in favor of a comforting bath.

I ran the water steaming hot and filled it with a fresh-scented bubble bath. I poured myself a scotch, then stopped in the den to look at my bookshelves. There was an old volume of Poe – not the stories, just the collected poems – and I pulled it down to take with me as I soaked and sulked.

My mood was maudlin. I couldn't blame Mike for shutting me out, yet it was difficult to be kept at arm's length when he was so very alone. He would have to go through much of his grieving by himself, and I understood that completely.

I turned up the jets on the whirlpool and started flipping the pages. So many of the poems were written to dead and dying women – various names, all meant to be Poe's Virginia – and so many had as their theme the loss of a loved one. I started to read them aloud, one by one, matching the somber cadences to my mood.

I finally came to 'The Raven.' It had been years since I had read the poem in its entirety. The editor of the anthology had written an introduction, proclaiming that this work had made an impression that had probably never been surpassed by any single piece of American poetry.

More than one hundred and fifty years had gone by since its publication. Reflecting on it, I viewed that a stunning fact.

I loved the poem – everything about it. The tale of the young man, devastated by his lover's death, visited on a bleak winter night by the stately ebony bird. The fact that the bird could talk (Poe eventually described in an essay his plan to use a creature that was nonreasoning but capable of speech). The pulsating rhythm of the stanzas building as the narrator recognizes the torture of his fate, realizing that he will not find peace in forgetting his beloved. And of course, the haunting refrain of the raven's taunting reminder – 'Nevermore.'

At the end of the poem there was a note, reminding the casual reader that Poe considered his bird 'the emblem of mournful and never-ending remembrance.'

I thought of all the deaths that had occurred in this last week – unnatural and unnecessary, each of them – and closed the book.

I dried off and got into bed, reading myself to sleep.

We had no idea what kind of schedule Aaron Kittredge kept, so Mercer had offered to pick me up at six-thirty on Sunday morning. We drove to the block where he lived, on West End Avenue, and parked at a hydrant in front of the stoop, waking ourselves up slowly with coffee from the corner bodega.

For almost an hour we talked about Mike and Valerie. Mercer had left him at his own apartment last night, and one of his sisters was waiting there. She had arranged to take him out to see his mother and spend the rest of the weekend with his family.

At seven-thirty sharp, I saw Kittredge come out of the

building and trot down the steps. Both of us got out of the car and I called his name.

He turned his head toward me but kept walking away, swinging his gym bag. I went after him, trying to keep up with his pace.

'Mr Kittredge, I've got to see you.'

'Another day. I'm late.'

'I need twenty minutes.'

'I told you what I know. Yesterday's news. Lay off me.'

Joggers and dog walkers were interested in the scene. I dodged between them.

I called out a single word: 'Ratiocination.'

Kittredge stopped and turned around. 'Now there's a word I haven't heard in a very long time. Who's your side-kick this time?' he asked. 'You trade in the wise-mouth for the strong, silent type?'

'Mercer Wallace, Special Victims.'

'Let's take this conversation off the street,' he said, removing his keys out of his pocket and leading us back to his apartment.

He let us inside and motioned us to sit in the living room, while he opened the bedroom door and whispered something – probably explaining our presence – to the girlfriend.

Kittredge didn't know what to make of us. 'So what's this? The book club of the Manhattan DA's office? Or are you reading fiction now to try to find out how to solve cases?'

He poured himself a cup of coffee but didn't offer any to us.

'Can we start with Emily Upshaw again?' I asked.

'Suit yourself.'

326

'The story she told you when you first met her, about the boyfriend who claimed to have killed a girl?'

'Yeah?'

'The day I was here with Mike Chapman, Edgar Allan Poe's name didn't come up in that conversation. What I want to know is whether Emily ever mentioned that she thought the murder she was telling you about had anything to do with Poe.'

He shook his head. 'You know what kind of reception she got from the desk sergeant when she walked in the station house and started talking about a woman holed up alive behind a wall of bricks? Nobody thought she was wrapped too tight. The last thing I think she woulda done is make literary allusions to try to impress a bunch of harebag cops.'

'But you,' I asked, 'when she spent time with you, didn't she mention it?'

'Emily introduced me to Poe. That was much later on, though, when she was hanging out here, trying to get her act together.'

'And was it in the context of this murder her boyfriend had told her about?'

'I guess it was. You know the short stories?'

'Some of them,' I said.

'I'd never known any of them. Emily had an anthology. She made me read a few tales – "The Cask of Amontillado," "The Black Cat."'

'Both of those are about people who were bricked up alive. Didn't that make you take her more seriously?'

'Me? Hey, Ms Cooper,' he said, refilling his mug. 'I may have been the only guy in town who gave her the time of day. Quite frankly, between the booze and the blow she ingested, and the fact that there was no missing victim and no crime scene, even though I tried to help her at first, I began to think she was just lifting the crap she was telling me right out of the fiction she liked to read.'

'But you must have gotten enough into Poe's work to become interested in ratiocination, didn't you?'

'What makes you think so?'

'Your visit to the New York Botanical Gardens, Mr Kittredge,' I said. 'Your meeting – or your aborted visit – with a man called Zeldin.'

Kittredge put the coffee down in the sink and bent his head before turning back to me.

'I guess the department spit up the old story to you. Is that fool still around?'

'You want to tell us why you wanted to see Zeldin?' Mercer asked. 'Did it have anything to do with Emily Upshaw?'

'She'd been out of the picture for a decade when that shooting happened,' Kittredge said, thinking for a minute before he spoke. 'I guess you're right, in a sense. Emily had nothing to do with it directly, but she left that book of short stories here. I picked it up about ten years later, when someone told me it was Poe who wrote the first detective stories in literature.'

'Emily hadn't talked about those?' I asked.

'Nah. She was interested in the bizarre and macabre. It was "The Murders in the Rue Morgue" that got me hooked.'

'On what, the techniques of Monsieur Dupin?' I asked, referring to Poe's amateur sleuth.

'I liked a character that used his brain to solve crimes.'

'But he ridiculed the Parisian police, didn't he?'

'He thought like a detective. It fascinated me. You know the others?'

'Poe's other detective stories? Only that there are three that feature Auguste Dupin,' I said.

'Yeah. "The Purloined Letter" and "The Mystery of Marie Roget,"' Kittredge said. 'What most people don't know is that Marie Roget was based on a real case – on a murder that occurred in New York. You knew that?'

'I had no idea. I mean, if I remember correctly, he makes a reference to coincidences between his story and an actual murder here, but I assumed that was just a fictional device to hook the reader.'

'It made me curious, so I looked it up. There was no cold case unit at the time, and it was before I'd started painting. I just thought it would be interesting to take a stab at the original case, since it had never been solved.'

'But it must have happened over a hundred—'

'Eighteen forty-one. So what? People are still trying to figure out who Jack the Ripper was, aren't they? Who killed Cleopatra? Was Alexander the Great murdered?'

'Who was the victim?' I asked.

'Mary Rogers,' he said, smiling. 'Poe just added a French accent and moved her to Paris.'

'And she was a shopgirl, too?'

'She worked in a tobacconist's store, selling cigars, down on Broadway near Thomas Street,' Kittredge said. 'Right up the street from where police headquarters and your office stand today.'

'And are the facts similar?'

'Pretty close. The beautiful Miss Rogers failed to return home one evening. There was no such thing as a missing persons bureau, so her family put an ad in the New York *Sun*, asking for information about her disappearance. A few days later – bingo.'

'They found her?'

'Raped, beaten, strangled to death with a piece of lace from her petticoat. Somebody came upon her body in the Hudson River, on the other side, right near Hoboken.'

'How'd she get there?' I asked.

'Mary probably took the ferry over with a suitor. There was a kind of lovers' lane then, called the Elysian Fields.'

How ironic that the place in Greek mythology where those blessed by the gods went after death – the eternal ideal of happiness – became the murder scene for a beautiful young woman, forever memorialized in Poe's story.

I thought of the solution that Poe had worked in his brilliant tale of deduction. 'Was it a sailor who killed Mary Rogers?'

'Some thought that,' Kittredge said. 'There was a rock tied around her waist to weigh her down, and it was made with a sailor's knot. But nobody was ever caught.'

'You have any theories?' I asked.

'Did you know there were people who speculated that Edgar Allan Poe was the killer?'

I was shocked. 'You must be joking.'

'He had enemies, Ms Cooper. Lots of enemies.'

'Yes, but—'

'This was a new form of fiction – the detective story – so some journalists misunderstood it. Thought it displayed an unnatural obsession with the crime. Poe himself was known by many to be an odd young man – personally antagonistic, frequently drunk and depressed, with a chronically sick wife who couldn't have offered him much social companionship. He was known to take long, rambling walks in the woods, ferry rides across the river. The story he wrote had the most incredible detail about the murderer and his methods – things that had never been printed in the newspapers.'

'That's hardly enough to link him to killing someone.'

'And the bottle of laudanum found near Mary's parasol and scarf? Poe was well-known for his flirtation with opium, in all its forms.'

'Not all that unusual at the time.'

'Yeah, Ms Cooper. But put those coincidences together with the fact that he knew Mary Rogers, that maybe she trusted him enough to go—'

'Wait,' I said. 'Poe actually *knew* the dead girl?'

'James Fenimore Cooper, Washington Irving – and yeah, Edgar Allan Poe – they were all her customers at the little cigar shop. If I were investigating this case today, I'd have to say Eddie is someone I'd want to talk to. A person of interest.'

'So at some point you made a phone call to Zeldin. Was it about Mary Rogers?'

'Yeah. I'd been online doing research, and also up at the public library on Forty-second Street. Half of the articles I read mentioned this Zeldin character. Makes himself out to be the world's leading expert on Poe. I called him and asked if I could talk to him.'

'And he invited you there, to the Bronx?'

'Yeah, to the snuff mill,' Kittredge said, turning his attention to Mercer. 'You ever smell a setup, Detective? Ever walk into a trap?'

'That's what you think happened?'

Kittredge had been hostile when Mike and I first

encountered him, but had warmed considerably when talking about Poe. Now he took on the appearance of a paranoid personality, his eyes flashing between us to see if we credited what he was saying. He fidgeted with everything on the countertop, playing with a pack of cigarettes and twisting a napkin till it shredded in his hands.

'Cost me my job and almost my pension. Somebody set me up.'

'In what way?' I asked.

'I was jumped by a pack of kids outside the gate.'

'Yeah?'

'They were waiting there for me. Someone must have told them what kind of car I was driving, what I looked like, and that I had a gun.'

'How do you know that?'

''Cause they were yelling to each other when they knocked me to the ground – one was calling out the orders to find the gun. Those kids had no other reason to be there.'

'They worked at the gardens, I thought.'

'You thought wrong. Two of them used to work there a few years back. These kids all had addresses in Queens. None of them had anything to do with that neighborhood the night this went down.' Kittredge fired the words at me.

'Were they armed?' I asked.

'They had knives. All of them had knives,' he said, pushing up his jacket and shirtsleeve in search of a scar to display. 'Then one of them got my gun.'

Mercer pressed on. 'But it was one of the kids who got shot, wasn't it?'

'I carried a second pistol on my ankle. An old habit,

Detective, from working narcotics. They didn't find that one.'

I wasn't a fan of the nuts on the force who thought one gun wasn't enough to do the job.

'Was the boy shot in the back?' Mercer asked, having the good sense to leave out the question of the distance for the moment.

Kittredge walked to the sink, his back to us, and turned on the faucet, running water and rinsing his mug. 'Who told you so? That crackpot Zeldin? He's the one that didn't want me in there to begin with. He probably set the whole thing up.'

I glanced at Mercer. Kittredge spotted me and called me on it. 'You think I'm making this up, huh?'

'No. No, I don't. I can't imagine a reason someone would invite you there, but then not let you in.'

He walked toward me and pointed a finger in my face. 'Before you go thinking I'm some kind of psycho, spend a little more time checking out that group of screwballs.'

'I assume you've already done that, Mr Kittredge. That's why we're here.'

'I knew what the rumor was. Zeldin probably thought I was there to investigate him and his cronies. The Raven Society or whatever they called themselves.'

'What—?'

'After I got jammed up I didn't give a damn. I didn't care about police work – real or fictional. I started taking art classes for therapy. Anger management,' Kittredge said, waving his arm around at the various incarnations of his favorite nude. He was wild-eyed now that we had stirred up these unpleasant memories.

'But what was the rumor about Zeldin? I don't know what you mean.'

'Not just him. His whole little secret society. For somebody who thinks she's pretty smart, you don't really know much about this, do you?'

'I'll take all the help you can give me.'

'A very select membership, with very special rules. There are people who believe, Ms Cooper, that if you want to be admitted to the Raven Society, you have to have killed someone,' Kittredge said, walking to the door of his apartment and opening it, to signal the end of our meeting. 'You have to have taken a page out of Edgar Allan Poe.'

Chapter 36

'Ready to give up on this?' Mercer asked. 'I know you'd rather be curled up at home with the crossword puzzle.'

'Time to pull out that list of names again and see what kind of birds these ravens really are before we keep ruffling their feathers. C'mon, we've got places to go and people to see.'

We were back in the car by nine and Lieutenant Peterson was beeping Mercer. He returned the call and gave me the news.

'Loo can't raise anyone over at the UN on a Sunday. Thinks we ought to drop in and start the ball rolling. You got his attention with this diplomatic mission connection to a suspect.'

The Sunday-morning ride back through Central Park and over to the FDR Drive was quick. The February chill was powerful as we drove south along the East River. We passed under the Roosevelt Island tram cables, and I avoided glancing off to my left at the elegant remains of the old Blackwell Hospital site that sat on the island's southern tip – the scene of a case we had worked several years back.

Mercer turned off the highway at Forty-eighth Street

and squared the block to come around in front of the vast complex that fronted on First Avenue. After the Second World War, when every large American city was competing to host the headquarters of a new international organization to replace the League of Nations, the deal was clinched for New York by John D. Rockefeller, Jr's gift of $8.5 million which allowed the purchase of seventeen prime acres of real estate in midtown Manhattan's Turtle Bay.

The United Nations opened for business in 1950 with the completion of the now familiar tall and sleek Secretariat Building – our destination this morning – followed later by the General Assembly and conference buildings.

As Mercer shut off the engine and stuck his laminated parking plaque in the car's windshield, we were both conscious of the fact that the UN, technically, was not within the jurisdiction of the United States. It had its own police force and post office, and operated with a unique set of rules and regulations.

Forty minutes later, passing through layer upon layer of internal security, we presented ourselves to the second assistant to the chief of protocol for the United States mission, the duty officer in charge on a quiet Sunday morning.

Ralph Barcher wanted to know more about our inquiry. Mercer told him only that we were at the preliminary stage of an investigation that was confidential, but might involve an employee or relative of someone assigned to the world peace organization. Barcher balked at the idea of releasing any information to us without permission from the protocol chief himself.

'Why don't you phone him?' I asked. 'I'll be happy to explain what we need.'

He looked at his watch and thought better of placing the call. 'You know you can go to our website and get a listing and mission location for every member state,' Barcher said, somewhat nervously.

'You can be sure we'll do that. But it's the home addresses and contacts that I want as well.'

'Don't you understand the security issues we have when it comes to the release of that sort of personal data, Miss Cooper?'

'We'll be sensitive to those, of course. We represent the two most important law enforcement agencies in the city. We're not terrorists. Who's the chief?'

'Waxon. Darren Waxon.'

'That must be a recent promotion. I did some work for him when he was the deputy, just six months ago,' I said. 'I can't imagine he won't be willing to help us.'

My unit was frequently called for help in training the staff of foreign missions that came to this country with a myriad of clashing cultural values. We had stepped in to prosecute a tribal leader who had brought the horrific practice of female genital mutilation from his sub-Saharan hut to West 112th Street, counseled rape survivors attacked by opposition rebel troops in Eastern European civil wars, intercepted teens brought from Southeast Asia in juvenile sex slave practices, and handled domestic violence incidents for women from countries in which they were still treated as the property of their spouses, even though they were married to businessmen and not camel herders.

'I'm afraid that since you won't brief me on what you're

going to do with these names, there'll be nothing Mr Waxon can help you with either.'

'Look, I can't tell you exactly what case we're working on, but you can see from our business cards we're both assigned to highly sensitive matters. We don't intend to embarrass anyone.'

Barcher reexamined the cards we had handed to him.

'I suppose, Miss Cooper,' he said flatly, 'that you've given some thought to the concept of diplomatic immunity.'

'You're really jumping the gun. To tell you the truth, that hadn't crossed my mind yet. I'm not even close to saying that you're going to hand us a crime suspect on a silver platter. We'd just like to make sure we don't ignore any possibilities.'

Mercer tried to be helpful. 'Maybe Ms Cooper didn't make herself clear. We're not looking at any of your ambassadors here as a target. What we're doing might eliminate the chance of drawing your people into the investigation.'

'What do you know about immunity, Detective Wallace?'

'Not much.'

'It's an ancient principle of international law, sir. It dates from the early Greeks, who allowed messengers and envoys to travel freely through neighboring countries, so they weren't subject to punishment, even when they carried bad news.'

'That was then,' Mercer said.

It seemed so unnatural not to have Mike at my side. I smiled just thinking of his typical comeback. He probably would have told Mr Barcher that the Greeks had left us a legacy of some other interesting habits, too.

'Same theory as today. Representatives of foreign government officials are exempted from the jurisdiction of local courts and authorities. They're allowed to operate under the laws of their own countries.'

'That extends to their families, too?' Mercer asked.

Barcher bristled. 'Diplomatic agents as well as their immediate families are immune from all criminal prosecution.'

'Unless their home government waives that immunity, isn't that right?' I asked.

'Certainly. It's not a license to commit crimes. If you think you've got evidence to charge someone, the first step is that the State Department advises the proper government involved and requests a waiver to take the case to the proper court.'

'How about diplomatic staff?' I asked, thinking that our perp might even be attached to a mission for some other purpose.

'Consular employees have less protection, Miss Cooper. They only get immunity for acts performed as part of their official duties.'

'Well, I suggest you spend a bit of your spare time today getting together the list I asked for. I'll have a grand jury subpoena up here first thing tomorrow morning.'

'I don't mean to be an obstructionist. There must be – well, as we'd say here – a more diplomatic way to go about this. If you're talking about some egregious criminal matter, you know we have had charges result in deportation in the past.'

'That's a pretty unsuccessful solution, Mr Barcher,' I said. 'When you deport a major felon, he's never brought to justice in our courts, there's no punishment for him here at all, and usually he works his way back over our borders in no time, if New York City is the place he wants to be.'

He tried another route. 'You know, one of the things we do here at Protocol is work with the injured, the aggrieved party to try to secure some kind of restitution for them.'

'Money? For victims of violent crime?' Mercer asked. 'You think that women who've been sexually assaulted are just looking for money? They want this bastard off the streets, Mr Barcher, whoever he is. They want him behind bars. Now maybe our case will turn out to have nothing at all to do with the United Nations, but we're expecting your help.'

Barcher walked to a file cabinet and opened the drawer, retrieving two copies of a document from a large stack. 'One hundred ninety-one member states. I can't provide you with home addresses, but these are where their missions are located.'

We walked to the elevator as we both scanned the alphabetical list, looking for names of African countries. I took out a pen to check the ones I recognized.

'Angola. That was Portuguese, I think. Not British,' I said, thinking of Annika's comment about the perp's accented word. 'Benin. What's that?'

'Used to be Dahomey back when you took geography. French West Africa.'

'Botswana. Now that used to be under British influence,' I said, marking the page. 'Burkina Faso. Where the hell is that?'

'Upper Volta. Part of the French Union at one time.'

'Burundi. I think that was German or Belgian,' I said, buttoning my coat as the guard let us out of the building.

'Cameroon,' Mercer said. 'Check it off. That had both British and French divisions.'

'This is going to take more manpower than I guessed. We're not even out of the C's yet.'

We got back into the car and Mercer called Lieutenant Peterson. 'Alex will shoot a subpoena up to the chief of protocol in the morning. I can't say we were greeted with open arms here. You might put in a request for some backup from the Nineteenth Precinct. With any luck, we'll be knocking on a lot of doors tomorrow afternoon.'

Mercer seemed attentive to Peterson's reply. Then he listened to something else the lieutenant had to say, grabbing the pen from my hand to write down an address.

'Here's our chance for that second chat with Emily's friend Teddy Kroon. Emily's child, the one she gave to her sister Sally to raise? She showed up on Kroon's doorstep an hour ago, trying to find out from him who her father is.'

Chapter 37

Mike Chapman would have been pushing me out of the way if he were with us, telling Teddy Kroon to stop whining. Mercer and I took the more compassionate approach, hoping to gain his trust and elicit more candid responses than we had in our first meeting.

'Amelia. Amelia Brandon,' Kroon said, repeating the girl's name over and over again as he rocked back and forth on his living room sofa. 'I opened the door and I swear it was like seeing Emily's ghost. Amelia. It was Emily's little girl.'

'You just let her walk away?' Mercer asked.

I was sitting next to Kroon and patting him on the back to help calm him.

'What else could I do? She came in and talked for ten, maybe fifteen minutes. I, I think she had figured out that I might be her father,' Kroon said, forcing a smile. 'I guess I convinced her that wasn't possible.'

'But why didn't you give her some coffee – find some way to stall and keep her here – and go inside to call the precinct?'

Kroon looked at Mercer quizzically. 'Detective Wallace, this whole thing came at me as such a surprise, I'm sure I didn't do a lot of things you would have thought of.'

Mercer had the opportunity he wanted. Kroon was caught in a lie. The draft of the letter from Emily Upshaw to her sister was one of the files that had been opened on the computer the night of Emily's murder. Amelia and her appearance could not have been much of a surprise at all.

Mercer pushed the coffee table out of the way and lowered himself onto an ottoman that he pulled up directly in front of Kroon.

'Now one of the things we'd like to do this morning, Teddy, is to establish some ground rules,' he said, his huge frame boxing the smaller man into place beside me. 'You haven't been entirely honest with us about—'

'Yes, I have. Yes, I have from the very beginning. It's my fingerprints; didn't I tell you they'd be everywhere in Emily's apartment? I, I knew that was going to be a problem from the first time the police started questioning me. Is that what you mean?' Kroon looked over at me to be the good cop in this conversation, but I stared back at him without offering any comfort.

I remembered that Mike had been even more suspicious of Kroon when he got the confirmation from the autopsy that no sexual assault had been completed on Emily. The killer's sexual orientation was of little moment if the whole scene had been staged for the purpose of misleading the investigators.

'You gotta do better than that, Teddy. You gotta convince us you weren't the one waiting in the apartment for Emily when she came home from the theater the night she was killed.'

Kroon was practically doubled over. 'But I told you the name of the bar I was in. People saw me there. Lots of people.'

'In a crowded bar where you were a regular. No one can swear to the time you arrived or when you ordered your second drink or whether you went out and came back during the course of the evening.'

'I'd never have hurt Emily. She was the dearest friend I've ever had,' he said, resting his head in his hands.

Mercer tapped a long, thick finger against the top of Kroon's knee. 'Look at me when I'm talking to you,' he said, his deep voice the only sound in the room.

Kroon slowly lifted his head to meet Mercer's eyes.

'Don't mess with me, Teddy. There's a little chip inside the hard drive that recorded the exact minute someone went into a bunch of files from Emily Upshaw's computer,' Mercer said, rubbing his fingers together in front of Kroon's face. 'And there were enough skin cells on the computer mouse to tell us that person was you. So it suggests that you were either there with your friend at the time she was attacked with – correct me if I have this wrong – *your* carving knife, or that you interrupted your mourning after her death long enough to log on to her machine. Neither one of those is a pretty picture.'

Kroon's head snapped back and he leaned it against the rear edge of the sofa, gazing up at the ceiling.

Mercer was getting to him. 'Start with the crap you gave us about leaving messages on her answering machine. There were none.'

'Maybe I dialed the wrong number. I'm telling you that I called Emily several times.'

'Try harder. You knew she was very upset. You lied about that, too. She told you she was frantic when she called you at the store in the afternoon.'

'Like I said, she only left a message with one of my sales—'

'Teddy, her phone records show she was talking with someone at your shop for almost five minutes.'

It wasn't warm enough in Kroon's apartment for any of us to be sweating, but small, watery beads were forming on his forehead.

He pulled himself upright and snarled at Mercer, 'Emily Upshaw was scared to death when she called me that afternoon. She had a premonition that she was going to be murdered.'

Mercer and I hadn't expected that answer.

'All right, Detective? Would you have believed her if she told you that? Would you have taken her any more seriously than I did?'

'It depends what she was talking about.'

'Someone was trying to find Emily. Someone she didn't want to hear from ever again.'

I thought I knew where he was going. 'Amelia Brandon. Her daughter?'

Kroon was silent.

'Look, Teddy, we know the letter that Emily wrote to her sister about Amelia is one of the documents you opened the night of the murder. That's why I don't believe you were all that surprised when Amelia showed up at your door this morning. There's got to be a different reason you turned the child away.'

'Fear, Miss Cooper. Plain and simple fear. Can you understand that?' He pushed himself up from the sofa and walked away from the two of us.

'Of course I can accept that.' Better than you'll ever

imagine. 'But it would help if you told us who you're afraid of.'

He balanced himself against the windowsill as he shouted at me, 'How the hell am I supposed to know if you people can't figure it out?'

'So what did you do?' Mercer asked. 'Send the kid back out on the street as a test balloon? See what kind of trouble she attracts? I want to find that girl, Teddy, before we have another tragedy on our hands.'

Kroon exhaled. 'Emily had been sick since she got that phone call from Amelia, maybe a week or ten days before she was killed. She'd promised her sister never to have any contact with the child.'

'We know that. Sally Brandon talked to us when she was here. But Amelia's got to be out of college by now – she was bound to find out sooner or later.'

'Some sort of legal papers had been arranged for the Brandons when Emily gave up the baby, but apparently no one ever destroyed the original birth certificate on file at the hospital. Amelia hadn't gone looking for trouble. She simply wanted to come here to meet Emily, to find out why her mother had abandoned her. She wanted to know who her father is.'

'Wasn't his name on the birth certificate, too?' I asked.

'No. That just said "unknown" in the space for the father's name.'

'Do you know who he is?'

Kroon nodded his head up and down. 'Emily told me that same week. The NYU professor whom she slept with the time she came to the city for her college interview. Noah Tormey is his name.'

'Did Emily actually speak to Amelia?'

346

'Only once. You see, the child didn't have a phone number for Emily. Her home phone is – was – unlisted. So Amelia rummaged through her mother's papers but the only things she came up with were some occasional clippings of articles with Emily's byline that Sally must have saved. The girl began to call the editorial departments of the magazines, and once she did that, Emily got calls from her former colleagues, telling her that someone named Amelia Brandon was trying to reach her.'

'So Emily phoned her?' Mercer asked.

'Absolutely not. She'd made a promise to her sister that she wasn't going to break. But she was tormented by the fact that Amelia was determined to track her down. There was no way to put the cat back in the bag. I guess one of the other writers on the magazine staff finally gave the child Emily's phone number.'

'Take us to Saturday afternoon before the murder,' Mercer said, 'when Emily called you with her – what did you say – premonition?'

Kroon wiped his brow. 'I was at work, like I told you. The store was busy and I'm afraid I didn't take her as seriously as – well – as it turned out I should have.'

'You couldn't have known what would happen to her,' I said.

'Emily had been at home all morning, sleeping late, I'm sure. She went out for the papers and some groceries, and when she got back there had been a series of calls. Three, I think she said. All of them hang-ups.'

I looked at Mercer, who had studied the outgoing and incoming activity on Emily Upshaw's phone records. He nodded his head and mouthed the words 'pay phone.'

'Emily couldn't imagine who had called, but she was concerned that it had something to do with Amelia's attempts to find her. Every time we had met during the week, she'd been soliciting my help with what to do about telling her sister.'

'And your advice?'

He shrugged. 'Be honest with her. There was nothing to hide anymore.'

'The hang-up caller, did he or she phone back?'

'Yes. That's what prompted Emily's panicked call to me. It was that doctor – you know, the one with the Asian name who was found dead last week.'

'Dr Ichiko?' I asked.

'Exactly.'

'Did Emily know him?'

'No,' he said. 'She told me that she'd never met him.'

Mercer walked over to Kroon. 'But you just told us her phone is unlisted.'

He sniffled and answered, 'Emily's name was in the file the doctor had kept on Monty, when Ichiko had treated him back in his college days. Apparently, Monty had talked about her in session, as the woman he lived with, the person he confided in when he had the flashbacks that he had killed someone. The doctor had an NYU alumni directory. Emily's number is printed in that.'

'What did he want?'

'First he spooked her by just expressing relief that she was alive – that she hadn't been murdered long ago. Ichiko asked whether she had seen the newspapers, the headlines about the skeleton in the building basement. Emily had just come home with the papers – the *Times* and the tabloids. He told her to look at the *Post* follow-up story, that he was convinced he knew whose bones had been discovered. And certain that the killer was Emily's old boyfriend, the one she called Monty.'

'What did Emily do?' I asked.

'Ichiko wanted her to tell him where Monty was, what had become of him. She swore she didn't know, that she hadn't seen him in over twenty years. He pressed Emily hard – he really scared the daylights out of her.'

'How?'

'He told her that once the skeleton was identified, Emily wouldn't be safe in New York. That she had to help him figure out what had become of Monty or they'd both wind up dead. Dr Ichiko wasn't wrong, was he?'

'And you, what did Emily want from you?' Mercer asked.

'Money. Money to get out of town. And advice about where to go.'

'What did you tell her?'

'That she couldn't run because she didn't know where in the world this man Monty had gone.'

'Hadn't she thought of that before?' I asked.

'Often,' Kroon said. 'She often wondered what had become of him. How do you support yourself if you're a poet, Detective Wallace? Nobody can make a living that way today.'

'The pages you opened from Emily's computer, Teddy, what was that about?' Mercer asked.

He bowed his head. 'That was such a stupid thing to do.'

Heartless, I wanted to add.

'What was so important to you that you opened computer files before you even called nine-one-one?'

Kroon walked to his desk drawer and returned to the sofa, sitting next to me and handing me a thin manila folder. 'You can look. I mean, when I found her body, I assumed she'd been killed by the Silk Stocking Rapist. That it was just a rotten piece of bad timing and bad luck. I – I guess I just wanted to be a hero.'

'It never occurred to you that the killer was Monty?'

'Call it denial, Detective. I had read about the rapist back in the neighborhood, stabbing a woman. I – I guess I didn't think things were moving so fast, since the doctor had only called Emily that very day. I didn't think Monty was anywhere around yet, so I thought I could find information about Monty that I could turn over to Dr Ichiko, that would help the police solve the old case.'

I opened the file that Kroon had printed out the night of Emily's murder and shuffled through the papers to see whether anything struck me as relevant or useful to our investigation. I hadn't had the chance yet to study the police forensics report on the computer.

Teddy may have claimed a close friendship with Emily, but for some unfathomable reason he had purloined some very personal writings. There were pages of meditations on the emotional upheaval she had undergone because of Amelia's contact, and intimate recollections that the dead woman had written about her parents and sisters.

Then came a lengthy manuscript, titled 'Poetic Injustice,' which listed both Emily Upshaw and Noah Tormey as its authors. It appeared to be the academic treatise on Poe's flirtation with plagiarism that she had researched and written for the young professor – the one that had scotched his ambitions at the Raven Society.

Next came a paragraph of single-spaced prose. I lifted the page from my lap to read it.

Kroon saw what it was. 'See? I thought I could give this to Dr Ichiko, to show that Monty – whoever he was – had confessed to Emily.'

I read the lines:

I determined to wall it up in the cellar, as the monks of the Middle Ages are recorded to have walled up their victims. For a purpose such as this the cellar was well adapted. Its walls were loosely constructed, and . . . I made no doubt that I could readily displace the bricks at this point, insert the corpse, and wall the whole thing up as before so that no eye could detect anything suspicious . . . by means of a crowbar I easily dislodged the bricks and, having carefully deposited the body against the inner wall, I propped it up in that position, while with a little trouble I re-laid the whole structure as it originally stood.

'Stick to gourmet cooking, Teddy. That's vintage Poe. "The Black Cat." Another burial behind brick walls,' I said.

He looked crestfallen, as though he had actually found a clue of significance.

The last pages included the draft letter that Emily was working on to send her sister Sally, telling her about Amelia's discovery.

'Is this your handwriting?' I asked, pointing to the edits and corrections that had been made in pen along the margins.

Kroon said yes without looking up.

'Why did you write Noah Tormey's name at the top of the page?'

'I wanted to be sure I'd remember it. I'd heard his name from Emily for the first time, just a few days earlier.'

'But why?' I asked. 'What were you going to do with this letter, with this information?'

'Well, nothing. I – uh – I just felt I knew the truth and ought to keep a record of it, for Amelia's sake.'

'And then you brushed her off at the door when she arrived this morning?' Mercer asked.

I read the page again while Mercer questioned Kroon. The changes he had made to the draft made no sense to me. It was no longer intended to be a letter to Sally Brandon.

'Where did you send the girl?'

'Nowhere in particular. I couldn't deal with her is all.'

'Did you give her Tormey's name?' Mercer asked. 'Was that your plan?'

'No, not yet. I didn't think she was ready for that. I didn't know what to do with her. She wanted information about Emily's life, about who would be able to help her. I – I told her about the detective who had befriended her mother—'

Mercer was steaming. 'Kittredge? Did you give her Kittredge's name?'

'Yes.'

'What else? Did you talk about Monty?'

'Only that I don't know who he could be. I wasn't suggesting she try to find out.'

'But she's desperate for information about her birth parents. For all we know you've sent her out in harm's way. Now how the hell do you help us find her again?' Mercer asked. 'At least if you'd given her Tormey's name, maybe he'd have taken her in and we'd know she's safe.'

Now the written words made more sense, came clearer on the page when Kroon answered Mercer's questions.

'Of course you didn't want her to get to Noah Tormey quite yet,' I said, looking up at Kroon. 'You were hoping to extort a little money from him in order to let his secret go to the grave with Emily.'

Chapter 38

From Kroon's apartment, I placed a call to Sally Brandon. Amelia had come to New York to look at graduate schools, but had never told the Brandons what she had learned about her birth mother nor about her efforts to reconnect to Emily's world. Sally's distress and pain rang through the telephone wires as clearly as her voice.

We waited while Sally tried to reach Amelia on her cell, without success. Mercer called Peterson to start in motion efforts to find the girl before she knocked on the wrong door.

Mercer and I stopped at Swifty's for a late lunch. Neither of us had received any messages from Mike, and we were both distracted by our thoughts of his grief.

'What do you make of Dr Ichiko contacting Emily Upshaw the day she was murdered?' Mercer asked.

'I've been thinking about his last phone call – the one to the Raven Society. What if something Emily said in that conversation pointed him in that direction, caused him to make the call?'

'To Zeldin?'

'Or to anyone else who's a member. The number he called wasn't Zeldin's personal phone. It was just his recording on the answering machine. It can't be a coincidence that the doctor phoned the Raven Society. Maybe Emily unwittingly provided a clue that Ichiko followed up on. A fatal one.'

I walked back from the restaurant at four in the afternoon, splitting with Mercer so that he could spend a long evening with Vickee and Logan. Grace's Marketplace featured jumbo stone crab claws flown in from Florida, and I took home half a dozen, already cooked and cracked, as an effortless attempt at feeding myself a good dinner.

I changed into causal clothes and stared at the display on my own answering machine. No messages. When I didn't take time to remind most of my friends that I thrived on human contact, they ceased calling, believing that I was too consumed by my cases to socialize.

I cocooned myself in the den with a couple of old movie DVDs and let the week's weariness overtake me. The dull headache I'd been lugging around with me since our visit to Poe Cottage had faded to an occasional thud. I picked at the meaty crabs when I got hungry and put myself to bed early after a few chapters of the latest biography of Marie Antoinette.

I was still claustrophobic and opened the window wider, despite the midwinter chill. I left the light on in the hallway, newly uncomfortable in the dark. My last thoughts were about Mike and how lost he must have been feeling.

The cop on the security desk was the only person in the lobby of the DA's office when I pushed through the revolving door at seven-fifteen. There was a lot of catching up to do. Getting in ahead of the troops would allow me two hours of work with no phone interruptions, and the added advantage of not having to see everyone's expression of surprise as they passed me in the hallway, back on the job at Hogan Place.

The routine business of the sex crimes unit had gone on under the meticulous watch of my deputy, Sarah Brenner. The in-house cold case experts, Catherine and Marisa, had left memos detailing the eight DNA hits that came back from CODIS in a single week, solving crimes committed as far back as eight years ago. The line assistants – forty of them who specialized in this sensitive work – had responded to crime scenes and hospital beds dozens of times, interviewed scores of witnesses at their desks, and answered 'ready for trial' – the three magic words that jump-started the process of jury selection – on six felony sexual assault indictments.

I read all the new screening sheets, which summarized the facts of the cases for me, so that I could get a sense of every assault and each assistant's caseload. We had been working around the clock to stop the Silk Stocking Rapist, to identify Emily Upshaw's killer, and to put some flesh on the entombed skeleton in order to learn her backstory.

In the movies, cops and prosecutors working the big case never seemed to have to worry about other old or new business. In fact, burglars still climbed up fire escapes and raped sleeping victims, women who separated from abusive partners were stalked and assaulted as they left their jobs, college students were preyed on by peers who plied them with alcohol to make them more vulnerable, and children were molested by pedophiles in places they should have been most safe – their homes, houses of worship, and school grounds.

When Laura arrived at nine, I spent half an hour with her, dictating correspondence, listing phone messages for her to return, and organizing memos to be filed. The first paper to go out was a subpoena faxed to the protocol chief at the UN, to be followed by a hand-delivered original. In lieu of an appearance by 2 P.M. at this afternoon's grand jury, he could make the home addresses of the requested representatives available to Mercer Wallace.

The morning filled up as Sarah and I reviewed the new cases and she advised me of the direction each was going, and the assistants who wanted to discuss their investigations rolled in and out in response to Laura's summons.

Mercer called me from the protocol office at 1:45. He was holding the list of residential addresses. 'We're talking more than thirty countries,' he said. 'It looks like eleven of them fit nicely inside our geographic range.'

'Is the lieutenant on board?'

'Yeah. He went to the top on this. The chief of d's is pulling in guys from the street crime unit to sit on each house starting with today's four-to-twelve shift.' Those cops patrolled in plainclothes and unmarked cars, usually saturating high crime areas, without the obvious labels of the distinctive blue and white RMPs to give them away.

'Any other ideas?'

'Next call is to INS, to see if we can get pedigree information on all the family members who have visited or lived here.' That would have been impossible to do a few short years ago, before the Immigration and Naturalization Services had computerized their systems.

'Great. Battaglia wants to conference everything we did last week at four. Tell Laura to pull me out if anything develops,' I said. 'And, Mercer, you hear anything from Mike?'

'I've left some voice mails on his cell, just rambling and telling him what we've been doing. No callbacks yet.'

Pat McKinney walked into my office at 3:55. He told the assistant with whom I was working to come by later on and said Battaglia had asked him to pick me up. The meeting was long, as I had expected. Battaglia was a detail man, always wanting to have the most current theories of major investigations so that he could repay media favors by planting discreet leaks when he thought they were reliable enough to release.

'I don't care what time of night, Alex. You get anything connected to the UN, I'm the first to know.'

'Of course.'

'And the rest of the week?'

'We've got to go back to some of the people we talked to briefly – Gino Guidi, Noah Tormey, the men at the Botanical—'

I must have missed a signal from McKinney to the district attorney.

'That reminds me,' Battaglia said. 'Ellen Gunsher goes with you on some of that, okay? You're down Chapman, and he's the source of some friction there. I want Ellen to get some exposure on this. You got guns involved in the professor's shooting, you got the ex-cop who killed a kid with a gun. Ellen rides with you.'

I smiled and told him that was fine before he dismissed the two of us.

'You must have delivered big to get that included in your package, Pat. Battaglia telling me to partner up with your girlfriend. What's your secret? You doing more than just lighting his cigars these days? Moved on to wiping his fingerprints off a murder weapon that you've hidden somewhere?'

He ignored me and pushed open the door to the men's room. It was his favorite way of ending our conversations.

Laura was gone, but she had taped a message on the tall head-rest of my desk chair:

Mercer's on his way to the 19th squad. He wants you to meet him there.

It was already close to six o'clock. I closed up my office and went out in front of the courthouse to hail a cab for the rush hour ride to Sixty-seventh Street.

I flashed my ID at the officer on the desk and before he could scan it, the sergeant called over his shoulder, 'They're waiting for you on the second floor, Miss Cooper. Go right on up.'

I'd spent many fruitful hours in the squad room over the last decade. I'd interviewed crime victims, interrogated suspects, puzzled over facts with detectives, and napped on the hard wooden bench behind the bars in the holding pens when short evenings had turned into long overnights.

Lieutenant Peterson looked up as I opened the door. He put his finger against his lips before I could greet him or the half dozen detectives standing around, and motioned me to follow him into the captain's office.

Mercer was behind the desk, ending a telephone conversation. He handed me a copy of the sketch of the Silk Stocking Rapist – I knew the image as well as I knew Mercer's features – and then gave me a copy of the official United Nations newsletter with photographs of recent receptions and conferences.

'I picked this up when I was waiting for the list of names this afternoon. Look at the delegate speaking at the December meeting on trade sanctions.'

The man in the photograph looked remarkably like the composite drawing, except that he appeared to be in his mid-sixties. The hairline and round-shaped face, even the size of the nose and outline of the lips were identical to the rapist's physiognomy. The skin color was the deep ebony that witnesses had described.

'Who's your friend?'

'Sofi Maswana. Representative to the United Nations from Dahlakia.'

'Enlighten me, Mercer.'

'Like Eritrea, it was once part of Ethiopia. Broke off in the nineties and became an independent republic. Northern Africa, on the Red Sea, prized for its pearl fisheries.'

'And Mr Maswana?' I asked.

'He's downstairs with his number-one son, waiting to talk to us.'

'I'm impressed. That's why all the guys look so wired out there?'

'They know something's up,' Peterson said. 'They haven't seen the pair yet.'

'What do you know?'

'Maswana's a perfect gentleman,' Mercer said, flipping open his notepad. 'He's got business degrees from the University of London – don't go smirking there, Alex – and the Sorbonne. Sixty-eight years old. Been in the diplomatic corps for almost thirty years and has been posted here for six.'

'What's the address?'

'Town house on East Seventy-fourth Street, between First and Second Avenues.'

'I hope our profiler likes that for a "jeopardy center." Couldn't be better. What does he know at this point?' I asked.

'By four-thirty, INS confirmed visa information for other family members. There's a wife who splits her time between here and home, and five kids, all in their twenties. Three sons, two daughters. They've all come and gone from the States over the years. I got an agent to meet me at Maswana's office in the Secretariat building so I didn't have to use any ID that linked me to Special Victims. I thought immigration questions would be less threatening than telling him we were looking for a serial rapist.'

I liked the sound of this. My adrenaline was pumping, just like the detectives who paced in the adjacent room. 'Good start. What did he tell you?'

'The agent explained to Maswana the latest updates in airport security procedures for United Nations personnel. The government's working on a form of identification to create an express VIP service for all diplomats who've submitted to extensive anti-terrorist screening procedures. Then, it seemed natural we had to take him through the family members step by step.'

'Was he cooperative?'

'One hundred percent. Help the good old USA, and grease the wheels to get through the airport more speedily. Mrs Maswana, he told us, is here until April. Both girls are at college, one at Princeton and one at Georgetown.'

'And his sons?' I asked.

'The youngest one is named after him. Sofi, Junior.

He's twenty-three. Goes to graduate school at Harvard but he's been home since Christmas, doing an independent study project. Went back up to Cambridge just this past weekend, but Mr Maswana will make him available for anything we need.'

'Timing is everything,' I said. 'It puts him in the 'hood for the recent series, but he's a bit young for the 'scrip, especially going back to the earliest cases. How about the two older ones?'

'The middle son, David, is the one who's here with the father tonight. Twenty-seven years. He works in a family export business run by an uncle – Dahlakian pearls – on Fifth Avenue, near the diamond district. He's been in and out of town lots of times in the past five years.'

'That fits with the subway stop on Fifty-first Street,' I said, thinking of the MetroCard and the Forty-seventh Street hub for wholesale jewels that had stretched to the surrounding blocks.

'He's twenty-seven, lives at home with Mom and Pop. He's the spitting image of his old man. I'm not jumping to any conclusions but he looks awfully, awfully good, Ms Cooper.'

'How about his big brother?'

'Comes and goes as well. He'll be thirty on his next birthday. Has a wife back home, with twin daughters. Mr Maswana says that Hugo's involved in private banking, but he hasn't been in the States since a brief visit last summer.'

'Did you check that out with INS?' the lieutenant asked.

'It fits what they've got. All the Maswanas are present and accounted for, except Hugo.'

'And he wasn't here when the pattern started up again, even according to the computer records, am I right?' I asked.

Mercer nodded.

'How'd you take the next step? How'd you tell Mr Maswana you wanted to talk to his son about a criminal case?'

'When we'd come to the end of the general questioning, the INS agent and I stepped out for a minute. I checked with the lieutenant, who already had a team sitting on the town house, in case our subject was inside. So I went back in to the ambassador and told him the truth. I'm sure he wanted to put out my lights, but he was the model of diplomacy. Quiet, dignified, restrained. If the kid's inherited anything of his character, then I'm wrong to suspect him. Maswana said he'd produce his son at the precinct as soon as he could locate the young man, and he kept his word.'

'So what's the plan?' I asked.

'Bring David up here. If we get really lucky, he spills his guts,' Peterson said. 'Otherwise, you try to develop some probable cause. Worst-case scenario, he sucks on a coffee cup, we keep him under surveillance tonight, and this time tomorrow we've got our DNA results.'

Mercer Wallace went downstairs to bring David Maswana up to the squad, but the father was not so easily separated from his son. The three of them entered the cramped office in a row.

The lieutenant stepped outside to make room and Mercer introduced me to the two men, who sat opposite me across the captain's messy desk. I explained that I wanted to question David out of Sofi's presence. The father was polite but firm.

'Is my son under arrest for anything?'

'No, sir, he is not.'

'Do I need to get him a lawyer?'

'No, he's not in custody. You have my word on that. Of course, if you'd like to have a lawyer present, we can certainly wait here until you've reached one.'

Maswana checked his watch for the time. 'I'd prefer to get started. We have nothing to hide.'

'Then I'm going to ask you to step out of the room. Lieutenant Peterson will give you a comfortable place to—'

'I intend to sit right here, Madam Cooper, beside my son.'

It was too early to start butting heads. 'That's not going to work, Mr Ambassador. You're welcome to have a seat down the hall, but I will not conduct the questioning in your presence. I'll be right outside when you two have had a chance to decide what you'd like to do this evening.'

No serious interrogation of an adult suspect could be carried on with a parent sitting next to him. If David were psychologically ready to unburden himself about his criminal conduct, the company of his prominent father and the rectitude of his upbringing would put the chill on any chance of a confession. The entire dynamic changed when the target was alone.

I went out to the squad room and gave Peterson some cash to order in a sandwich for David and some coffee for all of us. Like the superstitious ballplayers who left their pitchers alone on the bench between innings, none of the detectives approached me to banter or offer suggestions. Mercer and I huddled in a corner to discuss strategy.

Ten minutes later, Mr Maswana emerged from behind the opaque glass door.

'I shall accept your rules, Madam Cooper. But I would ask you to suspend what you're doing anytime David requests that you do.'

'Of course.'

Mercer and I returned to the room, and while we were explaining the purpose of our questioning, a uniformed cop brought in the package from the local deli.

I placed the sandwich in front of Maswana along with a cup of coffee. Once he drank from the container and left it on the desk, it would be abandoned property that I could submit for DNA analysis before the end of the evening, without the need for a search warrant or confession.

I opened the lid of my coffee and sipped at it. 'How do you take yours, David?'

He pushed the food and drink away. 'Nothing for me, thanks. I'm not hungry.'

Mercer began by asking some basic pedigree questions. The young man was nervous – he avoided making eye contact, his voice had a slight quiver from time to time, and he kept his hands clasped in his lap – but I would expect anyone to be frightened in this situation.

When he talked about his education, David made no mention of any schooling in England. 'When were you at Harvard?'

I wanted him to answer with the year of his class, so that I could see if that slight accent that Annika heard would surface in the same three letters as the word 'ass.' He not only said that word, but the word 'pass' as well, and there was no hint of a British pronunciation.

Mercer worked David on dates and times of year. He was vague about much of it, but then we were talking about events that were quite remote in time. Statutes of limitation had been written into our laws because people couldn't be expected to account for their whereabouts five or six years after the fact.

While Mercer did the heavy lifting, I tried to measure the guy's responses. At times he seemed earnest and as candid as he could be, and at moments when his facial expressions seemed identical to the police artist's sketch, I was ready to lock the door on the cell and throw away the key. The brilliance of DNA meant that science would resolve any of our uncertainty within twenty-four hours.

Forty-five minutes into questions and denials, Peterson knocked on the door and smiled at me, offering a pack of cigarettes, his lighter, and an ashtray. 'I forgot the captain got rid of his illegal paraphernalia a year ago, at the mayor's request. We'll bend the rules for you a bit.'

He had remembered the cigarette butt recovered from the stoop in front of one of the crime scenes. The perp was a smoker, and the remains he left on the desk would be another easy source of DNA analysis, from saliva.

Mercer and I each took a cigarette from the pack to make the activity inviting to our target. David Maswana wrinkled his nose at the smell of the match lighting. 'Thanks. I don't smoke.'

Maybe he didn't. Maybe he was smart enough not to make the process of evidence collection any easier for us.

At the end of an hour, Mercer was ready to play hard-ball. The vague answers about recent dates and times – those that would key into the January assaults – were unacceptable. Mercer pressed for firm answers, for information undoubtedly recorded in this generation's ubiquitous PalmPilots and desktop calendars.

He asked David to voluntarily give a DNA sample, to allow us to swab the inside of his mouth with a Q-tips. The young man welled up with tears before refusing the request, saying that he would ask his father about that before leaving the precinct later on.

Then Mercer removed a slip of paper from the folder. He turned it face-up and placed the composite of the Silk Stocking Rapist's face under the nose of our prime suspect.

David recoiled automatically and started breathing heavily. 'It's – it's like me a lot, but then, who made this? White women? A lot of the characteristics would, well – look like any, um—'

Mercer's dark brown skin was almost the same shade as David's. He leaned in and pointed at the kid. 'Don't let me hear any we-all-look-alike-to-them bullshit, okay? This sketch looks more like you than the photo on your driver's license.'

Another knock on the door and Peterson cracked it enough to motion me out. I thought Mercer had David on the ropes for the first time, making progress and softening him up. My annoyance at the interruption was visible.

'Sorry, Alex. I assumed you'd want the call. Darren Waxon, the chief of protocol says he has to talk to you.'

I took the receiver and spoke brusquely into the phone. 'Yes, Mr Waxon?'

'Miss Cooper, I'm wondering how much later you're going to keep the ambassador and his son in the police station. It's after eight-thirty and if you're planning to take any kind of action, I'll need to know about it as soon as possible.'

I hesitated, afraid there had been a leak from someone in the department who saw the two men waiting downstairs earlier in the evening. 'Who told you Mr Maswana was here?'

'He called me himself, to thank me and let me know what was going on.'

'Thank you? For what?'

'For telling him why the district attorney subpoenaed the personal-residence information in the first place and what the investigation concerned.'

My annoyance was fast turning to anger. 'Exactly when did you tell him that?'

'Miss Cooper, I gave each of the missions the courtesy of informing them that we had no choice but to respond to the proper legal process. Protocol requires—'

'But what time? At what hour did you tell that to Mr Maswana?'

'This afternoon, shortly before I gave Detective Wallace the list of addresses.'

The whole time that Mercer thought that he had pulled a fast one on Maswana with the ruse of getting information from him via the INS agent, the ambassador knew we were looking at one of his sons as a possible serial rapist.

'You had absolutely no business revealing that—'

'Miss Cooper,' Waxon said, meeting my ire with his own, 'I wasn't about to cause an international incident over a – a handful of hysterical women.'

Mike Chapman would have called him a frigging idiot, would have threatened to lock him up for obstructing governmental administration.

'Hysterical women? What kind of misogynist are you?

Well, if you've disturbed the domestic tranquillity by giving one of the other Maswana sons the time to get out of the country this evening before we could get our hands on him, I'll bring a few of those victims by your office so you can explain the concept of diplomatic immunity to them face-to-face.'

I told Peterson to carry on the interrogation and to ask the wily Mr Maswana for his permission to swab David, in order to exclude him as a suspect. 'Keep someone with him all the time. He's likely to be talking to his son Hugo by cell phone. And let him think we got called out to the scene of a new rape. Stall them here as long as you can.'

I opened the door and asked Mercer to step out. 'You and I are headed back to the airport tonight. Tell the ambassador anything you want – anything but that. Tell him we've been called out on another case. We've got a flight to catch.'

Chapter 39

Shortly before 9 P.M. we were in Mercer's car, at the intersection of Sixty-seventh and Park Avenue.

'Which way, Alex? JFK or Newark?' he asked.

I had called my travel agent's office in hopes she was working late, but got her voice mail. 'Just go south. If our best bet is Kennedy, we can take the Thirty-fourth Street tunnel, and if it's Newark, we get the Lincoln at Thirty-ninth Street.'

I dialed Information for American Airlines. We had crossed Fifty-seventh Street by the time I got through the recorded menu prompts and was put on hold for a live human being.

'The night we went to the airport to get Annika Jelt's parents into the country,' I said to Mercer, 'there was that guy at Kennedy who finally helped us work it out. Did you keep his name?'

He pulled the leather case that held his gold shield out of his pocket. 'The newer business cards I've picked up are behind the badge.'

I found the one for the Port Authority supervisor and tried his cell phone. He answered on the second ring and I gave Mercer a thumbs-up.

After I reminded him who I was and the urgency of our purpose, I asked him to find out what airlines had late-night European flights to cities that would connect to something that flew near Dahlakia, like the Ethiopian capital of Addis Ababa.

Mercer steered up the ramp that encircled Grand Central Terminal and pulled over while we waited for an answer.

'Most of your European flights departed between six and eight o'clock. We've only got a few going out between now and midnight.'

'Where to?'

'London, Paris, Rome with American. Stockholm on SAS. Moscow via Aeroflot. And it looks like Rome has been canceled because of a mechanical problem.'

'Newark. Can you get us a fix on Newark?'

'London and Paris. Both on Continental. They go out around eleven, too.'

'This is a police emergency. There's a felon – possibly a murderer – that we have to stop before he leaves the country. If I give you his name, can you check the manifests?'

The supervisor was silent. 'Will you cover me in writing? You know it's forbidden for us to give out passenger information.'

'You have my word, you'll get whatever you need.'

'Just the flights that haven't left yet?'

'Start with those,' I said. 'Then you can work backwards.'

There was always the possibility that if the older Maswana son was actually our man, and was warned by his father in midafternoon to get out of town, he had done it by train to another city or by shuttle to other airports that also serviced Europe. I crossed my fingers that the array of available flights was so much broader from New York than any other Northeastern port that he would have taken his chances by staying local.

'Who am I looking for?'

'The surname is Maswana. Hugo Maswana.'

Mercer corrected me. 'What if he's been using his younger brothers' passports? What if he's taken off as one of them to screw up the computer records? Tell your guy to check for all three names – Hugo, David, and Sofi.'

For five more minutes we idled at the top of the ramp until our contact got back on the line. 'Skip Newark. How fast can you make it out here?'

'Half an hour,' I said, turning to Mercer. 'It's JFK. You got a bubble?'

He reached under the front seat of the department car and pulled out a red plastic dome. He opened his window and extended his arm to stick the magnetized light on the roof of the car, accelerating to high speed and whelping his siren to move cars out of our way.

'Miss Cooper? Give me your phone number. Your party's been playing games with us. He first booked on the ten P.M. Paris, then switched to Rome, and when that canceled he put himself back on the midnight to Paris. He's not ticketed yet. London leaves at eleven and it's wide open. He hasn't checked in anywhere as of this moment. I'll get the Port Authority police on the gates and security checkpoints. He may be waiting to make a last-minute dash for the flight so he doesn't raise a flag once he's formally ticketed and checked in.'

The tunnel was practically empty and Mercer sailed

out on the Belt Parkway, making time I wouldn't have dreamed possible if I had to make a plane on a tight schedule.

'No wonder the ambassador came into the station house like such a lamb,' I said. 'He must have had Hugo banned from the household for a few years, thinking he'd outgrow his penchant for raping women. Wife and children back home in Dahlakia would settle him down.'

'I'm sure you're right. That's why the cases went cold four years ago. Maswana probably called Hugo at his office today and told him not to pass Go, not to collect his two hundred dollars, but hightail it to the airport and head for home.'

'And the father was smart enough to bring us a decoy – the middle son, who looks enough like Hugo – and the sketch – to make us salivate. It whet our appetite, it stalled us from looking anywhere else, and Maswana knew there'd be no risk because even if we held David overnight, the DNA results would exclude him tomorrow.'

By nine-forty, Mercer parked the car in a no-standing zone in front of the sprawling American Airlines buildings. I called my Port Authority contact, who told us he was inside Terminal A. The flights to London and Paris both departed from Concourse C, at gates only fifty yards apart.

We walked inside slowly and separately, in case Hugo Maswana was looking for a pair of investigators that his father may have described to him.

I walked past Mercer and whispered under my breath, 'I'll check the Admirals Club to see if he's waiting up there.'

Mercer turned off to the concourse, in the direction of the security screening.

I took the staircase to the club, and smiled at the hostess who tried to stop me to show my identification. I scanned both sides of the room and saw only a handful of bedraggled business passengers waiting for their late-night departures.

My phone rang at the same time I heard the PA system: 'Announcing the last boarding call for American flight 605, nonstop to Paris Charles de Gaulle. Final boarding, please.'

I flipped open the cell and it was our Port Authority contact, telling us Maswana just bought an e-ticket at a kiosk in the terminal and was confirmed on AA 605.

I ran back down the steps and up the incline to the security gate.

As I approached, I could see Hugo Maswana seated in a plastic chair just beyond the screening machine. He was dressed in a suit, but had removed his shoes to put them through the system. He reached into the basket to lift out a brogue and replace it on his foot.

At that very moment, Mercer got the attention of one of the Transportation Safety Administration screeners. He must have been trying to explain that he was a cop and had a gun that would set off the metal detector when I saw the man put the palm of his outstretched hand against Mercer's chest.

Hugo looked up at the commotion and seemed to realize that Mercer was there to intercept him. He stood up and dropped the pair of shoes before he bolted toward the gate.

Where the hell were the Port Authority cops? There was no one in sight, and I could only hope they were waiting for us at the boarding gate.

I caught up with Mercer, who had his badge in his hand. 'It's the damn gun, Alex. He won't let me in with it.'

I looked at the TSA agent, paralyzed by the bureaucratic necessities of his job, and trying to figure out whom to call to help him. I turned away from Mercer and made a dash through the frame of the metal detector. It screamed its alarm – maybe my gold watch, my belt hook, or my underwire bra had set it off – and I kept on running past the newsstand and fast food concessions after Maswana.

I was glad for the ringing bells, sure they would bring someone to capture me as well as my fleeing target.

The only advantage I had over Hugo Maswana's greater speed was the slipperiness of the flooring under his socks. Twice I saw him slide and fall to one knee as I gained on him, running in my rubber-soled loafers.

Now people were screaming and guards were charging from both directions – some coming at both of us from the departure gate and others overtaking us from behind.

Two of them lunged at Maswana first and wrestled him to the ground. Another one grabbed at my shoulder and tried to twist me around. I shook him off as he pushed me down and I fell on top of the suspect's back.

Maswana writhed on the ground and shoved me away, still kicking at the guards. As I grabbed his hand to keep it from striking me, I scratched at it with my nails and a thin line of blood trickled out on the surface of his knuckles. I wiped at it with my jacket.

Mercer Wallace and the PAPD supervisor jogged into sight, confirming to the men who had brought Maswana down that he was, in fact, the suspect we were after.

'Is he under arrest, Detective?' one of them asked Mercer. 'You taking him in?'

'Not exactly,' Mercer said, motioning the agent to step to the side, explaining – I was sure – that we might just be detaining him here for questioning until we could establish probable cause for his arrest.

I stood up and joined their conversation. The agent was non-plussed. 'I mean, we can hold him for a security breach at the airport. It may only keep him a day or two.'

'That's all we need,' I said to Mercer. 'Between the blood on my sleeve and the skin cells under my nail, we'll know this time tomorrow if we've got a case.'

Chapter 40

'You're late,' Laura said, following me into my office. I glanced at the clock and saw that it was ten thirty-five.

'I didn't get home until almost two. Just couldn't move myself this morning,' I said, reaching for the message slip in her hand.

'I think your body is trying to tell your brain to take—'

'Check the personals, Laura. My brain wants to rent new space. A body with a lower metabolism, no stress, one that moves at a slower rate of speed. Sluggish would be good for a couple of months. Maybe there's someone in appeals who wants to get on this treadmill for a while. Judge Tarnower?' I started at the message on the pink slip of paper. 'Did he tell you what it's about?'

The chief administrative judge rarely dealt with anyone other than Battaglia. I was afraid I'd gotten into his crosshairs over the lockup of the phlebotomist at the Midtown Community Court a week earlier, but Paul Battaglia hadn't warned me about any effort by Tarnower at interference.

'Only that it's urgent. I told him you were on your way in.'

I dialed the number and waited for his secretary to patch him through. Ellen Gunsher walked into my office and I held up a finger to suggest that she wait till I finished the conversation.

'Judge Tarnower? Alex Cooper, returning your call.' I used my right hand to flip through yellow-back complaints to find the file on the phlebotomist's case.

'How've you been, Alex?'

'Fine, thanks.'

'I'm calling to try to save you a bit of embarrassment. You and Battaglia.'

That was about as likely as me signing up for a gynecological exam with Pierre Foster, the defendant in the case. 'Always nice when someone's looking out for me, Judge. Whose toes did I step on?'

He chuckled, and we seemed to be vying to see whose voice sounded less sincere. 'No damage done yet. Any publicity in the pipeline on your matter?'

'Pierre Foster won't be arraigned on the indictment until next week. I'm sure the district attorney will prepare a press release. It's likely there are other—'

'Who's Foster? That's not what I'm talking about. It's the fellow they're holding out at the airport. He's halfway home, Alex. Why can't you just let go?'

I turned my back on Ellen Gunsher. 'May I ask, Your Honor, who got to you on this?'

'Got to me? That's a hell of a way to put it, young lady. Nobody got to me. We're talking about diplomatic immunity, the Vienna Convention. The ambassador and his family are immune from all criminal prosecution.'

'Not if the State Department asks the Dahlakian government to waive immunity. Any publicity in the pipeline is what you want to know? If the DNA matches my case samples, as I expect it will, we're talking one of the biggest serial cases in the city in years.'

'I have an assurance from the premier's office, Alex, that if the Maswana kid is the perp, he'll be taken care of by the authorities in his own country. It may even be a more appropriate kind of sentence, if you get my drift. Hell, I've never been to Dahlakia, but they may still believe in public castration in the town square.'

What was this man thinking? 'I'd rather have a life sentence without parole, Judge, and so would all of my witnesses. A long, miserable life upstate.'

'You know how expensive it will be to mount a trial like this, and then pay for sixty years of prison time?'

'The way I figure, Judge, is that the mayor eliminated the longtime exemption for diplomatic parking plates last year, so the thousands of dollars the city gets in fines from the UN neighborhood and all the consulates around town can pay for Mr Maswana's bologna sandwiches till he croaks.'

Tarnower was silent. 'Can you forward me to Battaglia?'

'Sure.'

'And Alex? Foster – that guy you were talking about – he's the one at the Midtown Community Court, right? I wouldn't spend too much time on that press release. The Dumpster your cops took all their evidence from is MCC property. They should have thought to get a warrant. Your case against him might go right out the window.'

The judge cut me off before I could forward his call to the district attorney. I hung up and sat down in my chair as Ellen approached me.

'Rumor has it you guys made a big score last night.'

No point asking how she knew. Battaglia had undoubtedly told Pat McKinney about Maswana, who was incapable of keeping professional secrets from his main squeeze.

'Fingers crossed. As soon as the lab has a preliminary read on the DNA, we'll know,' I said.

'I tried calling you at home around nine o'clock.'

'There were no messages on my—'

'I hung up after three rings. Silly to bother you when you weren't available.'

'About what?'

She smiled at me. 'Gino Guidi. He's coming around a bit.'

'How do you mean?'

'He'll be here any minute. I pushed his lawyer to give us more, just like you asked me to.'

I returned Ellen's smile. 'Nice work. Conditions?'

'You know there always are, Alex. Sort of a queen-for-a-day,' she said, referring to a deal prosecutors often dangled before targets of criminal investigations. A onetime offer of the opportunity to come in and tell what they know, with the guarantee nothing they say can be used against them in the courtroom.

'What do you figure he's got to hide?'

'Kirby says only his morbid fear of publicity. He thinks if Guidi can point us in some useful direction, you won't need to involve him if you wind up with someone to charge in any of these crimes. I tried calling Chapman when I couldn't reach you.'

'You won't get through to him, Ellen. He's withdrawn from all of us.'

'Oh? Maybe I assumed something I shouldn't have. I thought Mike would have told you about this by now. He got right back to me early this morning.'

I couldn't conceal my surprise. 'Mike?'

'Yeah. I mean, I understand he took off for the week, but he reached out to Scotty Taren for me. I feel so badly for him,' Ellen said. 'We obviously want a detective in on this meeting, so Scotty's here in my office. And I reserved the conference room down the hall. All this okay with you?'

I was still stuck on the fact that Mike had returned Ellen Gunsher's messages but wouldn't respond to any of mine.

'Alex?'

'What?'

'You ready to have another go at Gino Guidi?'

'Sure. Did you say we're doing it in your office?'

'No. He and Roy Kirby are in the conference room.'

'Give me a few minutes, okay?' I asked.

Ellen walked out and I dialed Mike's home number. I left a message on the machine, telling him that if it was too difficult to discuss personal things, I wanted to give him the good news about Maswana and get some direction in dealing with Guidi. Then I beeped him and tapped in my number, followed by 911 to tell him it was urgent.

'I'll be in a meeting with Ellen,' I said to Laura. 'Hold everything – except Mike or the boss.'

The three men got to their feet when I entered the room. Guidi and Kirby were seated together on one side of the rectangular table, facing Ellen Gunsher and Scotty Taren. I took my place at the far end and let Kirby go through the usual spiel about how forthcoming his client really wanted to be but how little he had to contribute.

'Here's a list we've prepared of some other people who were in the SABA program at the same time as Mr Guidi,' Kirby said, passing each of us a photocopy. 'Mind you, Ms Cooper, these are nicknames. There are only two with complete surnames.'

'They were guys I ran into later on. The others I never saw again.'

'Did you keep a journal at that time?' I asked.

'Well, not exactly a—'

'He's struggled to remember what he can,' Kirby said, interrupting his client when he realized I was going to ask for the original paperwork – apparently more than Kirby wanted me to see.

Scotty was taking notes. Guidi had something in writing that his lawyer was holding back and we would angle a way to get it.

'You want to flesh out something about these people for us?'

Guidi's answers were bland and fuzzy. I'd bet that the two SABA members identified specifically led lives cleaner than hounds-teeth by now or he wouldn't have put them forward. The ones who might be more useful – and potentially more embarrassing to him – remained obscure and would be impossible to find.

'Let's go back to Washington Square. The guy from your program who sat next to you on the park bench – Monty – that time he confessed to you that he killed a girl,' I said. 'You told us last week you didn't know he was referring to Aurora Tait then, is that right?'

'Absolutely. I had no reason to then.'

'But when, exactly when, did that occur to you?'

'Oh, I don't know, Ms Cooper. I hadn't thought about Aurora in years, until I read the story and saw those initials in the newspaper. The approximate time of her disappearance, the fact that the building where the skeleton was found was owned by the university – and frankly, it reminded me of Monty's story – another addict, another rich boy like me who'd screwed up his life.'

'You mentioned he talked about boarding school in some of your sessions. Do you remember where? What school or even what part of the country?' I asked.

Guidi shrugged and held his hands in the air, palms up. The sun gleamed off the gold on his cuff links. 'Maybe New England. Either Andover or Exeter. Could have been St Paul's. In the boonies, it was. I remember he talked about how he liked being near the woods and the peacefulness of the more remote countryside.'

'He was orphaned, you told us. Do you know how or when? Any details about his family that would help us figure out who he is?'

Guidi looked at me. 'That's mostly what he talked about in the meetings. Typical junkie's denial, blaming all his problems on everyone else. He never knew his father. I think his mother had a menial job, working as a servant – maybe even the housekeeper – for the scion of an old industrial family. When she died – some blood disease, it was – he was still a kid, taken in by the fat cat who'd been her employer. Richest man in town, that's who sent him off to boarding school and paid for his education.'

'This man who adopted him, didn't Monty talk about him at all?'

'That was part of his resentment. He was never adopted.'

Neither was Edgar Poe, I remembered. The Allans wouldn't give him their name. I had to wonder whether Monty knew the parallels between his own life and the tormented poet's.

'Was he bitter about it?' I asked.

Guidi checked with Kirby, who must have given him a green light to keep talking.

'Remember when I said that Monty told me he had killed a girl for betraying him?'

Ellen and I both said, 'Yes.'

'I – uh – I guess after I left the station house last week I began to think more about it. I thought of a few other things I – uh, I guess I asked him at the time. Sorry I didn't press myself a little harder that night.' He tried to muster an earnest smile.

'That's all right, Mr Guidi,' Ellen said. 'Anything you give us now will be helpful.'

I wanted to kick her under the table to keep the pressure on him rather than try to use her short supply of charm to stroke him, but I restrained myself.

'I know I asked what he meant by betrayal, by what this girl had done to him to make him fantasize about killing her,' Guidi said, focusing his attention back on me. 'You must understand that at the time I heard his story, Ms Cooper, I assumed it was a fantasy, a product of his dope-induced hallucinations. We all had them.'

I looked away from his face and while he continued to talk, gesturing to me with his left hand, I noticed the thin shape of a rifle barrel forged out of gleaming eighteen-karat gold in the fold of his French cuffs.

'He knew I came from a wealthy family. For me, starting over after I screwed myself up meant getting a job in a mail room in a fancy firm, as I think I mentioned. For Monty, it was out on the street doing physical labor, some kind of construction work. Here was this guy who came to every meeting with a book of poetry jammed in his back pocket, quoting everything from the classics to Philip Larkin and James Wright – but meanwhile his hands looked like he'd been sentenced to dig ditches ten years earlier.'

'But the girl,' I asked, 'Aurora – what did she do to him?'

'Monty's benefactor had given him one last chance. He'd flunked out of boarding school, managed to get into college from public school, but then hit the skids with drugs and booze once he got here to the city. When Aurora found out who had been supporting Monty, who had enabled his lifestyle – not knowing all the money was going down the toilet – she got on a bus and went up to his home, wherever that was, and spilled the beans.'

'Why?'

'To try to shake down the old man. She'd guessed wrong, was the problem. She thought if she told him the truth about Monty's addiction, she could score enough money – pretending it would go for private rehab and readmission to school – that she could take off and leave Monty in the dust,' Guidi said. 'With the rest of us.'

'The straw that broke the camel's back?' Ellen asked.

'Exactly. The old guy had been threatening to disinherit Monty anyway. Even though he had never adopted the kid, he had pledged the dying mother that he'd secure her son's financial future. As a result of what Aurora told him, he wrote Monty out of his will – not a single cent of inheritance – and before Monty could clean himself up and plead for another chance, the fat cat had a stroke and died a day or two later. Revenge,' Guidi said, his voice dropping to a whisper.

'What did you say?' I asked.

'Revenge, Ms Cooper. That's why Aurora Tait wound up in a brick coffin. I might not have been as creative in disposing of her, but more than a few of us who crossed her path would have been only too happy to have had our revenge. I'm sure that's what Monty had in mind.'

He tugged at the tip of his shirtsleeves to align them with each other and rested his clasped hands on the table.

'Do you shoot, Mr Guidi?' I asked.

'Sorry?'

I pointed to his cuff link. He twisted his wrist to look and remind himself what he was wearing.

'Oh, these? Upper Brookville Hunt Club. It's their logo.'

Ellen Gunsher found a new purpose for herself, trying to make her pathetic little firearms unit relevant. 'Are you a good shot?'

'Been shooting all my life.'

Scotty Taren looked puzzled. 'In the Bronx? What are you, a friggin' squirrel bagger?'

'Quail, mostly. Game birds. At the club. But my first kill was back when I was a teenager, Detective, right in Van Cortlandt Park. D'you know it?'

'North Bronx, right next to the high-rent district in Riverdale.'

'That's where I grew up – Bailey Avenue,' Guidi said. It was still a neighborhood of large fieldstone houses that

386

looked more like suburbia than New York City. 'I was fourteen and had just gotten a new puppy for Christmas. We were in the backyard and I was throwing sticks for him to fetch. A coyote came out of the park—'

Little Miss Texas was incredulous. 'A coyote?'

'There's eastern coyotes all over the state,' Taren said. 'Sometimes they slip down here through the woods when they get cold and hungry farther north. Real pain in the ass for Emergency Services to tranquilize them and ship 'em out before they start running in packs and attacking domestic animals – and little kids.'

Guidi went on. 'I thought it was a German shepherd running into the yard to play so I didn't panic at first. Then I saw that grizzled gray neck and the tail hanging down – you know the way coyotes do? – and he just snatched my puppy, a small brown Lab, and made off into the park. I went after him with one of my father's deer rifles, hanging in the garage, and dropped him before he could do any serious damage to the dog.'

Ellen seemed pleased with the story's happy ending. Scotty Taren raised an eyebrow at me and moved his lips. I made out the words 'Professor Tormey.' Aaron Kittredge was no longer the only marksman on our list. Guidi could just as easily have been the one who shot at us that day at the Hall of Fame, and Kirby didn't know enough to stop him from telling a story of his childhood that set up his marksmanship for us.

There was a knock on the door and Laura opened it. 'Excuse me, sorry to interrupt.'

'It's fine,' I said, getting to my feet with the expectation that she had Mike Chapman on my phone line. 'I can step out.'

'It's for Ellen,' she said, shaking a finger at me. 'Mr McKinney needs to talk to you, dear.'

There was a pause while Ellen left the room, and I decided to wait for her before going on with any more questioning.

'It's an odd set of circumstances,' I said to Guidi. 'Aurora's body found in the basement of the house on Third Street, and now the possibility that someone you knew bricked her up there to pay back a betrayal. Nobody in literature served up revenge better than Poe, and here we have a real-life copycat. On top of that, you're one of the most generous supporters of Poe Cottage. I don't think I've even thanked you for getting us in for a private tour last week.'

'Did I do that?' he said, apparently surprised to hear it.

'Perhaps it was your secretary. Zeldin set it up for us, after we left the Botanical Gardens. I noticed your name on the plaque in the cottage.'

'No coincidence there at all, Ms Cooper. My name is on a lot of Bronx institutions. Zeldin himself can tell you that. I've donated a new magnolia garden in my mother's memory, which will open in the spring. And the two of us traipsed all over the conservatory just before the holidays. He's shameless about looking for naming opportunities, and some of us are vain enough to oblige him.'

'Traipsed? What did you do with Zeldin?' The man couldn't traipse, from what I'd seen of him.

'Have you been to the conservatory since it reopened? It's spectacular. He walked me through the whole thing after hours one night.'

'I didn't think he could walk,' I said. 'I've only seen him in a wheelchair.'

Zeldin's immobility had kept him out of my main focus as a suspect.

'He only resorts to his iron buggy when his gout kicks in. That makes it too painful for him to get about very much, with the muscle deterioration condition he suffers from. But most of the time he can walk just as well as he can talk.'

Chapter 41

The meeting had broken up by noon. I called Mercer at his home in Queens and suggested we meet at Zeldin's office at the Botanical Gardens up in the Bronx at two o'clock, for another go at him.

When I dialed Mike's cell phone it dumped me into voice mail. Sympathy and concern hadn't worked to get him to respond to me, so I tried another route. 'Look what you've reduced me to, Detective Chapman. Now I'm getting information from you through Ellen Gunsher. I'm insane with jealousy. You knew it would have that effect, didn't you?

'Well, she's playing so nicely with me in the sandbox that I'm going to take her along this afternoon. See how she does in the gardens. Scotty will drive us up to the Bronx and Mercer will meet us there. I'm not trying to tempt you to come back to work, but I thought maybe you and Ellen were beginning to bond and you'd want to show her all your old Fordham haunts.' I paused, thinking my tone had been too flip. 'Take care. I'm not very good at getting the bad guys without you.'

Scotty Taren's bulky outline blocked my doorway. 'Zeldin's there. I gave him some crap about wanting to discuss Mr Guidi's connections and contributions. We gotta enter through the back gate on Mosholu 'cause the front entrance is closed today.'

'I thought they only shut down on Monday.'

'Usually. But they're setting up a giant tent behind the conservatory this week. Most of the staff is off 'cause they'll be doin' overtime for the benefit. Friday night's their big fund-raiser – Winter Wonderland, he called it. He's gonna leave our names with security. I'll give Mercer a shout and let him know.'

Shortly before 2 P.M. the three of us – Ellen, Scotty, and I – drove through the tall wrought-iron fencing off Kazimiroff Boulevard and stopped at the gatehouse. The guard pulled back the plastic window to tell us that Zeldin was expecting us in the Haupt Conservatory, the stunning crystal palace that was the jewel of the gardens' exhibition space.

There was no sign of Mercer as we parked in the designated space – the only car in the deserted row – and climbed the walkway against the fierce February wind. The pathways were empty but for the golf carts that employees used to get around the miles of roads and sidewalks inside the gardens. There was no one to inquire of at the ticket desk inside the front door of the enormous building – one full acre under seventeen thousand panes of glass. It was very still inside, and eerily quiet.

We must have been there almost ten minutes before a custodial worker trudged from a hallway into the circular lobby area, where we waited under the Palm Dome. It was a thicket of New World palms that reached over ninety feet up into the building's cupola, circling a reflecting pool that mirrored their elegant limbs as they stretched toward the sunlight.

'Excuse me – have you seen Mr Zeldin?'

The man didn't speak but pointed behind him, in the direction of a sign that announced the entrance to a tropical lowland rain forest.

Scotty started walking and Ellen and I fell in behind him. 'Outside, I'm freezing my ass off,' he said. 'In here, it's like hangin' out at my mother-in-law's trailer park in Lauderdale. I think I'm gettin' a hot flash.'

He unbuttoned his overcoat and loosened the tie around his neck.

The newly refurbished cement path wound through thousands of densely planted trees and shrubs. I would have thought we had entered the heart of a Brazilian jungle had the ground beneath us not been paved. Large leaves and fronds hung over our heads, brushing against my hair as I ducked to avoid them. The only sound was the whisper of the misting device that sprayed water from behind the trees.

Scotty was impatient. 'Zeldin? Anybody home?'

His voice echoed and I heard a shuffling noise in a small thatched hut that bordered the path ahead of us. 'What's that?' I asked.

Ellen read from the large illustrated signage that showed a photograph of a dark-skinned woman crushing leaves between her hands. 'It's a healer's house.'

'I'll give the bastard something to heal. This place is too hot for me,' Scotty said, wiping the sweat that was rolling down his forehead with the back of his hand. 'They got monkeys in here, too?'

There was noise above us, now, and we each looked up to find its source. A mesh metal staircase, painted dark green to camouflage it against the foliage, wound up more than fifty steps around a huge empty tree trunk, leading to a skywalk that trailed along the length of the rain forest. A worker in khaki overalls got up from his knees and leaned over the railing, picking brown tips off the ends of thick growth.

'Yo, pal. You seen Zeldin?' Scotty asked.

The man cocked his head and squinted. '*No comprende, señor. No lo sé.*'

'I'm telling you, I feel like we're in frigging Santo Domingo. You think that guy's an exhibit or he's really working here?'

A sharp right turn led us out of the rain forest and into a room that looked like it was built for a Victorian estate. The humidity level lowered immediately, while hanging vines hovered over a long rectangular pool, full of aquatic ferns and plants that surrounded a statue of naked goddesses spouting jets of water over tiered fountains.

Scotty bent over and dipped his handkerchief in the murky green liquid, mopping his brow before I could urge him not to put the slimy stuff against his skin.

The room ended at a ramp that curved down between a wall of lichen-covered boulders. At the foot of it, we seemed to have left the natural habitat for the intrusion of a twenty-first-century convenience – a dark, narrow tunnel several hundred feet long, connecting the arms of the conservatory to each other via an underground passage that was made out of an ugly form of corrugated siding. I wondered if it was just my own recent brush with a dank enclosed space that made this space seem uncomfortably creepy, or whether my companions were bothered as well.

When we emerged at the far end, we not only found Zeldin, but had transported ourselves into the middle of a simulated African desert as arid as the rain forest had been damp.

Scotty had to pause to catch his breath after mastering the uphill section of the ramp. Ellen and I approached Zeldin, who was seated in his wheelchair but turned his head at the sound of our footsteps.

'I hope you didn't have any difficulty finding me.'

Ellen and I answered politely before Scotty could complain, and I introduced them to each other.

'The detective told me you've got more questions for me,' Zeldin said with his distinctive drawl. 'Why not fire away?'

There was the sound of laughter coming from the next corridor, and I looked up to see its source. Two teenagers, each dressed in baggy jeans and hooded sweatshirts, were being chased by a third who wielded a watering can in his hand.

'I assumed we could do this in your office,' Ellen said.

'There's no one here to bother you, young lady.'

'Those kids – is it a school tour or something?'

'Heavens, no. Just a few of the local boys who do chores around here. I was showing them the carnivorous plants in the next room – they were fascinated,' Zeldin said, smiling.

'Who's carnivorous?' Scotty asked, catching up with us and shaking Zeldin's hand.

'The Venus flytrap, the pitcher plant,' Zeldin said, starting to wheel in the direction of the rowdy teens. 'They're not dangerous to humans, Detective. They don't really eat flesh. The leaves respond to the pressure of insects that land on them and they spring closed. It's the secretions that kill the bugs, who rot inside or starve in a pool of fluid until they dissolve. Not a pretty death.'

'I haven't seen many that are.'

'If you don't mind, sir,' Ellen said, 'I'm not here for the plant tour. We have some questions that will probably require you to consult your records.'

I couldn't read Ellen as well as I could my usual partners – Mike and Mercer – but what had seemed from the outside like such a benign setting now enveloped us in an oppressive atmosphere that was stifling and unpleasant.

'Records? From the Raven Society? I've already shown them to Ms Cooper.'

'Not those,' she went on. 'We'd like to talk about Gino Guidi and his involvement here, at the Botanical Gardens. Perhaps his financial contributions.'

'Ah, he told you, then, about the Bronx River cleanup?'

I listened to Ellen while she led the questioning. I was exhausted, both physically and emotionally, and distracted while I waited for a call about results on Maswana's DNA from the chief serologist.

Ellen had been drawn into today's outing because of Guidi's self-proclaimed marksmanship and its possible connection to the Tormey shooting. Now Guidi's name was dragging her in the direction of Dr Ichiko's death site.

I let her run this, in part because of my fatigue, and in part because I thought it would lead nowhere. Guidi's admission about his shooting ability probably had little significance.

'No, sir, he didn't,' Ellen answered.

'I'm sure you've seen signs alongside the highways from time to time, where individuals or businesses have paid for the maintenance of a particular area.'

We all nodded.

'Mr Guidi likes his name on things. I hadn't paid any attention to it the day I heard how Dr Ichiko died, but I was reminded of it more recently, after your visit to Poe Cottage. Con Edison does the environmental upkeep farther downstream of the gardens, and several local corporations have adopted parts of the river that flow through their neighborhoods. But Gino Guidi chose that strip of rapids himself – the part with the waterfall – because he used to play there when he was a child. Knows the area quite well, Ms Gunsher. I'd forgotten about that, because the sign bears the name of his company rather than himself.'

'Providence Partners,' I said.

'Yes, yes. I'd forgotten that connection when I first heard of Ichiko's death,' Zeldin said, wheeling his chair around.

'That's why I'd like to conduct this meeting in your office.' Ellen was attempting to be more aggressive now.

Scotty Taren's face was drained of all color. Again he was sweating profusely and I thought he was beginning to look ill.

He coughed a few times and then spoke to Zeldin. 'Why don't you get up out of that buggy and walk over with us?'

Zeldin's answer was sharp and loud. 'Don't be absurd, Detective. I can't do that.'

The three boys stopped horsing around when they heard the tone of Zeldin's voice. The tallest one started to walk toward us.

I was sweating, too. Maybe it was the intense heat inside the conservatory, or maybe it was the proximity of rough-looking teens coming toward me.

'Get me Sinclair,' he yelled out to the hooded boys. 'Get Mr Phelps for me *now*.'

The three looked at one another and spoke in Spanish, but they were too far away for me to understand.

Ellen reached for the handles of Zeldin's wheelchair. 'I'm sorry, sir. Let's all just calm down and go back to—'

'Get your hands off there, young lady,' he said, raising the volume another few notches.

Scotty started wheezing and clutching his chest.

'Scotty? Scotty?' I put my arm around him and tried to find a bench to seat him on, but as I leaned in close to talk to him, the teens came running toward us. One broke for a side door that led out to a large sculpture garden, turning to lock it behind him and remove the key before rejoining the others.

The three raced in our direction. They shouted something to Zeldin as they came by him, while one of them grabbed Ellen and lifted her off her feet, tossing her onto a large shrub with branches that stretched out five feet in each direction. They kept on running past us, back to the long tunnel and toward the front entrance.

Ellen's screams should have shattered the hundreds of glass panes that surrounded us.

I let go of Scotty and ran to where she lay, facedown, as though something was holding her in place.

'Ellen!'

She stretched out an arm to me and turned her face. There was blood everywhere.

I stepped off the paved walk and onto the rocks that

ringed the giant plant. *Encephalartos horridus – a ferocious blue cycad* was the way a nearby sign described this unlikely weapon.

Every long arm of the green monster was lined with spikes, from its root down to its very tips. Ellen's face and torso had been impaled on them with the force of the kid's thrust, and I had to literally lift her off its center, thorns hanging from her skin like rusty nails from an old railroad tie.

I sat her on the ground and waited for her heaving cries to stop. Behind me, Scotty – also in some kind of physical distress – kept murmuring apologies about not being able to help.

'Call nine-one-one, Scotty. Can you do that?'

Ellen started to pull the prickly pieces out of her forehead. 'Don't touch them,' I said to her. 'Let me try it.'

I could see she was ripping the skin on her face in an effort to get out the thorns. The pain must have been excruciating, and I tried to spread the wounds apart with my fingers to release the embedded needles without further lacerating the surface.

Again I looked over my shoulder. Scotty had rested his bulky body against some kind of small tree trunk. The overweight, out-of-shape detective was fumbling with his cell phone as though it was a struggle even to open it. He looked like he was in the middle of suffering a heart attack.

I grabbed the phone from his hand and dialed 911.

'It's just my angina, Alex. It'll pass.'

'Operator? Yes, it's an emergency. At the Botanical Gardens. Inside the Haupt Conservatory.'

Now the battery of questions.

'No, operator. I have no idea what cross street. It's a police officer *down*. Two officers, badly injured. We need an ambulance and we need cops.'

'I don't understand, miss. Is this a crime or a medical emergency?' the 911 operator asked.

'It's both, damn it. We're wasting precious time.'

I gave her the information and hung up. I dialed Mercer's number. 'Where the hell are you?'

'I'm over in front of the administration building. I just arrived but nobody's around.'

'The conservatory – the crystal palace, remember? Get security and get over here as fast as you can. There's an ambulance on the way. I'll explain.'

I dropped the phone on the ground and tried to stop Ellen from pulling more thorns out and scarring her face.

In all of this, it suddenly occurred to me, Zeldin had never opened his mouth to offer help. I twisted around to confront him, but he was nowhere in sight.

Chapter 42

'Is it taking them as long as it feels?' Ellen asked.

I had removed all the thorns from her face. Blood had streaked down her cheeks and lined her neck. It caked on my hands as well.

'Are you okay if I go back to the door? Maybe Mercer's having trouble getting in.'

She nodded.

'Scotty – don't even think about moving a hair until Mercer and I get back,' I said, but he didn't seem capable of trying. I balled up my bloody scarf and tucked it beneath his head.

I retraced my steps through the African desert. The late-afternoon sun was casting shadows now, and all of the plants seemed more sinister than they had before Ellen's assault – branches and tendrils and leaves as large as elephant ears reaching out over the path as though to slow my retreat and grab on to me.

I broke into a trot as the walkway sloped downhill, tree limbs grazing the top of my head and catching on the sleeves of my jacket. The long cylindrical tunnel was dark and claustrophobic, almost like an empty subway tube. I kept looking behind me because it sounded as though I were being chased, but it was just the noise of my own footsteps echoing off the metallic walls.

Out of Africa now, and passing through the end of the tunnel, I slipped in a puddle of water that had dripped from an overhead sprinkler, and grabbed the moss-covered rocks to stop myself from falling. Their surface felt hairy and damp, like a handful of caterpillars resting in the shade.

I pushed off and jogged up the curving ramp, snagged on the head by hanging jade vines and the pods of cacao plants. The Victorian reflecting pool was like an oasis in the middle of the other, overgrown faux environments, but it took only seconds for me to dash through it before being launched back into the dank humidity of the tropical jungle.

There was no sign of human life in the dense growth, but as I ran around the base of the huge tree trunk, I could hear feet pounding on the skywalk above me. I ducked off the path and into a mass of ferns, looking up and fearing another encounter with the three young thugs. It was only the same workman I had seen on the way in, oblivious to everything but the browned tips of his plants. He seemed anxious to find out who was racing through his sanctuary this time, and from the expression on his face was more frightened by the encounter than I.

By the time I reached the Palm Dome, I could hear pounding against the front door, and through the glass windows could see Mercer, a security guard, and two EMTs. Once I let them inside, I started to double back – out of breath myself – and told them what they would find as they ran on ahead, pointing in the direction where I had left Ellen Gunsher and Scotty Taren.

Mercer stopped me and tried to calm me down. 'Why did you call for medics?'

'Ellen's cut up pretty badly, but I think it's all superficial. I'm worried about Scotty, though. He's got some kind of coronary history and he's just collapsed in there like a lump.'

'Take some deep ones,' he said, as I bent over, my hands on my knees, trying to regulate my breathing. 'You never met with Zeldin?'

I straightened up. 'Yeah, he was here. Didn't you pass him on your way in?'

'No. The security guard said I just missed him. He sped off the grounds in one of those minivans.'

'Who was driving?'

'According to the guard, Zeldin himself was behind the wheel,' Mercer said.

'What about kids? Did you see any "wild child" types?'

'Yeah. When the guard opened the gate for me, a trio ran out. Hoodies?'

'Exactly. We've got to get the local precinct on it. They're the ones who pushed Ellen, and it seemed to me it was on some kind of signal from Zeldin.'

A blue and white squad car pulled up in front of the conservatory with its lights flashing. Uniformed cops got out on each side and we met them at the door, repeating the story and suggesting that they get started in case the three teens were still moving through the neighborhood in a pack. They radioed out the generic description with orders to bring the group in for questioning and then took off to sweep the area before darkness enveloped the city streets.

'There's a second ambulance on the way. You want to

stay here by the door while I see if they need a hand with Scotty?' Mercer asked.

'Sure. But if you pass one of the gardeners on your way through, send him back to relieve me. Ellen's a mess. I might as well help with her – she's hysterical.'

I stared out the tall windows and watched as the setting sun threw long shadows across the frozen flower beds. Looking at the bleak landscape I found it hard to believe that within two months' time, a dazzling array of chrysanthemums, zinnias, and peonies would color every inch of these same borders.

The vibrations of my cell phone startled me and I pulled it out of my jacket pocket to answer it. Maybe a DNA match to the rapist we'd been calling John Doe would brighten the bloody afternoon.

'Hello?' I said tentatively, hoping to hear a cheerful reply from Dr Thaler.

'Maybe your skinny little ass fits through this gate, but I'm too big to squeeze in and too old to climb over.'

'Where are you, Mike?' The sound of his voice was the best antidote to my fatigue and depression.

'You told me ol' Gun-shy was here, didn't you?' he said, referring to Ellen by the nickname the office trial dogs had given her for her well-noted fear of the courtroom. 'I kind of missed abusing her. Thought you two broads might need a hand. I went to the gate, exactly where Mercer told me to be, only nobody was there to let me in. So I drove back around to the other entrance on Fordham Road. Same story.'

'Damn it, he's got the security guard from the Mosholu gate in here with him. There's been a bad scene – I'll tell you about it. Are you – do you think you're ready—'

'C'mon, Coop. Commandeer one of those golf carts the staff scoot around in. Pick me up and get me inside.'

I started back to find Mercer, but first walked right into the gardener he had sent to take over my post. 'Do you speak English?'

'No, señora,' he said, shaking his head.

'*Mi amigo, el detectivo?*'

'*Sí.*'

'*Lo dice que yo soy buscando un otro amigo. Yo soy buscando Mike.* Okay?'

I didn't know whether I came close to making sense but counted on the quiet man to tell Mercer that I had gone to find Mike. It was the best I could do under the circumstances.

I pushed open the door and ran down the path. Three electric golf carts were lined up on the roadway. I sat in one and turned the key in the ignition, pressing down on the pedal to get onto the main drive, heading east and looking for the road signs that marked the direction of each of the gates. I was bound to run into another guard along the way.

I traveled a few hundred yards before the road forked, one arrow pointing to the Twin Lakes and the other toward the children's adventure garden. One thing I didn't need was another adventure, so I skirted around behind that plot of land in the direction of the new visitors center.

The paths were meant to be scenic. Rock gardens gave way to gazebos that were surrounded by vast swaths of seasonal plantings that would bloom when these dismal days gave way to spring. The daylight was dimming and I had to stop in the middle of the next intersection to read the signs.

I dialed Mike's number as I drove near the conservatory gate. 'I can't spot you,' I said. 'Do you see the headlights on this thing I'm driving?'

'Where the hell are you?'

'Near the ticket booth, in the middle of a big parking lot. I'm the only jalopy in the joint.'

'Wrong gate. C'mon, blondie. Try finding the building that Zeldin took us to, where he's got that Raven Society office. I'm over on that side. How can you possibly lose Fordham Road?'

Two hundred and fifty acres of pristine land in the middle of the Bronx – absolutely deserted – and I couldn't find a street sign for one of the city's largest thoroughfares.

I stepped on the pedal and chugged along until the next intersection, where Azalea Way crossed Snuff Mill Road. The latter led, I knew, to the building we had visited with Zeldin, and near the carriage house in which Sinclair Phelps lived.

I flipped open the phone again. 'Now I got it. I'm on the bridge crossing the river. Get back in your car – you must be freezing. I'll get Phelps to help me. He can call someone from security if he hasn't got keys himself.'

'I got the heat on. Make it snappy, kid.'

'I'm flooring this buggy, Mike. Mercer and I have been worried about you.' Then I said quietly, 'I've missed you.'

I could hear the river running over the rocks below me, and the roar it made as it dropped from the gorge just beyond me drowned out whatever Mike whispered to me in response.

I steered on past the snuff mill, which was as completely dark within as it was getting to be outside. I remembered that Sinclair Phelps's carriage house was not much farther along, so I kept driving around the curving path until I made out its outline, pulled up behind it, and turned off the cart's motor.

The stone building standing alone on the wooded grounds looked like a small English manor house in the Cotswolds. I knocked on the back door several times and called Phelps's name, but no one answered.

I tried the handle, which was not locked, so I let myself into the kitchen. A phone was mounted on the wall next to the refrigerator, and there was a list of the organization's telephone extensions beside it, so I assumed it to be a direct connection to the gardens' employees.

I dialed zero and waited several rings before someone on the switchboard picked up.

'Yes, Mr Phelps?'

'I'm, uh – I'm sorry – I'm not Mr Phelps, obviously. But I am calling from his house. Can you connect me to security, please?'

'Is there a problem at the carriage house, ma'am? I'll get someone right—'

'No, no. There's a New York City detective trying to get into the gate on—'

'The police are already inside, ma'am. We're aware of the commotion at the conservatory. Can you hold? That's another line ringing.'

She was back to me in thirty seconds.

'I'm talking about the Fordham Road gate.'

'Yeah, we just heard about that other guy. You stay where you're at. Security will bring him to you there, okay?'

I hung up and called Mike again on my cell phone. 'I gave up on you, Coop, and called Mercer,' he said.

'He's got a couple of guards on their way to get me. You inside? Stay warm – see you in ten.'

'Did he tell you what happened?'

'Yeah, I know you've been looking to smack Ellen in her long, sour puss for years, but dumping her into the briar patch? I hope you saved a little of your strength for the next guy.'

'What do you mean?'

'Mercer said Gino Guidi's on his way over here. You amateurs must have pissed him off this morning. He's all fired up – without his lawyer this time – no holds barred.'

'Remind me, Mike. Is there anyone I haven't annoyed lately?'

'I'll be right there, kid. Just relax.'

I replaced the receiver on the wall hook. I didn't want to rub up against anything in the house with my bloody ski jacket, so I took it off and put it on the back of a kitchen chair.

After three or four minutes of dead silence, I pushed open the swinging door and entered the living room. It looked like Phelps had been called away suddenly. There was a tall floor lamp that was on, next to a worn leather chair, and resting on a table between them was a book, turned upside down with its spine splayed. A half-filled coffee cup rested on a coaster.

I walked over and picked up the book. It was an academic treatise on the London plane tree. I flipped through the pages and as I did, a small stack of green bills fluttered onto the carpet. I bent over to pick them up – they were all hundred-dollar denominations – and stuck them back between two pages, replacing the book on the tabletop.

I was too restless to sit.

The room was rather impersonal. There were very few signs of homeyness for someone who had been in residence here for so long.

I walked to the mantel over the fireplace to look at the photographs displayed there. All of them were studies of gardens and trees, presumably favorites of Sinclair Phelps.

I was pacing now, walking from the front window, where I looked in vain for signs of the groundskeeper or Mike and Mercer, back to the bookcases on the far wall.

I returned to the window, parting the thin lace curtains again to search for headlights, then crossed the room again.

There were more photographs on one of the shelves. A rugged-looking young Phelps on skis, and another of a child in a young woman's arms – his mother's, perhaps. I smiled at her outfit, which so clearly dated the picture to the sixties – bell-bottom jeans, a peasant-style blouse, long stringy hair parted in the middle, and a peace symbol patched onto the arm of the child's jacket.

A car door slammed in front of the house, but before I could get to the entrance, Phelps had opened it and found me in the middle of his living room.

'Miss Cooper? Is there something wrong?'

'I apologize, Mr Phelps. I – uh, we had a problem over at the conservatory—'

'Yes, I've just come from there. Everything's going to be fine. What are you doing here?' he asked, his eyes scanning the room to see if anything had been disturbed.

'Well, I was trying to tell you that one of the detectives got sort of stuck outside—'

'Chapman? He's on his way in. Zeldin wants you all to meet over at the office in the snuff mill and—'

'But Zeldin's gone,' I said.

'I just saw him, Miss Cooper,' Phelps said. His tone seemed to get more stern as we talked. 'He's asked me to bring the detectives to meet with him. You might as well join them there.'

I started to back up toward the kitchen door as he made a move toward me.

The sudden knocking on the front door startled both of us.

'I'll just step out a minute to take care of this. One of the staff must have a problem.' Phelps walked toward the door, but before reaching it he turned back to the table and chair. He picked up the open book, stopped to make sure the money was still in place, and continued on his way to the door. I noticed his large hands, covered with calluses, dried and cracked from years of physical labor.

I was frozen in place – uncertain about what to do – one hand on the bookshelf and the other poised against the kitchen entrance.

I glanced beside me at the floor-to-ceiling array of books. The bottom shelves were all to do with plants and landscape gardening. The ones above my head were a neatly lined-up collection of volumes of poetry.

I tried to listen to the voices outside as I read the familiar names: Yeats, Eliot, Spender, Auden, Owen, Roethke, Thomas, Heaney. Edgar Allan Poe.

The man Gino Guidi knew as Monty – Aurora Tait's killer – was never without a book of poetry in his back pocket. Even in his teens and twenties, the jobs he had taken to support himself had imprinted their physical hardship on his hands.

The voice of the man that Phelps was talking to was

raised a pitch. They were arguing about something. The visitor cursed, and the words were spoken in Spanish. The visitor stepped back away from the door, and through the gauzelike curtains I could make out a dark-hooded sweatshirt covering his head.

Packs of marauding teenagers. Aaron Kittredge had encountered a similar group outside the back gate a decade ago when he tried to visit Zeldin to talk to him. Others had attacked me at Poe Cottage while the rest of their gang caused a distraction at the bandshell. Today, a threesome assaulted Ellen when Zeldin ordered them to go and get Sinclair Phelps. Maybe Phelps was running them the way a spymaster would send his agents out on missions. Maybe the money stashed inside the book was a payoff for a job well done at the conservatory today. Maybe.

I made a sudden decision. I pushed against the kitchen door, padded across the linoleum flooring as quietly as I could, and let myself out into the cold, dark February night.

Chapter 43

I turned the key to start the golf cart. Without flipping the switch for the headlights, I jammed the pedal and swung the small machine around in a tight circle. Instead of driving out as I had come in, I followed the stone wall behind the house in the opposite direction – certain that I could avoid Phelps and the hoodie and just as sure that I could connect around to one of the main paths.

The strong afternoon breeze seemed to have died down with the sunset. I was grateful for the cart's overhead cover and windshield, which sheltered me somewhat from the winter chill. I hadn't stopped to retrieve my jacket from the kitchen chair, but I was glad for the silk camisole I had put on beneath my cashmere sweater and slacks when I had dressed so many hours ago.

The road looped around a fenced-in area of several acres in which bushes were covered with a large tarp to ward off the frost. I was racing through an urban oasis – the most natural of settings in the most unnatural neighborhood – hoping to find homicide detectives from whom I was separated by fields of rose gardens, lilac bushes, and a conifer arboretum.

Had I identified the murderer, who was indeed hiding

in plain sight, whose bold imitation of Poe's fictional brick crypt had been revealed accidentally by the destruction of the old building in which the grand master of crime stories had lived for a brief time? And had the tragic circumstances of his own childhood led him to live out the fictional tortures of the literary master of revenge?

I took no chances with lights, and slowed down only to look at the path markings at the first intersection. From the direction of the carriage house I heard shouting – perhaps Phelps and the young man still arguing or – maybe worse – commands being given to the thugs to hunt me down.

In the distance I could hear the gurgling sounds of the river, and I followed the pavement toward the noise, as it intensified into a pounding of water against rock.

There was a sign to the snuff mill, and I veered off in that direction before the small overpass, hoping to see familiar NYPD Crown Vics parked nearby.

I paused above the driveway entrance to the three-story building. It was completely dark with no cars in sight. Of course Phelps had lied to me about Mike and Mercer wanting to meet me there.

I juiced the machine and was about to retrace my route when I saw headlights coming from the direction of Phelps's carriage house. I didn't want to take the chance of crossing his path, so I drove away from the mill instead. Anxious to get back to the conservatory and a populated area of the gardens, I turned left at the first possible break in the road. It was a larger stone structure – the sign said Hester Bridge – and as I ramped up and over it I could hear the rushing noise of the waterfall at the foot of the Bronx River Gorge where Dr Ichiko had met his death.

There were only two choices as I rolled down the incline. A left would lead me to the farther bridge, toward which I had seen Phelps or his cohort heading just minutes ago. According to the arrow on the signpost, the straight-away would take me back to the conservatory and administration building – after a drive through New York City's only native forest – fifty acres of undisturbed stands of hemlock, birch, and beech.

I was pushing the cart as fast as it could go, and it bounced me around on the seat as it rattled over branches and rocks that winter storms had thrown down in its path.

The birds and animals that populated the dense trees and exotic park in warmer months had either flown south or hibernated, and there was a dreadful silence that hung over the dark woods – a quiet appropriate to a greenhouse, but not one that I had ever known before on a city street.

Ahead of me, between bare brown tree trunks and filtered through the evergreen branches, I could make out the headlights of another cart. They were coming my way.

I turned the wheel sharply and tried to make a U-turn on the path, hoping to find a foot trail on which to drive. The little machine lurched and threw me forward against the dashboard, stalled in place. I played with the ignition but there was not even a flicker of life. The cart had run off its charge. It was dead.

The blunt nose had bumped against the curb on the left-hand side of the road. I jumped out and looked around to get my bearings, and decided to run for cover in the opposite direction from which I had come.

The ground was firm when I stepped onto it. I was

glad the snow had melted from its edges so that no tracks would be obvious to anyone heading along this way. I looked for a clear path between the trees, and set off racing when I found a narrow hiking trail. A small sign identified a grove of Himalayan white pine, and their flexible branches covered with long green needles gave as much protection as I could have hoped for. I ducked and took myself as far off the roadway as I could navigate without much visibility.

The pair of lights got closer to me now and came to a stop in what I assumed was the vicinity of my abandoned cart.

Certainly, Mike and Mercer would be searching for me. There was no point in my trying to peer out of the foliage and see who had approached. If he were friend and not foe, he would have been calling my name.

The headlights cut off. My pursuer had decided to look for me on foot. I didn't hear him getting closer – maybe he had been fooled briefly by the direction in which the empty cart had been facing and started his search on the far side of the paved road. But I took the moment to climb deeper and higher into the woods, certain I would find an egress on the far side of the trail I had entered.

Seconds later, the intense beam of a high-powered flashlight made a 360-degree arc from the roadway where the man – probably Phelps – was standing. I crouched behind one of the fat pines. My clothes were navy blue and black. There was nothing shiny or bright to catch the attention of a flashlight, so I tried to stay calm and motionless.

When the glare no longer looked like it was focused on me, I found the trail again and kept walking, up a hilly slope and into a denser plot of trees. I patted my pants for my cell phone, but realized it was back in Phelps's kitchen, in the pocket of my blood-soaked jacket.

As I climbed higher I thought of Mercer and Mike. They knew I was inside the gates of the Botanical Gardens and they would know I would not have left here without them. Mike had sworn to me at the hospital after my spell beneath the floorboards at Poe Cottage that he would never again leave me behind without a thorough search. I expected to hear sirens any minute, and I knew they could call in choppers with infrared lights that were capable of finding my warm body in the darkest forest if it came to that.

I stopped for a few minutes, still spooked by the total silence of the woods around me. A groundskeeper who had lived on this property for more than twenty years would know every inch of the terrain, while I was feeling my way around like a blind person. I could walk myself in and around trails that Phelps would be able to trace from memory until I dropped from exhaustion, or I could shelter myself in the warmest place possible and let the NYPD come to me.

The long green fingers of the pine needles seemed as likely a cushion as anything I would find in this wilderness. I pulled at a few of the low-hanging branches, knowing I'd infuriate the garden's high-rolling contributors for destroying their plants and counting on their forgiveness if I survived the chase.

I covered the surface of the ground with several fronds and then seated myself atop them, pulling others over me as further camouflage. But the frozen turf beneath them was filled with the residual dampness of the winter's earlier storms, and fifteen minutes of sitting still chilled me more than I could bear.

On my feet again, I traipsed down the far side of the hill, hoping to find some way back to civilization. Now I could make out two sets of headlights, tearing across the roadway like a pair of bumper cars at an amusement park. What if Phelps had called on his army of teenage bandits to ferret me out?

Time to get off a comfortable path, I told myself. I bent beneath the boughs of several trees and started traversing the hillside. I wanted to be in a place where I couldn't see lights, and nothing short of night-vision goggles could spot me.

My cheeks tingled with the cold, and I wiggled my toes to make sure they were still moving. I soldiered on between and among the thick pine trees.

About thirty feet ahead, a dark gray mass seemed to loom behind the green foliage. I worked my way toward it, dragging several branches behind me to serve as a blanket, wondering whether spaces between the large boulders would offer any better respite for me.

I held on to a tree trunk and pulled myself up the last few feet, leaning on the side of the first rock I came to, gulping in the cold air to catch my breath.

A series of huge stones towered over that one, so I stepped around it to see whether there was a niche in which I could lodge myself. I was standing at the mouth of a small cave, and without thinking twice I stepped inside the black hole to get shelter from the elements – and from my pursuers.

It was dry inside, and I felt immediate relief as I tried to adjust my eyes to an even darker field of vision.

Looking at the ground so as not to twist an ankle or stumble on a rock, I got about eight or ten feet back into the cave, so that even a strong light beam would not catch me at the edge of the opening.

I didn't look up until my forehead brushed against something large and hairy dangling from overhead. I knelt on the floor in a panic as dozens of bats let loose with a volley of high-pitched squeals, routed from their roosts by my unexpected invasion. Some dove directly at me with their bared little teeth and extended claws displayed to my horror. Others flapped around my ears, ominously flaunting their four-foot wingspan before taking off out of the cave, leaving me quivering on its filthy floor.

Chapter 44

I was flying now, flying downhill as fast as I could move myself, with furry little mammals shrieking above me as their own fear forced them out of hibernation into the bracing shock of cold air. They blackened the sky beyond the treetops and swarmed like an angry army as they tried to organize into some kind of formation.

In what direction could I find safety? I brushed at the wings that neared my scalp, worried that a bat would become entangled in my hair. Worried also that the most aggressive ones were likely to be rabid.

Suddenly, I had a more important fear. Even if the detectives were scouring the park, a flock of brown bats would have no significance to them. Sinclair Phelps would know their seasonal habits, would know I had disturbed the roost, and would know exactly where on the property the bat cave was located.

As I approached the roadway from halfway down the slope, a minivan without headlights pulled into view and braked to a standstill. I doubled back and ran uphill to the boulders, climbing up on top of the lowest ones, rather than reentering the cave, as I heard heavy breathing and something charging up the underbrush toward me.

Panting at my feet were two dogs, German shepherds who barked furiously as they tried to scale the rocks. The bats that fluttered overhead made passes at them, too, and the dogs raised their snouts at the creatures that taunted them.

'Down!' shouted a voice a few feet farther down.

At the sound of Phelps's command, both animals squatted on all fours and impatiently waited for their master. The shrill screech of the bats, some beyond the range of human hearing, must have been disturbing to the canines, both of whom whined and growled as they lay in place.

I glanced again at the sky: treetops, bat wings, and not too far overhead the steady stream of flights landing and taking off from La Guardia Airport, directly across nearby Long Island Sound. No sign of any helicopter above, nor any police flashers below.

I was wedged into place in the crevice between two boulders, the dogs twelve feet below me, snarling and salivating as they waited for orders to attack.

Phelps took his time climbing up to meet me. He used the high beam of his flashlight to feature me as the bull's-eye within his target. When he reached the dogs they seemed to whine even louder, as though asking his permission to take a piece out of one of my legs.

'Shut up!' he said, and the whimpering stopped as they put their heads on their outstretched paws.

I saw that he was carrying a shotgun. I thought of the professor – Noah Tormey – and the marksman who had nearly taken him out that day at the Hall of Fame. How logical to need weapons – and a marksman – in an urban park like this, where so many vermin were likely to have wreaked havoc on the precious plant life.

'Now, I think you're going to have to climb down from that perch, Miss Cooper. We've got work to do.'

I didn't respond. I thought I could hear police sirens in the background and I wanted Phelps to think the game might be over for him.

'I do hear that noise, Miss Cooper. But it's not for you the bell tolls. My boys are out stirring up a little trouble on Fordham Road. It's a very dangerous city beyond these gates. You know that better than anyone.'

So his teenage thugs would create a diversion on a Bronx sidewalk and 911 calls would flood the switchboard. Even Mike and Mercer might think it was I who was in trouble out on the nearby street, that I had somehow been spirited off the garden grounds or had been stupid enough to follow the kids who had attacked Ellen Gunsher after Mercer told me he had seen them leaving the gate.

'Call off your dogs,' I said, stalling for time. Some of the bats were still circling above us while others had settled on tree branches, wizened little faces staring into mine from their upside-down positions.

'They're so hard to discipline, Miss Cooper. Coydogs, actually. I breed them. It's one way to keep the deer population down. Gets rid of the rabbits and moles that are so destructive to plants.'

A mix of wild coyotes and feral dogs. They were rumored to be a vicious hybrid.

'Let's go,' Phelps said, louder this time.

I heard an engine turn on and saw the minivan start to move. One of his young troops, no doubt, getting rid of the car so the police wouldn't make our location. My eyes followed the vehicle till it disappeared around the bend, but I didn't move.

'You can sit up there. You can even keep climbing to the top. But then where do you go? Besides, I've got hiking boots on and can overtake you in a couple of minutes,' he said.

I wanted to tell him to shoot me – it would be faster than whatever he had in mind – but I didn't mean it. And I knew it wasn't his first choice of disposing of me because anyone out searching would hear the gunshots echo throughout this quiet preserve.

I started to inch myself backward up the large boulder but couldn't get a toehold without looking down. By the time I had raised myself a couple of feet, Phelps had put the shotgun on the ground and was making his way up to me. He grabbed my left ankle and wrenched it around, pulling me toward him. He lowered himself off the rocks and kept tugging at me until I landed in the dirt on my tailbone, smacking my head against the stony surface behind me.

'I certainly didn't mean to knock you out,' he said, kneeling beside me. 'Not before you help me carry a few of these.'

Phelps gestured to the loose rock piles that some glacial movement had thrown off as it passed through the river gorge and woodlands a few thousand years earlier.

'Of course,' he said, standing and extending a hand to me, 'you're probably thinking I could just let the coydogs have a go at you. You've never seen them take down a deer, have you? They can each grab hold of a leg and head off together on a brisk run – and when you find the carcass in the woods a few days later it looks like it snapped in half as easily as a wishbone might at a Thanksgiving dinner.'

I was on my feet, rubbing the back of my head.

'The problem with that is the poor dogs would suffer for it in the end. I've got them so well trained at this point, and Zeldin or someone else in the administration here would decide they'd have to be put to sleep for hurting you. Wouldn't that be a sorry trade?' Phelps said, shaking his head. 'So what does that leave me instead?'

I didn't have to say it aloud. There could be only one thing he wanted to do to me in the cave.

'Perhaps you knew this, Miss Cooper, that the very first crypts were in caves? Deep, cool, wonderful recesses in which to entomb people. We're going to custom-make a crypt for you, Alex. Poe's way.'

Chapter 45

There was no point screaming. Not yet. I didn't want to be gagged or bound until I had exhausted every other possible means of helping myself get out alive.

'Start over there.' Sinclair Phelps poked me in the back with the point of the shotgun. 'You're a big girl – you can carry a few of those.'

I could see his plan. He would arrange this to look like a rock slide, as though I had been trapped inside – running away from goodness knows what – had panicked and was unable to get help. That would only work if he thought no one else had put together the facts, as I had, that linked him to his victims.

I bent down and picked up a large rock – it must have weighed more than twenty pounds – and slowly walked with it to the mouth of the cave.

'Go in. Go on in,' he said, prodding me again with the gun. 'All those stories about bats are just myths. They're very timid creatures. Last place they'd want to be is in your hair.'

I walked a foot or two into the cave, pushed farther by Phelps, who told me exactly where to drop my first load. Now I could see rows of the furry beasts hanging from their roosts.

'"A midnight vigil holds the swarthy bat," Miss Cooper. You know that one?'

I shook my head.

'Poe's "Coliseum." A lesser-known work.' He watched me as I maneuvered the rock into place.

'Did Aurora Tait have to make her own coffin, too?' I asked.

Phelps laughed. 'No, no. But then it was so much easier for me to get Aurora into my lair, Miss Cooper.'

'I suppose all you had to do was promise her heroin.'

'High-test. Best shit on the street. She came to me like a baby for its bottle.'

'Why there? Why that building? Because it was Poe's house?'

'Keep moving,' he said, conscious that I was stalling but pleased to show off what passed for his intelligence, after serving for all these years in a job that belied his educational background and knowledge of literature. 'That was just a richly ironic coincidence. You know the story? You know "Amontillado"?'

I was lugging another rock now, pretending to limp because I had twisted my ankle. 'The ultimate tale of revenge,' I said. 'Of course I know it. You mean it was just chance that your construction work was in that particular basement?'

'The landlord was always having work done there. That dump probably wasn't fit for occupancy a century ago.'

'And Aurora, she saw what you were doing?'

'She wasn't quite as sober as you are, Miss Cooper. Nor as well read. She found it amusing that I was a day laborer. She liked to watch me work, as long as she was high. I

424

gave her the dope that afternoon and she obliged me by shooting up, getting herself into a stupor, as I knew she would. By the time I lifted her over my shoulder and stood her up behind the wall, she was almost ready to come around. Can you imagine the look in her eyes when she realized what I was about to do to her?'

At this very moment I was able to imagine it perfectly well.

'Betrayal. She earned every exquisite second of her miserable death. She was responsible for depriving me of everything I'd been promised from the time I was four years old. The bitch had tried to extort money – a lot of money – from my step—' Phelps stopped to correct himself. 'From the man who raised me. She screwed up the whole plan, and in doing that she condemned me to the gutter.'

I was on my third small boulder, peering out into the black-green forest for any sign of a rescuer.

'I'd spent my entire youth trying to please a man who never really wanted me under his roof anyway. He'd taken me in when my mother died,' Phelps said.

I had heard much of the story from Gino Guidi, but I figured it would anger this strange man to let on that the detectives and I knew more about his past – without knowing his identity – than he might have liked.

'It doesn't make any sense that he took you in if he didn't want you.'

'I was too young to know. My mother was his house-keeper, and the woman who took care of me after my mother's death also worked for him, on the kitchen staff. She claimed he was keen to do it at the time. The rejection came much later on, when I was eight or nine. When he finally got married the new bride wanted her own children. Of course she didn't want the illegitimate kid of the parlor maid anywhere in the mix.'

'Who – who was the man?'

Phelps was watching me build my coffin, eyeing me as I ferried heavy rocks from the hillside into the cave. He was leaning against the side of it, shotgun tucked under his arm, a jacket zipped up to his chin and a scarf and hat on his neck and head that seemed enviably warm.

'Phelps. Sinclair Phelps.'

We'd been told that he'd been disinherited and disowned, that like Edgar Poe he'd never been formally adopted by his benefactor. 'His name? He gave you his name?'

'I took his name, Miss Cooper. Not long after Aurora and I parted ways. I didn't think I'd have the luxury of twenty-five years without anyone discovering her body – well, her remains. I never thought I'd get away with it so cleanly. I did, after all, confess to any number of people that I had killed the poor girl,' he said, grinning at me. 'It's not my fault they didn't take me seriously.'

'So your real name?'

'That hardly matters, does it? You see, if anyone put Aurora's disappearance together with the former NYU student who hallucinated about killing her, they'd be out of luck if they tried to find him. He just ceased to exist. One less junkie the world had to worry about. One less dropout never even likely to make an alumni contribution.

'But Sinclair Phelps? However you try to find him – the best private investigator, the most determined Cold Case Squad, even – what do you call it? – Google him on the Internet – and all it comes back to is a dead man, with no male heirs, who hardly ever left Keene, New Hampshire, when he was alive. There are so many periodical and philanthropic records that connect to Sinclair Phelps, owner of the largest paper-manufacturing company in the region, that a humble groundskeeper at a city garden doesn't even pop up on the screen. I simply reinvented myself.'

On the distant roadway below us I could see headlights moving slowly along. The red bubble flasher on top of it illuminated the blue and white colors of a patrol car.

Phelps pivoted and pushed me back inside the cave, pinning me against the wall and holding the shotgun to my cheek.

'They'll find us, you know. They're good at that,' I said. 'There's all kinds of equipment they can use to search for bodies in an area like this.'

'It worked long enough for bin Laden, didn't it? My bet's on the guy inside the caves.'

'Why here, Mr Phelps?' I asked softly. 'Why a groundskeeper at the gardens?'

'It's the perfect solution, don't you think? At least it was for a good while. I like working outdoors – that part never bothered me. And it's as close as I'm going to get to living like a Phelps. A nineteenth-century carriage house surrounded by hundreds of acres of the most glorious park and plantings in North America. Time for my poetry, and then there's Zeldin himself, who dropped into my lap with the world's greatest collection of Poeiana. I had access twenty-four hours a day to all those privileges of the Raven Society. It's not a bad way to go, Miss Cooper, if you've got to work for a living.'

Phelps had stepped back and ordered me to continue lifting and carrying rocks. The car had passed through without any sighting of us.

'You identify with Poe?' I knew there was a name for this syndrome in the psychiatric literature but I was too terrified to pull it up.

'I'm not foolish enough to think my own writings can compare, but he was always, shall we say, my inspiration.'

'He's the reason you killed Aurora?'

'Not at all. I had reason enough of my own to do that. It's just that he had composed the most brilliant manner in which to do it. It still excites me every time I think of what her final thoughts must have been when she realized that I was sealing her behind that wall. Alive.'

The rock slipped from my hands. I was losing my focus.

'Every time there was another insult in my life, another rejection, another defeat, I consoled myself by the thought that Poe had overcome all those similar things and more to become the greatest writer of his time.'

I thought about the tragedies that had overwhelmed Poe's life from infancy. He had all the psychological torment that could have created a monster, a serial killer. Aaron Kittredge believed he might have been one. It seemed more plausible to me with every second in Phelps's presence.

'Don't I get any credit for my rehabilitation, Miss Cooper? After Aurora's death, I was – well, nearly a model citizen for a very long time.'

'Until you murdered Emily Upshaw.'

'Emily knew too much.' Phelps sighed. 'Once the newspapers showed such an interest in the skeleton, it wouldn't have taken long for her to spill her guts about me.'

'She knew you as Phelps?'

'It's not the name I used in those days,' he said, 'but she certainly knew who my stepfather – well, whatever you want to call him – she knew who he was. She knew my story.'

And that led to Dr Ichiko, I thought, stacking another rock on the pile. Undoubtedly the shrink had all the information in his old patient files to help him piece together who 'Monty' really was.

'Dr Ichiko?' I asked.

'Now there's a man who wasn't all that clever. Information isn't of any value unless you use it properly. Dr Ichiko was just unfortunate.'

'He was smart enough to find you,' I said, wiping some debris from the corner of my eye.

'He got partway there. He knew enough to look for someone named Phelps. He remembered my affinity for Poe – some kind of psychological transference, he liked to say it was. So he did his research and called information for the Raven Society number, just to see if perhaps there was a member with my name. There's a Manhattan listing that goes to Zeldin's home, Miss Cooper. But if you check the Bronx directory, the same number rings at the mill. And when he dialed over here, I just happened to answer the phone. He didn't know that at the time, so when I heard the nature of his inquiry, I pretended to be the great Zeldin and invited him here to discuss the information he thought he had so brilliantly uncovered. He should have watched his step more carefully.'

Once the cover-up had been set in motion, Sinclair Phelps had not been able to stop. It was the fear that someone would come here to his sanctuary – whether it was Aaron Kittredge more than a decade ago, or Dr Ichiko or Noah Tormey most recently. Someone with a connection to Aurora or a link to Emily, someone who would expose the quiet life he had created for himself and connect him to the murder of Aurora Tait, someone who would walk through these gates and shatter the illusory world in which he lived.

'And your little punks – why did they attack Ellen this afternoon? What was that about?'

'Quite frankly, Miss Cooper, they had orders to go for *you*. I didn't know they'd be creative enough to impale someone on that gruesome plant, but they're good at being bad. I told them you'd be the woman asking all the questions – the ever-inquisitive Alexandra Cooper,' Phelps said, shaking his head in my direction. 'I understand you were uncharacteristically quiet today. They mistook that other lady for you.'

The boulders were stacked waist-high now. My time was running short.

I stepped back out into the fresh air and looked in vain for any sign of human life. I stalled for a minute, reaching into my rear pants pocket and realizing for the first time that I hadn't left my gloves in the ski jacket back at Phelps's house. Something stung me sharply as I tried to withdraw my hand.

Stuck tightly to the fine knit of the woolen gloves were several leaves of the plant – the ferocious plant – that I had pulled from the wounds on Ellen's face. The long thorns pierced the tips of my fingers and I winced in pain.

I had pocketed the treacherous needles so they wouldn't accidentally injure anyone coming to Ellen's aid. Now they might be my only defense against Sinclair Phelps.

Holding the gloves in my hand, I picked up a smaller rock, one that I could carry with a single arm. Phelps was leaning against a large boulder and had placed the shotgun on top of it. He was toying with a piece of material that I assumed would be my gag and binds – ripping it into several lengths of cloth.

There would be no second chance for me. If I didn't make a clean strike, it would be my very own, very premature burial.

I approached the mouth of the cave and walked directly in front of Phelps. He started to say something to me and as I turned to look at him, I shifted the rock to my left arm. With a single thrust, I rammed the thorn-encrusted black gloves into his eye with my right hand, pushing as hard as I could.

Sinclair Phelps howled as the prickly needles embedded themselves in his eyelid. He doubled over, covering his face with his hands. I lifted the rock and brought it down as hard as I could, pleased with the sound it made as it cracked against bone. Blood trickled from his ear as he fell to the ground.

The two coydogs leaped to their feet and charged at me.

I grabbed the shotgun from the boulder, pointed its barrel straight overhead, and discharged several rounds into the quiet night.

The dogs whimpered and circled each other in distress, frightened by the blasts of the gun. Dozens more bats swooped out of the cave, dipping their wings and blackening the sky above us. I clutched the weapon in my hand and ran down the slope as fast as I was able to move.

Chapter 46

'Ratiocination, my dear Coop. Edgar Poe would have delighted in your use of it.'

Mike Chapman was leaning against a bookshelf in the basement of the snuff mill, surrounded by ravens of every shape and size.

My shotgun volleys had rallied several pairs of police officers in the direction from which I had come running. Two intercepted me on the roadway and took me into their patrol car. They brought me back to Zeldin's office, the place from which Mike and Mercer had been tracking the search mission.

'Once I saw Phelps outside the door of his cottage paying off one of the kids, it all started to come together. It was a gang of teenagers who had assaulted Aaron Kittredge when he tried to visit here almost ten years ago. Phelps must have feared, then, that he might be spotted. He didn't want to risk an accidental encounter with someone who could link him to his other life. It was kids who hit me over the head, and who tried to – to bury me.' I paused to take a deep breath. 'Who put me under the floorboards at Poe Cottage.'

Mercer refilled my water glass. 'And the same kids –

Sinclair Phelps's roving band of bad boys – who mistook Ellen Gunsher for you in the conservatory.'

'He could have lived out the rest of his life here, undisturbed, if no one had been able to connect him to Aurora Tait. Or to Emily Upshaw,' Mike said, folding his paperwork in quarters and tucking the pages in his blazer pocket. 'Or to his own miserable past.'

'Did you guys find Zeldin?' I asked. 'Do you think he knew anything about Phelps?'

'He's all fired up, Coop. We even got him out of the wheelchair tonight, pompous old stiff that he is. I think he was in the dark about Phelps. I mean, he knew that the little hoodlums did all the groundskeeper's dirty work, but I don't think he figured murder. When Ellen was attacked, he got himself out of there like a rocket, but he phoned Phelps to call off his boys. If Zeldin had known, he might have let Phelps into the Raven Society,' Mike said.

I looked over at him to see whether he was joking. 'You still think that's a prerequisite for membership?'

'I think Edgar himself would have liked it that way, don't you? I intend to find out.'

The brick coffin had been inadvertently opened and everything Phelps thought had been entombed with Aurora Tait had begun to spill out.

'Where are you going?' I asked Mike, who had turned his back to me and was walking toward the door.

'Just lie there and mope as long as you want, kid. Let somebody else handle your big case for you. If you hadn't run off into the woods, you'd have heard the good news.'

'What?'

'Hugo Maswana. The DNA's a match. Annika's family

433

is going to stay with her another week so you can put together a lineup and arraign him on the indictment. Substitute his name for John Doe.'

I tossed back my head and stared up at the ceiling. For almost five years I'd been trying to put that bastard out of business.

'That means the ambassador is waiving diplomatic immunity?' I asked Mercer.

'No such luck. It means you've got to get back in the ring and fight him, Coop. Then you got to get Noah Tormey to sit down with Amelia Brandon – his daughter. She took the bus back home, but she's entitled to some answers.'

'So am I.'

'What's stumping the normally know-it-all prosecutor?' Mike asked.

'When did Phelps have time to set up the attack on me at the cottage?'

'He must have heard Zeldin make the offer to call Gino Guidi's office to get us in. We sat in the coffee shop for almost an hour waiting for clearance. That gave him plenty of time to do it.'

'But what were they going to do when they came—?'

'Idle thoughts. You don't want to go there,' Mike said. 'Anyway, it would have distracted us from any bad business at the gardens. It would have looked like a mugging in a tough neighborhood. Who knows where we would have found you.'

He continued on his way to the door, waving a hand. 'I'll give you a call, Mercer.'

'We're not done,' I said, standing and rattling a porcelain bust of the great poet as my elbow struck against the side table.

'Oh, yeah? I am. The Upshaw murder is solved. How does it go in Clue? It was Colonel Mustard, in the conservatory, with the knife. Case closed.'

'The arrest, Mike. You've got to stay to get all the facts from me so you can take Phelps to his arraignment.'

'Make yourselves comfortable. Stick around for the next meeting of the Raven Society.' He pointed at Mercer. 'Detective Wallace is taking the collar.'

I looked from Mercer to Mike. 'But it's a homicide. It's your case.'

'Not this time.'

'Why not?' I could see that I was losing him. He was tired and distracted, running his fingers through his thick, dark hair and resting his arm on the mantel over the fireplace.

'Police brutality.'

'What are you talking about?'

'Phelps stands up – if he can – in front of the judge tomorrow morning. He'll be a full turban job, his shattered skull packaged in layers of bandage and gauze wrap.'

'Yeah, but I'm the one who hit him.'

'Some court-appointed asshole looking for his Clarence Darrow moment sees my name as the arresting officer and spots his opportunity. Makes me the dupe, stringing my personal life into the middle of the mess. "Detective Chapman went over the edge this time, Your Honor. He's lost control of himself, taken it out on my client." Asks for all kinds of privileges for the murderer with the cracked cranium. Maybe even gets him bail for medical treatment. I'm not in the game, kid. I'm outta here.'

'Don't be ridiculous. I had to hurt Phelps to save my own life.'

'That'll be the footnote after the trial, Coop. Right now, nobody'll believe it was anything except excessive force by a homicide cop who's got no focus at the moment. You're not the one who stands next to this scumbag at the arraignment – one of us dumb dicks does that. I'm not giving the tabloids the chance to bring Val . . .' Mike's voice trailed off. 'To make this frigging case personal.'

I tried to maneuver myself to stand in Mike's way but he sidestepped me and kept walking. 'They'll blame Mercer for it. You don't want that, do you?'

'The gentle giant? Nah. They won't play the race card. Nobody thinks he'd hurt a fly. It's me they'd be gunning for.'

'Nobody's going to let you be held responsible for Phelps's injuries.'

'Alex Cooper used her glutes and pecs instead of her brains to bring a guy down? I'm not being the patsy for you tonight.'

'Why, Mike? I disappointed you?'

He turned back from the doorway of the snuff mill. 'Yeah, Coop. You did. Too bad you didn't finish the job tonight. One less shitbird for the State of New York to house and feed for another forty years. One less miserable excuse for a human being to suck the life out of every appeal and excuse in the book. You should have hit him harder when you had the chance.'

No need saying I didn't believe Mike meant those things. I knew he did.

Mercer had his notepad ready. 'Let's get back to it, Alex.'

The front door was open and Mike was silhouetted in its frame. Behind him was a phalanx of department cars with bubble flashers on their hoods surrounding the quiet house, casting red streaks of light against the backdrop of the dark forest.

'Tomorrow? Want to have dinner with me, Mike?'

He stopped to answer. 'I barely have the strength to get myself through the night. I can't help you this time, Coop. I just can't do it.'

I heard Lieutenant Peterson's voice in the front yard, ordering one of the men to escort Mike's car out the gate on the far side of the gardens to avoid the reporters and cameramen waiting at the nearest exit.

I started through the doorway to go after Mike. There was something else I wanted to tell him. I had a need to make some kind of physical contact with him as badly as I wanted him to embrace me.

'We've got work to do, Alex,' Mercer said, clamping a strong hand on my shoulder to hold me in place.

I looked up at him, ready to plead my case, but he gave no ground. I turned away from the flashing lights, let him close the door behind us, and walked back to sit in the armchair, surrounded by Poe's dark birds.

Mercer pulled up a stool opposite me and stroked my head until I lifted my eyes to look at him. 'Let the man go, Alex. Just let him go.'

You can now order superb titles directly from Time Warner Books: